OBLIVION

A STARFIRE NOVEL

★★★

STEVE WHITE &
CHARLES E. GANNON

OBLIVION

This is a work of fiction. All the characters and events portrayed in this book are fictional, and any resemblance to real people or incidents is purely coincidental.

A Baen Books Original

Baen Publishing Enterprises
P.O. Box 1403
Riverdale, NY 10471
www.baen.com

ISBN: 978-1-4814-8401-5

Cover art by Dave Seeley
Maps by Randy Asplund

First printing, May 2018
First mass market printing, May 2019

Library of Congress Control Number: 2018005090

Distributed by Simon & Schuster
1230 Avenue of the Americas
New York, NY 10020

Printed in the United States of America

10 9 8 7 6 5 4 3 2 1

OBLIVION

A STARFIRE NOVEL

★ ★ ★

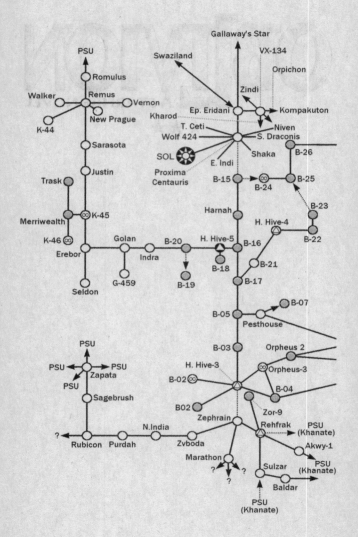

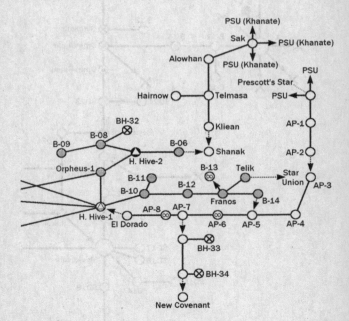

Star Union

B-27   B-28   B-29

PSU (Khanate)
Sak → PSU (Khanate)
Alowhan → PSU (Khanate)

Prescott's Star → PSU
Hairnow → Telmasa → PSU
AP-1

Kliean   AP-2

BH-32
B-08
B-09
Orpheus-1   H. Hive-2   B-06 → Shanak   AP-3

B-13
B-11   Telik
B-10   B-12   Star Union
Franos   B-14
H. Hive-1   AP-8   AP-7
El Dorado   AP-6   AP-5   AP-4

BH-33

BH-34

New Covenant

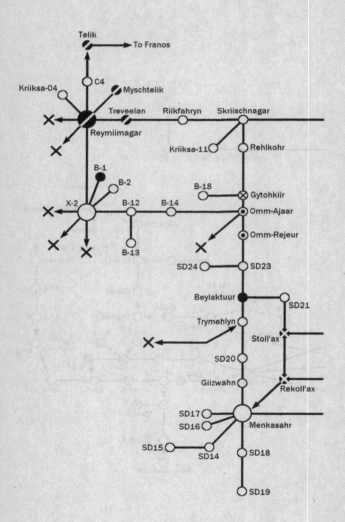

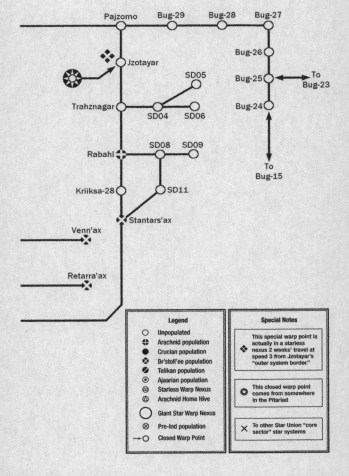

Pajzomo   Bug-29   Bug-28   Bug-27

Jzotayar

SD05

Trahznagar   SD04   SD06

Bug-26

Bug-25   To Bug-23

Bug-24

SD08   SD09

Rabahl

To Bug-15

Kriiksa-28   SD11

Stantars'ax

Venn'ax

Retarra'ax

Legend

○ Unpopulated
▦ Arachnid population
● Crucian population
⊗ Br'stoll'ee population
◪ Telikan population
⊙ Ajaarian population
⊗ Starless Warp Nexus
◉ Arachnid Home Hive

◯ Giant Star Warp Nexus

⊗ Pre-Ind population

→○ Closed Warp Point

Special Notes

❖ This special warp point is actually in a starless nexus 2 weeks' travel at speed 3 from Jzotayar's "outer system border."

● This closed warp point comes from somewhere in the Pitariad

✕ To other Star Union "core sector" star systems

PART ONE
A Time
To Gather Stones
Together

PART ONE

A Time
To Gather Stones
Together

CHAPTER ONE

All conversation on TRNS *Zeven Provinciën*'s flag bridge ceased when the Marine sentry rapped out "Attention on deck!" and a tall man in fleet admiral's uniform entered.

That uniform was not the standard space-service gray coverall that could serve as a spacesuit liner. For this occasion, Ian Trevayne wore the deep-blue and white and gold service dress of the Terran Republic Navy. To most people in most times and places, there would have seemed something strangely incongruous about his apparent age—early thirties at most, appropriate perhaps for a lieutenant commander—and the rank insignia of a broad gold stripe and four narrow ones on his sleeves. Not to these people, though, and not to anyone in what was currently left of human space, for his unique story was too well known.

In part, it was that story, with its mythic resonances that seemed to create a palpable aura around him, that caused the flag bridge to hold an even more profound hush than his exalted rank could account for. But only in part. These

3

days, in his presence, people tended to take refuge in silence, not knowing how to behave around a man who had suffered such a loss as he sustained at Bug 17, two systems behind them.

As he approached the chair that was sacred to him, he spared a glance at the outside viewscreen. At a distance of almost fifteen light-minutes, the primary sun of Harnah was a faint orange-tinted gleam, for it was only a K-type main sequence star. As such, it was not a naked-eye object from the Solar system, although no one but astronomers gave a damn about how many light-years from Man's birthworld it lay in normal space. The distance that mattered was measured in warp transits—three of them, a distance that had become terrifyingly short.

Four light-minutes from the primary, and quite invisible from here, was a planet that had once been Earthlike. In fact, it still held some hardy and by now wildly mutated forms of plant life. But it had been a world of the misnamed Arachnids—the "Bugs" to all who had ever encountered them—and as such had been blasted clean of that universally loathed and dreaded form of life in the Bug War of the 2360s, a little less than two centuries ago by the standard dating of Old Terra. It was the same treatment that had been meted out to every Bug planet, and when it was over everyone had truly believed that Creation had been cleansed of the Arachnid abomination, an insensate hive consciousness that existed only to expand and consume like some obscene melanoma eating at the body of galactic life. Trevayne's mind shied away from the memory of that belief, now so cruelly disproven.

Trevayne stood beside the chair but did not sit down.

He turned to a ruddy-faced man with the massive build imparted by many generations lived in low temperatures and high gravity. "Is all in readiness, Captain?"

"Aye, Admiral," rumbled Flag Captain Janos Thorfinnssen in a voice which held only a trace of the dialect of his native Beaufort. "All elements of Combined Fleet are linked into the hookup, and all personnel are standing by."

"Very well." Trevayne turned to his operations officer, currently doubling as acting chief of staff in the absence of Captain Elaine De Mornay, who was two warp transits away in the Alpha Centauri system supervising the mustering and refitting of the Heart Worlds' reserve fleets in this hour of ultimate need. Ever the traditionalist, he gave the immemorial naval courtesy promotion. "Commodore Singhal, let's proceed."

Captain Gordon Singhal stepped in front of the comm screen and activated it. "Attention. Grand Admiral Trevayne wishes to address all personnel." He stepped aside, and Trevayne took his place.

The screen was split three ways, showing the faces of the admirals commanding Combined Fleet's three national components: Rafaela Shang for the Rim Federation, Mario Leong for the Pan-Sentient Union, and Adrian M'Zangwe for the Terran Republic. But, Trevayne knew, thousands and thousands of beings, human and otherwise, could see *him* and would be hearing his voice (not all at the same time, as the transmission flashed across a wide swath of the Harnah system at the velocity of light), with sophisticated translation software for the Orions and Ophiuchi.

In his resonant deep baritone, and in a Standard

English which held the still-prestigious accent of Old Terra's Britain, he began without preamble, for none was needed.

"Even after all that has occurred, many of us still cannot comprehend what has happened to the world we knew and believed to be immutable. Despite this, you have all behaved magnificently in a long and grueling campaign. Keeping up morale despite being continuously forced to retreat is one of the hardest things warriors can ever be called upon to do." Which, Trevayne reflected, was why he had decided it was high time to give this little talk. "You have not wavered or failed. You have done your duty. But you may find it hard to fully understand what that duty means anymore, in a time when so many unthinkable things have happened and continue to happen, and so many assumptions have been shattered. Confusion and bewilderment are understandable.

"Therefore I wish to review the events that have brought us to this pass. I will be telling you things you already know, but which you may not have fully assimilated.

"Our world first began to change in 2524 when the Arduans arrived in the Bellerophon system, having crossed *normal space* in immense generation ships—the first known interstellar voyagers ever to do so—to escape a nearby supernova that threatened to make their planet uninhabitable. Even greater shocks were in store: their seeming lack of regard for their own individual lives, and the apparent impossibility of communicating with them. To us, these suggested one horrifying thing: a hive mentality like the Bugs. We didn't know then that the former arose from their absolute belief in reincarnation, and that the latter was due to the fact that they communicated using their empathic *selnarm* sense—and that our lack of that sense caused them to regard us as not fully sentient.

"It took a war to get both sides past their misconceptions. But now the Arduans we fought are our friends." Trevayne's face and voice grew stern. "Despite everything that has happened, we must remember that. The Arduans as a *race* are not our enemies. Our Arduan allies of the First Dispersate are marked for genocide just as surely as we are.

"For, as we subsequently learned, the vast exodus we had encountered was only the first of many. On their doomed home planet, the Arduans had continued to send forth one diaspora after another in an effort to save their entire race so that there would be sufficient new births for everyone to be reborn." Not for the first time, Trevayne wondered glumly if humans could have done as well under the circumstances. "But the Arduans of those later diasporas regressed and devolved in some manner foreign to us, and the *Destoshaz* warrior subspecies had become dominant, and taken to calling themselves 'Kaituni' rather than Arduans. Convinced that the first diaspora had turned traitor, and aided by information from those of their number who had already established themselves in the Zarzuela system, they prepared a war of extermination. In the course of their long slower-than-light voyage they developed new technologies and broke up their generation ships into kinetic projectiles."

Trevayne grew even more somber. "We all remember what ensued. Without warning, swarms of relativistic rocks swept through many systems of the Pan-Sentient

Union, devastating planets and in some cases disrupting suns. The Khanate of Orion bore more than its share of the brunt, and all humans of all our star nations appreciate and admire the fortitude with which this calamity has been borne." Trevayne wanted to especially emphasize that point for the benefit of his Orion personnel, for he knew the destruction of the artificial "Unity" warp point, which he had ordered in an effort to contain the damage had occasioned certain amount of ill-feeling, as though the humans were casting the Khanate adrift.

"But even worse was to come," Trevayne continued inexorably. "As the Kaituni war fleet began to advance along the warp lines, we were confident that their much lighter ships, however numerous, would be meat for our devastators and superdevastators—the ships that had won the war against the first Arduan Dispersate. Too late, we learned that those titanic ships were precisely the ones that cannot live inside the range of the Kaituni's newly developed relativistic acceleration weapon, or RAW, employing focused quantum entanglement to teleport particles to within the volume occupied by a sufficiently massive target. Thus it was that Admiral Waldeck's fleet was gutted in Home Hive Two. And it was in that same system that we received an even greater shock, when a nightmare from which we believed we had awakened reappeared."

Trevayne didn't need to say what that nightmare was, and he saw no purpose to be served by doing so. No one in Combined Fleet had ever quite recovered from the moment when ships of the supposedly extinct Bugs had come boiling through a concealed closed warp point from a hidden Hive system where the Kaituni, presumably through some application of their *selnarm* faculty, had somehow made contact with them.

"Since then," he resumed, "the Kaituni have hovered behind the Bugs, 'herding' them along as they have forced us back from system after system, allowing them to take losses that would be appalling to any other species. And the closer to Sol they have forced us, the less we have been able to risk taking a stand. For far too long, the most we have been able to do is inflict the maximum possible losses on them while maintaining a fleet in being . . ."

For an instant, Trevayne's voice faltered. No one on the flag bridge breathed—nor, in all likelihood, did anyone in Combined Fleet. By now everyone knew what Trevayne had sacrificed on the altar of a "fleet in being" in the Bug 17 system. For it had been there, two warp transits back along their dismal line of retreat, that his wife, Admiral Li-Trevayne Magda, had staged what could only be called a mutiny, leading a covering force to shield the fleet's withdrawal because it had been the only way to prevent Trevayne from doing it himself. And when a fresh Bug horde had appeared from an unsuspected direction, she had been cut off and was now presumed dead . . . by everyone but her husband.

Everyone knew all of this. But no one understood the full depths of Trevayne's torment, for people tended to forget about Han Trevayne, now six years old. Slightly more than a year earlier, he and Magda had sent their daughter to stay with Magda's godparents on Novaya Rodina, their adopted home, while they themselves had departed on an expedition against the Tangri corsairs. But then they had been caught up in the unimaginable catastrophe that had engulfed the known galaxy and had never seen Han since. Trevayne had had to content himself with very rare interactive messages to her, and the knowledge that Novaya Rodina was unharmed. And now he could look forward to the prospect of explaining to the little girl what had happened to her mother.

The pause was only momentary. When Trevayne spoke next, his compelling voice slowly and steadily built up from the somber depths it had been plumbing. "So now we are here in Harnah, only two warp transits from Alpha Centauri. Our long fighting retreat is coming to an end, because it must. The time is approaching when we must stand and fight, for we will have no choice. Alpha Centauri is not expendable. It is the gateway to all the Heart Worlds . . . and to Sol, and Old Terra."

He paused again, to let that sink in. To all humans, wherever born and of whatever political allegiance, there was something unutterably sacred about humanity's birthworld. And only once, in the Bug War, had it been this threatened.

"Even now," Trevayne went on, "all the available reserve forces in the Heart Worlds are converging on Alpha Centauri. We will continue to delay the enemy, here and in Bug 15, to give them as much time as possible." His voice dropped an octave. "In these decommissioned ships, with their proud histories, it is as though we are summoning up ghosts. And I know, better than most, how what may seem to be dead can sometimes arise in times of great need."

The silence took on a new depth, for all knew to what he referred. In 2443 he himself, the hero of the loyalist side of the Fringe Revolution, had been almost physically destroyed in the Revolution's climactic battle at the age of forty-nine. For eight decades he had lain in a cryogenic stasis from which he could not be awakened without killing him. Finally, a means had been found to transfer his brain into a youthful full-body but anencephalic clone of himself—and, in a way that had tapped into very deep wellsprings of myth, his reawakening had occurred just before the first Arduan Dispersate had arrived and the dogs of war had been let slip again.

"But it is not enough that we summon up decommissioned ships." Trevayne's voice became a clang. "We must summon up from deep within ourselves all that we are. But that is not enough. We must summon up all that we ever *have* been. But that is not enough. We must summon up all we have ever *thought* we were. But that is not enough. We must summon up all we have ever thought we *ought* to be, or that we might become.

"In this apocalyptic hour, nothing less will serve. And I know nothing less will be forthcoming from each of you." A final pause. "That is all."

In the midst of a profound silence, Trevayne turned to the flag captain. "Janos, I want you to have your communications officer prepare a new courier drone for Elaine De Mornay. I have new instructions regarding the work on the reserve units—and, in particular, on the deployment of the orbital fortresses."

"At once, Admiral."

"In addition," Trevayne continued, as much to himself as to Thorfinnssen, "I want an update from her on how the work is progressing. Yes, I know she's doing her best."

He really did. De Mornay was that rarity, a warrior of fiery—sometimes even rash—instincts who was also an organizer *par excellence*. "But I need for her to expedite the refitting of those bloody old hulks! I expect a strong Bug probe into this system at any time. Quite simply, I need to know how much longer Combined Fleet needs to draw out its fighting retreat."

"Yes, Admiral. I'll—"

At that moment, readouts above the sensor station began to flash, and other lights awoke at the communications center. Singhal, alarmed, turned and demanded a report. Trevayne had a pretty good idea of what it all portended before the acting chief of staff returned to his side.

"Admiral, there is a sudden irruption of sensor drones through the Bug 16 warp point."

Bug 16, thought Trevayne, where humanity's old demon crouched, with its new demon following behind. "Captain, sound general quarters immediately. Gordon, put all elements of Combined Fleet on full alert immediately. We all know what is coming behind those drones, don't we?"

SBMKAWK missiles at first, capable of warp transit and prepared to launch gouts of anti-mine munitions to clear the way. Next, the inexorably advancing phalanxes of Bug warships that would come through in multiple warp transits, stolidly indifferent to the losses occasioned when two of them materialized in the same volume of space.

"And Janos," Trevayne added, "please expedite that courier drone. I believe the clock has started ticking again here in Harnah."

CHAPTER TWO

At the time Ian Trevayne had dispatched Elaine De Mornay to Alpha Centauri, he had been putting the finishing touches on his address to the fleet. He had spoken of summoning ghosts.

He had no *idea!* she now thought, as she stood before a large viewscreen and watched the latest antique glide soundlessly past. For this was—God help them all—an *Athabasca* class superdreadnought from the Bug War, just arrived from Epsilon Indi.

The image of the new arrival was being transmitted across almost ten light-minutes, for it was pulling into one of the orbital shipyards in Alpha Centauri A's asteroid belt. She herself stood on a balcony in the cavernous control chamber of the great space station that was the Pan-Sentient Union Navy's command center for the Alpha Centauri system, the second most important system of that polity's human worlds—and, by some estimates, not even second. She manipulated the screen's controls

13

and it went to actual outside view. Before her were the magnificent twin planets of Nova Terra and Eden, whose common center of mass the station orbited at a little over a light-second. Beyond, at seven light-minutes, was the Sol-like type G2v yellow sun Alpha Centauri A. The secondary component of this binary system, the K1v type star Alpha Centauri B, was visible only as a superlatively bright orange star, for it was currently almost two hundred and forty light-minutes away, well out toward apastron in the highly eccentric orbit which, at periastron, brought it within ninety-four light-minutes of Component A.

When the exploration ship *Hermes*, bound for Neptune in 2053, had blundered through Sol's solitary (and utterly unsuspected) warp point, its crew had naturally been more than a little surprised to abruptly find themselves thirty light-minutes from Alpha Centauri A. But further surprises were soon to come. In the heady years of the early twenty-first century, when extrasolar planets were first being discovered in wholesale lots, an Earth-sized world had been detected around Alpha Centauri B, orbiting far too close to be a habitat for life. But no such discoveries had been forthcoming around Component A, and there had been a tendency to write off Sol's nearest neighbor. It turned out, however that Alpha Centauri B II had simply been easy to find, whipping around its primary so rapidly as to induce an easily observed "wobble." Component B's other planet—a small gas giant with a marginally terraformable moon—had gone unnoticed. So had the entire planetary system of Component A, which turned out to have an extremely dense Kuiper Belt, obscuring observation of the inner planets, including the life-bearing twins which were of somewhat less than Earthlike mass but were denser and therefore smaller. (This was a somewhat younger system that Sol's, and had thus coalesced from a more heavy-element-enriched interstellar medium.)

Thus Alpha Centauri had turned out to be an unexpected treasure trove of colonizable real estate. But the *real* reason the system was a prize had emerged when humans, who now knew what to look for, had explored it for other warp points. They had found *seven* of them, leading to various nearby stars with warp points of their own. (Only much later, during the Bug War, had yet another warp point—a "closed" one, undetectable until someone came through from the other side—come to light, with all its freight of both terror and strategic opportunity, for it had connected to Bug space.) All at once, the gates of the galaxy had seemed to burst open, and human expansion had exploded outward in a series of surges, punctuated by wars, for other toolmaking species had also discovered the enigmatic warp network that brought the stars within reach.

Commander Andreas Hagen joined her on the balcony, interrupting her thoughts. Trevayne had sent him to Alpha Centauri before her, to prepare the way. To some, it might have seemed an odd assignment for Combined Fleet's staff Intelligence officer. But he and Trevayne went back all the way to the latter's unique resurrection from near-death, for Hagen—then a lieutenant commander, recently seconded from the Rim Federation's Bureau of Ships to the faculty of its naval academy—had been assigned to the newly reborn living legend as a special liaison officer, charged with bringing him up to speed on the technological developments of eight decades which he had spent, as he himself put it, getting well and truly freezer-burned. Now Hagen had reverted to his old area of expertise. In Combined Fleet's present pass, rigid occupational pigeonholes counted for no more than the fact that he and she belonged to two different (and historically hostile) star nations. Having one's head on the block confers a certain sense of proportion about the true relative importance of things.

Now Hagen wore a wry smile. "I just thought you'd like to know that we've gotten another message from Assemblyman Morosini out at B, demanding passage back to Sol for his junket."

A jag of irritation shot through De Mornay. The current crisis had caught a delegation from the PSU's Legislative Assembly on Alpha Centauri B II (a), investigating the cost-effectiveness of investing in that moon's terraforming. Ever since arriving here, her concentration on far weightier matters had been periodically interrupted by their squawks of indignation.

"You tell him I said exactly what I've said before," she said through clenched teeth. "There are only a finite number of time-slots available for transits through the Sol warp point. All of them and more are earmarked for the foreseeable future for the Mothba . . . that is, the *reserve* fleet. I will not disrupt our schedule for their convenience. They can bloody well cool their heels out there." (She had picked up a number of expressions from Trevayne.)

"Will do." Hagen's smile was now one of pleasurable anticipation, for he knew the politicos' wails of anguish and bellows of outrage would be in vain. There were, of course, far more senior officers than a mere captain in the Alpha Centauri system. But Trevayne had made it very clear that his chief of staff spoke with his voice on all matters pertaining to the preparation of what was being derisively dubbed the "Mothball Fleet." In fact he had broken one insufficiently cooperative rear admiral *pour encourager les autres.* Regarding the use of Alpha Centauri's warp points, Elaine De Mornay's word was law.

After a moment, De Mornay switched the screen back to the pickup from the shipyards. The venerable superdreadnought she had been observing was now being nudged into a construction dock.

"At least," Hagen commented, "we've got adequate dock space since we terminated new construction. Not that everybody agreed it was a wise decision."

"No, they didn't," De Mornay acknowledged. "But it was an easy one in the case of the devastators and superdevastators. It was a harder call for the lighter ships that haven't become death traps for their crews. But it's a matter of resource allocation. When the choice is between building one new ship or upgrading ten old ones, it's no choice at all. Especially considering how many old ones we've got."

Hagen nodded. They both knew the history of space-warship design philosophy. Most of that history could be summed up in the phrase *bigger is better.* At the beginning of the First Interstellar War in the early twenty-third century, the largest warship had been what would be considered today a light cruiser. By its end, the superdreadnought had ruled the skies. There had been a hiccup of sorts in the Third Interstellar War, when the late unlamented Rigellian race had introduced the one- or two-seat strikefighter, with its ability to maneuver into the "blind zone" that reactionless drives created aft of the big ships. But countermeasures had kept pace, and a well-handled battle line with adequate fighter support had continued to be the decisive factor. The trend had continued in the Bug War, with the introduction of the monitor, twice the tonnage of a superdreadnought, and on into the Fringe Revolution, when Ian Trevayne had unveiled the supermonitor. And it had accelerated when the invention of phased gravitic propulsion—the "Desai Drive"—had robbed the fighter of its speed advantage. The devastator and then the superdevastator (the largest hull capable of warp transit) had followed; and with the development of the gravitic disruptor, which those titanic ships' engines could use effectively, it appeared that the warship of space had reached finality . . . and invincibility.

But then had come the Kaituni RAW, within whose range no devastator or superdevastator could live. Abruptly, the proudest ships ever built had been relegated to the role of glorified long-range missile platforms. And, just as abruptly, the superdreadnought had once again become the ideal warship size, too small for a RAW targeting solution, and with reasonable speed and cloakability.

"Yes," said Hagen. "And thank God the upgrading is relatively simple. It's largely a matter of ripping out modular systems and sensor arrays and plugging rapid-firing energy torpedoes and up-to-date sensor and targeting arrays into the existing power systems. At least we don't have to install new engines." He frowned at the viewscreen. "Of course, with museum pieces like that one, that don't have Desai Drive . . ."

"They can still be useful for system defense, within the Desai Limit," De Mornay reminded him. Within twenty light-minutes of a stellar mass, or two light-minutes of a planetary one, the Desai Drive would not function and ships that mounted it were reduced to an even footing with those that did not.

Still, she reflected, it was no wonder that the term "Mothball Fleet" for what she was assembling here from the various Heart Worlds was approaching semi-official status. People who used it, she thought with a certain asperity, ought to be grateful that mothballing was very simple in the vacuum of space.

Hagen's mention of the installation of energy torpedoes reminded her of something. "How is the re-installation of the old stuff progressing?"

"Very satisfactorily, as you'll see when you get your regular report on it in a couple of days. Fortunately, there are a *lot* of asteroids around here."

"And a lot of skilled labor in the belt," De Mornay nodded. Long ago, the invention of artificial gravity units had meant that the resources of asteroid belts could be exploited with no nonsense about having to build spin habitats or genetically engineer a human subspecies specialized for life in microgravity—the latter not free from ethical issues in any case. By now, Sol's belt was highly developed indeed, and Alpha Centauri A's little less so.

Ian Trevayne had resolved to take full advantage of that

fact. The obsolete weapon systems being removed from mothballed ships and replaced with energy torpedoes—all the force beams and hetlasers and standard missile launchers and so forth—would not go to waste. Following his instructions, De Mornay had been remounting them on robotic weapon buoys (to the extent they were available) and asteroids (whose availability was effectively infinite). The density of such improvised defenses was growing impressive. Any invader of this system would, she was grimly determined, have to hack his way through a thicket.

The thought of passive defenses brought another thought to the surface of her mind. "I keep expecting to get a courier drone from Admiral Trevayne , augmenting his instructions about the fortresses. Some of the things he's said seem to suggest that he's had some new ideas on their deployment."

Like all populous, highly developed systems of the PSU, Alpha Centauri was defended by massive orbital fortresses. Unfortunately, that very mass—typically somewhere between a devastator and a superdevastator—made them meat for the RAW. Trevayne had ordained that they should not be shackled immovably to their orbits. Here, again, the system's extensive asteroid developments provided a solution. There was an abundance of tugs, mounting powerful tractor beams. De Mornay had commandeered as many of them as possible and was having them slaved to the fortresses. They would never be anything but slow, yet the arrangement could provide them with a certain strategic repositioning capability, though not a realistic tactical one.

Simultaneously, the fortresses were being turned into pure long-range missile batteries—all other antishipping weapon systems were being ripped out to make room for more launchers and missile storage.

"Well," Hagen reminded her, "we're not quite due for one of his regular communications just yet—" At that moment, his wrist communicator beeped for attention. It was the comm officer.

"Commander, a courier drone has entered the system through the Bug-15 warp point. The contents are already coming in via *selnarmic* relay." A pause. "It's from Admiral Trevayne, sir."

Hagen and De Mornay exchanged a meaningful look. "The chief of staff and I are on our way," said the former. They departed, not quite at a run.

By the time they reached the comm center, Trevayne's message had already been downloaded, even though the Bug-15 warp point was a good twenty-seven light-minutes distant, by grace of the instantaneous *selnarmic* relay developed by humanity's Arduan allies. They read it in silence.

"So," Hagen breathed, "the Bugs are already attacking Harnah."

"At least the Bugs," De Mornay cautioned. "As usual, we don't know whether the Kaituni are ready yet to participate directly or are still hanging back. But either way, the point is that Admiral Trevayne wants to know how long he needs to fight a delaying action there. In other words, how much more time do *we* need."

"Shall I have the various departments submit reports?"

"No time for that. And no need, I think. You and I both

know more or less where we stand, And the longer we delay in replying—and the more time we ask for—the more of the Admiral's people are going to die in Harnah." De Mornay paused as though inviting Hagen to disagree. But he said nothing. She turned to the comm officer. "Prepare a courier drone—right now."

As soon as it had become horribly obvious that devastators and superdevastators could not be exposed to the possibility of contact with the Kaituni, Trevayne had formed his into a special task group under the command of Commodore Hugo Allende and stationed them far back from any threatened warp point, in close proximity to a warp point of egress. But in Harnah he had, to Allende's fierce satisfaction, risked placing them a little closer to the Bug-16 warp point than usual. Thus, before they had gotten very far in from that warp point, the lead Bug formations entered a blizzard of long-range missiles .

In the meantime, fighters swarmed around and through those formations, seeking ship's blind zones. It was clear to Trevayne that the fighter, like the smaller warship classes, seemed destined to make a comeback. His pilots were all veterans by now, and they included avian-descended Ophiuchi, the best fighter jocks in the known galaxy. They also included Orions, risking themselves with the fearlessness demanded by the warrior code of *Theernowlus* and afire to avenge their shattered homeworld.

Yet still the Bugs came, and came, and came. It was the kind of stolid, insensate advance, totally without regard to losses, that had always horrified humans, who felt themselves to be in the presence of some inexorable natural force with no resemblance to intelligent life as normally understood. It couldn't even be called suicidal. The Arachnid hive consciousness was very much concerned with its own survival. When it lavishly expended individual units, it was no more being suicidal than a human was being suicidal when he trimmed his hair or fingernails.

Little by little, Combined Fleet pulled reluctantly back. Disregarding Allende's frustration, Trevayne ordered him to take his slow behemoths back first, giving them a head start in crossing the thirty-two light-minutes to the Bug-15 warp point, where they were to take up position. This, of necessity, robbed the defenders of their firepower. But the delaying action continued.

It was still continuing when a courier drone from Alpha Centauri arrived, considerably sooner than expected. After Trevayne and Gordon Singhal had read it, the acting chief of staff looked up with a smile. "That sounds like Captain De Mornay, doesn't it?"

"It does indeed," Trevayne agreed in a tone of quiet pride. "And it was because I more than half expected something like this that I got the devastators and superdevastators started back when I did." He drew himself up. "Commodore Singhal, Combined Fleet will commence the withdrawal to Bug-15 as planned—immediately."

CHAPTER THREE

Commodore Ossian Wethermere, commander of the Relief Fleet's Special Recon Detachment, saw the blip appear in the holoplot the same moment that his sensor officer Katherine Engan shouted, "Warp point activity confirmed, and bogey on the scope."

At last, Wethermere thought, *the pendulum of luck is swinging our way again.* "Lieutenant Schendler," he muttered to his comm officer, "tell *Viggen* to stand ready. Then signal Cluster Leader Temret aboard the *Fet'merah* that he must ensure that his *selnarm* link to us remains precise and clear. This operation depends upon that data conduit—at least until we come out of stealth."

"Cluster Leader Temret signals his understanding and that he is sending the bogey a *selnarm* hail."

"Any sign the bogey is getting twitchy?"

"None, sir. No way to say for sure, but I'd lay odds the Kaituni don't suspect that *Fet'merah* is an Arduan ship masquerading as one of their own."

"Not yet, they don't—but they will, eventually. Lieutenant Ross, stand by on the primary beam. Zhou, is our plant ready to juice it?"

"Been waiting for hours, Commodore."

Evidently the bogey was not entirely trusting of *Fet'merah*; it had increased speed on an oblique heading, keeping distance while also remaining in range to scan and react.

"Temret reports that the bogey is replying to his hail, asking for identification."

"What kind of ship is she?"

"Armed courier, sir. Pretty much a twin to the one we grabbed at Mymzher a few months ago."

So, the bogey didn't have much in the way of armaments, but was fleet of foot. Of course, so were Wethermere's other—and currently stealthed—ships, particularly the corvette *Viggen*. But the objective here was neither to chase nor destroy.

"How's our reciprocal *selnarm* comm link to *Fet'merah*, Schendler?" he asked. This would not be an auspicious time for the Arduan telepathy-based relays to fail in either direction. Being stealthed, Wethermere's own Q-ship—a former freighter they'd christened the *Woolly Impostor*—would be deaf, dumb, and blind if that occurred. Although stealth fields kept any sensor-alerting radiant energy from escaping or being reflected by the hull, it was a two-way blackout curtain: you couldn't see or sense anything outside of it, either.

"*Selnarm* links steady," Schendler replied. "Not enough data for pretargeting, though, sir."

"Tell me when there is, and patch the telemetry

through to Lieutenant Ross. And tell Commander Knight to ready Bloodhound One."

"Captain Knight reports Bloodhound One is prepped and ready to deploy."

I can just imagine. "Very well. Mr. Lubell," he ordered the helmsman, "bring us to course thirty-seven by—and maintain speed."

"That will have us converging with the bogey's own trajectory in just over four minutes, sir."

"I'm counting on that, Sam. We want to be as close as possible when we start this party." *And we can't afford any screwups, not with so much at stake.* It shouldn't have been such a critical mission, but fate had decreed otherwise, and had started issuing those harsh decrees weeks ago.

Having trailed the Arachnid fleet through the attenuated warp links that joined together the various species of the now gutted Star Union, the immense Relief Fleet had finally surprised a small rear guard force that the Bugs' Kaituni drovers had left monitoring the warp point between the systems known as Bug 29 and Bug 28. It had been the break that fleet commander Miharu Yoshikuni had been waiting for: a source of current intel and a better glimpse into the possible intentions of both the Bugs and the Kaituni, who were clearly not allies and often seemed to clash—violently—over the course they should follow. She and her two vice-commanders, Arduan Narrok and Orion Kiiraathra'ostakjo (an old friend and comrade of Wethermere's), had not been pleased with what they had learned. The main fleets blocking the primary advance of the Kaituni from Pesthouse to Earth been dealt several sharp defeats by superior numbers and a surprising new weapon that used quantum entanglement to materialize matter within the same space occupied by the armored hulls of the largest classes of vessels (with the predictably catastrophic results).

Worse yet, the Kaituni drovers propelling the Bug fleet through the Star Union had imposed their will not by compelling arguments but by daunting numbers. An entire Dispersate worth of warships had arrived unannounced in the Star Union itself, ready to take charge of the lesser Arachnid horde that had streamed out of their hidden system toward their historical "feeding grounds" in the Star Union. The purpose of the Kaituni's brusque shepherding of the Bugs: to drive them through the back door access to the main warp-line that led to Earth, and so into the rear of whatever formations were holding back the larger advance along that route. In short, they were to sever the one link between Earth and its main defense fleet, now known to be under the legendary Admiral Ian Trevayne.

This put the strategists of the Relief Fleet upon the horns of an often contentious dilemma: should they forge ahead to engage the combined enemy forces as quickly as possible, or attempt to trail them more closely to better learn their composition and also to buy time for several specialists to perfect what might prove to be a decisive new weapon? Tentatively combat-proven in the last engagement, this weapon held the promise of enabling Relief Fleet to disrupt key Kaituni *selnarmic* command and control links. A more polished version of that system would almost certainly mitigate the numerical disadvantages of the Relief Fleet in contending with two such multitudinous foes, but it was unclear if Trevayne and Earth had enough time left to justify any delay for the sake of further technological refinements. Ultimately, Admiral Miharu Yoshikuni had decided to pursue both strategies simultaneously: to attempt to catch the enemy fleets as soon as possible, but to do so carefully, while the research leaders—human Captain Chong and Arduan Lesser Cluster Leader Lentsul—strove to put the finishing touches on their game-changing technology.

But this was precisely where Fate had foiled their plans. After shattering a Kaituni cruiser and capturing a destroyer at the warp point that joined Bug 29 to Bug 28, the fleet had been at pains to probe Bug 28 with great care, not wanting to alert the enemy to their presence. However, it had taken several days to disarm a tripwire system on the other side of the warp point, comprised of a matrix of *selnarmically*-connected automated couriers— only to discover that the rest of the system was empty.

So, whereas the Relief Fleet had undergone the necessary evolution into assault order, it now had to go through yet another evolution into the fastest possible warp point transit formation that would also allow them to speed across the B 28 system. And with each passing day, they fretted the increasing possibility that the enemy fleet would pull too far ahead of them to catch.

Once through the warp point, the fleet did make extraordinary time: Bug 28, like Bug 27 beyond it, was a starless patch of space, remarkable only for the fact that it had both a warp point into it, and a warp point out to another destination. Consequently, the ships were able to use their Desai drives, which essentially doubled their speed.

But as they drew near to Bug 27, they confronted the same challenge they had faced while contemplating the warp point into Bug 28: how to enter without losing the element of surprise?

Fortunately, technical intelligence provided the answer. Having dissected the tripwire courier elements while the Relief Fleet sped across the inky black zone known as Bug 28, the two most expert Arduan analysts— Mretlak and Lentsul—discovered data indicating that the Kaituni had detached a single ship to remain behind to check the status of the tripwire at regular intervals. And that interval was within 36 hours of rolling around again. It was also implied that the bulk, if not the entirety, of the Kaituni fleet had come to a stop in the Bug 27 region. Reason: unknown.

Collectively, this meant that meant that the Relief Fleet's most urgent and lacking combat necessity became adequate tactical intelligence: where were the Kaituni situated, how were they deployed, how were they positioned in relation to the Bugs they were driving before them? Happily, the Kaituni had now delivered what was very possibly a repository of information that would answer those questions and many, many more.

"Commodore," Lieutenant Ross announced from her weapons console, "we have closed to optimal firing range on the Kaituni courier."

"Lieutenant Engan, any sign that the bogey suspects our presence?"

"None, sir, although I think they are becoming

suspicious of the false credentials that the Arduans came up with for the *Fet'merah*."

"Then it's time to start the party. Lieutenant Ross, show me your firing solution. Absolute precision is required."

Ross aimed her well-veined hand at the new primary beam relays that had been rigged to her gunnery panel when the weapons were retrofitted into the *Woolly Impostor* only five days earlier. "I have ninety-nine percent plus reliability, sir. It's helpful that we've seen this class of ship before and know right where to fire."

Indeed it is, Wethermere thought. *It's not a hugely lucky break, but a damned welcome one, even so.* "Very good." Leaning toward the intership, he asked, "Captain Knight?"

Knight's response from the *Viggen* was immediate. "Waiting for your go signal, Commodore."

"Watch your sensors; you'll need to do some precision flying."

"Just as we rehearsed it, sir. I've got a bay full of eager Marines, so the sooner the better. Before long, they won't care whose ship they tear up."

"A figure of speech, I hope, Captain."

"Me, too," Knight grumbled. "The adrenaline is running pretty high back there."

Which, given the specs on this op, was perfectly understandable. It was the sort of mission that generated a flight or fight response—and Marines were chosen, in part, because their temperament invariably leaned toward the latter. "'Sandro Magee can keep them in line. Just remind them of the objectives. And promise them extra beer."

Knight gruffed through a throat clearing; that may have been as close to a laugh as Wethermere had ever heard emerge from the laconic career officer. "That should do the trick. Waiting on you, *Impostor*."

Ossian turned to his helmsman, Sam Lubell. "Does our telemetry match the bogey's?"

"Zero point zero deviation in all axes for the last fifteen seconds, Commodore. It doesn't get any better than this."

No, it certainly doesn't. "Lieutenant Engan, prepare to drop the stealth field. Lieutenant Ross, as soon as your instruments confirm the *selnarm*-relayed target lock we've been getting from the *Fet'merah*, engage the pretargeted components of the bogey with the primary beam. Shift to secondary target immediately—but, do not execute until I instruct."

"Yes, sir."

"Mr. Lubell, you will rig our drive to automatically cut out .0001 seconds after the gunnery board processes Lieutenant Ross' firing order. Prepare to maneuver to position Drillbit, as outlined in the OpOrd."

"Aye, sir."

"Lieutenant Engan—drop stealth. Ross: fire."

Wethermere waited for the sensors to tell him if what they had rehearsed thirty times had actually worked. If it had, it would mean that *Woolly Impostor* would suddenly become visible to the Kaituni bogey, and in almost the same instant, its primary beam would be firing at less than twenty kilometers range. Closer than point blank in space battles, this was analogous to putting a pistol against an adversary's forehead before pulling the trigger. If the adversary had been an armor-sheathed elephant, that might not have been so effective, but against this fragile opossum-sized opponent . . .

The primary beam—a weapon which had long since been superseded by more destructive systems, but remained unmatched for the precision of its annihilatory energies—licked out at the Kaituni armored courier and sliced a neat gash through the core of her drive coils without even nicking the power plants driving them. With shocking abruptness, the courier was at a dead stop in unfolded space.

And according to the holofeed that rose in a column alongside his command chair, Wethermere confirmed that the *Woolly Impostor*'s own drives had cut out the desired fraction of a second later, thereby preventing an overshoot while the residual power in the target's drive coils expended itself.

"One hundred eighteen kilometers off her starboard quarter," Engan shouted.

"Correcting to assault position Drillbit," Lubell said calmly over the end of her report. "And—fixed at sixteen kilometers, same relative attitude."

"Excellent," Ossian replied with a general smile for his bridge crew. "Ross, neutralize the enemy weapons that can bear, and watch for her to roll to change her facing. Captain Knight, you have the green light; execute Keyhole."

"Aye," was all that Knight said as his own ship, the smaller but incredibly swift *Viggen*, seemed to materialize out of thin space just three kilometers over the dorsal midship section of the enemy. Clearly visible in the monitor, the Marine boarding team Bloodhound One came hurtling out and toward the stricken enemy, propelled by EVA maneuver packs. In the half minute that had elapsed, the enemy ship had done little other than attempt to rotate turrets toward *Woolly Impostor*, with the net effect of having those turrets disappear in actinic flashes of atomically disrupted matter.

"Lieutenant Ross, engage secondary target with primary beam."

"Engaging, sir."

White-blue coruscations flared at a single point on the slightly curved back of the Kaituni ship. Bloodhound One was diving straight toward it.

"Report on effect, Lieutenant Engan."

"Estimates put hull-vaporization aperture at four meters, sir."

Good, but not good enough. "Continue firing, Ross. Radially swivel the aimpoint, as we discussed."

Ross hesitated. "The effect of that was not wholly proven, Commodore."

"Do it." *Because if we don't, there could be some Marines slamming into that Kaituni hull at too many gees.*

"Executing," Ross had murmured. The primary beam traced a slightly widening gyre now—invisible except for where the rim of the prior aperture sparked and fumed as more matter was torn into subatomic froth.

"Bloodhound One passing final commitment waypoint, sir."

Wethermere nodded. "Steady hand on the beam, Ross. Schendler, patch me through directly to Major Magee. Open channel."

"You are on open tactical, sir."

"'Sandro, how's the ride?"

After a moment of what might have been stunned silence, the deep, bear-like voice of Alessandro Magee muttered, "Exhilarating, sir. Particularly since we don't know how it ends."

Ossian studied the close-up of the dorsal spine of the ship. "I do. Commence retroboost. Weapons free. Boarding aperture, Lieutenant Engan?"

"Five meters. And change. Sir," she reported.

"Ross, terminate beam. 'Sandro, it's your show from here on in. But stick with the rules of engagement: don't kill any you don't have to, but if it looks like they are trying to self-destruct the ship, or burn out the computer—"

"Understood, sir. RoE will be followed. With extreme prejudice, in the latter circumstances."

In the monitor, the Marines of Bloodhound One had slowed from a high speed blur to a fast rush toward the glowing, ragged edges of the five-and-a-half meter hole in the back of the Kaituni ship. As their EVA packs flared brightly with sudden retroboosting, Wethermere could hear a couple of grunts: the deceleration to make safe entry and landing inside the crippled enemy was sharp enough to compress ribcages.

Then, like a flock of diving raptors, the Marines of Bloodhound One were through the keyhole that had been bored into the courier from *Woolly Impostor*'s standoff fire at position Drillbit.

"And now what, Commodore?" Schendler asked.

"And now, we wait." *And hope 'Sandro takes the Kaituni alive, and their computers intact.*

CHAPTER FOUR

Admiral Miharu Yoshikuni shook her head, seemed unwilling to glance down the table at him—or so Ossian thought. *Probably afraid she'll smile. Must be tough having your not-so-secret lover sitting at the same flag briefings.* He tried to keep a mischievous grin off his own face.

Yoshikuni turned toward Least Fang Kiiraathra'ostakjo. "Least Fang, your reaction to the outcome of today's mission surprises me."

"In what way, Admiral?"

"You don't seem surprised that Commodore Wethermere's insane plan worked."

"I am not," the Orion remarked with a casual pass at his vaguely felinoid whiskers.

"But just yesterday, you were tireless pointing out the risks of the operation," Admiral Narrok reminded him. The Arduan's three eyes had opened a little wider; the vocoder that rendered his voice registered surprise.

"That is true. It is also true that the logic which applies

to and governs my life does not seem to apply to nor govern Commodore Wethermere and his plans. But that is hardly surprising, since they seem to originate from amidst the grey crags that, in the myths of my people, separate the dark lands of madness from the shining plains of inspiration."

Yoshikuni rested her chin on her hand—an unusual posture for her, but necessary, since she was evidently determined to hide the incipient grin there. "We have some axioms that evidently resonate with Orion myths," she commented a moment later.

"So we *Zheeerlikou'valkhannaieee* have learned. But despite the improbable means whereby we gathered enemy data today, the Kaituni are aware that we have it. At least for now."

Yoshikuni nodded. She glanced down at the Arduan contingent in her conference room aboard the RFNS *Krishmahnta*. As ever, they sat quite still, surveying the proceedings calmly with all three of their independently-focusing eyes, the larger central one ever open and unblinking. "Councilor Ankaht, is there any chance that the data in the Kaituni courier's computer is disinformation, that the Kaituni fleet ahead of us suspects our presence due to our recent neutralization of the ships they left guarding this warp point?"

Ankaht leaned forward slightly. Her hairless body, humanoid but far more sinuous than a human's, seemed to flow into the new position. "You are concerned that the Kaituni suspect they are being followed, and so, hope to mislead us?" Ankaht assayed the human gesture of shaking her head in negation—but the action recalled a person with a severe tic, verging toward a petite mal seizure. Arduans' dependence upon *selnarm* meant they relied even less upon body language than vocalizations. Consequently, their attempts to mimic human gestures were often arresting.

Ankaht may have discerned that her motion generated more alarm than understanding; she ceased and raised both semi-sinuous arms, the tentacle clusters at their ends pulsing into wide, emphatic asterisks. "No, we may be absolutely certain that the data gathered today is genuine. The content and style of the communications—much of which was personal or minor reports from the enemy fleet's campaign through the Star Union—are consistent with what we decoded from the data banks on the Kaituni destroyer we took partially intact several weeks ago."

In response to Yoshikuni's dubious frown, Ankaht's three eyes narrowed slightly and her lesser clusters rose faintly: an appeal to listen to reason. "Admiral, it would require much time to explain how and why I may say that content of the armored courier's databanks was entered without the anticipation of unwanted *selnarmic* inspection, but trust me when I say that it was. I offer a crude analogy: in the same way that you have reflexive body actions that are almost impossible to purposefully mimic,"—the vocoder's rendering of her voice suggested a wry self-reference—"there are *selnarmic* gestures in the courier's various logs that simply would not be present if they had anticipated that we Arduans might come to inspect their data. Similarly, there is a great wealth of personal messaging, bound for the other Dispersates. Much of its content is particular to my people."

"Particular in what way?" asked Kiiraathra's immense, one-eyed second-in-command, Rrurr'rao.

Ankaht's intelligence chief, Mretlak, writhed the smaller tentacles at the tip of his left arm. "You are aware that we Arduans do not permanently die—*zhet*—but, instead, discarnate? And then are reincarnated to resume our lives?"

Rrurr'rao's ears laid back slightly. "I have heard this." His tone did not impart the impression that he had much confidence in this Arduan claim.

Apparently, Mretlak detected the same mixture of uncertainty and dubiety. "It was this difference between us and the many races of your Pan-Sentient Union, or PSU, which led many of the more reactionary Arduans of our First Dispersate to judge you as, collectively, nonintelligent. It was deemed that our *shaxzhutok*—remembrance of past lives—and the *selnarm* that links us are the defining characteristics of sentience, a prejudice that became ubiquitous in the later Dispersates with which we now contend. This is, of course, nonsense. But these telempathic phenomena are the defining characteristics of our species' existence, both individually and collectively."

"And how did this engender the especially characteristic communications you detected among the Kaituni data?" Yoshikuni's frown was no longer one of doubt, merely intense concentration.

Two of Ankaht's tentacles rolled over each other in a desultory gesture. "As these later Dispersates arrive, the Kaituni populating them attempt to contact loved ones in the other fleets."

The brow-tuft above Rrurr'rao's remaining eye contracted into a furry bush. "But these Dispersates departed your doomed homeworld over the course of many centuries, and their populations were not cryogenically suspended. How could any hope to be reunited with the kin they remembered?"

Mretlak's tone was calm, patient. "As you suggest, my people have not merely been scattered across the vastness of space, but separated by deep rifts of time. However, for us, this does not signify that we mourn for those we knew and who discarnated during our separation. Rather, we look for their reincarnated return.

"But, with our race divided among so many Dispersates that have been out of communication with each other for so long, there has been no way to determine which of our loved ones are presently reincarnated, and if so, among which fleet they returned to life. A great deal of the personal message traffic that we discovered on the armored courier are attempts of past lovers and children and parents to locate each other, once again. It is—" Mretlak paused; the vocoder's depiction of his voice trailed off in something that sounded very much like sorrow. "It is," he resumed, "quite poignant. Particularly since many of these attempts to restore old bonds are tinged with tones of confusion and bewilderment."

"Why?" Wethermere had not been aware he was going to ask the question until it emerged from his mouth.

"Because they cannot understand what has happened to our people," Ankaht answered, turning her three eyes upon him, the central one widening as it did: a sign of affinity. "When last they were incarnate, all in our race cherished *shaxzhutok*, reveled in the lessons and recollections of past lives, sought the union in *selnarm* that we call *narmata*." Her voice saddened. "They have awakened into an existence where this no longer defines the fleets into which they are born. The *Destoshaz*-controlled culture of the Kaituni eschews *narmata* and *shaxzhutok*, and has often euthanized those of my caste, the *shaxzhu*, whose gift it is to reclaim and reveal the more distant memories of both individuals and of our race. They are like lost children."

"Whom we are set upon killing," Mretlak finished darkly.

"And whom will return from that discarnation to be returned into our race as we Arduans rebuild and restore it," Narrok reminded him.

Mretlak let his eyes close in slow acquiescence that, to Ossian's limited understanding of Arduan kinesics, seemed grudging.

Rrurr'rao was nodding too. "Our lives may be different in many particulars, Senior Group Leader Mretlak, but be assured that I understand the longing and drive to find missing kin. The Kaituni have savaged most of the Khanate's major worlds, and many of the others besides." He drew up stiffly; it did not seem confrontational, but more the rigidity of careful self-control. "None of the *Zheeerlikou'valkhannaieee* in this fleet have any knowledge of whom amongst their kin survive. If any. And as you point out, we do not reincarnate."

Kiiraathra glanced at his lieutenant, whose tone had gone from dark to borderline menacing in the last sentence. He, along with many others among the various

PSU races, found it difficult, if not specious, to make distinctions between the Arduans and the Kaituni. Kiiraathra did not allow a pall to gather in the wake of Rrurr'rao's conclusion: "We also lack *selnarm*, which has proven to be an unlooked-for advantage for this fleet."

Commander Rudi Modelo-Vo, Admiral Yoshikuni's Fleet Tactical Officer (in name, at least), frowned. "An advantage, Least Fang? I'd say our lack of *selnarm* puts us at a constant and severe disadvantage. Our enemies can communicate instantaneously, control remote assets from any distance without time-lag, and exchange information using a quantum-based medium that we can't even detect with our best instruments."

There was silence as, once again, the collected senior staff separately decided how best to react to Modelo-Vo's tone deafness when it came to tactical nuances: a significant deficit in a fleet tactical officer. Kiiraathra folded his large, tabby-furred "hands." "All of what you say is true, Commander, but we must consider one further variable: that the Kaituni do not know the Arduans are with us. Which means they do not suspect that we can intercept and understand their signals, can send target data to our stealthed ships before they reveal themselves to attack, and have devised means of subverting and compromising their *selnarmic* command and control links. Indeed, the latter phenomenon is the very basis of the weapon system upon which Captain Chong and Group Leader Lentsul have been working. About which: is the device ready?"

With Chong absent, Lentsul alone was left to reply. Still nervous in the presence of humans, he straightened in his chair, two small tentacles switching spasmodically.

"It is ready. I believe. And as Admiral Kiiraathra'ostakjo points out, the Kaituni presumption that we cannot discern nor manipulate their *selnarmic* elements constitutes an immense tactical advantage. But, I warn you—as has Commodore Wethermere—it is fundamentally a one-time advantage." With a glance at Ossian, he leaned forward into his explanation. "The commodore's care in ensuring that our actions would remain unreported, both when we have tested the weapon and have used *selnarm* as a remote targeting guide for stealthed warships, has been resisted by some." He may have glanced at Yoshikuni and Modelo-Vo. "But that resistance was not wise."

Yoshikuni bristled at Lentsul's characteristic lack of tact. The lids of the two smaller eyes flanking Ankaht's larger, central one sagged in exasperation.

Oblivious, Lentul pressed on. "Once the Kaituni realize that this Relief Fleet has Arduan allies, they will change their operations accordingly. So the advantage we currently enjoy will end along with their ignorance."

Narrok leaned forward, thereby silencing Lentsul, which may have been his intent. "In essence, we possess an enormous advantage, but one which we must protect each time we use it by ensuring that no enemy escapes to report its existence. And so, we cannot utilize it on an open battlefield until we are poised to enter a combat of decisive strategic importance."

Surprisingly, Lentsul also seemed inured to the cue from his own Arduan commander. "Exactly so," he affirmed. "However, before we leave the topic I must correct another of Commander Modelo-Vo's misunderstandings."

Regardless of species, every being in the room shifted

uncomfortably in their seats. Yoshikuni glared at Ankaht. Wethermere had seen library patrons stare at the parents of boisterous children in just that same manner.

Unaware of the wake of annoyance his behavior was leaving behind, Lentsul continued. "Commander Modelo-Vo characterized *selnarmic* phenomenon as taking place in a quantum-based medium. This is erroneous."

Modelo-Vo sounded as though he was gargling with lye. "That's odd. I thought I'd heard you describe its properties as akin to quantum entanglement, occurring without regard for the normal laws constraining all physical phenomenon and information exchange to the speed of light."

"You evidently were inattentive and did not discern that my reference to quantum phenomenon was couched as an analogy, not a physical property of *selnarm* itself." If Lentsul understood that Modelo-Vo's flushed face and widened eyes indicated a sudden upsurge of rage, he gave no sign of it. "In fact, the agency underlying the operation of *selnarm* remains a mystery even to us Arduans. We liken it to quantum entanglement because it shares the relativity-defying characteristics you have invoked, Commander. On the other hand, it demonstrates properties which are wholly distinct, as well. For instance, quantum entanglement seems to operate—as best we can tell—between particles or other quantal elements that are somehow paired, either due to shared origins or other more transient similarities in their present state. *Selnarm* evinces no such reliance upon pairing. Its effect is expansive and thoroughgoing: an accomplished *shaxzhu* such as Councilor Ankaht could establish mental contact among a great number of minds instantaneously throughout a solar system. She could send a more generalized empathic pulse—a mood or feeling, in your limited lexicon—to almost all Arduans in that same sphere. There is nothing in your or our understanding of quantum mechanics that can account for this pervasive effect. Nor is there any indication that particles of any type—even at the sub-quark level—are involved in actuating these phenomena. Our theories lean more toward what your physicists have labeled string or wave theories, which propose that what we deem matter and energy are all simply expressions of common components, distinguished only by waveform characteristics. However, we have never determined a means of testing these theories, and so, the mechanism underlying *selnarmic* activity remains hypothetical. At best."

Yoshikuni brought her hand down flat on the table: the sound was noticeable, but not quite a slap. "Thank you, Lesser Group Leader Lentsul. Your explanations have been most illuminating. If we have need of more, we shall surely ask for them. Now, Councilor Ankaht, the floor is yours: tell us what you and your intelligence team have learned regarding the deployment and plans of our opponents."

A ripple passed along Ankaht's greater tentacles, which Ossian knew signified that she had mixed feelings about the data she was about to present. "Firstly, as we conjectured, the enemy fleet is still in the system immediately beyond this one: Bug 28. However, they are rapidly preparing to continue on to Bug 27 and ultimately Earth. Indeed, they sent the courier we intercepted because their departure for Earth was accelerated in just the last few days."

If possible, Yoshikuni sat straighter. "They've accelerated their timetable? Your people assured us that prior intel indicated they were still just regrouping to herd the Bugs onward."

Ankaht did not quite sound arch as she replied. " 'My people' did indeed report that, because that was what we discovered when we deciphered the databanks on the wreck of the *Degruz-pahr*. But circumstances have changed. Dramatically."

Yoshikuni leaned back, frowning. Whether from Ankaht's effortless rebuff of her aggressive demeanor or at the promise of unwelcome news, Ossian could not tell. "Very well. How have the circumstances changed?"

"The Kaituni ahead of us—they call themselves the Fourteenth Dispersate—were expecting to split the Arachnids into two groups. One was, as we feared, to be pushed to arrive at system Bug 17 before Admiral Trevayne did, thereby cutting off his fleet from Earth and bottling it between two forces. The other half of the Omnivoracity force was to continue on to Bug 15 in front of the Fourteenth Dispersate, to achieve the same end, in the event the first half of the Arachnid fleet arrived in Bug 15 too late."

"So they were pursuing both options," Narrok observed with a calm sweep of one major tentacle. "Sensible."

"Yes," Kiiraathra agreed. "They certainly have the superiority of numbers that allows them to explore all strategic options."

Ankaht signaled assent. "Yes. This was the premise

upon which their orders were based, and which had been *selnarmically* issued to them years before their Dispersate arrived here. Again, as we conjectured, the Dispersates' collective actions and intrusions were coordinated long before they arrived."

"So what was the dramatic change?" Yoshikuni's voice was not quite sharp, but it was not amicable. Although the admiral respected Ankaht, she did not seem to like her much. Which, Wethermere reflected, made little sense, unless the human admiral was jealous of the easy friendship the Arduan councilor had with Wethermere himself. Who, until this moment, had never considered it probable, let alone sane, that Miharu Yoshikuni could feel jealously possessive of her romantic relationship with him—and above all, jealous of an alien with whom there wasn't even the possibility of emotional, let alone physical, intimacy. But, now, Ossian wondered if—

"Ironically," Ankaht answered, "the change was in how profoundly *cooperative* the Arachnids became. Too cooperative, as it turned out. Once the Kaituni's small leading flotilla had completed shepherding them into Bug 26, and was thereby separated from the rest of the Fourteenth Dispersate, the Arachnids raced ahead. Their entire fleet. Their drovers followed and, despite the marked Kaituni technological superiority, just managed to keep up as the lead elements of the Arachnids raced along the warp line leading from Bug 25 to Bug 17."

"So . . . no more Bugs? They're out of our way?" Modelo-Vo sounded as though he could hardly believe such a stroke of good luck.

"Correct."

"But did the Arachnids emerge into Admiral Trevayne's rear area?" Narrok's voice was tense. An inherently strategic thinker, he, like Wethermere, did not see this as a tactical windfall. The Arduan admiral was entirely focused upon the strategic consequences of whether Trevayne had escaped to withdraw further toward Sol, or whether the enemy had now bottled him up along that route of advance. Because if the Bugs had trapped him there, the job of defending Earth would fall solely to the much, much smaller Relief Fleet: a hopeless task.

"No," Ankaht answered to several audible exhalations of relief. "The Kaituni drovers who followed the Arachnids reported that Admiral Trevayne was in the process of conducting an orderly withdrawal from the Bug 17 system when they emerged from the warp point that joined it to Bug 21. Their arrival did not inflict significant additional losses to his fleet."

"But now the full weight of the Arachnid fleet we have been following has joined with the larger one preceding the main Kaituni force. Which is, as we conjectured, comprised of approximately seven whole Dispersates." Narrok's three eyes were focused on something well beyond the bulkhead.

"That is correct. We have also determined that they are led by a *Destoshaz'at* by the name of Zum'ref. However, only two-thirds of the Arachnid ships that we were following actually reached Bug 17."

Kiiraathra's nose wrinkled slightly. "Then where is the other third?"

"Most of it remained behind in the system you

designate as Home Hive Four. Two small Arachnid flotillas—picket elements, according to my military analysts—remained behind in the flanking systems of Bug 21 and Bug 22. And apparently, not all the Kaituni drovers made it back through these systems to deliver their reports."

Jennifer Pietchkov, Alessandro Magee's wife and the only human with a reasonable measure of pseudo-*selnarmic* ability, leaned forward from where she had pulled away from the lip of the conference table. "The Arachnids turned on them?"

"Yes, although that should not surprise us too greatly," Ankaht said mildly to her colleague and friend. "They have resisted the herding attempts of the Kaituni before."

Wethermere nodded. "Yes, and their reasons are probably the same this time, too."

Mretlak's central eye closed and reopened slowly: profound agreement. "They are reclaiming their old systems. The system they most heavily invested was one of their Hives."

"Which we devastated over two hundred and sixty years ago," Yoshikuni pointed out irritably.

"So you did," Narrok agreed. "But what caches might they have there that you did not find, but of which they still have record? What data, archives, resources are there that, in their tireless industry, the Arachnids secreted in cometary orbits or amidst the litter of a belt, or on any one of thousands of nondescript planetoids? In the quest to reestablish themselves quickly, these assets could be crucial to them now."

"And beyond logic, there is the reflex of tradition,"

Rrurr'rao added with a nod. "It is their place. They will go to it. Perhaps out of instinct as much as reason."

Yoshikuni leaned two, fine-fingered fists on the table. "So we are now aware how the circumstances have changed. And I am presuming that the Kaituni fleet ahead of us is now racing to do the job that they had originally envisioned for half of the Bugs that they lost: to cut off Trevayne by getting to Bug 15 before he does."

Ankaht's vocoder-voice was calm. "Yes. Or at least, to enter it and interdict the warp point to Alpha Centauri before he reaches it."

"Wouldn't Admiral Trevayne's fleet just push one Dispersate out of the way?" asked Jennifer Pietchkov. Her voice sounded as though she already doubted whether such a task would be as easy as her phrasing made it sound.

"No, Ms. Pietchkov," Narrok answered solemnly. "Certainly, Admiral Trevayne would prevail. He might not even lose that many ships. But he would lose many, many precious hours while a much larger foe was close at his heels. Battles are lost just as often due to running out of time as running out of resources."

"Admiral Narrok, I could not agree more." Yoshikuni sat very straight. "And that is why we will be changing our own strategy to match the Kaituni's."

"In what way, Admiral?" Ankaht asked.

"In the only way that will help Admiral Trevayne's defense of Earth: we're going on the attack."

CHAPTER FIVE

While the various admirals and their adjutants were still silent, Admiral Yoshikuni waved a hand over the center of the table; a holoflat of the local warp network winked into glowing existence. "We have an excellent chance to catch them while they are sorting themselves out in Bug 27. The timing will be close, but we can do it.

"And we'd better. If the Fourteenth Dispersate reaches Bug 26, our problems multiply. That system has a star in it, so any battle fought there would involve maneuvering around its Desai limits. That usually favors defenders.

"It would also mean that any Kaituni who are dispatched from there to inform others of our presence have two ways to escape the system: the warp points to both Bug 24 and Bug 23. So the odds of us keeping them bottled up once they get to Bug 26 are pretty unpromising.

"On the other hand, Bug 27 is a starless system with only two warp points: the one leading to us here in Bug

28, and the one that goes to Bug 26. And if any stragglers get through to Bug 26, we'll have a free field of maneuver in which to cut them off and hunt them down. And I will reemphasize what Commodore Wethermere has been stressing from the moment we began shadowing the enemy: every time we get into a fight, keeping our existence a secret is every bit as crucial as winning. So, we cannot afford to have our presence revealed by leakers who'd run further down the warp-line to Bug 15 or Bug 17."

Rrurr'rao leaned back from the table. "I do not wish to contend with the Admiral's assessment," he said carefully, "but how do you plan to enter a system that the Fourteenth Dispersate already occupies, yet reach and block the next warp point before their lead elements begin to move through it?"

She nodded to acknowledge the pertinence of the question. "By counting upon their demonstrated apathy when it comes to setting adequate rear-guard patrols in place and by sending in our fastest stealthed ships to reach the far warp point, unnoticed, before they reform their fleet for their next movement down the warp-line." She waved her hand; a strategic map of the Bug 26 system replaced the warp line diagram. "Admiral Narrok and Least Fang Kiiraathra'ostakjo, along with Commodore Wethermere, have been aiding me in refining the relevant concept of operations for several weeks, now."

Ossian felt, as much as saw, the resentful glare that Modelo-Vo sent his way. The commander's exclusion from the planning of this maneuver demonstrated to everyone in the room what had long been suspected: that he remained the Fleet Tactical Officer in name only. His inability to think outside the box of conventional military doctrine had made it necessary to cut him out of a loop that his inclusion would only have weakened.

Jennifer Pietchkov put up a hand. "You've been working on a plan for weeks? But you only learned about these changed circumstances today."

"True, Ms. Pietchkov," Yoshikuni answered with an abrupt nod, "but the relevant conops were going to be employed eventually because no matter when we had to move aggressively, or where, the problem facing us was going to be the same: to trap the Kaituni in a system *before* engaging them. Anything else gives them the chance of sending a warning further down the warp line. And that warning could include intelligence on our special tactics or advantages which, as were pointed out earlier, become useless once our enemy has general knowledge of them." She leaned back. "No. We have to catch them here. And it is our good fortune that the news about the Bugs breaking ranks and leaving them in the lurch apparently caught them off guard. The Kaituni will be busy restructuring their forces, going through an evolution into formations more suitable for the changes in their upcoming warp point transfers."

"What changes are you referring to, Admiral?" Modelo-Vo asked glumly.

"Mostly, they are having to adopt a more traditional formation. Up until now, they haven't had to worry about reconnaissance or about breaching strategies if they discover that a warp point is held against them. All those problems had been handled and absorbed by the Bugs. But not anymore. So now the Kaituni have to contemplate which ships they're willing to pull out of their van and dedicate to those routine operations."

"Wouldn't they have contingency plans for that?" Pietchkov wondered.

"No doubt," Narrok replied. "But a fleet under way is a ponderous beast to control, and must be shaped appropriately for the many tasks it might be called upon to perform with little warning. The Fourteenth Dispersate must now shift into those new formations and run through readiness drills as well. In general, this will both delay them and force them to adopt a more attenuated shape, with advance elements further ahead and the vulnerable logistical tail further behind."

"Which determines our tactics for the coming engagement," Yoshikuni explained to the faces around the table. "Our first move will be to retrofit some of the courier drones we captured today to get a positional update on the Kaituni and detect any buoys or automated defenses they might have left behind to watch, or simply monitor traffic, that uses the Bug 28-Bug 27 warp junction. Like the tripwires we encountered before entering this system. If they have such assets in place, we'll send in our Arduan ship, the *Fet'merah*, to override those monitoring devices. Just like last time.

"The first actual combat forces we send through will be our fastest, stealthed superdreadnoughts. Their energy output is low enough that they can make almost full speed to the other warp point."

"They will coordinate their approach vectors by brief *selnarmic* contacts?" Mretlak asked.

Narrok nodded. "If any deviation is required from their

set path, yes. This vanguard will ultimately position itself between the main body of the Fourteenth Dispersate and the warp point to Bug 26. Then we shall bring up the bulk of the fleet behind them."

Modelo-Vo cross his arms. "And if they see our numbers and turn tail immediately, trying to scoot through the warp point?"

Wethermere nodded. "That worried us, too. So we're going to keep some of the larger, slower lead elements of the main body stealthed, also. That should make it look like we, too, are attenuated and with less imposing numbers. With any luck, they will think they can take us on, ship to ship, long enough for their error in judgment to prove fatal to them. If not—well, that's why we're going to have the cream of our stealthed SDs and SDHs holding the far warp point. Our main body is going to close with theirs as quickly and as hard as possible, and we do have a slight speed advantage. So the battle around the warp point itself could get pretty fierce for a while, but we consider it unlikely that the Kaituni will be able to bring enough weight to bear to slip any of their ships through. And if they do, we'll have faster ships right on their tail. Which is why we need to hit them while they're in Bug 27: so we have a whole other system's worth of space in which to hunt down any who get around the superdreadnoughts and heavy superdreadnoughts with which I'll be holding the warp point."

Wethermere, along with Narrok, and Kiiraathra, detected the pronoun Yoshikuni had used a split second before the others; all three of them snapped forward at the same instant. "*You'll* be holding the warp point?"

Miharu's green eyes swiveled to meet his. The almost tortured vulnerability he had often seen in them as they looked down, or up, at him during intimate moments was utterly gone. "Yes, Commodore. That's my place in this fight."

"Admiral." It was Narrok; the tone from his vocoder was extremely level. Extremely careful. "Granted that this is your decision to make—"

"Exactly correct. And it is made."

Kiiraathra'ostakjo's slit-irised eyes were wide. "A commander's place is at the head of the fleet."

"Admiral, I don't lecture you on what you already know. Do not presume to lecture me. At the head of the fleet is exactly where I'm going to be. And exactly where I will be needed: where the fighting is going to be the trickiest, the closest, the most unconventional." She looked around the table; her expression dared any of them to interrupt her. Wethermere was considering how best to do so when she took the initiative once again. "Frankly, none of you have my credentials for this kind of operation. During the war with the Arduans, every major engagement in which I was the ranking or executive fleet commander was one that I fought as an underdog." She glowered at Wethermere, anticipating the objection he had his mouth open to utter. "And I was commanding a whole fleet while doing it. No one else here has that kind of experience. Admiral Narrok is an excellent strategist and will arguably do a better job than I will wielding the van of our fleet against the main body of the Fourteenth Dispersate—not the least because we'll be employing special tactics which require a nuanced understanding of what *selnarm* can and cannot do. Admiral Kiiraathra'ostakjo is among the finest carrier commanders I've ever met or heard of—but all his carriers will be with our main van. And with those assignments, we are fresh out of admirals."

As the horrible logic of her arguments sank in, Yoshikuni's tone modulated into a more conversational tone. "It's not as bad as some of you are thinking. Remember, we'll be able to seed the area in front of the warp point with *selnarmic* microsensors. Thanks to the Arduan ships in my task force and on my own ships, I'll have pretargeting on the approaching enemy hulls before they even know we're there. And if we're fortunate, they will see Admiral Narrok bring our main van through before they detect me. That means that they won't all come at me at once, but in penny packets as you push and then break them from behind."

Narrok's tentacles were very still. "Even in those ideal circumstances," he said slowly, "you will still have the weight of steel very much against you."

Yoshikuni shook her head; her shining black hair described a brief, gleaming wave. "Not if you come in quickly enough. And hit them hard enough."

Wethermere knew that tone, the one that indicated that Miharu Yoshikuni had made up her mind. It also meant that she was no longer interested in counterarguments. For reasons he had not yet discerned about her, Miharu often reached a point where she seemed to feel that analysis would only serve to undermine her resolve. And the Iron Admiral never let anything undermine her resolve. But she also hated insufficient planning, so—"Admiral, I'd like to suggest adding an additional safeguard to your concept of operations."

Miharu's eyes cut back in his direction, wary; she had experienced, both in the wardroom and the bedroom, how Ossian's willow could often outbend and, so, outmaneuver her oaken stiffness. "Yes, Commodore?" She said it as if she was expecting a trap.

"Admiral, even if the Kaituni don't have a holding force at the warp point we must enter through, we have to expect that they'll leave a set of tripwire buoys and automated couriers there as well. At least enough to monitor any proximal activity and transit traffic. Which will alert their main body once we send something through."

She frowned. "Commodore, we've already discussed the contingency for that. We send through a captured courier drone of our own to take a look around. It will register as authorized, since it comes from the enemy ship we just seized."

"Yes, Admiral. That will tell us what's just on the other side of the warp point. And approximately where the bulk of the Fourteenth Dispersate is located. And, *if* we can tap into and control the reporting elements of their tripwire, we can prevent it from reporting the transitions of your stealthed, superdreadnoughts, battleships and smaller vessels."

"Correct. So what's the problem?"

"Admiral, what happens if we *can't* tap into and control the tripwire they've left behind?"

No one answered because the question was clearly rhetorical. The Kaituni would be alerted, and, failing to detect the hulls that triggered the transit alerts from the tripwire system, would no doubt begin suspecting what they had no reason to suspect up until that moment: that they were being followed by foes who possessed a technology which rendered them virtually invisible. The result of that realization—patrol and detection sweeps, alerts sent further down all accessible warp-lines, defense of the further warp point from both the near and far sides—were responses as predictable and inevitable as the falling of dominos. And potentially disastrous to the execution of Yoshikuni's plan.

The admiral leaned back, her face unreadable. "I don't see that we have any alternative to that risk, Commodore— here or elsewhere. We might not be able to prevent detection."

"I agree, Admiral. But perhaps that fact should shape our tactics."

One of Yoshikuni's fine eyebrows elevated. "In what way?"

"We send in an unstealthed advance element that will appear to explain all the transits, in case we're detected."

Lentsul frowned. "Do you mean to send in a carrier and its fighters?"

Wethermere shook his head. "Unfortunately, that wouldn't work: something as small as a fighter won't trigger the warp point. Besides, Bug 28 is starless and therefore, all of its space is suitable for Desai drive. Meaning that fighters lose their speed advantage. However, a small number of medium-sized ships carrying smaller ships within them could be used to mislead the Kaituni."

Kiiraathra'ostakjo groomed his whiskers briskly. "Yes.

If a freighter goes through, it would only create one transit signature. But if it then released five smaller ships—couriers or pinnaces—from its bay, the Kaituni would have no reason to suspect that all those craft came in through a single transit unless they have dedicated very precise monitoring assets to their tripwire."

Wethermere nodded. "Which we have not observed thus far. So if we bring through that kind of advance group, the Kaituni would see a number of transit-capable hulls that far exceeds the number of transits it took to get them in the system."

Yoshikuni leaned forward. "And so, my stealthed task force could use that transit deficit to conceal, or rather 'account for,' its own entry. The Kaituni would see a number of unstealthed hulls that equal the number of transits. So since the number of visible ships and recorded transits match, they wouldn't know to look for my stealthed flotilla."

Wethermere nodded. "That's the concept, Admiral. You slip in between the elements of that advance group of freighters and quickly race ahead under stealth on preplotted courses, confirmed as clear by the courier drones and the *selnarm*-capable elements within the group. Then you set up your task force between their main van and the warp point on toward Bug 15."

Modelo-Vo looked as though he'd swallowed a cup of vinegar. "And if the Kaituni are already most of the way to that warp point? Sending in an unstealthed advance group might chase them out."

"Not if most of the advance group is comprised of Kaituni—or Arduan—craft and running Kaituni transponder codes. The enemy will tweak to the sham eventually—they always do—but the further away they are, the longer it will take them to do so, and the less concerned they are going to be about activity at the warp point they've already left far behind."

Kiiraathra'ostakjo was nodding in the abrupt fashion of his species. "This additional precaution fits well with the concept of operations we devised earlier. We shall insert the Arduans who will attempt to gain control of the tripwire as the lead element of that first group. If they succeed in commandeering the buoys and alert system so that it will not report transits, all may proceed as in our best-case scenario. However, if they fail, the rest of the advance group will come through, with Admiral Yoshikuni's task force interspersed among them. Either way, the Kaituni will have no reason to suspect that she is stealthed and making best speed for the other warp point. And that is the crucial advantage we must gain."

Yoshikuni nodded. "I agree. This gives us a good set of contingencies with which to adapt to different operational outcomes. We will employ them and use the Special Recon Detachment that Commodore Wethermere has assembled to function as that advance group. Now, unless there are any further questions, I want to commence detailed planning with the command staff." As the nonmilitary personnel rose to leave, Yoshikuni glanced—almost reluctantly, Ossian thought—at him. "Commodore, you will leave with Commander Modelo-Vo and brief him on the operational particulars of the recon detachment immediately. He'll want some time to settle in with them."

"I beg your pardon, Admiral?"

Yoshikuni's glance returned to him as a hard—unnecessarily hard—stare. "Commodore Wethermere, don't be obtuse. You are being relieved from command of the recon element."

CHAPTER SIX

The room was silent except for the faint hum of the lights. Then, Kiiraathra pushed back from the table. Narrok's tendrils flinched once. But it was Ankaht who had the courage to ask, "Is that wise, Admiral?"

Yoshikuni's look was as direct and piercing as a rapier thrust. "Councilor Ankaht, since you're not here in a military capacity, I can't give you a demerit for asking that question. I'd like to, though. As much for its lack of insight as for your temerity. But instead, allow me to answer your question with one of my own. Who is the ranking PSU officer in this fleet? And who is senior among its commodores—both in calendar years of service and combat experience in two wars?"

The more relaxed voice that emerged from Narrok's vocoder resonated with his suddenly less rigid posture: understanding had supplanted his initial surprise at Wethermere's removal from his post. "Commodore Wethermere is the senior PSU officer with our fleet. By a considerable margin."

"Exactly," Yoshikuni snapped, eyes still on Ankaht. "In short, I am not relieving Commodore Wethermere of his current command because of insufficiencies in his performance, but because this is an extremely dangerous mission and he is not expendable."

Ossian rose slowly. "Admiral, with all due respect—"

"Commodore, let me save you the trouble of pointing out that we have another rear admiral with the fleet. Because that point is moot. In the first place, Admiral Voukaris is another Rim Republic officer, so he cannot take your place as a senior representative for the PSU. And as far as he might be considered a replacement for any of the other admirals in their current roles, well— there is the matter of his combat record."

"What is wrong with his combat record?" Ankaht asked.

"The fact that he doesn't have one," Yoshikuni replied sharply. "He was the only other flag officer I could lay my hands on when we left Bellerophon. And his role there— chief administrator and inspector for all our groundside and orbital installations—marks him for what he is: a supremely capable bureaucrat. He has been an outstanding logistics organizer for us, has excelled at frontier provisioning—but he's not a combat officer."

Ankaht's tentacles lay flat and motionless upon the table before her. "But let us return to the logic you have applied to Commodore Wethermere's status. Applied to yourself, it means you shouldn't be leading the advance element in the attack, Admiral Yoshikuni. No matter your credentials. You, too, are not expendable."

Her retort—"Not true,"—was punctuated by a finger

that she jabbed at Narrok and Kiiraathra'ostakjo in sequence. "These two admirals both rank Voukaris."

Kiiraathra stiffened slightly. "Admiral Yoshikuni, my given military rank is Least Fang. That makes my rank equivalent to a human rear admiral. I am the same rank as Voukaris."

"Maybe in the eyes of the Khanate, but not me—and not the PSU either. I wasn't in this campaign for twenty-four hours before Commodore Wethermere provided the rationale and *de facto* authorization for brevetting you up one rank. So whatever we call you, you are above Voukaris on the fleet's table of organization. Besides, both you and Admiral Narrok have exceptional skill as combat commanders and excellent organizational and strategic qualification. Under either one of you, the Relief Fleet would remain in excellent—er, hands," she finished with an abashed glance at Narrok's arm-ending tendril clusters.

"True," he replied, "but as an Arduan, I am neither a member of the PSU or the Rim Federation, yet. Which touches on another aspect of your indispensability, Admiral. Eighty percent of our fleet swears allegiance to your government. They should be led by their own commander. At all times."

Yoshikuni's expression was as dogged as a determined street-brawler. "As you say, Arduans are not full members of the Rim Republic—yet. But you Arduans are provisional members, and you've been out here, willing to fight and die alongside us. Under these circumstances, that's good enough for me."

Ankaht had leaned backward in her seat; an Arduan

posture that signified well-controlled surprise. "That may be good enough for you, Admiral, but will it be good enough for the thousands of human personnel who were locked in a life-and-death struggle with those same Arduans just under seven years ago?"

"It will have to be. And before you go pointing out that Commodore Wethermere can be risked on the line because Admiral Kiiraathra'ostakjo is also a PSU officer, you might want to ask the Least Fang why he hasn't raised that objection himself." Yoshikuni looked down the table at the Orion. The others followed her gaze. Wethermere simply looked away; he knew what was coming.

The Orion inclined his head slowly, unwillingly. "Admiral Yoshikuni is, unfortunately, quite correct. According to the founding documents of the modern Khanate, a flag officer may not also hold a political position of any kind, even if it is solely titular. The internecine wars of our first starfaring centuries were often caused—and extended—because single individuals occupied both such positions of power. This led to recurrent warlordism, as always occurs when military and political dominance are combined in the same individual. It becomes impossible to check their actions, to hold them responsible to any authority other than their own agendas or . . . caprice. As was too often the case in the early history of my people. So, for me to be able to fulfill a political role, I would have to immediately resign my commission and my duties with this fleet."

"Which we cannot afford, either in terms of Relief Fleet's command structure or morale," Yoshikuni added. "Conversely, as I understand the PSU articles of incorporation and the military protocols that have been established over the years, this topic has not been specifically addressed in its naval regulations. That is probably because the democracies that left their legacy in the form of Earth's current government did not have to deal with the Orion tendency to consolidate power in a minimal number of persons and institutions. Instead, human government is characterized by the separation of powers and checks and balances. So political figures holding a military rank did not materially threaten civic stability."

She stood. "So Commodore Wethermere is indeed the senior PSU representative in this fleet. That makes him indispensable, if our actions are to have the de facto approval of a representative of that polity, into whose space we have now entered. Accordingly, this matter is closed. You are dismissed."

Mretlak almost stumbled into Captain William Chong as they met at the secure ingress to the Confidential Technical Intelligence Cluster, the human exiting, the Arduan entering. Mretlak started, more surprised than the human. Growing up among other *selnarmic* beings, it was rare that one ever was physically surprised by the presence of another. Like dim beacons, their telempathic links were not completely blocked by walls or other sightline obstructions, and so, the subconscious of the Arduan was not so perpetually alert for unanticipated stimuli as was the human.

"Leaving for the day, Captain?" Mretlak inquired.

Chong hefted a box in his arms meaningfully. "Leaving

for good, I guess. Lentsul arrived just a minute before you. Told me the time had come to clear out."

Mretlak's smaller tendrils drooped momentarily; other Arduans would have perceived in that gesture what humans perceive in an exasperated sigh. "I apologize for Lentsul, Captain. He means well, but he is not well attuned to the emotions of others. Even among his often less personable caste—the *Ixturshaz*—he is notably, well, abrupt, on occasion."

Chong's lips quirked in what Mretlak had come to interpret as a wry smile. "He is abrupt on every occasion, it seems to me. But I don't take it personally. And the two of you don't need me much any more: the project has moved into pure *selnarmic* manipulation now. Way above my head—even if I was a sensitive, like Jennifer Pietchkov."

Mretlak attempted a human bow, reflected that he probably appeared to be spasming in reaction to a cramp. "I am sure we shall have continued want of your input, Captain. You have been an excellent colleague in our endeavors."

"The feeling is mutual, Senior Group Leader. Now, if you'll excuse me—"

Mretlak stepped aside; the human nodded his thanks, made for the first corner in the corridor, was gone.

Lentsul's *selnarm* reached out from beyond the door into the research labs. "The human's departure stirs currents of regret in you, Senior Group Leader. Why?"

Mretlak made his way into the secure area, stopping to satisfy the various biometric and genetic security monitors and checks. "He was a hard worker, insightful, attentive to detail, and not a bigot. Why would I not regret having such a colleague as a daily fixture in our laboratory?"

Lentsul sent (puzzlement). "Because he is a human. Because however well-intentioned he may be, he will never understand us. And because we constantly had to slow our communications down to the pace enabled by the cumbersome, limited vocalizations that his species mislabels 'speech.'"

Mretlak was tempted to renew their old debate: that sometimes, the speed or utility of communications was not as important as the fellow feeling it might nourish, and with it, a chance for genuine and lasting amity and peace. But Lentsul, although never mounting definitive counterarguments, likewise never felt that Mretlak's were decisive. Lentsul simply accepted—where perhaps he might not need to—that Arduans and humans were fated to coexist but without any genuine understanding or mutuality of opinion or experience.

But Mretlak was too tired, and too worried, to once again contend with the inflexible *Ixturshaz*. "So we have come to the final phase of Project Turncoat?"

Lentsul's three eyes widened in response. "Yes. And the Kaituni technology we seized today and several weeks ago is accelerating the research wonderfully. If only we could get our tendrils on several of their intact automated fighters."

Mretlak sent (agreement), reflected that it would be quite difficult to get their hands on an intact Kaituni robot wingman (as Chong, a former fighter pilot, had dubbed them). Two of them were always paired with a *selnarmically*-controlled remote-operated, or "ROV," fighter, and the humans had nicknamed these small three craft formations "triads" "We will not secure an automated fighter in time, now," he asserted.

"No, we will not," Lentsul agreed. "As Yoshikuni made clear, it will not occur until the salvage operations after a major engagement. Which is ill-timed: it would be better to conduct a detailed analysis of the robot-fighter's control systems beforehand."

"It would, Lentsul, but we are not expected to deliver Project Turncoat until after this coming battle. The admiral understands that we cannot reveal its existence to anyone until we are ready to field test it. And we cannot do that without more data, more intact examples of the Kaituni command and control elements."

"Which seem crude, in many ways," Lentsul sent with a wave of (disappointment, disapproval). "For instance, their equipment relies far less on *selnarmic* relays than ours do. One would have thought that, being thirteen Dispersates after us, their systems and technology would have been more elegant, more advanced."

Mretlak sent (partial accord). "Yes, but from what we have now seen of their histories, Ardu became desperately inhospitable in the last centuries, and so, regressed. In almost all ways."

Lentsul's tentacles stopped their tentative probing into the guts of a Kaituni remote probe. "Why so? Pre-supernova flares?"

"That, too, but mostly because those who followed us had no choice but to strip the world of all its useful resources without spending the time or energy to control the effects of that process. They knew that they were living in a biosphere that would soon be vaporized; there was no logic and no benefit to preserving what was left of it." Mretlak peered over Lentsul's shoulder; the Kaituni device was, indeed, more primitive than those of earlier Dispersates. "And just as their environment became more harsh, so did they. There is evidence that this Dispersate and the one before it had largely turned away from *selnarm* and *narmata* before they left Ardu."

"It was no longer utile to them?"

Mretlak sent (uncertainty, resignation). "Perhaps. But more so because it was deemed a distraction. As time grew shorter, and our people grew more desperate, they became narrower in their interests, in their actions, in their concerns. Seeing past lives through *shaxzhutok* was no longer a source of wisdom, but disappointment: they were bitter to be alive in such dire, joyless times. Their inner worlds were stunted and they grew accustomed to a kind of psychological isolation and alienation that is all too akin to what the humans experience in their normative existence."

"How terrible. And terrifying," Lentsul affirmed. "It is perhaps a mercy, then, that we shall relieve our brothers and sisters from their torment when we meet them in battle."

Mretlak physically winced. "Even though we shall meet their souls again in a subsequent life," he commented, "I cannot bring myself to be so blithe at the thought of discarnating so many millions of our kin."

Lentsul sent (surprise, objection). "No, Senior Group Leader. I speak of relieving them from the torment of their autocratic *Destoshaz-as-sulhaji* leaders and ethos. I suspect that the systems we are working on here in this lab will be so effective against their ships that it will paralyze them, prompt the *Destoshaz* to realize that they have no choices other than surrender or suicide. And since suicide will not change anything, surrender is the only logical option."

Reasoned like a true Ixturshaz, *reflected Mretlak. If only the world was driven by the rational inevitabilities that his caste likes to imagine.* Unfortunately, there were other powerful, irrational variables in social equations. Illogic, passion, reflex: these, too, were behaviors that shaped history, often to grim ends. But as usual, Mretlak did not bother to add that depressing, leavening perspective to Lentsul's monochromatic worldview. "I will need some privacy, at this juncture. I must install a backdoor subroutine before you and the technicians begin to finalize the programming for the Turncoat system."

Lentsul looked up in the midst of a *befthel*: a simultaneous blink of all three eyes that signaled great surprise among Arduans. "A backdoor? What is that?"

"It is a common provision among human software systems. It is a subroutine whereby a knowledgeable user can alter or wholly disable the program that has been built around it. Or into which it has been built. Consequently, this will allow any knowledgeable user to deactivate Turncoat."

"Why would you weaken a system by incorporating a means whereby it may be illicitly terminated?"

Mretlak paused, closed his *selnarm* slowly so that

Lentsul would not notice, would not detect the many misgivings that stirred beneath the answer. "It is essential if we are to ensure that Turncoat cannot be . . . misused."

"Misused by whom?"

Mretlak wondered at himself; he had not adequately prepared for this moment. He had known that he could not keep the backdoor into Turncoat a complete secret. He had to share it with Lentsul, who was, in the course of overseeing the final software design for Turncoat, sure to detect signs of it, anyhow. Nevertheless, Mretlak had not reconciled himself to sharing so crucial a secret with a confidante who lacked nuance as profoundly as Lentsul. But the moment of disclosure was upon him, and Mretlak could not turn back now. "Well, one possibility is that the humans might misuse it."

Lentsul's reaction was surprisingly swift and unremarkable. He sent a brief wave of (accord) which overlaid his response of, "Prudent. A coup among the humans, or the other *zheteksh* races, could result in their using it unnecessarily."

Now it was Mretlak's turn to be perplexed. "How would they use it unnecessarily?"

Lentsul's response was (surprise) that his superior did not innately understand his assertions *a priori*. It was a trait which had no doubt endeared Lentsul to many of his prior commanders. "As I pointed out earlier, if Turncoat allows us to paralyze as many Kaituni units as we suspect, there is no reason to destroy so many of our kin. But the humans might doubt the genuineness—or continuation—of our cooperation, particularly if we were to learn that they secretly plan to use Turncoat as a means whereby they can turn a mostly bloodless victory into an opportunity for genocide against our kin."

Mretlak emitted an involuntary pulse of (horror, surprise, outrage). "If Turncoat did enable such a one-sided victory, we would not permit them to conduct such a slaughter."

"With respect, Senior Group Leader, there are those among the humans and Orions who would be certain to ensure that we Arduans were the first to be slaughtered. Many do not trust us. Many still hate us."

Mretlak nodded, although he differed with Lentsul over the magnitude of the hatred and danger he perceived among the humans. "These, too, are circumstances for which we should be prepared. Happily, the backdoor subroutine gives us a way of disabling the program before it can be used to such evil ends." *And so will protect us all from other dangers which you are both too myopic and too idealistic to perceive, good Lentsul.*

Jennifer Pietchkov entered the stateroom she shared with Alessandro Magee and did not stop to talk or even glance around. She strode toward him where he stood next to their outsized bunk and did not stop until she rammed into him, chest to chest, her arms snapping around his broad back. "Tank, this is killing me."

She felt her otherwise unflappable Marine major husband stiffen in immediate fear. "What? What's killing you, Jen?"

"The not knowing. The waiting. The nightmares about me returning alone to Zander to tell him that his Dad— dad is dead. Or the nightmare where everyone else is coming home to parades and medals—but Zander's still standing there, waiting for his parents. And they never get off the ship. And he just stands there, waiting, until—"

Tank hugged her so close that it was almost painful, but that was good: it pulled her out of the dream-memories, back into the moment. "That's not going to happen," he said.

She reared back, looked him in the eyes, looked for any doubt, saw none—which alarmed her more than if she had. She held him at arm's length. "Alessandro Magee, you are not indestructible. You do not have some halo of endless good luck hanging over your head. You do things like—today—long enough, often enough, and your number will come up."

He put his hands over hers, where she held him by the shoulders. "Jen, we didn't ask for this war. But it's here. And I have to see it through. That's what this uniform, what this insignia of rank, mean. I don't get to stop just because I've done it enough to tempt fate—whatever that means."

"No, but you don't have to be in the lead, all the time."

"And I'm not. There's Harry Li, and a bunch of the new officers we're bringing in to the Bloodhound SpecRec group—"

"All of whom you rotate out of the field command slot when you know the mission is going to be hot."

"They have to live long enough to know how to lead well, without losing their heads—figuratively or literally."

"That's bullshit, Tank. You were a newbie, once, too. And you managed to survive this long without such careful mentoring. No: you just can't bring yourself to make them take the same risks that you do. Harry says—"

Tank's eyebrows raised. "Oh? And just what does Harry Lighthorse Li have to say on this particular topic?"

Shit. Well, no going back now—"He says he wishes you'd let him lead more often. That you're too busy taking care of your men, that you don't properly take care of yourself." Seeing the frown building on Tank's face, she played her trump card. "And he says that you need to remember that you're a father now, but that you've given above and beyond the call for so long that you don't know how to step back. That by risking yourself again and again to keep your men out of danger, you risk forcing your son to grow up with a blank space where his father should be."

Tank's frown broke, and his strong, rough-hewn features seem to fold in upon themselves, painfully constricted as if he was suffering a heart attack.

Jennifer grabbed him in a hug again. "Tank, Tank: look at me. I'm sorry. But it has to be said. Because it has to change. It has to. Zander needs you; I need you. The time has come for you to teach your men by letting them lead, letting them shoulder the burdens you've carried for so long."

'Sandro's immense torso expanded and contracted through a long, deep sigh. "Jen, I'll do what I can, but I can't make any promises. I'm not calling all the shots. Just like today: I got my marching orders directly from Captain Knight and Commodore Wethermere. They had to be sure there were no screwups, that we succeeded in taking that Kaituni ship, no matter what—"

"No matter what," Jen repeated darkly, running her

hands down Tank's chest before stepping away. "That's pretty much the defining phrase in all this, isn't it?"

"You know it is," he answered miserably. "You've known that from our first date. I'm a soldier. When we weren't at war, I could choose to resign or not when my tour was up. Now, being so far from home and with all enlistments extended until the resolution of the crisis, my choice is to serve or desert in wartime. And you know what that means."

Jen nodded, felt safer on the other side of the compartment while loathing the distance she had had to put between them so that she could think, so that she could be an advocate for herself and their son and their family. Balanced on the razor's edge of life during wartime, all she wanted to do was be as close to him as possible, as long as possible. But if, instead, she kept reminding him, kept pushing for him to relent just a little, then maybe he wouldn't go on some missions. And one of those missions he missed might be the one that would have otherwise had his number on it, that could mean—

She felt his hands on her shoulders. "I'm sorry, Jen. I don't want to—"

She turned and held him so close that he couldn't finish his sentence.

Which was fine, because she didn't want him to speak.

Neither of them did for several hours.

Ankaht was waiting for Ossian as he emerged from the conference room in which he had briefed Rudi Modelo-Vo on the disposition and standard operating procedures of the Special Recon Detachment. Had Ankaht been pressed to define the human's expression, she suspected the word "glum" would have been appropriate. "It has been a difficult day, Ossian?" she asked.

"I'd say that's a fair assessment," he answered in a voice that was more clipped and precise than usual.

They walked together in silence for the better part of a minute, but it was a comfortable silence. Unlike many humans, Wethermere was truly capable of being companionable without speaking; he radiated fellow-feeling the way few of his species did. It was almost as if he sensed a *narmata* among his own kind, even though they were blind and deaf to its existence. She wondered what turns their relationship might have taken had he been a sensitive like Jennifer, or more interesting still, an Arduan himself—

She recoiled from the thought. However admirable some humans might be, they were nonetheless *zheteksh*: creatures that lived and then died, once and finally. They did not reincarnate, they had no telempathic bonds between them, and they had no race memories. Although in the case of Wethermere, she was tempted to wonder: the admiral who had been his mentor, Erica Krishmahnta, had reportedly called him "Old Soul" on several occasions. Given the significance of that label in the late admiral's Neo-Hindu faith, Ankaht wondered if, just maybe—

But no: whatever more sublime mysteries might lie beneath their alien consciousness, humans were still ineluctably the products of their short, finite, and ultimately brutal lives. Their entire existence was suffused with a sense of breathless urgency, racing against the clock of their own mortality, engendering all the acts of desperation that one might reasonably, if tragically, expect from such creatures. With no hope of better things in a later life, they were profoundly and ruthlessly self-seeking: they lied, murdered, cheated, and stole with alarming frequency and from the most selfish of motives. *Although,* Ankaht wondered, *would we Arduans be any different if we had but one journey through the halls of existence? If compelled to walk in their shoes, would we not find many, if not all, of their motivations and foibles becoming our own?*

But whatever the answer to that question, and whatever the relative moral merits of their respective species might be, it was folly to even attempt to imagine how relations with a human might be different if that other person was not, in fact, human. The particulars of a species left its imprint so deeply and pervasively upon each of its members that it was a pointless speculation to wonder how they might be different. *Because if Ossian had been born an Arduan, he would not be Ossian. He would be something else. And so, ironically, I might not feel this strange kinship with him, because there would be no joy in bridging the speciate gulfs between us. For those gulfs would not exist and neither would our joint triumph in bridging them.*

Perhaps that extraordinary bridge of amity and trust between the two of them was what Miharu Yoshikuni sensed, without fully realizing that she did. That could certainly explain why the admiral's relationship with Ankaht had subtly but steadily eroded in direct proportion to her growing intimacy with Ossian. Yoshikuni's was not a sexual or romantic jealousy—the mere thought of what that implied brought Ankaht to the verge of nausea—but an envy of her interpersonal intimacy with Wethermere. Which was possibly fueled by the fear—or worse, the knowledge—that Yoshikuni knew that she would never allow herself to share such easy and profound closeness with him. And perhaps Ossian sensed that, as well.

So: best tread carefully when inquiring after the events of this day. "You did not seem to expect being removed as the commander of the recon detachment."

He looked sideways at her with a rueful smile. "You don't miss much, do you?"

The understatement was not meant as an ironic insult—not quite; Ankaht decided to ignore the slight barb buried in it. "My perspicacity is unrivalled." He smiled more fully at her willingness to play along in the same vein. "But did she give no intimation of this impending change as you and the admirals developed your basic concept of operations?"

"None. Although now I understand why she left some features of the plan vague." He shrugged. "I presumed that she saw no reason to fill in the details until we knew exactly where and when we were going to have to carry out this maneuver: the specifics of the scenario would logically determine the specific tactics we'd employ. But now I suspect she was ruminating on taking this step from the very start." He shook his head. "I just don't know why she put off telling me. I mean, I take her point about my being the PSU representative, even though I don't agree that it is a sufficient basis for her to relieve me of it. What I don't see is why she didn't make her concern clear from the start, so we could plan appropriately, maybe get Modelo-

Vo up to speed when the time came for him to take over. Or better yet, get someone else to sit in that chair. Like Knight, for instance: he's the officer for that job."

"I conjecture that Admiral Yoshikuni did not mention it earlier because she had not made up her mind about what she was willing to do. So she put it off."

Wethermere smiled again. "You mean, because she was worried that I'd pester her endlessly about changing her mind?"

"That, yes. But also because I think she needed to be certain of *why* she was taking the step of removing you from command."

Wethermere slowed, turned to stare at her. "What do you mean, 'why?' She told us why."

Ankaht slowed to match his pace but did not match his stare. "All beings, particularly those without *selnarm*, often have many reasons for their actions—more reasons than they are willing to share openly."

"Are you suggesting that she was influenced by— 'personal' considerations?"

"Ossian, she may be the Iron Admiral, but she is still a feeling being. I would be startled if her emotions were not conflicted in this matter. Given her dedication to duty, my suspicion is that she wanted to be sure that she was transferring you out of the recon detachment for the correct reason—the fact that you represent the PSU in this fleet—rather than out of personal attachment and fear for your well-being."

Wethermere raised an eyebrow. "Trust me; Miharu Yoshikuni would *never* allow her personal feelings to influence a command decision."

"I didn't say she would. But I do not share your apparent surety that she would never find it difficult to summon the resolve to do so."

Wethermere stopped at a T intersection. Ankaht did also, studying his face. Wethermere rarely looked perplexed, but he did now, glancing first at the left hand turn and then at the right.

"What confuses you?" Ankaht asked him.

"Not sure which way I should go." Turning to see her unblinking stare, and shifting his two eyes in a fruitless and somewhat spasmodic attempt to engage all three of hers, he explained, "Usually I go left. That leads to dinner with Miharu in flag country." He glanced to the right. "But tonight, I'm wondering if I should just make myself scarce. Get back to *Woolly Impostor*, prepare the crew for the change in management. And give Miharu space. It might be pretty awkward having me around right now, and she's got to keep her focus on mission planning."

"Of which you are customarily a part."

"Yes, well—but I haven't received any message to stay on board for a tactical review after finishing with Modelo-Vo."

"Yes. Perhaps she is putting off further planning until tomorrow. It is rather late, after all."

"It is," Wethermere agreed, still looking down the right hand branch of the T intersection.

After several moments of silence, Ankaht asked him. "What do *you* want to do?"

"Me?" he asked, as if that consideration was so novel as to be surprising. "I'd go spend time with her. I think— I think this is hard on her. But Miharu doesn't seek others when the going gets hard; she gets inside her shell and seals it up. Doesn't open it until she's sorted everything out."

Ankaht curled one tentacle in slow understanding. "Yes, that is consistent with what I have seen of her. But it may be different now. Different with you, at least. Particularly here on the eve of battle and great uncertainty."

"Maybe, but there's no way to know that."

"You are correct. And there is no way to learn without asking her directly how you might help her most, right now. She might ask you to take your leave. She might ask you to remain with her. But if you do not ask her the question, you will never know how she would have answered."

Wethermere stared at Ankaht as if he was just seeing her for the first time. Then a slow smile spread across his face and he nodded faintly. "Good night, Ankaht. And thank you."

"You are welcome," she said to his back as he turned to the left with a purposeful gait.

CHAPTER SEVEN

Stealth field engaged, the RFNS *Krishmahnta* emerged into the unmarked expanse of deep space that stretched between Bug 27's warp points into Bug 26 and Bug 28. But, the *Krishmahnta* being a monitor, Ossian Wethermere could not afford to open her engines up wide; that would quickly overload the field's energy-absorptive capacities. "Report," he demanded.

"All clear ahead, Commodore, just as the Arduan-reprogrammed courier drone reported. Getting *selnarm* transmission from Cluster Leader Temret aboard the *Fet'merah* now."

"Patch him through to me."

"Yes, sir. Switching."

"Temret?"

"Here, Commodore."

"Is the hot-wiring job you pulled on the enemy tripwire buoys holding steady?"

"'Hot-wiring,' sir?"

Wethermere smiled at himself despite the tension on his bridge. "Are the Kaituni warp point sensors firmly under your control?"

"Yes, sir. They would have been impossible to compromise using real-space commo channels, but their *selnarm* links had very modest crypto and firewalls. Easily breached. Control is assured."

All of which confirms Ankaht's assertion that the Kaituni really don't suspect that anyone is tailing them. "Sitrep on the entry groups."

"Our remote probe caused no alarm. Given its Kaituni origins, it was polled by the tripwire buoys and its codes were accepted as legitimate. It used that link to reciprocally feed our control software back up that datastream. Upon entering in the *Fet'merah*, we activated that software remotely and commandeered the sensors around the warp point. Passive sensors have detected the closest Kaituni elements to be over eighteen light-minutes distant, making surprisingly leisurely progress toward the far warp point."

Which explains why Miharu took in not only her flotilla under stealth, but the recon detachment as well: at that range, the Kaituni are not going to detect the warp point activation. Of course, if they have some cloaked ships nearby—"Any sign of cloaked Kaituni?"

"None, sir. *Fet'merah* has done nothing but search for them since entering this system. That, and wait for you and the rest of the Relief Fleet."

"Have the Kaituni attempted to contact you?"

"No, sir. Our best estimates indicate that we were able to exert control over the tripwire system before it was able to send notification of our arrival to the Fourteenth Dispersate. In which case, they only know that the courier drone arrived. They have no discernible alternate means to have detected us, or anything that arrived afterward."

Which was all perfect. Which made Wethermere nervous. "Are you currently in contact with Admiral Yoshikuni?"

"Not at this moment, sir. We have kept to the commo intervals set out in the initial conops: one compressed *selnarmic* packet every three minutes on the average. That interval is further modified by a shared plus or minus fifty second randomization algorithm."

"The admiral's latest sitrep?"

"All clear. All forty-eight capital ships of her stealthed strike flotilla report full function. No evidence of enemy detection, and no projected intersection between her telemetry and the courses being followed by the Kaituni. Whose own use of *selnarmic* communications is much lower than we expected; they are unusually reliant upon lascom and even radio."

Wethermere rubbed his chin: was this more evidence of the speciate recidivism that Ankaht had anticipated among the later Dispersates? Possibly, but Ossian had more immediate concerns: "And you're sure that our own use of *selnarm* will not be detected by the Kaituni?"

"Not unless we wish it to be, Commodore. At these ranges, only a *shaxzhu* or a very, very powerful *Selnarshaz* would detect other sources of *selnarm* stirring in their perception of our species' collective *narmata*. And they would have to specifically focus on trying to discern such a presence. Unless they already suspect that there are

Arduans following them, they would have no reason to extend and strain their awareness to undertake such a draining exercise of *selnarmic* detection."

Yes, but once we show up and start engaging them with precision fire, coming straight out of stealth . . . "Once they know we're in-system, they'll have plenty of reason to suspect that we have Arduan help. Have you learned anything since entering Bug 27 that would cause you to revise Ankaht's assessment about their inability to, well, hack into our own *selnarm* links?"

"No, sir. Please be at ease about this. As Ankaht explained, only machine-relayed *selnarm* can be 'hacked' at all, because the relays lack consciousness and therefore lack the ability to screen out telempathic signals they do not wish to receive. However, our own mechanical *selnarmic* relays have been heavily encrypted. We conservatively estimate that it would take weeks to breach them, maybe months. On the other hand, we have now had months to analyze various samples of Kaituni technology, including multiple systems employed by the Fourteenth Dispersate itself. Since they expect no *selnarmic* contact in these salients, their encryption is not much more challenging than that of the tripwire system we just compromised and controlled. So our links remain secure. And our enemy's remain extremely vulnerable."

"Thank you, Temret. *Krishmahnta* out." Wethermere frowned, leaned back in the large chair overlooking the immense bridge. Well, it wasn't anywhere near as large as those of the devastator-classes, but it still felt more like an amphitheater than a bridge. He glanced at the holo-plot. The main van of the Relief Fleet continued to pour through the warp point that connected Bug 27 to Bug 28, spreading quickly into a fast attack formation that would drive on the unsuspecting Kaituni like a pile driver. Kiiraathra'ostakjo would be through in moments, Narrok a minute or so after him. Everything was going perfectly according to plan.

Which usually meant that something was about to go desperately wrong . . .

Admiral Yoshikuni glanced at her commo officer, who nodded. Good: Modelo-Vo was on the secure channel. "Report," she demanded.

"*Viggen* has reached the warp point into Bug 26. Found one buoy. Dormant, apparently activated only when it senses the warp point throwing off incipient transit anomalies. It has been disabled via a *selnarmic* virus."

"Good. Your job is now to hold the warp point, in case any leakers get through." She smiled. "Think you can do that, Rudi?"

She could hear the answering smile in his voice. "Well, ever since you beefed up the recon detachment with destroyers and a few cruisers, I think we can take care of anything that comes our way."

"Good, but I'm going to give you a little more stiffening, in case some bigger leakers come your way."

"Sir?"

"I'm sending Captain Knight back with his pennant of heavy and standard superdreadnoughts."

"Admiral, does that mean I'm no longer in command of—?"

"Commander," Yoshikuni interrupted, trying to keep the impatience out of her voice, "let's keep our egos on a leash today. Captain Knight still reports to me. He has been tasked to hold the warp point. And only that. You are my free safety. As such, you have the discretion and freedom to use the recon detachment to add to his efforts or to pursue opportunities we cannot foresee, until and unless you receive new orders from me. So Captain Knight may rank you, but you are not under his direct command until I say so."

"Understood, Admiral."

More like "relieved," *judging from the sound of your voice*, she thought. She gave the hand sign to close the channel. "Tactical, any change in the approaching threat force?"

"None, sir." Lieutenant Yaris gestured into the holoplot; a tapering lozenge of red motes crept lazily toward the thin, stacked wafers of blue ones that signified Yoshikuni's flotilla. "They continue to show no awareness of our ships or of the *selnarmic* microsensors we let drift out of our stealth sphere."

"Readiness of our scramblers to attempt interdiction on their *selnarmic* fighters' 'wingmen?'"

"The EW sections on all ships report full function. We should be able to take all their conventionally linked robot fighters out of the battle within the first few minutes."

"That's fine, but keep reminding our overeager electronic warriors that after the Kaituni fighters launch, we still have to let their main body close and commit to a tactical formation—before we yank the rug out from under their autonomous wingmen. Taking away two-thirds of each of their fighter triads at a single blow is only half the objective; ensuring that the balance of their main formation is made vulnerable by gutting their fighter assets is the other."

"Yes, Admiral. I shall keep stressing that point."

Yoshikuni nodded, watched the growing mass of blue motes at the opposite end of the holoplot shift position in a single jerk; the *selnarmic* update, now cycling every sixty-seconds, had just come through. She scanned the density of contacts, knew what it signified: almost the entirety of the Relief Fleet was now in-system, the monitors pressing forward as quickly as possible while being careful not to exceed the capacity of the leading ships' stealth fields. Soon enough, the Kaituni would detect the other unstealthed formations behind them, apparently dangerously attenuated, and turn to attack those seemingly outnumbered craft.

And until then, Miharu Yoshikuni had to keep reminding herself not to drum her fingers in impatience.

Captain O. A. Knight leaned over to look in the plot. "Bring us five degrees to starboard, and zee plus three."

"Aye, sir." Sam Lubell—part of the bridge crew whom Knight had brought off the *Woolly Impostor* to serve under him aboard the superdreadnought RFNS *No-Dachi*—turned with a single raised eyebrow. "Any reason for that new course, sir?" Seeing Knight's frown, he hastily added, "Just so I am aware of any changes you foresee in the tactical picture, Captain."

Knight frowned. "Sitting right in front of the warp point isn't optimal, Lubell: we're positioned astride their traffic conduit. So I want to put us in a flanking position. No matter how they approach the warp point."

"Understood, sir. Thank you, sir," Lubell said as he made the course change. Knight watched the holoplot as the blue mote signifying *No-Dachi*'s twin, *Gladius*, swung over to follow . . . and almost started in surprise when Lt. Engan shouted. "Warp point surge; transition imminent! Checking if proximity of *Viggen* has triggered—"

Knight's eyes flicked toward the purple hoop designating the warp point, noted *Viggen*'s position, shook his head. "Belay any confirmatory *selnarmic* pings to our remote sensors, Lieutenant Engan. The last navplot update shows that *Viggen* did not maneuver too close to the warp point."

"Then what—?" began Schendler at the comm station.

"Traffic moves through warp points in both directions," Knight muttered. Even to his own ears, it sounded as though he had gravel stuck in his throat. "Schendler, one top priority *selnarm* squeak to Admiral Yoshikuni on RFNS *Broadside*: we have incoming hostiles."

Miharu Yoshikuni nodded when the comm officer relayed Knight's report, resisted the impulse to slap her palm down on the armrest of her conn in frustration. She glanced at the wide, unblinking eyes of the officer. "No return signal. No alert to our strike force. They'll see it themselves. For now, we stay silent."

"Admiral," began the ship's skipper, Captain Ibrahim, "the Arduans have assured us that as long as their presence is not suspected in this system, their *selnarm* exchanges would only be detected by chance. We could—"

"We could send a general signal, yes, Captain," Yoshikuni interrupted staring into the holoplot. "And we could prove the power of chance by sending that signal and having it intercepted by this newly arrived enemy ship. A ship, I point out, that will be passing between us without any ability to detect our hulls and with no realistic chance of running into any of them." Even though Yoshikuni's strike force was in relatively close formation, that meant that even her most closely located hulls were still separated by well over fifty thousand kilometers.

"But if one of our commanders gets anxious—"

"I trust that our officers will continue to show the same self-control that they have to date. They know the OpOrd: hold position and hold fire until they get a flag signal to the contrary. I expect them to follow their orders. The enemy admiral is going to see what appears to be empty space all the way to the warp point into Bug 26. That presumption of local security will make the Kaituni just that much more vulnerable." She did not turn to look back at Ibrahim. "Are my orders clear?"

"Crystal, Admiral."

Yoshikuni nodded, glanced at the Comms officer. She kept her voice low. "Lieutenant Bazin?"

"Yes, Admiral?"

"Have our *selnarmic* microsensors pinged us with a compressed update on the enemy bogey, yet?"

"No, Admiral. Twenty seconds until the next remote sitrep."

"When that data comes in, I want you to pay close attention to any mascom, lascom, or tight-beam RF emissions from the bogey. Give me as much directional data as possible."

"Admiral, that will be mostly differential analysis."

"I hope it will be," Yoshikuni muttered in reply. *Because the only way we'd get a direct read is if we're unlucky enough to have an enemy comm link graze across one of our stealth fields or microsensors . . .*

Captain O.A. Knight was extremely grateful for the tactical edge that stealth technology furnished him. But the deaf-and-dumb waiting that it conversely imposed was also driving him slowly, quietly mad.

With no way to see beyond the globe of energy absorption that was the hallmark (and tell-tale sign) of a stealth field, Knight and his crew had no choice but to count down the seconds until the remote sensors sent a *selnarm* squeak that would provide a brief view and assessment of whatever enemies had actually come through the activating warp point. And since he was in the commander's chair, he was the only one on the bridge who could not afford the slightest sign—even that of a slightly more rigid posture—of anxiety while waiting for that information.

"Five seconds to update," Schendler announced.

If I needed a cuckoo clock, I'd have had one installed, Knight thought uncharitably. He only nodded, made himself suppress a yawn that was more affected than actual . . . and glanced at the holoplot.

An almost invisible red speck appeared near the purple hoop that marked the location of the warp point.

"We have the update," Schendler exclaimed. "One

bogey, bearing zero-zero-three by three-fifty-nine at a range of seven light-seconds, making straight for the Kaituni van at .06 cee equivalent. Tentatively identified as a courier-escort. She is broadcasting on one of the customary enemy frequencies, sir. Decryption proceeding. The transmission is comprised of short strings with a lot of repeats. I'm guessing basic transponder and security exchanges, Captain."

Knight nodded. "A dog barking because it's in sight of its kennel."

"What do we do, sir?" asked Lubell.

"We sit in our silent ball of blackness and let him pass."

Engan was studying her sensors intently. "Sir, the bogey is cycling through a variety of direct-beam comm links. Apparently updating the buoy we compromised earlier and select enemy vessels through lascom transmissions . . ."

No different than our own standard operating procedures, reflected Knight.

". . . but they are sending some signals into empty space. Unless, of course—"

"Unless they've seeded their own microsensors around this warp point." *Probably updating some suitcase-sized passive sensor platform made mostly of plastics. Which we never spotted. Which could be floating somewhere behind one of our own hulls. Which increases the chance that one of their comm beams will get clipped off by that hull's stealth field and cause the bogey to investigate—* "Ross, I want six *selnarm*-retrofitted heavy bombardment missiles soft-deployed to a range of two kilometers. Do it now."

"Yes, sir." Ross' reply sounded more like a question than a confirmation. "Deploying now. Do I maintain a link to them?"

"Yes. For now, use their attitude control thrusters to keep them near us, well within the stealth field. But keep your finger ready on the firing switch."

"Sir, I'm sorry; I'm not following you."

"For now, you don't need to, Lieutenant. And if we get lucky, you *won't* need to. But be prepared to route our *selnarmic* sensor data to the missiles and to activate them."

"Aye, sir."

But Knight barely heard Ross' reply: he was watching the bogey intently, waiting for the next, imminent update . . .

Miharu Yoshikuni saw the bogey jump forward in the updating holoplot—but not far enough. In the intervening minute, it had slowed, veered aside. Something had made it change course. *Damn it.*

Well, now we have *to take a chance with real-time updates.* "Sensors, send *selnarmic* activation protocol beta to our tier one array of passive microsensors." That would furnish every hull in her flotilla with streaming sensor updates. "But hold the tier two array in reserve." That would give them a backup in case the Kaituni started finding and neutralizing the tier one platforms.

"Aye, sir."

"Comms, I need to speak to my task force leaders."

"Getting Captain Knight and Commander Modelo-Vo on *selnarm* link ASAP, Admiral."

The real-time system display brightened, unfroze the varicolored mayflies which had been jerking their way through the navplot, minute by minute, for the past two hours. Several smaller lead elements of the Fourteenth Dispersate were moving forward more rapidly. There were less definitive signs that the rest of the formation was, conversely, slowing. Well, that much was good news: the longer it took for the enemy van to get to her strike force, the more time the body of the Relief Fleet had to catch it and grind it down from behind.

"Admiral, I've got Captain Knight and Commander Modelo-Vo on the command channel."

"Acknowledged. Gentlemen, you're closest to the warp point: any guess why the bogey started getting twitchy?"

Modelo-Vo started making an uncertain sound; Knight interrupted brusquely. "My sensor ops caught indications that the bogey was signaling to proximal receivers that were beneath the volumetric sensitivity of our scans: we conjecture Kaituni microsensors. Our best guess is that they grazed one of our stealth fields, didn't get the ping-back they expected, have become wary. They may suspect nothing more than a dead sensor, but they're proceeding with due caution. They're not stupid."

"You've got a good jump on this, Captain. Have you taken steps?"

"I have, Admiral. I followed protocol Charlie X-Ray."

Excellent: Knight had cut loose some *selnarmically*-steerable ship-killer missiles for remote launch. He'd ultimately move his ship so they fell outside of his stealth field. Once the enemy tweaked to them, his own ship would be well away. The Kaituni might wonder where the missiles had come from, or if they had somehow been undetected as they were lying doggo—but there would be nothing pointing back to their source from within a stealth field. "Just what I would have done, Captain. Good thinking. And it looks like we're going to have to put your precautions to immediate use. The bogey seems to be starting a widening spiral sweep."

"Yes, ma'am. They're looking for something. Might as well satisfy their curiosity. I can be ten thousand kilometers away from the missiles in a few seconds, and I'm told we already have a hard lock on the bogey since they've started running active sensors."

"If your on-board *selnarm* specialists have tested the missiles' responsiveness to their links, you are cleared to begin."

"Yes, Admiral. The missiles were confirmed as responsive within the first half minute we soft-deployed them."

Yoshikuni suppressed a smile; Knight's seasoned professionalism was as evident as he was laconic. "Show them the missiles and engage the bogey as soon as it sees them. You are to remain under stealth. You, too, Commander Modelo-Vo."

The two men answered her with a chorus of "Aye, aye, Admiral." The channel closed.

In the holoplot, the blue icon denoting Knight's *No-Dachi* scooted further to the side of the purple hoop of the warp point. Six small cyan pinpricks remained behind, hovering motionless in the space it had vacated: the missiles he had soft-deployed for remote operation. For a moment, the bogey did not react—then it straightened out of its slow, cautious recon sweep into a high-speed sprint back toward the Kaituni van.

"Sensors?"

"The bogey is sending on all channels, using all comms."

Ibrahim, leaning forward from the captain's conn, gestured toward the six blue pin pricks. "Why is Knight not activating the—?"

"He's giving that bogey a chance to stammer out a full report about the missiles. Making sure that the Kaituni have no reason to suspect this was anything other than some lurking mines they missed on their earlier sweeps. But any second now—"

As those words left Miharu Yoshikuni's lips, the six cyan midges brightened and raced after the enemy escort. Reports bounced back from one section to another on her bridge: transmissions from the bogey had redoubled; it was deploying a recorder buoy; it had begun emitting chaff and image-makers; but only one missile had fallen for the bait and veered off target.

Two of the remaining five blue pinpricks winked away as Sensors announced, "Enemy point defense fire has commenced; scratch two."

The remaining three missiles closed. The red bogey danced erratically. The closest blue point flickered and died, but had apparently been close enough to injure its target: the enemy icon faltered in its course, slowing slightly—

The last two blue glints drove into the red icon. All disappeared.

"Target destroyed," announced Sensor Ops.

Yoshikuni leaned back. *Textbook*, she thought, suppressing a smile. *We didn't show our hand or true forces, but gave them a completely convincing automated ambush scenario. Now, if they follow the customary playbook, they'll send forward some light hulls to sweep the area, like sappers going ahead into an enemy minefield, while the van slows and hold back, waiting for the "all clear."*

But in the next moment, Yoshikuni was leaning forward, rigid, eyes widening.

Because that's not what the Kaituni were doing. Instead of just frigates and destroyers probing forward at a leisurely pace, they were racing for the warp point at flank speed—every single red mote that comprised the Fourteenth Dispersate. An angry scarlet wave building momentum toward the thin blue dike of her currently invisible strike force.

"Er . . . Admiral," began Ibrahim.

"Send to all ships; stand to general quarters," she ordered the Comms officer. "Sensors, ETA of enemy lead units?"

"Given the performance statistics of the ship classes assumed to be comprising their vanguard, we project thirty-seven minutes, Admiral. The leading edge of the main body will be trailing by about five minutes, assuming they hold present course and speed."

Sensor Ops shouted into the end of the report. "Relief Fleet's first echelon of monitors is coming out of stealth, not far behind the rearmost ships of the Kaituni formation."

"Any Kaituni reaction to that?"

"None observable yet, Admiral. It's all unfolding pretty quickly."

"Continue to report. Gunnery, start compiling a target list for distribution throughout our control net. Sensor Ops, keep refining those projected firing solutions; inform me when we are close to achieving hard lock."

Respectful assents answered her as she leaned back, frowning at the holoplot.

Ibrahim who had never sunk back into his chair, was watching the plot carefully. "Certainly some of their larger ships will fall back to protect the auxiliaries at the rear of their fleet."

Yoshikuni shrugged. "Captain, I only know one thing for certain right now."

"And what is that, Admiral?"

She pointed at the swollen wave of red icons. "Here they come."

CHAPTER EIGHT

Ossian Wethermere stared at the small holographic image of Admiral Narrok that was being projected to the left side of his conn on the RFNS *Krishmahnta*: it was another convenience particular to the monitors in the fleet. "This looks like the worst case scenario about which you warned us, sir."

Narrok was motionless but the vocoder transmission announced, "I suspect so."

Kiiraathra'ostakjo's presence was voice-grade only; Orions were less enamored of what they considered communications frippery. "It is difficult to conceive this madness of theirs as a strategy. You are certain they will sacrifice their auxiliary craft merely to slow us down?"

"I am now," Narrok replied. "Consider the holoplot. The Kaituni's rearmost and slowest craft are hanging back even further, clustering along the route of our most direct pursuit."

"And they are hopelessly outgunned. They shall be annihilated in moments."

Ossian shook his head. "Maybe less quickly than if they ran, Least Fang. Look at what's coming back to help them: the bulk of the Kaituni monitors. Which are launching waves of fighters."

Kiiraathra made a noise that sounded like he was both choking and huffing. "Their fighters. *That* should prove amusing."

"Granted, they cannot anticipate how profitless that part of their strategy will be. But if you consider the position of their monitors and auxiliaries, I suspect they mean to dare us to run a gauntlet of debris."

"I see no debris gauntlet, Ossian Wethermere."

Narrok's voice sounded grimly amused. "I believe the Senior Commodore is referring to the auxiliaries. For if we destroy them in their current positions, we will be creating a debris field in front of us, flanked on all sides by the monitors. However, if we choose instead to work around the auxiliaries, we will find ourselves in a head to head combat with the monitors. And if we try to outflank their monitors, we shall find ourselves in a long, running battle—which, for the Kaituni, is exactly the outcome they wish."

"They cannot win such an engagement."

"Their monitors will not survive," Narrok agreed. "But all their other craft—particularly the superdreadnoughts and all the lighter classes of ships now racing for the warp point to Bug 26—shall surely escape. And once they have, we cannot prevent them from achieving what is now their primary objective."

"To reach and warn their main fleet along the warp-line to Earth."

"A possibility we considered from the start," Narrok agreed, tactfully omitting that he had been the one to point out and detail this potential problem. Ossian wondered if Miharu would have been so tactful had she been in Narrok's place. "But I did not foresee their employment of this formation, this particular delaying tactic."

"How could one foresee a fleet being willing to sacrifice the infrastructure that allows it to remain an effective fighting force?" Kiiraathra sounded as disgusted as he was irritated.

Wethermere frowned. "There could be a benefit to this situation, however. Remember: we have assets that *they* cannot foresee. And we may be able to use those to leverage their plan to our advantage."

There was a long silence. Narrok, motionless, asked. "What do you have in mind, Commodore?"

"You should not have asked that question," Kiiraathra sighed.

"Why?"

"Because Wethermere will answer with one of his insane schemes. And down that path lies madness."

Narrok sounded amused. "That path has also led to quite a few victories."

Kiiraathra's sigh was even deeper. "That such irrationality also leads to triumph is the greatest source of the madness he engenders. But I suppose we have no choice: what bizarre plan do you envision this time, Wethermere?"

Ossian leaned back, smiling. "Sorry to disappoint, Least Fang, but I'm afraid this time, my plan is mostly conventional." He felt his smile widen, savoring the response he knew his final qualifier would elicit. "*Mostly* conventional."

Kiiraathra'ostakjo grumbled, almost growled. "You do this to torture me, human."

"Most assuredly, Least Fang. Now, let's consider our alternatives . . ."

Miharu Yoshikuni watched the approaching red horde; the closest of the icons were almost in contact with the outermost blue points of her own staggered grid of defenders. Wei at Sensor Ops was calling out the range. "One point five million kilometers and closing. Enemy shows no sign of adjusting maneuver, no awareness of our formation."

"Hard lock on all primary, secondary and most tertiary targets, Admiral," Yaris inserted into the reports from behind her screens at the Tactical station. "Links fully integrated and strong. Automated PDF protocols continuing to adapt to enemy configuration."

"One million kilometers and closing," Wei announced. Yoshikuni glanced at the closest bogeys. They were destroyers and cruisers, the fastest hulls in the enemy fleet. And she would let them pass her front rank. Her own third rank would emerge from stealth to engage them. The enemy heavies behind the Kaituni skirmish line—the battleships and dreadnoughts of various marks and classes—were sure to begin evolving their formation in response. Which was just what Yoshikuni was waiting for.

"Five hundred million kilometers and closing," Wei

said, voice somewhat strangled. Behind her, she could hear Captain Ibrahim swallowing nervously. To date, no one had had the nerve to attempt this tactic: to reveal successive layers of stealthed ships, starting with the rank *furthest* from the enemy and ending with the one that was closest to—or already interpenetrated with—the threat force. But it was also arguably true that no force so large as Yoshikuni's had ever enjoyed so complete a measure of surprise . . .

"Enemy craft now moving through defense layer one," Wei commented, more calmly now that the most tense moment had come and gone.

Yoshikuni nodded, studied the plot. "Defense layer three: weapons free. Engage designated targets."

Miharu Yoshikuni had fought in many of the hardest, harrowing battles of the prior war with the Arduans. She had watched scores of supermonitors reduced to junk in the first half hour of their ultimately successful attempt to secure a toehold around the warp point into the BR-02 system, her own ship ultimately included in the hulls lost that day. She had seen reversals in which their Arduan foes were blasted by the dozens under withering fire from devastators. But never had she witnessed so abrupt and so bloody a reversal as the one she saw unfold in her holoplot, and could visualize out in space.

The leading wave of smaller Kaituni craft simply ceased to exist in the space of ten seconds. Emerging from stealth at the equivalent of point-blank range, the more advanced ships of the rearmost defensive screen in Yoshikuni's task force raked their fire across five times their number: in the holoplot, it was like watching a scythe of death sweeping the enemy motes from the color of active hulls—red—to motionless maroon dots.

The Kaituni reacted almost immediately; the leading ships of their next rank—battleships, mostly—slowed, trading fire tentatively as they waited for the heavier marks and classes of dreadnoughts to catch up. As defense layer three peppered them with missiles, the enemy craft dressed their formation so as to optimally engage this new threat, which had begun to give ground slightly. Sensing irresolution, the Kaituni resumed their approach—

—and so entered the close range firing envelope of Yoshikuni's defense layer two, which added its own close range missile barrage blind, its birds guided by the fire control net of defense layer three. Still stealthed, the ships of defense level two then dodged away to new preplotted positions.

Again, the Kaituni formation drew up short. Then as if resolving itself to uncover these hidden ships and bear down upon the more distant visible ones, it rushed forward, the first of the enemy dreadnoughts hard on the heels of these harriers.

Which put them within half a million kilometers of Yoshikuni's heaviest strike group: defense layer one.

"Bazin," she said to the Comms officer, leaning back. "Signal to all hulls in our group: drop stealth and execute preprogrammed firing solutions. Defense layer three is to pick off any threat hulls that still exist behind our position. Second layer is to be fed targeting updates and wait as a stealthed reserve." She turned to face Ibrahim. "Captain, fight your ship."

★★★

O.A. Knight remembered to relax his fingers where he was clutching the arms of his conn aboard RFNS *No-Dachi*. Admiral Yoshikuni was wreaking incredible havoc among the Kaituni—probably racking up the most one-sided kill-to-loss ratio in naval history, at the moment—but the weight of steel was still strongly against her. He scanned the stacked disks of blue motes that comprised her formation's three-tiered defense structure. They were still almost completely intact, but they seemed terribly thin compared to the mass of red that had piled up against them, surging like an immense, wounded amoeba. If more of the inbound Kaituni did not reverse course to engage the approaching Relief Fleet—

"Captain Knight," called Schendler, "Commander Modelo-Vo on secure channel two."

"Patch him through."

The circuit hissed open. Modelo-Vo sounded calm and collected, but his words didn't match that impression. "Captain, I suspect you're seeing what I am. If we don't add our weight to Admiral Yoshikuni's defenses, I'm concerned that she could be overrun."

"Commander, I want to help her as much as you do. But we have our orders and our primary objective: defend this warp point and prevent any leakers from getting through."

"Acknowledged, but the smaller craft that have the speed to slip through her defenses have almost all been neutralized. Our job here—"

"Remains both crucial and our sworn duty—until we are told otherwise."

Modelo-Vo's pause was not promising. "Captain, I will

remind you that I was granted full autonomy over the Special Recon Detachment. While I would like us to move forward together—"

"Commander, stow that. You have freedom of action to exploit unforeseen opportunities. What you're watching in your navplot is not an opportunity: it's a meat-grinder. And if you take your light hulls into that fray, they will be pureed in a minute's time. I understand your desire to help the admiral,"—*by God, do I ever!*— "but that's not our call. Do you understand?"

Modelo-Vo sounded less than convinced. "I don't fully agree with your interpretation, Captain, but for the time being, I will hold position. Modelo-Vo out."

Knight drew a deep breath. He had two superdreadnoughts and two heavy superdreadnoughts under his command. He knew better than to wade into that knife-fight up ahead, not without getting integrated into the fire control links first. Modelo-Vo might be loyal and brave, but that wasn't going to thicken the skins or increase the firepower of his ragtag collection of escorts, frigates, destroyers, and disguised civvie hulls. The light cruiser he'd been given as his command ship might last long enough for him to get in a few telling shots of his own, but that was the sum total of combat impact he could bring to bear.

"Captain," Schendler asked carefully, "Commander Kundra from *Gladius* is sending a coded message on secure one. Wants to know if you wish to exercise command change prerogatives as senior officer in the detachment. Just as a precaution."

Kundra, second in command of this pennant, had been

listening in on the conversation with Modelo-Vo, as per general quarters commo redundancy protocols. In short, communiqués between detachment commanders were too important to be lost along with either of the ships exchanging them, so there was always a "listener" on the bridge of the designated deputy commander—in this case, Kundra on the bridge of *Gladius*. Knight rubbed his chin; it was tempting to relieve Modelo-Vo after that exchange. Admiral Yoshikuni's decision to keep the recon detachment as a free-response element was understandable, but her former Fleet Tactical officer was proving to lack the temperament—in addition to the experience—needed by a line officer. On the other hand, if Knight started acting as though he didn't trust the other senior officers around him . . .

"Signal *Gladius* actual that we will not be altering the command roster at this time. End of message."

As Schendler sent the communiqué, Knight glanced at the holoplot. Yoshikuni was still holding her own, largely because she had had almost all the enemy ships in target lock when she emerged. And now, as they threatened to breach apparent gaps in her line, she was revealing one after the other of the re-hidden hulls of defense layer two—thereby plugging each new hole and flanking the Kaituni who had hoped to exploit it. But if the entirety of the Kaituni fleet kept coming at her—

Knight moved his point of focus to the rear of the Fourteenth Dispersate's van. Maybe half of the enemy monitors had hung back to form what looked like a sleeve around their own auxiliaries, through which those lesser hulls were not even trying to flee. Rather they seemed to be loitering there. A good number of the Relief Fleet's monitors were moving to engage, trying to turn the flank of the enemy battlewagons.

It was a strange arrangement of ships and Knight was pretty sure that one of Wethermere's unconventional plans might be behind the peculiar tactical maneuvers— which had better show their effectiveness soon. Otherwise . . .

He glanced back at Yoshikuni's three warping, buckling defense layers. *Otherwise, there's not going to be anyone here left to save.*

Ossian Wethermere watched as the Kaituni monitors swung around to deny his own formation of similar ships access to their flank. The range between them was great enough that neither side was committing anything other than an occasional long-range missile, all of which were being knocked down by point-defense fire batteries.

"Sir," asked the lieutenant at the weapons console, "we could give them a hell of a warmer reception with the energy torpedoes—and not deplete our missile stocks."

Wethermere looked at the man briefly. "I'm very well aware of the offensive potential of our energy torpedo batteries," he commented drily. *I wonder if you even know that I'm the person who came up with the notional design for that fast-repeating version of the weapons.* Which had changed ship-to-ship warfare dramatically in the last ten years. "However, at this point, we're going through the dance of testing each other's defenses and capabilities. And there is a reasonable chance that they are unaware of our repeating energy torpedo technology, or are simply uncertain how extensively we have retrofitted our ships with it. Either way, I intend to acquaint them with our full armament all at once. I trust you have no further questions, Lieutenant?"

The officer heard the diminished affect in Wethermere's the last question, understood he was being obliquely admonished. "No questions, sir. Sorry, sir."

Ossian nodded, looked back at the holoplot. As the Kaituni monitors turned to face him, they were necessarily peeling away from the core of auxiliaries around which they had arrayed themselves, the protective sleeve of their formation widening and flaring at the outermost cuff. Perfect.

"Comms, *selnarmic* secure channel to *Celmithyr'-theaanouw* actual."

"Least Fang Kiiraathra'ostakjo is already standing by, Commodore."

Of course he is; no true Orion waits patiently to get into a fight. The closer they get to the moment of engagement, the more antsy they become. "Least Fang?"

"It is I. I am receiving regular *selnarmic* updates from within my ship's stealth field. The enemy has behaved as you predicted, and my detachment has reached the final waypoint undetected. The time seems propitious."

"Indeed it is, Least Fang. I say three times, we are now at activation conditions for Phase Two. And good hunting."

"You also, Ossian Wethermere. *Celmithyr'theaanouw* out."

Well, hunting wasn't exactly what Wethermere and his formation of over a hundred monitors were prepared to do; it would be more like dynamiting goldfish in a bathtub.

"Task Force Deep Fang now coming out of stealth, sir," reported Sensor Ops as a dense cloud of faint blue icons finished maneuvering into position behind half of the monitors comprising the Kaituni's defensive sleeve. Led by *Celmithyr'theaanouw*, almost two hundred superdreadnoughts, heavy superdreadnoughts, and battleships had slipped between the defensive sleeve of Kaituni monitors and the sluggish limb of auxiliaries that they were protecting. Now on the rear flank of their adversaries, the ships of Deep Fang—each an optimum compromise between speed, firepower, and maximum stealth performance—commenced an all-weapons bombardment into the blind spot—the drive cone—of each of their adversaries.

Kaituni monitors flared and died like strings of firecrackers before the majority of them could angle toward a new course that denied these new attackers firing solutions astern. But that course change peeled the enemy further away from the auxiliaries—and each other. The Kaituni's defensive sleeve was not only widening, but thinning, fraying.

"Now, Gunnery; groom data links with the other ships in our formation and fire all energy-torpedoes. Sustained barrage. Close the range. Watch for them to launch fighters."

Which the Kaituni did spasmodically. The triad formations—each one comprised of a *selnarmically*-controlled fighter attended by two smaller, automated wingmen—erupted both fore and aft of the desperate enemy hulls. But in this empty patch of space, they were actually slower than the craft that launched them; without any planet- and stellar-centered Desai limits to contend with, the larger ships were able to employ their immense Desai drives, which allowed them to travel twice as fast.

"Why are they launching fighters at all, sir?" asked Tactical as the enemy icons continued to die at an almost four-to-one ratio, compared to the number of code omegas popping up among the blue icons of the Relief Fleet.

"To get as many offensive platforms into the battle as possible, mostly in an attempt to overload our defensive systems and distract us with new targets. But I think we are just about ready to teach them the futility of that tactic." Wethermere glanced at the other end of the holoplot, where a red tide of smaller but more numerous red motes surged against the warping defensive disks of Miharu's task force. Sure enough, sprays of tiny scarlet spindles—fighters—were vomiting out of that Kaituni contingent as well, attempting to probe her lines, exploit gaps, overwhelm her comparatively thin defensive fire assets. "Comms, raise Admiral Yoshikuni on secure *selnarm* three."

"Her comms officer has just come on the line, sir."

"Very well." Wethermere raised his voice. "This is *Krishmahnta* actual, for the Flag."

"This is the Flag," Miharu said in her Iron Admiral voice. "Threat force has committed the majority of its fighter triads."

"Here, too. Ready to throw the off-switch?"

"Been ready for three minutes. What took you so long?" He could hear the rueful smile in her voice.

"Sorry; we were all taking a nap back here. Now

handing off scrambler activation to my electronic warfare specialist. Who will engage in ten seconds and . . . mark."

"Engaging mine in ten seconds," Miharu echoed, "and . . . mark. See you on the other side, Commodore. Flag out." The line snicked off before Ossian could reply. *Classic Iron Admiral brusqueness*, he reflected with a smile of his own. He leaned back, listened to the EW Officer's countdown concluding:

"Three. Two. One and engage."

The command disruption system that Lentsul and Commander Chong had devised to use against the Kaituni was deceptively simple in principle. The two automated wingmen that accompanied each remote-controlled enemy fighter were not coordinated by *selnarm*, but by conventional lascom. There was, however, an emergency radio backup in the event that the lascom sustained battle-damage or line of sight was blocked. Although carefully encoded, the enemy had neither lavished time or resources to foolproof it, nor anticipated that their adversaries would ever have the luxury of dissecting one of their robot fighters over the course of many months. The Kaituni war plan had been to attack relentlessly, swamping and overrunning all their objectives with overwhelming numbers and ferocity. And elsewhere, that had worked.

But Relief Fleet, having stayed in the shadow of the Fourteenth Dispersate, had been able to harvest and meticulously examine examples of the fighters. Having picked apart and assessed every subsystem, they had found the cryptographic element that the Kaituni had— quite reasonably—assumed would keep the backup radio links indecipherable to their foes: a digitalized *selnarmic* recognition failsafe. In short, while the automated "wingman" fighters were not controlled by *selnarmic* links, they would only recognize commands prefaced by a digitalized representation of a *selnarmic* code-string— something that non-*selnarm* using races would have almost no chance of understanding, let alone decoding.

However, Lentsul and the other Arduans in his technical intelligence cluster had managed to crack the code-string. With the automated wingmen thereby triggered to receive radio commands, the Arduans simply needed to generate a full bandwidth broadcast of a single decisive radio command that would be recognized by the wingmen as valid. Lentsul's intelligence cluster had settled on a deceptively innocuous command: they sent the signal that activated each robot fighter's self-diagnostic routine, minus one confirmation parameter. So when each wingman then discovered that the very command that initiated the self-diagnostic had possibly been corrupted upon reception, the craft's robot brain tripped into an endless loop of detect and check, detect and check, detect and check. And so, effectively paralyzed the unit, since the broadcast command kept altering slightly, according to a self-modifying algorithm.

Wethermere witnessed the effects with a growing smile. Throughout both of the Fourteenth Dispersate's main bodies, the scarlet spindles signifying enemy fighters came largely to a halt, a few incarnadine splinters—the *selnarmically*-controlled fighters—angling off to continue their missions. Which usually ended abruptly, as Relief Fleet's now overwhelming defensive fire and manned fighters swarmed and smothered each of these lone wolf survivors.

And best of all, from Ossian's viewpoint, the carefully structured formations of both Kaituni detachments were now hopelessly awry. Even though their fighters had been slow, they had represented crucial firepower and maneuver elements: a screening force and a slow but tangible counterattack resource—all suddenly gone. Meaning that whatever plans and formation changes the Kaituni had been evolving had now been, in the course of a few seconds, reduced to ruins.

Wethermere leaned back, called for secure *selnarm* channel two. "Admiral Narrok?" he asked of the thin air to his left.

A small holograph of Narrok materialized there. "Yes, Commodore, I have witnessed it myself. The theater-wide scrambler has performed as hoped. You will now press your attack from both sides?"

Wethermere nodded. "I'll be the hammer, Least Fang Kiiraathra'ostakjo is the anvil. And you, sir, can now run the gauntlet through the auxiliaries."

"I shall bypass them as planned, will deploy our own *selnarmically*-controlled fighters to disable and seize as many as possible."

"Excellent, but I wouldn't wait too long to commence that operation, Admiral." Wethermere glanced at Yoshikuni's three defensive disks; they had now compressed into one, severely warped shield, red icons having penetrated it at various points.

Narrok was apparently looking at the same image. "I shall make all haste. Narrok out."

★★★

Miharu Yoshikuni grunted against the sudden convulsion that ran through the *Broadside*; a near miss by an antimatter warhead, certainly within two hundred kilometers. "Where's my point-defense fire grid?" she shouted.

"Working to restore data-links," Gunnery explained, working frantically at his console. "We lost the ones that were routed through *Spatha* when she went Code Omega."

Code Omega. The dreaded term that meant another of her ships had died. She'd been hearing more of that term in the last ten minutes, and the rate at which those reports were accumulating was increasing steadily.

There had been a brief lull in her losses as the robot-fighter scrambler system came on-line. The Kaituni had veered or staggered in confusion, the careful tactical logic of their formation suddenly nonsense. They had wrought order out of that chaos like the professionals they were, but in the five minutes it had taken them to dress their ranks into a different configuration and press on, they had lost dozens of their biggest ships.

But there were still at least fifty enemy dreadnoughts of various classes and marks facing the thirty-one that remained combat effective in Yoshikuni's task force. And now she had played all her trump cards, including the ones she had hidden up her sleeve and tucked in the top of her boot. Now, it was just tired metal against tired metal.

Except that the enemy's remaining *selnarmically*-controlled fighters, finding large enemy hulls positioned on the approach vector to the warp point the gate, were no longer chasing behemoths that were also, paradoxically, swifter than they were. The gargantuas were now at bay, making them excellent targets for suicide runs. And while the Fourteenth Dispersate's fighters were comparatively slow, and were down to less than twenty percent of their original number, that meant there were still hundreds of them.

Yoshikuni watched them come. "Half our energy torpedo batteries will shift and link with our defensive fire assets. The other half is to keep attriting primary targets."

"Admiral, what leeway can you give me for evasive maneuvers?" asked the helmswoman.

"Damned little. You know the position we have to hold to maintain our part of the defensive matrix. You can go wherever you want within that footprint—but not beyond it." Which was essentially like telling the Helm to try to dodge and evade while staying in a broom closet.

Or maybe, more pertinently, a casket, Yoshikuni reflected as *Broadside* quaked again. And again. And again.

CHAPTER NINE

"Captain Knight, Commander Modelo-Vo on secure three, sir."

Knight repressed a sigh as the circuit opened, felt certain he knew what was coming. "What is it, Commander?"

Modelo-Vo did not disappoint Knight's expectation. "Captain, Admiral Yoshikuni is on the verge of being overrun."

"I see that, Commander; my holoplot is as functional as your own."

"Then sir, I recommend that we combine our forces and take some of the pressure off the defense line by maneuvering to waypoint Sierra Quebec with a full—"

"Commander," Knight interrupted wearily, "is your command channel to the admiral's flagship still active?"

"Yes."

"Do you have any reason to suspect that Admiral Yoshikuni has been incapacitated and is no longer directing the fleet's actions?"

"No, but—"

"There are no 'buts' in that case, Commander. I realize that you haven't logged many hours of duty conning a ship during wartime,"—which was a charitable way of saying, *you have zero experience during wartime*—"but I shouldn't need to tell you that as long as the admiral is in charge and in communication, we follow her orders. Unless and until she explicitly changes them."

"Captain, I'm quite aware of that. I'm also aware that as conditions change, so must responses."

"Yes, but that is the admiral's call, not yours. *Commander*."

If Modelo-Vo heard the emphasis on his comparatively humble rank, he gave no sign of being chastened by it. "Captain, you also heard the admiral designate me as a 'free safety.' I have broad latitude when it comes to determining the course of action for my recon group. Accordingly, I have opened this communication up to the general channel and am hereby instructing all elements of the Special Recon Detachment to make best speed for waypoint Echo-Three, staying under stealth until we reach—"

Knight leaned forward. "To all ships, Special Recon Detachment; this is Captain Knight. Be advised: it is my command directive that you are to disregard Commander Modelo-Vo's orders from this moment forward. He is willfully misinterpreting Admiral Yoshikuni's protocols and provisions regarding the disposition of your unit. You are instructed to consider him relieved of his command and your hulls attached to my pennant for the duration of this engagement."

Part of the general line seemed to cut out just as he finished.

"Captain," Schendler said quietly, "Commander Modelo-Vo is out of the link. I'm trying to raise him."

Knight waved the general channel closed, shook his head. "Don't bother. He won't respond. He'll be trying to privately convince the other ships of his flotilla to go with him."

Schendler nodded. "That's what most of them are reporting. All but two are refusing his hails."

Knight looked in the plot: Modelo-Vo's light cruiser was angling toward the furious melee of interpenetrated allied and enemy ships only one light minute off the shoulder of the warp point. One destroyer and one escort were following him. Two out of over thirty craft of different sizes and classes.

Knight felt Schendler's eyes on him, expectant. "What is it, Lieutenant?"

"Captain, duty requires me to point out that Commander Modelo-Vo disobeyed your direct order and then refused to acknowledge that you had relieved him."

Knight knew where Schendler was going, hoped the junior officer would have the good sense not to press him on the point.

But Schendler either lacked that sense or was a stickler for regulations. Or possibly both. "Captain, these are—serious infractions." At least he hadn't used the dread word "mutiny." "How would you like me to record them, sir?"

"I want you to record them *later*, Lieutenant."

Schendler looked baffled. "Later, sir? I don't follow. Shouldn't the report be entered as close to the occurrence as possible, in order to—?"

"Lieutenant Schendler," Knight said in a quiet tone. "Look at the holoplot. Look at Commander Modelo-Vo's light cruiser. Tell me what you see."

Schendler had at least enough subtlety to understand that he was not being asked to report the craft's position and vector. "I see it heading into a battle in which almost every enemy ship is several classes heavier than it is. At least."

"Does there seem to be much doubt about the final outcome for his ship?"

Schendler grew pale. "No, sir."

"Then let's not put anything on the commander's record that we might wish we hadn't, later on."

Wearing an expression that most humans wear when leaving a wake, Schendler nodded solemnly and turned back to his commo board.

Knight repressed a sigh, stared hard into the navplot himself. The distant engagement at the rear of the Kaituni van had turned into a slaughter. The enemy monitors had been split off from the auxiliaries, defeated in detail, and now the combined forces that had achieved that victory— almost ninety-five percent of the Relief Fleet—were driving forward, vaporizing what little resistance existed between them and the warp point. Knight measured their rate of advance, measured the intervening distance, compared the rate at which the remaining enemy icons were dying from red into maroon motes versus the rate at which Admiral Yoshikuni's blue icons were turning into the dread yellow and black horseshoe shapes signifying a Code Omega. He leaned back. "Mr. Lubell."

"Yes, Captain?"

"We will be activating contingency delta-whiskey-one."

Lubell's wasn't the only face that turned toward him in surprise. "We're going through the warp point, sir?"

"Is your hearing impaired, Mr. Lubell?"

"No, sir. Through the warp point. Very good, sir."

"Engan, passive sensors only as we go through. Ross; ready all weapons. We don't know what we'll find on the other side. Schendler, inform the rest of our pennant of our new course and integrate the Special Recon Detachment into our formation; they're operating under my flag, now."

"Understood and already accomplished, sir. However, Commander Kundra has a question."

"Which is?"

"Why delta-whiskey-one, sir?"

Knight rubbed his chin, lowered his voice. "Because I give equal odds that some of those ships are going to get through Admiral Yoshikuni's defenses. And if those leakers are superdreadnoughts, I'd rather catch them coming blind through the other side of the warp point, one at a time, rather than standing toe-to-toe with all of them on this side."

"And if there are Kaituni forces waiting for us when we go through ourselves, Captain?"

"Then, Mr. Schendler, we will have entered a world of hurt. Lubell, plot the course and take us through. Flank speed."

Miharu Yoshikuni knew, from the splatter of blood that

partly landed on her right sleeve and partly fell as a glittering spray through the holoplot to her right, that the divider truss which had narrowly missed her had impaled Captain Ibrahim where he had been standing behind her. "Helm, CO of *Broadside* is down. I am assuming direct command. Emergency damage control parties four and five to the bridge, on the double."

"Aye, ma'am," replied one of the fourteen persons still manning their stations on the smoke-filled bridge; the other eight were either killed or incapacitated.

She heard the damage reports as a distant yammer confirming what she already knew from glancing at instruments that she could read more easily and surely than a child's primer: heat dissipation was compromised, so the plants were overheating; a third of her energy-torpedo batteries were either destroyed or off-line; scattered decompression; hangar too damaged for fighters to launch or land; and most significantly, shields getting battered down faster than they could recharge.

The only good news was that these Kaituni had not been half as skilled as the opponents that the allies had first seen boiling out of the Zarzuela system, or that had savaged the Orion worlds. The ships and systems of the Fourteenth Dispersate seemed cruder, their crews' training and responses less crisp and decisive, their gunnery less accurate. Still a formidable force, of course—a bowel-shaking impact underscored that admission—but not the match of the earlier Dispersates.

"Admiral, some of their wrecks are getting past us, limping on partially functioning drives. Should we stop to—?"

"No time to catch them; let the second defensive layer deal with them." She reflected that second defensive layer had become more of a euphemism than a meaningful designation; it was now comprised solely of a few of Yoshikuni's lighter or damaged ships, hanging further back and engaging any enemies who tried to slip through what remained of her contracting, collapsing defensive shield. But, checking her plot, she saw three new blue blips—small ones—approaching from the direction of the warp point. And as she watched, the dim blue—thus, stealthed—ones of Knight's pennant winked out. "Did *No-Dachi* just lead her group through the warp point?"

"Apparently so, sir. We got a quick squeak the instant they did; awaiting decryption."

"And the other three bogeys, the ones heading toward us, are—?"

"Commander Modelo-Vo and two light hulls."

Good gods, what on Earth does he think he's doing? He'll get—"Commo, send to second defensive layer's acting CO: hold Commander Modelo-Vo's ships in reserve position. Make sure he—"

"Admiral! Wrecked enemy destroyer reactivating on our stern! We thought she was a dead hulk!"

Damn it, Rudi, your heroics distracted me at the wrong moment. "Steer fifteen degrees to relative port and plus ten on the zee axis; get my engine decks away from that—"

Broadside quaked sharply; half the system status indicators on the bridge went to red; decompression and overheat klaxons set up a chorus of dueling shrieks.

"Admiral, waves of fighters emerging from behind a gutted enemy superdreadnought. Range: four light-seconds, low off the starboard bow. All bogeys are on a collision course. Looks like they're set to—"

"To ram," she finished for her sensor operator. "Missiles batteries, all fire to rear and take targeting hand-off from second defensive layer's data links. That should give our missiles a lock on to that destroyer. Defense batteries; all that bear are to hit those fighters."

And while Miharu was hammering out those orders and saving her ship, three enemy dreadnoughts chose that moment to bear in upon *Broadside*, unleashing a well-coordinated salvo of HBMs: heavy bombardment missiles. Within the space of two seconds, over seventy were converging on her ship.

Miharu Yoshikuni felt her ship groaning as it danced through a crippled pirouette that spun it away from the suddenly revivified destroyer, saw the bogeys that marked the enemy fighters wink away one after the other, glimpsed the blue wall of the Relief Fleet's monitors only a few light minutes away, heard the frenzied cries of her bridge crew as they attempted to retask their defensive batteries to pick off the inbound HBMs. The edge of desperation in their rapid-fire exchanges compelled her to glance at the plot. She made a quick estimate of the remaining enemy missiles, saw all the red lights on the defense gunnery status boards, ran the numbers, and thought, *We're not going to make it.*

She was right.

Ossian Wethermere saw the icon of RFNS *Broadside*

go briefly yellow and then, in the next instant, transform into an omega symbol. *No. Not her, not now—*

Comms said quietly, "Admiral Narrok on secure one. Urgent."

Wethermere nodded at Comms, swallowed, made sure his voice would not waver. "Admiral."

"Commodore Wethermere, I trust you've seen—what has occurred."

"Yes, Admiral. Flag transfers to you, as per protocol."

"A protocol I regret having to activate. And over which I have grave reservations. But we have little time to reflect upon that now. Did you get an update on Captain Knight's position?"

"Only fractional, sir. Looks like he executed contingency delta-whiskey-one. Probably feared that the admiral's line would break before we got there."

"The issue does remain in doubt."

Wethermere assessed what was left of Yoshikuni's defenses and the Kaituni who had been pressing her: a deformed red dinner plate was grinding away against a paper-thin and even more deformed blue dessert plate. It didn't look like any decisive outcome was immediately imminent. "I agree, Admiral. I recommend sending our cruisers ahead at full speed. When the enemy dreadnoughts turn to protect the blind spots at their sterns, they'll lose precious minutes. And we'll be upon them before they can make up that lost time."

Narrok's vocoder reply was swift, decisive. "I concur. We shall continue to follow the operational orders, otherwise." He paused. As his stillness continued, Ossian could not fathom what it might mean; Arduans used little body language, and what little they did use was often mysterious and without human analog. "Ossian Wethermere," he said at last, "I am sorry. Admiral Yoshikuni was an excellent commander. And a good friend. To many of us." He stopped short of adding what was his clear intent: *and more than a friend to you, I suspect.*

Wethermere nodded and pushed all his personal reactions down deep inside, far away from his awareness of this moment and his duty within it. "Yes, Admiral, she was all that. And more. Now, let's finish this battle."

Ossian Wethermere was not used to walking around, conversing, making decisions, and yet feeling entirely detached from himself.

And yet that's exactly how he felt now, walking the corridors of the RFNS *Krishmahnta*. As news of the outcome of the battle spread—both of the Relief Fleet's extremely one-sided victory and Miharu's death—the various personnel he passed were all snapping slightly more formal salutes at him, all standing more rigidly at attention, all policing their eye contact more carefully. In some strange way, their strongest reaction to their admiral's death was not grief but a desire, even a desperate reflex, to replace her with a new command figure. And given Wethermere's presence on her hull, and his frequent visits there, he had become the undeclared yet unanimous recipient of their respect and regard. He wasn't sure he liked it very much, suspected that it was far less out of any particular regard for him than it was an unconscious expression of a social-mammal instinct: *if*

deprived of the alpha, promote another one, quickly.
Because leaderlessness felt too much like chaos.

But when he entered the flag conference room and
discovered that both Narrok and Kiiraathra'ostakjo had
arrived there before him, he detected the same subtle
change: he was no longer the most senior and trusted
advisor in the room. He was one of the flag staff, now—
even if his rank did not decisively indicate it.

Their greeting to him—single word acknowledge-
ments—had increased in careful regard but diminished
in the affable informality that had always allowed him to
move easily through any social strata, in any environment. Without any effort from him—indeed, against his
wishes, had he been asked—he had been elevated to a
position where casual speech and mannerisms were no
longer appropriate. If anything, it made him feel the loss
of Miharu even more keenly.

He realized they, as well as the others in the room—
Ankaht, Mretlak, and Jennifer Pietchkov—were standing,
waiting for him to sit. He waved at the chairs, sat just
after the admirals did. *Well, no reason to beat around
the bush . . .*

"Admirals, everyone, thank you for convening here.
Since you might be returning to your own hulls after the
dinner hour, I have taken the step of instructing the galley
to have meals ready for you at your convenience. Now,
Admiral Narrok," he turned to the motionless Arduan, "I
am going to presume that you will wish to transfer the
fleet flag to your vessel. So, in order to—"

"Senior Commodore Wethermere," Narrok's vocoder
intoned slowly, with extra emphasis upon the *Senior*, "I

do not believe it is necessary, or even wise, to make a formal flag transfer. Not at this time. Perhaps not ever."

Wethermere was so surprised that he could not keep himself from blinking. He turned to Kiiraathra'ostakjo, whom he expected to vociferously disagree: Orions were creatures who largely defined themselves by their place on a strict chain of command. But he was surprised to see his friend's nose wrinkling slightly: a sign of mild, reluctant disagreement. "I concur with Admiral Narrok; changing the flagship at this time would be— imprudent."

Wethermere looked from one to the other, wondering if they were both suffering from combat fatigue. "Gentlemen, I do not understand. A fleet needs a flagship, needs a headquarters and command locus. If it is a matter of *Krishmahnta* having superior command and control facilities, then we will simply modify it so that those systems are more amenable to Arduan—"

Narrok's tentacles flexed once. "No, Commodore Wethermere; I do not demur taking the flag to my own hull because I wish to shift it to this ship. My argument against moving the flag is strictly political."

Kiiraathra swept his whiskers back lightly, almost delicately. "More specifically, it is speciate."

Wethermere was baffled for a moment, then understood their implication—but could hardly believe it. "Do you mean to say that you feel it is unwise to move the flag to a non-human ship?"

Narrok's golden color deepened. "This is exactly what we mean to say. And if it seems to be an extreme, and awkward, accommodation to our current situation, I suspect we would be risking the entire fleet's cohesion if we proceeded otherwise."

Apparently reacting to Ossian's look of disbelief, Kiiraathra leaned forward, his eyes wide. "Ossian, my war-brother, you must hear this clearly—and it may be difficult since you have ever conceived and genuinely believed that all races are equal. But be aware: that enlightened view is not as prevalent as you might believe among humans. Or my people."

"Or Arduans," Ankaht added regretfully.

"In short," Narrok concluded, "let us consider the hard numbers we face in this matter. This fleet is comprised of slightly more than eighty percent human personnel. We Arduans make up slightly less than fifteen percent; the Orions, not quite five percent. How will your fellow humans feel if all symbols of control should pass to me, an Arduan—an admiral who was their opponent in the last war and who commanded fleets that killed millions of their siblings, children, or parents, less than ten years ago? They will not stand for it."

Wethermere saw that clearly enough, nodded, turned toward Kiiraathra . . .

Who shook his head. "No, Ossian Wethermere, I may not name *Krishmahnta* as my own flagship. My authority comes through the Pan-Sentient Union, whereas this ship is the pride and standard-bearer of a Rim Federation fleet. And as Admiral Narrok points out, my people represent less than four percent of this armada's personnel. You have a saying about the tail wagging the dog? It would be so here—monstrously so, if all signs and rituals of leadership were to pass from human hands to those representing the Khanate, or the Arduan Protectorate. And that would not merely produce a situation that is incongruous, but that is dangerously unstable."

"Because of—of bigotry?" Given his upbringing, given his close personal experience with both Orions and Arduans, the notion felt far, far more alien to Wethermere than either of those non-human species did.

Ankaht's lesser tendrils rippled fitfully. "Not simply bigotry but recent history. Given how recent the war between our species was, that distrust is understandable. Given that the enemy we fight is also of our species, that distrust is magnified. Enormously."

Kiiraathra released a sigh that sounded more like a growl. "And my own people—well, although my senior officers have made progress quelling the irrational resentment over Earth's decision not to send its fleets to the aid of our destroyed planets, anger and distrust remains on our hulls. And it has quickened a matching anger and distrust in the humans who have felt it in exchanges with them."

Wethermere felt all their eyes on him, realized that they meant for him to at least caretake and be associated with the flag's continuing presence on *Krishmahnta*. "But I'm not a flag officer . . . not really."

The voice that emerged from Narrok's vocoder was slow but firm. "As a senior commodore, you are a flag officer—by however narrow a margin that might be. Furthermore, you have direct standing in the Rim Federation naval formations, dating from your exchange posting and service with them during the last war. Your rank and command status is fully recognized here, both officially and popularly. And as the senior—well, only— representative of the PSU with this fleet, you have official standing that transcends your rank." He paused, apparently for emphasis: "This is your flagship, Commodore. Both by your own merit and rank—and by extension of the simple logic that it can be no one else's."

Wethermere shook his head. "No. There's Rear Admiral Voukaris. He is the ranking human flag officer from the Rim Federation. He must—" Ossian stopped when he saw the exchange of uncomfortable glances that ricocheted from face to face and ended, unexpectedly, upon Jennifer Pietchkov.

She squared her shoulders. "I suspect everyone is looking at me because no one wants to say anything— unpleasant—about a person from another race."

Wethermere frowned. "We say unpleasant things all the time, around here. That's in the nature of a command staff."

Jennifer sighed. "This is *personally* unpleasant." Her jaw squared and her eyebrows came down into a hard, straight line. "Look, Commodore: Admiral Voukaris is not fit for duty."

Wethermere did not think in time to stop from running his hand through his hair; a reflex that made him—and his hair—look adolescent. "What?" was all he could say.

Kiiraathra lowered his head so that his eyes did not meet Ossian's. Among Orions, that demeanor was observed when an outsider was charged with reporting the shameful act of one family-member to the rest of his/her presumably upright relatives. A deeply uncomfortable situation for all concerned since, among Orions, death was far, far preferable to dishonor. "I regret to report that we have just learned that Admiral Voukaris has been relying upon sedatives. Since the beginning of his arrival with the Relief Fleet."

"And no one noticed?"

Narrok's voice was measured. "It was noted by the chief medical officer aboard his own ship, but they had served together for years."

"Meaning that the CMO dispensed the sedatives off the record."

"Yes. However, in the last three weeks, as we have moved closer to engagement with the Fourteenth Dispersate, the dosage Admiral Voukaris demanded began increasing."

Wethermere slumped in his seat, tried not to judge the man, but could not suppress a sense of disgust. "And so the CMO finally came forward?"

"Unfortunately, no," Narrok said quietly. "Admiral Voukaris left his bridge shortly after the fleet received word of Admiral Yoshikuni's death. When he did not return to the conn, nor respond to hails, they located him by the transponder in his personal communicator. He was still in his quarters. He was . . . indisposed."

"He was unfit for duty and a disgrace to his rank," Kiiraathra declared in a flat tone which did not wholly conceal his discomfort in having to utter those words. "And cannot be trusted to retain any command position in this fleet." He inclined his head slightly toward Wethermere. "My apologies, friend, but I must speak plainly: this is one of the weaknesses of the bureaucratization of your warmaking classes. Those who are not in any way warriors may yet rise high in its ranks—persons whose greatest skill is in the shuffling of papers and making of lists." He saw Wethermere's raised eyebrow. "And yes, we in the Khanate have a system which has the defects of its own virtues. Our services only promote true warriors, but many of those have been leaders without patience, temperance, or balance. Each of our societies has, over time, paid the price of its command preferences. However, we are all paying the price of yours, at this moment. And the price is that we are now without a human admiral for a human fleet."

"So," finished Narrok, "in his absence, you must remain at the conn of Admiral Yoshikuni's flagship. It is both correct protocol, and an important symbol to the crewpersons of your species, Commodore. And it will be upon you to make a suitable statement, offer a suitable tribute, to the late admiral."

Wethermere was glad he had not eaten in several hours; his stomach had coiled into a tight, uncomfortable knot. From a considerable distance, he heard himself say: "I will have a statement within the hour. We will have a formal ceremony tomorrow at 0700. I will preside. Captain Knight will command the fly-by. All here must attend; anything less will start whispers about disrespect or disunity. We must eliminate those thoughts before anyone can think them."

"Agreed," said Narrok as Kiiraathra nodded sharply.

Wethermere looked around the room, realized he had new duties to perform; it was his ship, so he had to play the role of host, even though he was not the ranking officer present. He stood. "Unless we have further business, I thank you all for coming aboard *Krishmahnta*, and shall not keep you from your commands and responsibilities."

They filed out, Ankaht lingering behind a moment to regard him with all three, low-lidded eyes: a look he had come to understand as signifying great fellow-feeling and sympathy. He smiled and nodded to her; she slipped out of the compartment.

He looked around. It was not unusual to be the only person in a room.

But never before had he felt so alone.

PART TWO
For They Are Legion

PART TWO

For They Are Legion

CHAPTER TEN

Ian Trevayne had never expected to be able to hold the Bug 15 system. He'd known it was foolish to hope he could. And from Elaine De Mornay's assurances, he knew he didn't need to delay the Bugs there for any fixed period of time .

But he could and did bleed them as much as possible on his way out, while holding his own losses to a minimum.

It was an inherently useless system, a binary of two type K stars with planets that were either rock balls or gas giants. The Bugs had entered through two warp points, from Harnah and Bug 24, both of which warp points were fairly close to Bug 15 A. But the approach was so obvious that Combined Fleet had never been in any danger of being caught in a pincers. And as they withdrew, in order to pursue them the Bugs had had to pass through an asteroid belt which Trevayne had seeded liberally with laser buoys and cloaked carriers whose fighters had launched stinging attacks seemingly from nowhere. And then, as Combined Fleet had proceeded on outward to the Alpha Centauri warp point, twenty-nine light-minutes from the system primary (about as far from a star as warp points normally occurred), it had passed beyond the Desai Limit and become uncatchable by the Bugs, who lacked the Desai Drive. It had also meant that the retreating fleet could periodically pause, lash the pursuing Bug van with whip-crack attacks, and afterwards stay ahead.

And then, with Bug 15 A a mere bright orange star astern, they had drawn within range of Hugo Allende's devastators and superdevastators, which had been stationed near the Alpha Centauri warp point all along as per what had become standard doctrine. Under the cover of those titan ships' storm of long-range missiles, Combined Fleet had begun its transit.

Thus it was that Trevayne had arrived in Alpha Centauri. And he had a certain breathing spell, for the Bug hive-intelligence had by now learned better than to charge incontinently through a warp point in pursuit of his withdrawing fleet. So he called a conference—the last he would be able to call, he was coldly certain, before the final battle for Alpha Centauri began.

Unlike the superdevastator that had been Trevayne's flagship before the advent of the RAW had rendered its use for that purpose out of the question, a command superdreadnought like *Zeven Provinciën* lacked facilities for a virtual conference via holo projection. So Combined Fleet's senior officers were present in the flesh, sharing a large but overcrowded conference room with the local command structure. A two-dimensional display screen showed the Alpha Centauri A system with all its planets and warp points. The abnormal number of the latter made it busier than most such displays.

Trevayne opened the proceedings by addressing Elaine De Mornay, who had arrived to resume her position as his chief of staff. "Elaine, let me congratulate you on the job you've done getting the Mothball Fleet into shape." His lips quirked briefly upward at the name, which he had begun using simply to make himself understood. By now it had assumed semi-official status, having been adopted in a spirit of self-mocking defiance by its own personnel. "Its importance cannot be overstated. It is the only support Combined Fleet is going to have in defending this system. The Sol Reserve is formidable, but it cannot be committed here, at least not yet, lest the Solar System be left defenseless. This is why it has been the other Heart Worlds and not Sol that have been drawn on for the Mothball Fleet."

He paused to let that sink in. The expressions on the faces of Combined Fleet's officers reassured him. They were aware that they were on their own save for a collection of upgraded antiques.

"In fact, Elaine," he resumed, "you're only going to be back in your old billet for a short time, after which Gordon will again function as acting chief of staff. Very soon, I want you to go to Sol and do the same thing you've been doing here: supervising the upgrading of the Sol Reserve's mothballed ships, and mounting the removed obsolescent weapon systems on asteroids and buoys."

"Yes, sir. Given the level of development of Sol's

asteroid belt we ought to be able to do the latter much as we have here, only more so."

"Good. I want a *serious* kill zone created. Now, two other points concerning the defense of Sol. The first concerns the orbital fortresses here, with the tugs slaved to them. As I mentioned in my last courier drone from the Harnah system, I want the majority of them towed to Sol."

"Yes, Admiral. That operation is underway." It was, they both knew, a relatively straightforward matter. The warp line between Alpha Centauri and Sol had long since been "dredged" by the Kasugawa Generator (which could be used to increase the capacity of existing warp points as well as for creating new ones) and could accommodate anything up to a superdevastator.

Vice Admiral Zheng Sha, commander of the Alpha Centauri Defense Command, was visibly troubled. He had extended all possible cooperation to De Mornay, and never questioned any orders from Trevayne, Grand Admiral of the alliance. But this one had brought him close to the brink, and now he spoke up. "I've wondered about that, Admiral. Surely those fortresses could make a material contribution to—"

"I've no doubt of that, Admiral Zheng. But you see, I have a particular role in mind for them to play. And if, in the event, they have to play that role in Sol, they will do so more effectively if they are present in numbers larger than the enemy will expect on the basis of his experience with them here in Alpha Centauri. In other words, I don't want to tip our hand here.

"In a similar vein," Trevayne continued, this time

meeting the eyes of Mario Leong, commander of Combined Fleet's PSU component, which accounted for most of its carriers and "carrier/main combatant" supermonitors, "I plan to transfer a substantial percentage of our fighter assets to Sol." He did not say *human-piloted* fighter assets," although that was his intention. He did not distrust the Orions and the Ophiuchi among Leong's command, but he knew it was unreasonable to expect humanity's birthworld to mean exactly the same sacred thing to them. "Old Terra, after all, is inside Sol's Desai Limit, so the advantage that ships with the Desai Drive normally have over fighters is eliminated."

The silence in the room had seemingly been growing gradually more profound as Trevayne had spoken of the defense of Sol. Now it somehow seemed to plumb depths below the level of mere noiselessness, because he was forcing these people to gaze into the abyss to which their lives—and the lives of all the human race and its allies—had now come. Once they were driven back from Alpha Centauri into the Solar system, with its single dead-end warp point, any defensive strategy would be reduced the defense of a planet, and that planet would be Old Terra itself. There could be no more retreating. Humanity would, for the first time, truly be at bay.

Trevayne only allowed the moment to last a couple of heartbeats before speaking briskly to the room at large. "I now wish to discuss our deployment for the defense of Alpha Centauri." He turned to the screen and activated a cursor.

The display was a conventional one, with Alpha Centauri A at its center, and oriented so that the Bug 15 closed warp point in whose vicinity Combined Fleet still lay was at twelve o'clock of the imaginary superimposed clock-face in which humans still thought, at a distance of twenty-six light-minutes from the primary. A ring of tiny icons representing the asteroid belt circled the central sun at a radius of twenty-one light-minutes, just under twenty-five percent of the distance to Alpha Centauri B's closest approach so that gravitational perturbation had prevented the formation of a planet. Inside that hoop, the green icon of the Nova Terra/Eden binary planet system, whose billions could not possibly have been evacuated even given all the spaceships ever built, was currently at ten o'clock, orbiting at seven light-minutes. No less than six of the system's warp points, leading to Heart-World systems like Wolf-424, Epsilon Eridani and Sigma Draconis, were scattered to that side of the primary . . . including the Sol warp point, at seven o'clock and thirty light-minutes, placing it almost diametrically opposite their own position and fifty-two light-minutes distant. But the remaining two warp points, connecting with the Shaka and Niven systems, were in their astronomical neighborhood, at sixteen and twenty-five light-minutes respectively on a one o'clock bearing.

"One advantage the Kaituni have always possessed in this war," Trevayne began with seeming irrelevance, "is the immense volume of intelligence information which the Arduans of Zarzuela transmitted to them—and which they may or may not have subsequently passed on by some means to the Bugs. Essentially, they know everything about us, including our fleet lists. But the Mothball Fleet *isn't on those lists*; we've only just called it into existence. Therefore I mean to withhold it from their view as long as possible."

Admiral Adrian M'Zangwe's expression—not always easy to make out, against the almost coal-like darkness inherited from African ancestors genetically engineered to colonize a planet of an F type sun—intensified. "Do you mean concealment among the asteroids under stealth, sir?"

"More than that." Trevayne manipulated his remote, and the cursor flashed over the scattering of icons representing warp points. "Hasn't anyone noticed that this system contains quite a lot of . . . bolt-holes?"

One face at a time, understanding began to dawn in his listeners' features.

"I meant to break the Mothball Fleet into task forces and send those through the warp points to adjacent systems, from which we can summon them by pre-prepared courier drones. Appearing unexpectedly, they can launch flank attacks to break the Bugs' momentum and disrupt their organization, hopefully cutting their massive and rather unwieldy horde into smaller elements that can be defeated in detail."

All around the room, heads nodded. It was pure Trevayne.

"The Niven and Shaka warp points are obvious choices. And," he continued in carefully level tones, "if it should happen that we are compelled to withdraw from this system, the Epsilon Indi and Tau Ceti warp points can serve the same function, given our assumed line of retreat toward the Sol warp point. The others—" (he indicated a cluster of warp points in the nine to eleven o'clock region, out beyond the inhabited double planet) "—are less likely to be useful." His voice had now grown somber, and everyone knew why. No one voiced what they all knew but did not want to know. If the Bugs and/or the Kaituni could not be stopped short of Nova Terra and Eden, Combined Fleet could not linger to defend them, and they were doomed.

"I wish to emphasize," Trevayne went on, more briskly, "that I intend to hold these hidden forces in reserve as long as possible, and not reveal them any earlier than necessary. So until an opportunity arises that is too good to pass up, Combined Fleet will have to fight a conventional action, with the help of the defensive elements here. In particular, the tugged fortresses still remaining in this system will be positioned fairly close to the Bug 15 warp point, to provide missile coverage, but will commence a gradual withdrawal shortly after battle is joined."

"And my command, sir?" inquired Hugo Allende eagerly.

Trevayne gave him a somber regard. "The firepower of the devastators and superdevastators would, of course, be invaluable, Commodore. But it is my belief that it may very well be at this point that the Kaituni decide to take an active part. Now, we know their RAW generators are mounted on monitors—perhaps the smallest hull size that can accommodate them. These are not fast ships, but they do have a sufficient speed advantage over your vessels to overtake them in the course of a long stern chase across fifty light-minutes."

"Are we, then, to be stationed at the Sol warp point,

sir?" Allende's question was carefully respectful, but he couldn't keep an undertone of sullenness out of his voice.

"No. In our present extremity, that degree of caution is a luxury we can no longer afford. We *must* have your ships' firepower for the battle we are about to fight. I intend to station you in *this* vicinity." Trevayne indicated with the cursor a region sunward of the asteroid belt along the twelve o'clock bearing, about ten light-minutes from the Bug 15 warp point. "As the Bugs advance toward the inner system, you will engage them in a missile duel . . . *but*, you will gradually withdraw before them, in the same manner as the fortresses. We have calculated that this will give you enough of a head start to reach the Sol warp point ahead of the Kaituni, if you commence your withdrawal the moment we detect them emerging from the warp point. You will obey an order to do so instantly and unhesitatingly. Do I make myself clear?"

"You do, Admiral."

"Very well." Trevayne turned back to the meeting at large. "We will now go into the reorganization of the Mothball Fleet, and Combined Fleet's detailed dispositions. Captain Thorfinnssen, please ring the wardroom and tell them to have the stewards keep us supplied with coffee."

Destoshaz'at Zum'ref, unquestioned supreme leader of the Kaituni, gazed into the viewscreen with satisfaction, watching his ships emerge from the Harnah warp point into Bug 15, against the backdrop of the orange-tinted primary sun, only three light-minutes distant. (At least the humans described it as orange-tinted. His central eye also discerned a *murn* undertone that those sub-Arduan beings could not see.)

On a whim, he manipulated the controls to swing the view a hundred and eighty degrees around. Now he was looking away from Bug 15 A into the depths of space, in the direction of the Alpha Centauri warp point, twenty-seven light-minutes further out.

Of course, nothing was visible out there except the blazing backdrop of galactic stars. But he fancied that it ought to be possible to see the Bug fleet, such was the sheer number and total tonnage of ships now clustered at that distant warp point. It was a fleet that could only have been produced by the single-mindedness of a race for which the term "single-mindedness" was horribly apt.

He had long since adopted the human word *Bugs* for the Kaituni's somewhat-less-than-allies. It was short and to the point, and of course they had no verbal symbol for themselves. And even if they had, they had certainly made not the slightest move to communicate it—or anything else—in the course of the long advance along the warp lines from Home Hive II. Indeed, they had never evinced anything except an eerie indifference to the Kaituni fleet that followed along behind them, not precisely herding them but making certain that only a certain avenue of advance was open to them. Nor had they seemed averse to that avenue; they had advanced stolidly along it, unfeelingly absorbing losses that would have daunted even Arduans, assured of reincarnation though they were.

Zum'ref hated to admit it, but he could almost sympathize with the loathing the humans felt.

It had taken the Bugs some time to complete their

transit from Harnah, such were the numbers they'd had to feed through the warp point. But now they had finally massed their entire fleet preparatory to what even they must realize was going to be a climactic battle. After the last of those myriads of ships had moved off across the system to the warp point where they now crouched as though about to spring, Zum'ref had—as per what had become routine procedure by now—ordered his own fleet through behind them. He only had one Dispersate's fleet with him, but it would be enough for this purpose. The vastly greater resources at his disposal would catch up later.

"After all," he pointed out to his *ha'selnarshazi* intendent, fairly oozing (amused satisfaction), "once they enter the Alpha Centauri system, their motivations will be simple, straightforward and utterly predictable."

(Puzzlement.) The intendent gave the *selnarmic* equivalent of a raised eyebrow of inquiry.

"Don't you see, Inzrep'fel?" Zum'ref waved a tentacle cluster at a data readout of Alpha Centauri. "There is a long-colonized twin planet system, with billions upon billions of *griarfeksh*." He always took care to set the example for his subordinates by using that name for the humans: an unpleasant and ill-regarded scavenger of Ardu, their lost homeworld. "The Bugs won't be able to resist gorging on such an abundant protein source! It will attract them like a *bilbuxhat* turd attracts insects."

(Grim amusement.) "Indeed, *Destoshaz'at.* A veritable banquet!"

"And, of course, such a threat to those planets will make the *griarfeksh* Admiral Trevayne less inclined to withdraw. Even such vermin as they must have some feeling for their own kind. He will fight even harder and with more cunning than usual." (Renewed seriousness.) "I don't know whether he will be able to stop them or not. But if he does, his will be what the *griarfeksh* call a *Pyrrhic victory*. We will see to that."

"And if the Bugs win, their numbers will be so reduced that we'll be able to dispose of what's left of them with little trouble, given our technological advantages."

"Precisely." (Sudden decision.) "In fact, we will relax somewhat from our usual caution. As soon as the Bugs have all transited into Alpha Centauri and have advanced a certain distance, we will follow them without further delay."

(Hesitancy.) "Uh . . . *Destoshaz'at*, I remind you that as yet we have only the fleet of one Dispersate here . . ." Inzrep'fel trailed to a halt as her lord and master's central eye began to take on the hot flicker she had seen only a few times—but those few far too many.

(Mildness, neither deceptive nor intended to deceive.) "It will be sufficient, Inzrep'fel."

(Frantic agreement.) "Of course, *Destoshaz'at*, of course!"

So, at last, the Fleet had arrived at the gateway to what had been its real objective all along.

Neither the Old Enemies nor the Newest Enemies had ever guessed it. Indeed, the Newest Enemies had from the beginning flattered themselves that they were shepherding the Fleet ahead of them, allowing it to take all the losses against the Old Enemies. It was as well that they thought so. In fact, of course, driving back the Old Enemies had only been incidental to the plan—the plan that would assure the perpetuation of the Fleet for all time. Which set of Enemies annihilated the other was, of course, immaterial. Neither had any inkling of the Fleet's true purpose.

But they would soon learn. Now the Fleet was about to enter the system it had always aimed for.

CHAPTER ELEVEN

Traditionally, in interstellar space warfare the great advantage of the defenders had been that their attackers must come through a warp point whose location they knew precisely. (Ian Trevayne had once called the warp network one long series of Surigao Straits, to the puzzlement of most of his listeners, even those of Japanese or North American descent.) On the other hand, in the era before the Bug War the defenders had had no way of knowing exactly *when* an attack would come, and no military organization can remain permanently at the highest level of alert.

The introduction of warp-capable probes had changed that. Now it was routine for a defending force to periodically send the robotic scouts through the warp point through which an attack was expected.

Thus it was that Combined Fleet knew when the entire, inconceivably immense Bug armada—actually, the sum total of *three* armadas—was finally assembled in Bug

15, and when it was unmistakably gathering itself in a disturbingly organic way for a convulsive surge. So the attack on Alpha Centauri did not come as a total surprise.

Nevertheless, when it came it was a thunderclap of war which none of those who experienced it would ever forget, even if they lived long enough to forget everything else.

First came a wave of AMBAMs, or anti-mine ballistic antimatter missiles, sent through in unprecedented numbers. The space around the warp point fairly shimmered with the inconceivable energies of antimatter annihilation as swaths of mines were swept away. Then came waves of SBMHAWKs, belching forth their clusters of missiles, pre-programmed to seek out the ships of the screening force Trevayne had stationed around the warp point under Adrian M'Zangwe's command (for the Bugs had their own robot probes). But enough mines remained to take out most of those missile carriers. The screening force was largely intact when the dense formations of Bug monitors began to come through.

Trevayne had crafted a multilayered defense. First were the mines. Second was the screening force itself, comprised of superdreadnoughts and smaller vessels. Their lesser size was partly balanced out by the searing ferocity of the rapid-fire energy torpedoes that were their principal armament. They began to fall back when their losses reached a certain predetermined level.

Third were the carriers—further back from the warp point, but not very far, for they were so fast and maneuverable that they had no fear of not being able to dance away ahead of the lumbering Bug phalanxes in the manner permitted by reactionless, inertia-cancelling drives. Mario Leong commanded them, for they were mostly from the PSU, which had not progressed as far as the Rim Federation or the Terran Republic in equipping heavy fighters with the new scaled-down version of the energy torpedo. But those that had been so converted were teamed with missile-carrying fighters in the kind of tactical combinations they had honed to a fine edge in the course of a long fighting retreat. Slashing through the massed Bug array like demoniac spirits of destruction, the Orions among their pilot filling the comm networks with blood-freezing felinoid howls of triumph whenever a Bug ship blossomed outward in flame.

Finally, as the seemingly inexhaustible Bug numbers began to pile up faster than they could be destroyed, the second and third defensive layers fell back and merged with the fourth: the tugged fortresses and Combined Fleet's supermonitors, under Rafaela Shang's command. Together they laid down a barrage of the devastating heavy bombardment missiles Trevayne himself had first introduced during the Fringe Revolution, while gradually edging away at the snail-like speed of the fortresses. When the Bugs finally drew within tactical range, the big missile platforms switched to capital missiles and strategic bombardment missiles.

Eventually the Bugs, advancing in their sullen, insensate way through the missile-storm, closed the range. The supermonitors, still outside the Desai Limit, could withdraw ahead of them. But the fortresses had to be abandoned. Their crews were evacuated and they were left to fight on as best they could under autonomous computer control. Combined Fleet continued its fighting withdrawal.

By this time the Bugs' advance had brought their lead elements five light-minutes sunward from the Bug 15 warp point, and here they encountered Trevayne's fifth layer: Alpha Centauri A's dense asteroid belt, bristling with the weapon systems that had been ripped out of the Mothball Fleet to make room for today's energy torpedoes. Obsolescent those weapons might be, but most of the Bugs' armory was almost of the same vintage. Force beams wrenched at Bug hulls with their focused gravo-magnetic distortion of space. Primary beams, an even more tightly focused and energy-extravagant variation of the same principle, thrust home cylinders of destruction that were narrow in diameter but ignored all armor and defensive shields, like a rapier to the force beam's broadsword. Heterodyned pairs of x-ray lasers boiled armor away and sought for ships' vitals beneath.

Still, it wasn't as effective as it probably would have been against a human or Orion or even Arduan admiral, who would have been stressed and distracted by such a multitude of unexpected insect-bites. The Bug hive intelligence was immune to such things. They pushed stolidly on, taking their losses, and once they were through the asteroid belt Trevayne ordered the supermonitors to pull further back, for they had now entered Alpha Centauri A's Desai Limit and had lost their speed advantage. They continued to belabor the Bugs with missiles, switching back to HBMs, many of them configured as "laser torpedoes" capable of making multiple attack runs . The smaller ships continued to do battle at their weapons' most advantageous ranges, supported by the increasingly weary fighter pilots.

Some time earlier, the last of the Bug ships had completed warp transit. At last, the entire armada was in the Alpha Centauri system. And, well behind them but not as far behind as had been their practice so far, the Kaituni were beginning to appear at the Bug 15 warp point.

Gazing at the data readouts, Trevayne could not avoid a kind of awe. Even with the staggering losses the Bugs had taken—losses that would have ground down the will of any normal intelligence to continue—and the lesser but still all-too-high losses sustained by Combined Fleet, this was the probably the greatest number of warships ever to clash in a single system. It would certainly be so once the Kaituni completed their warp transit. And it would be incomparably so once the Mothball Fleet emerged from its extra-systemic hiding places.

Then, as he looked at the system-scale strategic display, he noticed something else . . . something not quite right.

"Gordon, something is not quite right."

"Sir?" Gordon Singhal joined Trevayne before the system display. It was oriented in the conventional manner, with the Bug 15 warp point near the top, on the twelve o'clock bearing. The swarm of icons representing the warring fleets were now below the broken ring representing the asteroid belt. A little further below that was the icon of Combined Fleet's sixth and last layer of defense: Hugo Allende's task group of devastators and superdevastators, positioned to send a torrent of long-range missiles into the Bugs as they proceeded on their expected sunward course.

Only . . . they weren't exactly following that course.

Trevayne manipulated controls. A line of light extended back from the Bugs' current position to the warp point though which they had come. Frowning, he keyed in a second command. Another line appeared, showing their anticipated route toward the Nova Terra/Eden binary. The former was perceptibly to the right of the latter . . . and the gap was widening.

"What are they up to?" Singhal wondered aloud. "And why haven't we noticed this before?"

"The deviation was slight at first," Trevayne pointed out. "As though they wanted to keep it inconspicuous as long as possible. But now it's growing."

"Could it be an attempt to disrupt our defensive strategy, sir?"

"Perhaps. But it's almost as though . . ." Trevayne entered another command, and the computer extrapolated the Bugs' altered course. "It's almost as though they're heading more or less in the direction of the Shaka warp point."

Singhal stared at him. "But . . . *why*, sir?"

"I cannot imagine. And the question is, at the moment, immaterial. Have comm raise Commodore Allende at once." At least, Trevayne reflected, there'd be no light-speed communications delay. *Zeven Provinciën* and her escorting light cruisers lay not far from Allende's formation. "He is to move his command so as to interpose it across the Bugs' new course . . . but only if he can do so in the vicinity of the Shaka warp point. With the Kaituni beginning to appear in this system, we can't risk moving the devastators and superdevastators any further away from the Sol warp point than they already are."

"Will that be possible, sir? I mean, as slow as those ships are . . ."

"I don't know. Run a computer projection. Knowing Commodore Allende, I think you can safely factor in the optimum expeditiousness on his part." Singhal hurried off. Trevayne fell silent, and for a time his brooding dark gaze did not leave the display screen.

The chief of staff returned. "Commodore Allende acknowledges his orders, Admiral. And I've got them working on that computer projection." He cleared his throat. "Ah . . . Admiral, may I make an observation?"

"Certainly, Commodore," said Trevayne without taking his eyes off the display.

"If this projected course is correct, and the Bugs are in fact, for some unfathomable reason, bound for the Shaka warp point, then the Mothball Fleet contingent in the Niven system—"

"—Will be in a position to appear on their port flank," Trevayne finished for him. And that contingent could, he knew, be summoned very promptly; prepared courier drones waited at each of the warp-points, needing only a signal to plunge through. "Yes, that thought has occurred to me. It's certainly an option. But I hadn't wanted to reveal those bolt-hole forces this soon. And I calculate that we don't need to make the decision just yet. We'll wait until we have definite word on Commodore Allende's potential to intervene effectively. In the meantime, all elements of Combined Fleet that are currently engaged with the Bugs are to maintain as close contact with them as possible, and take advantage of whatever tactical opportunities present themselves.

Whatever it is they are up to, we must continue to wear their numbers down."

"Understood, Admiral."

"Something is not quite right." Zum'ref's (irritated puzzlement) would have been palpable even without *selnarm*. He glared at the system display.

He had been preoccupied with the orderly emergence of his leading elements into the Alpha Centauri system, only occasionally receiving reports of the epic battle raging between the Bugs and the *griarfeksh*. With each such report he had exuded (serene self-satisfaction), for things were going according to plan. The human admiral, Trevayne, had prepared his defenses as brilliantly as expected, utilizing the materials at hand to the best advantage The Bugs were taking soul-shakingly horrific losses but, as usual, were ignoring them and continuing to advance. He thought back over the history of his exploitation of them. The breakthrough into understanding of their recorded thoughts . . . the realization that there was a surviving, concealed Bug hive, and the surreptitious use of human prospectors to locate the hidden warp point in the Home Hive Two system that led to it . . . the insertion of a timed biological *selnarmic* "beacon" into that hidden hive system . . . his, Zum'ref's subsequent strategic masterstroke, advancing so slowly as to assure that there would be as many *griarfeksh* ships as possible concentrated in Home Hive Two when it was time to unveil the RAW and unleash the Bugs . . . and, afterwards, his use of the great herd of ships ahead to do the work of pushing the *griarfeksh* back while letting them take the losses.

Yes, all had gone according to plan. The Bugs had made ideal tools, for they were so perfectly predictable.

Until now, when for once they were doing the unexpected . . .

Zum'ref turned his glare on his Intendent. Inzrep'fel said nothing and carefully kept her *selnarm* under tight leash. She wasn't about to be the one to remind the *Destoshaz'at* of his own prediction that the Bug armada would proceed mindlessly sunward toward the heavily populated twin planets, oblivious to everything save impatience to commence an orgy of eating.

After a moment, Zum'ref's expression and his *selnarm* both smoothed themselves out. "At the moment, there is little we can do except complete the transit of our forces through the warp point as planned, and continue to observe this . . . . anomalous behavior. Inform me at once if there are any further developments."

(Relief.) "Yes, *Destoshaz'at.*"

So the New Enemies—the ones defending this system— had noticed the Fleet's course change. It was clear that they had, judging from the reordering of their forces that was now underway, including an urgent-seeming repositioning of the very large ships that they had been holding back.

No doubt the Newest Enemies, still emerging into this system, would notice it, if they had not done so already.

Both must be very perplexed.

Soon their perplexity would be resolved. They would see what the Fleet was doing. And they might even understand why this system, with its array of warp points, had been what the Fleet had been aiming for all along.

★★★

"The computer projection is in, Admiral," Gordon Singhal reported. "Commodore Allende—even though he's been moving mountains—isn't going to be able to get his task group into opposition to do anything more than pick at the Bugs' flanks with missile fire at extreme ranges." He paused. "This assumes that the Bugs remain on their present course, and also that, as per your orders, he maneuvers in such a way as to not approach any closer to the Bug 15 warp point. If, on the other hand—"

"No." Trevayne shook his head, his eyes on the scarlet icons of the Kaituni forces streaming steadily into the system. "We don't know if these Kaituni ships include RAW monitors, and we can't risk putting the devastators and superdevastators into a stern chase they can't win. Remember, it's a long way to the Sol warp point." He drew a deep breath. "Order Commodore Allende to commence withdrawal at once—and yes, I know he won't like it. And activate the courier drone at the Niven warp point. I hadn't wanted to do it just yet, but we're going to summon Admiral Parnell."

CHAPTER TWELVE

Sometimes, in the history of war, a derisive nickname had been embraced by its victims and adopted as their own in a spirit of whimsical defiance and self-deprecatory pride.

Thus it was with the Mothball Fleet.

Rear Admiral Diego Parnell, PSUN, recalled a parallel Ian Trevayne had cited from the past of his own native island on Old Terra: "the Old Contemptibles." The Grand Admiral had mentioned it as he had placed Parnell in command of Task Group Niven, which would lurk a warp jump away from Alpha Centauri and await the courier drone that would summon it to come through and join the battle against the Bugs—or the Kaituni, as the case might be.

Parnell cherished a hope that it would be the Kaituni. He was a native of Orphicon, one of the Heart World systems that had been ravaged by a sleet-storm of relativistic projectiles, the dismantled fragments of Kaituni generation ships. It could have been worse. It could have been like Christophon, where a boulder of several tons had punched into and through the local sun. It hadn't created a supernova, of course, whatever the news media, scientifically illiterate as ever, had said; you couldn't do that with an ordinary main sequence star, the only kind that could have life-bearing planets. But from the standpoint of the system's inhabitants, the difference between a supernova and the unprecedented stellar event that had actually occurred had been academic.

Orphicon had gotten off relatively lightly, shielded to some degree by an outer gas giant planet. But a fist-sized chunk had plunged into an ocean at 0.67 *c*, smashing through the planetary crust beneath the ocean floor. The planet had been devastated by earthquakes, hurricanes, tsunamis and salt rain. No one knew exactly how many tens of millions had died. They had included Parnell's wife Marlena and his two children.

Yes, Parnell wanted it to be the Kaituni.

But if all tactical prognostications were correct, it was almost certainly going to be the Bugs. There would be no way to know until they actually emerged into the Alpha Centauri system, for the courier drone was preset with a simple order; there would be no time to reprogram it with any specific information about what Task Group Niven could expect to encounter.

Anyway, he thought, *the Bugs will do.* They, after all, had been cannon fodder for the Kaituni the whole bloody way from Home Hive Two, advancing through system after system like some inexorable, unfeeling force of nature. And anyway . . . they were *Bugs.* Parnell's gorge rose as there came into his mind, unbidden and unwelcomed, the image of a radially symmetrical, coarsely black-haired being with six upward-angled limbs around a central pod, two manipulative limbs, and eight stalked eyes . . . and a wide, disgusting gash of a mouth with rows of teeth, and wriggling tentacles to hold living prey still for mastication and ingestion. Like every other living human of the current era, Parnell had never seen an actual Bug. But the passage of almost a century and a half since the Bug War had been powerless to diminish the primal loathing felt by humans and all other races that had ever encountered that uniquely nausea-inducing life-form, seemingly an outrage against nature and sanity.

Partly to banish the flesh-crawling mental image, he reviewed his task group. Its largest ships were superdreadnoughts like PSUNS *Cyprus*, on whose flag bridge he stood. The Mothball Fleet's monitors and its few supermonitors had gone to strengthen Trevayne's fourth layer of slow missile ships in Alpha Centauri. Task Group Niven, like the other task groups concealed behind Alpha Centauri's warp points, was intended for swift flank attacks taking whatever tactical advantage the asteroid belt, just in-system, might afford, to disrupt the Bugs' momentum and cut their enormous horde into smaller segments that could be defeated in detail. So in addition to his superdreadnoughts, Parnell had battlecruisers, the smallest ship type that had any business in a modern fleet engagement as a main combatant. He had also been assigned a small fighter component, consisting of fleet carriers rather than the larger assault carriers that had largely replaced them in modern fleets. In short, the task group was designed for nipping at the flanks of three Bug armadas coalesced into an unwieldy fleet of staggering size.

Out of the corner of his eye, Parnell saw his flag captain approaching at a fast walk—or relatively fast, for Nadia Svoboda wasn't as young as she used to be. In this, she was typical of the Mothball Fleet. It wasn't just ships that had been brought out of mothballs, he reflected wryly. Many things about these ships were unfamiliar to the personnel of today's space navies. So a call had gone out for retirees, who had responded in their tens of thousands. Back on the active list, they now crewed ships out of their youth, ships they had never expected to see again.

Old ships and old people, thought Parnell sadly. He himself had been nearing retirement when the universe they had known had come crashing down. He and Marlena had been looking into a place on the bluffs overlooking the Naiad Ocean . . . a coast now turned into a brackish wasteland by tidal waves.

Svoboda came up, slightly out of breath. "Admiral, the courier drone has come through the warp point."

So it's time. Parnell didn't need to ask what message the drone was broadcasting. It had but one. And Task Group Niven's response to it was well practiced. "Very good. Go to general quarters at once. And alert all elements of the task group. We will commence our transit schedule immediately."

So a force of the New Enemies had emerged from the warp point to the left of the Fleet's course, just outside the asteroid belt. They evidently had positioned such forces beyond this system's warp points for just this purpose.

However, this presented an opportunity for the Fleet. There was no way to know what kind of opposition lurked beyond the warp point that had been the original objective. But now the New enemies had tipped their hand at this other warp point. Once the newly arriving force was destroyed, the way would be clear for the Fleet to fulfill its objective in this system—the objective that the Newest Enemies had never suspected, while the Fleet had permitted them to believe they were using it.

So it was now time for a modification of the plan, and a sharp alteration of course.

Gordon Singhal stared at the system display, watching the Bug armada, actuated by a single will, make the kind of ninety degree course change permitted by reactionless, inertia-cancelling drives.

"Admiral!" he gasped. "They're swinging to port and heading directly toward the Niven war point—"

"—And Admiral Parnell's task group," Trevayne finished for him. "Yes, I see."

A comm rating hurried up to Singhal and spoke rapidly. The chief of staff nodded and turned back to Trevayne. "Admiral, a message from Admiral M'Zangwe." As senior officer on scene, Adrian M'Zangwe was in tactical command of Combined Fleet in its running battle with the Bugs. "He reports that this sudden Bug course change has taken them somewhat off balance. And, of course, they're within Alpha Centauri A's Desai Limit, so they have no significant speed advantage. But he's confident that he can maintain contact with them . . . harry them from the rear, at least with long-range missiles and fighter strikes." He didn't add, or need to add, that without some such support Task Group Niven faced certain annihilation by the juggernaut rushing toward it.

"No." Trevayne's monosyllable was flat and cold. Singhal looked at him, startled. He looked closer to his chronological age than his biological one. He spoke like a machine as he gestured at the display. "If Combined Fleet pursues the Bugs, it will be moving *away* from the axis of advance leading from the Bug 15 warp point to this system's inhabited planets . . . and, beyond them, to the Sol warp point on the far side of the system. And more and more Kaituni ships are emerging from the Bug 15 warp point." He finally took his eyes off the display and turned to Singhal. His face wore an expression the acting chief of staff had never seen on it: he was clearly in agony of soul. But when he spoke, it was in a voice that could be heard by others on the flag bridge.

"No," he repeated. "Order Admiral M'Zangwe to take up position so as to interpose Combined Fleet between the Kaituni and the inner system. We cannot leave that route open."

"Aye aye, sir," Singhal said quietly. From the back of his memory, he recalled that this was the man who, during the Fringe Revolution, had given the orders that he had known must doom his own son.

He turned and strode toward the comm station. As he went, he could almost feel the dead silence spreading. Everyone in earshot knew that Trevayne had just sentenced Task Group Niven to death.

Diego Parnell had expected to fight a series of flanking

actions. He had felt this expectation confirmed when *Cyprus* had emerged from warp into Alpha Centauri space and he had observed the Bugs seemingly headed toward the Shaka warp point on a course at right angles to his own.

But then the Bug swarm—it was difficult not to think of it that way—had wrenched itself into a tight course change like a single amorphous organism. Now it was headed straight toward him, and he had received word that there would be no support from Combined Fleet. And as he looked at the tactical display, he knew he was looking into hell-mouth.

He shook off the thought angrily and commanded himself to concentrate on practicalities. He studied the readout of the Intelligence analysis of the sensor readings. He had gone to Niven knowing the approximate size of the Bug armada, or collection of armadas. Comparing that with what he was seeing now, it was clear that Combined Fleet had inflicted brutal punishment, at least to the extent that punishment could be inflicted on something unable to feel pain. Of course, what remained was still quite capable of swallowing up his task group without so much as a belch of indigestion.

They were now entering the outer fringes of Alpha Centauri A's asteroid belt. Unfortunately, this wasn't the region that had been sown with obsolescent weapon systems, as it hadn't been thought to be one of the more probable battlespaces. But the belt itself might be used to advantage.

He turned to face his staff, and the split comm screen that showed the faces of his subordinate commanders. "All right, people. There will be no head-on clash. Our original mission was to conduct flanking attacks, and that's exactly what I want us to go ahead and do, to the extent these . . . changed circumstances make it possible. I want us to disperse by squadron organization and take as much concealment as possible in the belt. They know we're coming, of course, but on the tactical level we ought to be able to confuse them some, given the improvements in stealth since the Bug War." In fact, he reflected, unless the Bugs had made radical advances in sensor technology—and there was no indication that they had—then ships within the closed bubble of a modern stealth field should be completely undetectable to them at any range beyond sixteen light-seconds. Not all of his ships had been retrofitted with such field generators, but all the carriers had. "In particular, I want the fighters to hit them as hard as possible as they pass through the belt."

"Yes!" exclaimed Small Claw of the Khan Zhreenow'-kharnak, PSUN, commander of Task Group Niven's carrier component, his luxuriant whiskers quivering. "And may our claws strike deep!"

A rumble of agreement arose from the others, all of whom were human, and Heart Worlders like Parnell. Most also shared his wrinkles and graying hair. He would not insult these people, who had already done so much for the Pan-Sentient Union, with any fatuities about possible survival. Nor did he need to. Looking into these aging faces, he saw nothing but steadiness.

"Now," he said gruffly, "let's get down to cases."

The reports from Task Group Niven were more and more interspersed with Code Omega signals—the traditional death-cry of human warships. Ian Trevayne received them all with a stoicism that masked his heartsickness.

Parnell was inflicting as much damage as anyone could have expected under the circumstances, making masterful use of his technological advantages. His ships might be old, but they were all of at least the same design vintage as the Bugs'. And their ECM and weapon systems had been upgraded to a higher order. The weapons officers of the Mothball Fleet, at least, were not oldsters, for those ships were now armed with up-to-date energy torpedoes that combined the best features of directed-energy weapons and any missiles except the very largest. Parnell's few fighters, emerging from their asteroidal hiding places, swooped around into the blind zones of Bug monitors and gutted them. His superdreadnoughts, flanked by swift battlecruisers, went toe-to-toe with the advancing masses of ships, blazing away with rapid-fire energy torpedoes.

But the Bugs simply continued their characteristic horribly unrelenting advance, taking their losses and grinding down Task Group Niven by sheer numbers, blanketing ship after ship with overwhelming firepower. And they held course unswervingly toward the Niven warp point.

Trevayne wished he had known Parnell better.

He became aware of Gordon Singhal at his side, watching the system display with bewildered fascination. "What are they doing?" he asked. "And why are they doing it?"

"I think I may know," Trevayne heard himself say, even as his idea was crystalizing.

"Sir?"

"I think the Kaituni—and ourselves—have been wrong in assuming that they've been allowing themselves to be herded toward Sol. No—I believe they have their own agenda. For them, all along, Alpha Centauri hasn't been a place to be conquered, but rather a place from which they can escape."

"But why, sir?"

"So the galactic cancer that is their species can . . . metastasize."

Diego Parnell lowered Nadia Svoboda's lifeless body to the deck. For just an instant, he laid a hand on her bloodied grey head. Then he rose and turned back to the chaos of the flag bridge, smoky and crackling with broken electrical cables, as damage-control parties put out fires and the remains of the crew tried to get control panels and readouts back on line.

It was over. There would be no more tactical finesse, no more maneuvers *Cyprus* was barely still underway, and some of her weapons were still operable, but that was about it. The few other remaining ships were in even worse case. The Bugs were simply obliterating them *en passant* as they moved stolidly on.

He felt a strange, almost listless fatalism as he passed an order to the acting flag captain, specifying a particular Bug monitor.

Cyprus would never reach that monitor, of course, limping her atmosphere-streaming way along. But the remaining rapid-fire energy torpedo batteries sent a barrage of destruction ahead of her. She shuddered as missiles smashed down the last of her defensive shields, and then shrieked with metallic agony as force beams tore and wrenched. Finally, at even closer range, came a volley of missiles in sprint mode, impossible to intercept even if *Cyprus* had still had anything to intercept them with.

By then, Parnell didn't see them. All he could see was Marlena's face, smiling gently, just before his universe turned very briefly to noise and fire.

The asteroid belt was astern, the warp point ahead. The Fleet could now commence transit, knowing nothing would oppose them on the other side, for the forces that had been there were now disposed of.

The Fleet had experienced radical depletion in this system—even more than expected. But that was of no moment. All that mattered was that some of it would break free of the Newest Enemies and proceed onward through warp point after warp point, seeding planets as it went.

That had always been the plan, in which the Newest Enemies had unwittingly assisted. This system had been the objective from the first, simply because of its multiplicity of warp points. That there would be one through which the Fleet could exit free of interference had been inevitable, and so it had proven. And now the great project could commence: the planting of new hives through the warp chains. The Omnivoracity, once seemingly destroyed by the Old Enemies and the New Enemies, would arise again, imperishable.

Arduans did not foam at the mouth. But the spasmodic twitching of the breathing slits on the sides of Zum'ref's thick neck conveyed much the same thing. And his Intendent and his staff officers flinched back from that which smoldered in the depths of his central eye as he watched, with impotent fury, the icon of the Bug armada vanish into the Niven warp point.

(Inexpressible outrage.) "The miserable, filthy vermin! What are they doing? Answer me that, you useless, Illudor-forgotten lumps!"

One of the staffers hesitantly exuded (mild protest). "We have no way of knowing, *Destoshaz'at*. Their action is inexplicable."

(Wild, unreasoning anger.) "Then what good are you? Must I do everything myself? I am surrounded by incompetents and traitors!" Zum'ref raised his arms, and his tentacle clusters twisted themselves into knots. "MY PATIENCE IS EXHAUSTED!"

After a moment, with a shuddering effort, Zum'ref got himself under control. Another staffer took advantage of the lull in the storm to speak up timidly. "In the long run, *Destoshaz'at*, it makes no difference. We don't need those repulsive creatures any more. They have served the purpose of inflicting major losses on the hu . . . that is, the *griarfeksh*." (Fawning flattery.) "With your supreme genius to guide us, we can sweep them aside as soon as all our forces are concentrated here."

(Sullen fury.) "What do you mean, 'all our forces'? This Dispersate has completed warp transit and is now present. We will commence our attack now!"

They all struggled to smother their (shock). Only Inzrep'fel spoke up. "Ah, *Destoshaz'at*, permit me to point out that we have only one Dispersate's fleet here.

Six more are on the way. Once we have them all assembled—"

(Cold contempt.) "Shut up, you coward! Aside from the losses it has sustained, the *griarfeksh* fleet has had its defensive organization disrupted and much of its depletable munitions expended. What we have here will suffice." (Rekindled wrath.) "Are you defying me?"

They all practically fell over themselves to radiate (disavowal of any such intent).

CHAPTER THIRTEEN

Throughout the course of the bitter fighting retreat from Home Hive Two, Ian Trevayne had repeatedly used, because he'd wanted no one in Combined Fleet to be able to forget it, the term *a fleet in being*.

He recalled the origin of the phrase. Admiral Arthur Herbert, Earl of Torrington, had coined it in his own defense on the occasion of his court-martial in 1690 for failing to risk his fleet by going to the rescue of England's Dutch allies at the Battle of Beachy Head—a battle which he had sought against his wishes and his better judgment, in obedience to orders. He had been acquitted, but his services had never been required by His Majesty again.

Trevayne had always felt a certain sneaking sympathy for Torrington. He had, by all accounts, been an exceptionally dissolute Restoration rake, but he had also been a fearless fighting man who had lost an eye to an Algerian corsair's scimitar, and he had been instrumental in assuring the success of the Glorious Revolution of 1688.

And, above all, he had been right: the existence of the fleet he had preserved had subsequently deterred the victorious French from invading England.

Now the term he had used so often had come back to haunt him, as he watched through the sensor eyes of recon drones as the Kaituni at the Bug 15 Warp Point organized themselves for an attack, and contemplated his own battered, exhausted, depleted forces. For he knew he must stand and fight here. Alpha Centauri could not be written off. And he hadn't yet come to such a pass that he could call in the Sol Reserve.

One good thing: Allende's devastators and superdevastators were by now only a few light-minutes from Alpha Centauri A, and would be able to reach the Sol warp point ahead of Kaituni RAW monitors even if the latter started out now and crossed the system unimpeded at their best speed—something Trevayne had no intention of letting them do.

He had had a certain amount of time to reorganize Combined Fleet's entangled elements into something resembling his pervious layered defense along the axis between the Kaituni and this system's inhabited twin planets. He had also had time to reflect on his options concerning the Mothball Fleet. Now he had reached a decision. He turned to the chief of staff.

"Commodore Singhal, have communications prepare new courier drones, to replace those now stationed off the Shaka, Sigma Draconis and Wolf 424 warp points. I have new orders for the commanders of the Mothball Fleet task groups in those systems, in the event that they are summoned into this system."

Singhal's eyebrows rose slightly. "You mean you're not going to recall them at once, sir?" This had been the general expectation among Trevayne's staffers.

"No. Recall Task Group Epsilon Eridani—that warp point's location makes it pretty much irrelevant to the battle that's going to develop, and the task group may be able to reinforce us here in time if it starts toward us now. But the three I mentioned may very well be able to play a very useful role." Trevayne didn't explain; he hoped Singhal would be able to figure it out for himself if he studied the positions of those three warp points relative to the expected Kaituni line of advance. "As for the Epsilon Indi and Tau Ceti task groups, they will remain where they are, under their original orders."

This time Singhal nodded, understanding. Those warp point lay almost directly along the route to the Sol warp point, on the other side of the system, well positioned for helping to cover a retreat.

"Aye aye, sir. I'll get right on it."

"Good. And Gordon . . ."

"Yes, Admiral?"

"Contact Nova Terra and Eden and inquire as to how the evacuation is progressing." Before the Bugs had appeared, Trevayne had advised the civilian authorities to commence using all available noncombatant ships to transport as many people as possible to Sol. He'd only hoped those authorities already had a plan worked out for selecting that tiny minority.

He suspected that politicians and their hangers-on would be overrepresented in that minority.

It was as though Singhal read his thoughts. "Aye

aye, sir. Oh . . . and Admiral, what about Assemblyman Morosini's party, out at Component B? He's sent another message—"

"I don't doubt he has. Well, we can't spare a naval vessel for them. And I doubt if the government at Nova Terra has much in the way of civilian transport for a voyage all the way out there. So tell him to possess his soul in patience, or words to that effect."

"Aye aye, sir."

As Singhal departed, Trevayne turned back to the system display and glared at the baleful scarlet icon at the Bug 15 warp point, wondering what the Kaituni admiral, or whatever he called himself, was thinking.

Zum'ref had calmed down as his organization had smoothly flowed into its attacking formation, although his subordinates still kept their distance as much as possible. Now, with the preparations complete, he sat studying the findings of the probe drones he had deployed earlier to watch the Bugs' battle.

The Intendent approached, fairly oozing (obsequiousness). "*Destoshaz'at*, all our forces are now deployed in this system." Just in time, he stopped short of saying *all our* available *forces*. "The only exception is the RAW monitors, which you ordered to be brought in last."

(Impatience.) "We won't wait for them. I have decided to leave them behind in Bug 15."

Inzrep'fel kept his *selnarm* scrupulously neutral and said nothing.

"They would have been useful," Zum'ref went on, "against the relatively few fortresses that the *griarfeksh* were employing, using tugs to give them limited mobility. But it is clear that the Bugs destroyed all of those. And I know this Admiral Trevayne well enough by now to know that he won't risk his devastators and superdevastators against us. Therefore, there is nothing here massive enough for a RAW targeting solution. So we need not delay while they make transit."

(Fulsomeness.) "As always, *Destoshaz'at*, your superior insight outstrips the rest of us."

"True," Zum'ref admitted. (Decisiveness.) "We will commence the advance at once."

The Bugs, in their passage through the asteroid belt, had thinned out the weapon emplacements there. But, as was clear now, their course had been biased slightly to port (that is, to the right in terms of Trevayne's system display). The Kaituni were moving, equally slightly, in the other direction, toward the current orbital location of the inhabited twin-planet system. So their course led through a region still bristling with widely dispersed weapon systems which, however obsolescent in term of today's military state of the art, could still kill you as dead as you could get. Furthermore, the Kaituni, unlike the Bugs, possessed Desai Drive, so there was no advantage in seeking engagement with them outside Alpha Centauri A's Desai Limit, which happened to lie just in-system of the belt.

This time, therefore, Trevayne made the belt his first line of defense. Not for the first time, he reflected on the fact—usually taken for granted by everyone, including himself—that warp points associated with a star, for some reason as obscure as everything else about them, invariably occurred in the same ecliptic plane as that star's planets. Thus, in the strategic though not in the tactical sense, the battlefield of space warfare was two-dimensional. Of course, it was not impossible to maneuver "above" or "below" the plane of the ecliptic, as it would have been with the rocket-propelled craft of the space age's dawn. But in practice it was very seldom done. And the Kaituni were certainly showing no inclination to do it.

The Kaituni also did not seem to be employing any of the tactical innovations they had sprung earlier—the recon pinnaces, the "stick-hives" for minesweeping, the defensive-fire modular ships, the heavy assault monitors, and the rest—simply because all of those were specialized for warp point assaults, and the Bugs had already taken care of that. So the oncoming array was a conventional-appearing one, including masses of monitors. Trevayne's recon drones couldn't tell him if those monitors included any of the RAW-equipped ones, but this didn't concern him; if they *were* there, they would find no targets.

He had dispersed his light units among the asteroids, and the Kaituni found themselves swarmed by cruisers and destroyers as they tried to shrug off the pinpricks of the emplaced weapons. These maneuverable ships did as much damage as they could with in-and-out attacks, but they could not sustain a stand-up fight with ships that could smash them with a single well-placed salvo. They continued to harass as the Kaituni advanced sunward from the asteroid belt and entered the Desai Limit.

Here Trevayne had stationed his carriers, heavily cloaked, and fighter squadrons that had had a little time to rest and resupply surged to the attack. It soon became evident to him that in one respect his enemies' order of battle reflected their new design philosophies: almost every capital ship carried at least one fighter squadron. A wild, confused dogfight snarled around the phalanxes of Kaituni ships.

Each side had certain advantages. Combined Fleet's fighters, and their pilots, were simply better than their Kaituni opposite numbers, and they were armed with scaled-down rapid-fire energy torpedoes. But the Kaituni had *selnarm*-enhanced command and control, and pilots who *knew* that they died only to be reincarnated and therefore had a kind of fearlessness that seemed suicidal by human or Orion or Ophiuchi standards. And, above all, the Kaituni had numbers, especially given the attrition their opponents had already suffered against the Bugs. The loss ratio was lopsidedly in Combined Fleet's favor, but the Kaituni could better afford their losses. The carriers fell back, continuing to launch their squadrons in shifts.

Further inward, the Kaituni came under long-range missile bombardment from Trevayne's monitors and supermonitors, knitted together into command datagroups that could concentrate a devastating time-on-target salvo upon a singles target. Meanwhile, his superdreadnoughts joined the cruiser-and-below classes that were tormenting the Kaituni flanks in cooperation with the steadily-diminishing fighters. The Kaituni fought back grimly, their monitor formations belching torrents of missiles and their lighter ships seeking close action with fatalistic perseverance.

And as the battle raged and losses mounted, Trevayne's eye kept going to the system display, where the green icon of Task Group Epsilon Eridani had by now put the twin planet system astern in the starboard quarter and was nearing the scene of battle even as Combined Fleet slowly drew back toward it. After a time, he did a quick mental calculation and nodded.

"Gordon," he said to Singhal, "I believe it is time to launch the courier drones to Shaka, Sigma Draconis and Wolf 424."

Singhal, who by this time knew the Grand Admiral's intentions, smiled grimly. "At once, sir."

Zum'ref also saw that icon—*murn*-colored on his system display—for he had *selnarm*-coordinated recon drones roaming this system.

He had a fairly good idea what it was, for by the same means he had observed the human force that had emerged from the warp point into which the Bugs had subsequently fled after annihilating that force. He had been puzzled, for his Intelligence staff's force estimates for Trevayne's fleet hadn't included any more than what had already been arrayed in the Alpha Centauri system. Evidently, Trevayne had summoned reserves from some unsuspected source. This new element must surely represent more of the same.

But then, as he watched, three more such icons sprang into being, at three of the system's warp points.

His Intendent saw it too. (Concern.) "They must have forces we didn't know about, in the systems with warp connections to this one."

(Grimness.) "Yes. These must be older ships, hastily recommissioned. As such, they wouldn't have been on the fleet lists we obtained from Zarzuela."

"Then surely, *Destoshaz'at*, we need have no concern about them."

"Don't be so sure. Remember—and there's no point in denying it—that the newest *griarfeksh* ships are, in most respects, somewhat more technologically advanced than ours. So even their less up-to-date ones are not to be entirely despised. Especially inasmuch as Trevayne has undoubtedly had their armaments and targeting systems upgraded as much as time has permitted." Zum'ref glared at the display. "I also see his fine hand in the selection of the warp points from which these new arrivals are emerging."

(Puzzlement.)

(Exasperation.) "Don't you see, fool? Look at the locations of those warp points relative to us."

Inzrep'fel studied the display, her rudimentary flanking eyes scrunching up closer to her large central one in concentration. And all at once, she understood.

From the Intelligence materials she had seen, she was somewhat familiar with the predominant human alphabet. And the pattern he had now grasped resembled an upside-down letter "T". The location of the battle now raging between themselves and the main human fleet, together with the newly appeared *murn* icons to left and right, formed its horizontal element. At the far end of the T's vertical was the Bug 15 warp point. And, even as she watched, the new arrivals began, at the very slow pace shown on this scale, to move toward that warp point.

"We can't let these new forces get behind us," she heard Zum'ref saying. "I'm sure they're not actually strong enough to cut us off from the Bug 15 warp point; we could blast our way through them. But having them in our rear while engaged with Trevayne's main fleet would complicate our tactical problems more than we can afford, since we're not in overwhelming strength." (Resignation.) "We will commence a withdrawal to the Bug 15 warp point."

"Yes, *Destoshaz'at*." The Intendent's voice was carefully neutral.

Zum'ref glared at her. *If you dare to mention that we would be in overwhelming strength if I hadn't ordered us to proceed with a single Dispersate's fleet, or even look like you're thinking it, I'll kill you, you crawling worm!* But Inzrep'fel remained silent and expressionless, her *selnarm* under a tight lid.

Zum'ref turned away, leaking a little (frustration) in spite of himself. *Anyway*, he told himself, *it's only a temporary inconvenience. All the fleets of our other six Dispersates will soon be concentrated in Bug 15. When we return here, Trevayne will never be able to withstand us—especially after the losses we've inflicted in this battle, and will continue to inflict as we withdraw.*

Yes, let him enjoy his "victory" while he can. It will prove to be what the humans call a Pyrrhic one.

Trevayne ordered himself not to slump as he received the report that the last of the Kaituni had departed Alpha Centauri space. He had to keep up appearances in the presence of the flag bridge crew, all of whom were as bone-weary as he was. It seemed hard to believe that only a week had passed since the Bugs had first entered this system.

Now, a week later, the phrase *a fleet in being* again rose, unwelcome, to the surface of his consciousness. He barely had one left.

The Kaituni leader had grasped his strategy with disobliging speed, and immediately began pulling back to the warp point from whence he had come. It had been a fighting retreat all the way, with Combined Fleet inflicting damage but also taking it, while the Mothball Fleet elements had strained to close in on the Kaituni flanks— or even, with suicidal heroism, to stand in the path of that withdrawing armada. The spatial "geography" of the warp points was such that Task Group Shaka had closed into range first, in the vicinity of the asteroid belt. The Kaituni had burned it out of the sky. Task Group Sigma Draconis and Task Group Wolf 424 had barely been able to link with Combined Fleet and join in the final clashes.

Now it was time to take stock. The Bugs and the Kaituni between them had accounted for well over half of the Mothball Fleet elements actually engaged—at least a third of its total strength. Combined Fleet's casualties were even heavier.

But, Trevayne was growing more and more coldly certain, he would have to fight one more battle at Alpha Centauri.

"Gordon," he said, "have a courier drone prepared, to send to Elaine. I need to know how far along things are at Sol. No . . . on second thought, I want her to leave matters to Andreas and her other subordinates for a time and come here in person. It's been too long since we've had a face-to-face conference."

"Aye aye, sir."

Trevayne rose and turned to go. Then he had an afterthought. "And Gordon . . . tell her that before she departs she should place the Sol Reserve on a second stage state of readiness. Just in case, y'know."

"Aye aye, sir," Singhal repeated, expressionless.

Then Trevayne finally allowed himself to depart the flag bridge and go to seek the almost forgotten pleasure of sleep. In his present state of exhaustion, he felt sure sleep would come quickly and not leave him alone with the image of Magda that haunted his solitary quarters— an image that he continued to sternly tell himself was a memory, not a ghost.

And, at any rate, he wasn't really alone with that image. There was also that of Han, gazing up at him with huge, slightly almond-shaped dark eyes that held nothing but unconditional love. More and more, that was what sustained him.

CHAPTER FOURTEEN

Ossian Wethermere nodded to the orderly. "Yes, I'll need the access restriction on the admiral's quarters removed today. You can leave the privacy override passkey with me. Dismissed." He turned to stare out the star-littered gallery window that stretched along the starboard side of *Krishmahnta's* flag briefing room like a living mural. In it, pinpricks glinted here and there: ships of the Relief Fleet, arraying themselves for entry into Bug 15. Arraying themselves for the coming attack.

The door page toned behind him. "Come in," Wethermere said, regretting—as he had started to, these days—the loss of solitude.

Narrok, Ankaht, Kiiraathra, and Mretlak entered. He gestured to the seats that had become habitual for them in the weeks that had passed since the Battle of Bug 27. "Shall I have a meal brought up?" he asked.

They demurred politely, unanimously. No surprise, there: time was growing short and they all had preparations to complete before the attack began. In another day or two, Narrok would send their first probes through the warp point into Bug 15—and god only knew what would happen then. This was to be the last face-to-face pre-assault status report.

Narrok smoothed the surfaces of his tentacles before beginning. "Mretlak, your prudence has always been beneficial, so we have been happy to wait for you to reveal your most recent findings in person, rather than resorting to comm channels and all their implicit security risks. Please share your developments."

Mretlak may have sent some *selnarmic* pulse of gratitude and respect to Narrok; their eyes met but, otherwise, neither one of them moved. When Mretlak's eyes finally engaged the others, his vocoded voice was calm, confident, but also a bit melancholy. "As suspected when we first detected them, the buoy and automated recon-courier we discovered near the warp point into system Bug 15 were not placed by the Fourteenth Dispersate, but by the immense Kaituni fleet that has pressed Admiral Trevayne up the warp line to Sol. We have fully decoded the buoy's data banks and have confirmed that no elements of the Fourteenth Dispersate ever reached this point. They made no direct contact with the seven Dispersates moving up that warp line."

Quiet sighs of relief sounded from most of the persons gathered there, Wethermere included. Had the Kaituni's main fleet been informed of the approach of their kin, they would have been likely to send scouts looking for it— and would have found the Relief Fleet instead, thereby ruining any chance of surprise.

"What method did you use to gain control of these Kaituni platforms?"

Mretlak waved a desultory tendril. "We hardly needed more than our initial ploy: we approached the warp point with one of the auxiliaries we commandeered and repaired from the Fourteenth Dispersate. Using its codes and *selnarm* links, we were granted updating and exchange access to both Kaituni platforms and so sent them routine housekeeping data in which our new *selnarmically*-based virus was embedded. The virus completely disabled the buoy and paralyzed the automated courier long enough for us to mechanically cut its power. These are, of course, pearls of great price."

"There's our sheep's clothing," Wethermere murmured with a faint smile.

"I beg your pardon?" Mretlak's eyes were somewhat protuberant, an Arduan sign of perplexity.

Ossian shrugged. "We humans have a saying—a wolf in sheep's clothing—which refers to being able to don a disguise that will convince your target that you are an ally, not an enemy. In this case, the Kaituni automated courier is our ticket into Bug 15. It is a craft that is on their rosters and which they expect to see. Using that as our entree, and assisted by the other ships we've salvaged from the Fourteenth Dispersate, I suspect we'll be able to pull the wool over their eyes—er, fool them—as to our true identity. At least long enough for us to get into the system and into position before mounting a general assault."

Narrok nodded, turned his eyes back toward Mretlak. "Did you have any difficulty inserting the *selnarmic* virus?"

"None, Admiral," Mretlak added with what may have a touch of pride. "Whatever difficulties we might have anticipated, given the variance between our First Dispersate codes and technologies and those of later Dispersates, have been completely eliminated by our access to extensive examples we captured as a result of our victory in Bug 27."

"And what, if anything, have we learned about the enemy forces beyond this warp point?" Kiiraathra asked, eyes narrowed and unblinking.

"Disappointingly little," Mretlak replied. "But this is hardly surprising. The buoy we discovered at the warp point was not placed there to disseminate data, but record it and send the drone back through to Bug 15 in the event of contact with hostile forces. However, what we have been able to discern from the buoy's secondary archives—mostly command routing and prior communiqués that were retained for purposes of internal referencing and authentication of new contacts—the Kaituni armada is indeed an amalgamation of seven Dispersates *and* the majority of the Arachnid swarm. Most of those elements are in the process of, or will soon be, assaulting Alpha Centauri."

"Damn, that's bad news," Wethermere breathed.

"But not unexpected," Narrok reminded the room. "It is a testimony to his proven skill—proven against me, I might add—that Admiral Trevayne has preserved a fleet in being and held back seven Dispersates and their Arachnid coursers for so long."

"It is a shame there is no data detailing the assets he still commands," Kiiraathra observed with a pass at his whiskers.

Wethermere shrugged. "If Trevayne has been pushed this far back, we can be sure he's taken heavy casualties, enough to make each withdrawal a grim necessity. If that wasn't the case, he would still be holding the enemy farther up the warp line. So we can broadly infer the magnitude of his losses from that."

"Yes," agreed Narrok, "and the further implication is not reassuring."

"Not at all," Ankaht agreed. "The more substantial Admiral Trevayne's losses, the more the outcome will depend upon us, small as we are."

Wethermere felt half of his mouth smile. "It is strange to think that the fourth largest human fleet in history should be called 'small.'"

Ankaht's two smaller eyes winked in mild amusement. "All things are relative."

"Even the size of a Dispersate is apparently a matter of relative perception," Mretlak intruded, his voice serious. "Specifically, we have a final report from the elements we left behind in Bug 27 to continue salvage and intelligence harvesting from the wreckage of the Fourteenth Dispersate. What they have discovered suggests that the enemy armada that we will encounter beyond this warp point may not be as large as we presume."

"Why not?" Wethermere asked.

"Because the later Dispersates apparently tended to be smaller. And less technologically advanced. So it may be inaccurate for us to always pair the term 'Dispersate' with a vision of the immense numbers of sophisticated ships which initially attacked us at the start of this war."

"I welcome any news that suggests the tasks before us may be easier, rather than harder, than we conjectured," Kiiraathra commented with more animation than he had shown in days.

"Unfortunately, despite the accuracy of Mretlak's quantitative analysis, that may not be indicative of a corresponding change in our adversaries' combat power, Least Fang," Ankaht said softly, carefully. "While the later Dispersates are smaller and somewhat more crude in their technology, they seem to compensate by accustoming their populations to a Spartan existence, and use the volume and resources typically reserved for amenities to carry deeper reserves of fuel and weapons, instead. Having considered the Fourteenth Dispersate's historical records at some length, our conjectures about the deteriorating conditions on Ardu—both due to the alteration of our home star and the despoliation of our planet's ecology—did not begin to compass the grim magnitude of the actual changes.

"Life during the last centuries became quite basic and even brutal, with all efforts and sacrifices dedicated to the construction of further Dispersates. Life expectation was halved; starvation was rampant, disease even more so. Draconian social measures were adopted; free choice went from being a rare luxury to an anachronistic oddity that was deemed inherently decadent. *Narmata* and *selnarm* were all but forgotten, except insofar as their occasional demonstration reassured the miserable masses that once their bitter life was over, they could expect to be reincarnated into a far better and brighter one."

"Gruesome," Wethermere mumbled. "It's hard to believe they didn't just lay down and give up."

"Some did," Ankaht said with a convulsion that may have been the Arduan equivalent of a shudder. "But the way the rest survived was to give up hope of anything better, and a ready acceptance of discarnation as an escape they welcomed rather than regretted." She looked around the room. "That is the culture of the later Dispersates. So be warned; if my people already seem inured to discarnation, these later Kaituni have made it a fondly desired end."

"Has their time between the stars, on their great space arks, not made them less bitter, more hopeful?" Kiiraathra wondered aloud.

"The conditions and accommodations on their ships are little better than those endured by the last generations born upon Ardu. Their food is vat-grown mush; they sleep four or five to a pod; they live, breed, and die in filth and squalor. They have embraced this kind of life as a means of readying them for whatever sacrifices they must make to settle a new world."

"Or to win a war to secure it," Ossian finished.

"Exactly," she affirmed. "Zum'ref could not have asked for more ready recruits, more willing suicide pilots, more hardened crews. These later Dispersates are now, if anything, the ultraorthodox among the Kaituni and will spend themselves with a readiness and abandon which makes them more threatening than their numbers seem."

Narrok lifted an authoritative tendril. "So, although these later Dispersates are cruder and less numerous, they are more ferocious and unflinching. Making them approximately as dangerous as the earlier ones."

"So it seems to me, Admiral," Ankaht said, glancing at Mretlak slowly. *Apologetically, even?* Wethermere wondered.

Kiiraathra leaned his large hands upon the table. "Let us attend to our numbers, as well as those of our foes. I received notification that the repair and salvage crews we left behind in Bug 27 have now concluded their labors. What, in sum, have they achieved?"

Mretlak straightened slightly. "Although we could not restore all the Kaituni craft we identified as salvageable, we have converted at least seventy percent of the high-priority enemy ships to serviceable prize hulls. This gives us an immense number of convincing q-ships—or, to use the Commodore's expression, wolves in sheep's clothing—with which to initiate entry into Bug 15 and any Kaituni-held systems beyond. Not only are the Fourteenth Dispersate's general ship classes and marks on record with the other Dispersates with which they coordinated their actions and production initiatives years before commencing this invasion, but we now have extensive access to the communication protocols and codes that the many Dispersates prearranged to identify themselves to each other once they came into physical contact. We also have relatively recent records of most of the Dispersates' senior command rosters: not more than two years old, in the worst cases. In short, we should be able to fool the genuine Kaituni for quite some time, after first entering a system that they hold. Presuming that we can keep word of our mimicry from spreading beyond each system in which we employ it, this should allow us to neutralize the defenses and tripwires of any but the most strongly held warp points prior to the entry of the bulk of the Relief Fleet."

Narrok's largest tentacles waved once, lazily: a sign of profound approval. "Your teams have done admirable work, Mretlak. Did the repair teams fare equally well?"

Mretlak turned to stare at Wethermere and Kiiraathra—his two smallest eyes focusing on the first, the central one upon the latter. "All reports indicate that they did. As per Commodore Wethermere's orders, first priority was given to restoring full mobility to those of our hulls which had suffered less than sixty-five percent damage. This means that while we do not have as many ready to enter the line as we would have had we focused on a smaller number of craft, we may ultimately hope to restore a much greater number once they have finished the repairs they are continuing while under movement. We estimate that the bulk of them will be ready within the week."

"So, not in time to be used in Bug 15," Kiiraathra mused, rubbing his knuckles along the under-crest of ruff that stood out slightly from the point of his chin to the base of his neck.

"No," Mretlak replied. "However, due to the staging instructions passed to us by Commodore Wethermere, all those which did not begin the campaign with stealth systems have been retrofitted with ones that were cannibalized from irreclaimable wrecks that were then scuttled. Retrofitting those stealth systems to new hulls will continue as the ships make their way here from Bug 27."

"Did the rearguard elements you stationed there encounter any new enemy or allied traffic?" Ankaht asked.

"No new ships have entered Bug 27 since the battle, so the security flotilla we stationed to protect our craft turned out to be an unnecessary precaution."

"Hindsight is the only way to truly see something with all three eyes," Narrok commented in a wry tone. "We could hardly afford to leave our salvage and repair auxiliaries unguarded—or fail to have units of all races on hand to make contact with and reassure any possible allied craft that happened upon us. If I recall the progress updates correctly, the relative calm in the system gave your on-site researchers ample time to examine the hardware and software utilized by the various elements of the Kaituni fighter triads."

Mretlak's main eye was half lidded. "That is correct, Admiral. We have now had the opportunity to examine large numbers of their *selnarmically*-controlled remote fighters, their autonomous drone wingmen, and the launch and control facilities upon the vessels that carry them. This has given us both the technical intelligence and test-beds to ensure that Project Turncoat, the final element of our anti-fighter software countermeasures and viruses, will succeed."

"You are certain of that?" Kiiraathra asked sharply, leaning forward in predatory eagerness.

Mretlak's drooping tendrils were an Arduan shrug. "Least Fang, certainty is impossible before success in combat has been demonstrated. However, we observed no failures during our last round of testing, and while this is the most ambitious element of our multitiered attempt to compromise and interdict the Kaituni fighter-triads, it will also be the most decisive. By far."

"Even so," Narrok intruded, "if circumstances permit, we shall not depend upon a full implementation of Project Turncoat during the battle for Bug 15. Instead, we shall isolate a safe test target before clearing your work for general combat use in subsequent engagements."

Mretlak lowered his lids briefly in respectful accord.

"Is there anything else of which we should be apprised? Any reservations over the data or conclusions you have shared with us, Senior Group Leader?"

"None except that which has concerned us all from the outset: the time we have lost researching and refitting while the enemy has been pushing further up the main warp line."

Wethermere shrugged. "True, but all the ships and intel we've acquired—to say nothing of the hulls we've repaired and upgraded—arguably make us stronger than we were when we engaged the Fourteenth Dispersate. And the intimate knowledge of our enemies' systems was just what we needed in order to ready our strategic lynchpin: Project Turncoat."

"Advantages which will be meaningless if we do not intervene in time," Kiiraathra objected calmly.

"True enough. But on the other hand, it could be suicide not to accrue every possible advantage. Let's not fool ourselves; we're going to be outnumbered the moment we enter the main warp line, no matter what has or hasn't happened to Admiral Trevayne's fleet. So since we're going to be puny compared to seven enemy Dispersates, we'd better be giant killers. Which means we need to have some unique and deadly weapons they don't expect, and we have to be able to hit them in critical locations. Because we in the Relief Fleet had better remember that, just like David in the bible, we can't win a toe-to-toe boxing match against the Kaituni Goliath."

Narrok nodded. "Agreed, although your reference is . . . obscure. Now, if there is nothing further, we should return to our preparations. I am holding us to a forty-eight hour window for the commencement of the preliminary operations that will enable our attack into Bug 15."

Wethermere and the others rose. Narrok did not. "Commodore, if I may have the use of your conference room for a few more minutes?"

Ossian, surprised, nodded. "Of course, Admiral."

"My thanks. Mretlak, I would inconvenience you to remain behind after the others have left."

CHAPTER FIFTEEN

Mretlak sensed Lentsul's presence in the secure work compartment of the Technical Intelligence cluster, the site where the finishing touches were being put on Project Turncoat. He turned in that direction, expecting to feel Lentsul's tentative *selnarmic* contact. However, his subordinate was apparently deeply engrossed in his current programming work, as was often the wont of the *Ixturshaz*: of all the Arduan castes, they were the most orderly and even myopic in focus. The human psychological lexicon had another suitable term: anal retentive—although that meant something different in the mind-body interactions of humans than it did amongst the Arduans. Retaining wastes was not connected to any behavioral predilections in his species, whereas in human infants, they evidently—well, what could one say? Humans were humans: enigmas wrapped in mysteries, all suffused with maddening inconsistencies. Well, many of them were, anyway.

Mretlak entered the compartment. Lentsul sent a distracted acknowledgement. Mretlak waited and then sent a wave of (importance, conclusivity) along with, "Lentsul, I have just come from the final preinvasion briefing. The outcome was not what we hoped."

(Diffident distraction) "What outcome do you refer to, Senior Group Leader?"

"The possibility that we might have been able to use Project Turncoat to effect the capture, rather than the slaughter, of our estranged Kaituni siblings."

"The humans persuaded Narrok of this?"

"No: Narrok needed no persuading. It was he who decided the matter. He asked me to stay after the briefing to explain why it was necessary."

(Mild surprise.) "Well, Narrok has been growing closer to the humans since the end of the last war. He works well with them. Almost as well as Councilor Ankaht."

Too well, was the implication lurking in Lentsul's *selnarmic* shadings. But there was nothing new in his possession of that sentiment. The tunnel-visioned *Ixturshaz* had never been sanguine about close partnerships with the strange, patch-furred species; he had merely resigned himself to it over time. "Narrok does work well with the humans, but I reiterate that they did *not* influence his decision this time. It was purely a matter of numbers."

Lentsul put aside his task, turned to regard his *Destoshaz* leader with all three eyes. "Which numbers would those be?"

"Estimates of how many Kaituni are in the seven dispersates we will face when we enter the main warp line to Earth."

Lentsul leaned back. "You told me that there were no tactical reports recovered from either the courier or the buoy we commandeered, no quantifiable references to those dispersates."

"That is true, but subsequent analysis indicated that they were driving an Arachnid horde before them, just as did the Fourteenth Dispersate. Consequently, we must presume that the Arachnids absorbed the majority of casualties that the human admiral Trevayne inflicted during his fighting withdrawal back along the warp line."

(Comprehension, concurrence.) "Yes, that would indicate that our most dangerous opponents—our own estranged Kaituni relatives—are largely undiminished."

"Precisely. Had they been much reduced in numbers, we might have been able to paralyze many of their key elements with Turncoat, and so force them to surrender in helpless multitudes. That option is no longer deemed safe. Narrok fears that if Trevayne's fleet collapses, we will have neither the resources nor the time available to spare on anything other than the outright destruction of our foes. The process of taking many thousands of captives and commandeering dozens or even hundreds of prize hulls is simply beyond the capacity of the Relief Fleet."

"Which, in such a combat, would be further encumbered due to its own casualties. No, sadly, Narrok's conclusion is utterly logical. It is also politically astute."

Mretlak suspected he knew what the small, black-skinned *Ixturshaz* meant, but sought certainty: "Astute in what way?"

"Insofar as this decision reassures our alien allies. With Narrok now in command of the fleet, the humans who fill its ranks will no doubt be wary of any decisions which could be interpreted as precursors to Arduan treachery, or merely an attempt to wrest more determinative power from them. Preserving any of the Kaituni who have wrought such havoc on human space would be a decision they might question in the best of times. Now, their suspicions will be primed to perceive any such initiative as a prelude to a coup, to taking away their preeminence. Narrok had little choice, I perceive."

Mretlak settled in the seat next to Lentsul, who returned to his work. "You seem quite unperturbed by this news."

"That is because it does not surprise me, Mretlak. With respect, you have always been inadvisably idealistic about the outcome of our relations with the humans. Our interactions with them are irremediably fraught. After all, they have little reason to trust us. Or us, them."

"Yes. I am disappointed. But if you are not surprised, you do not seem fearful or resentful, either."

"What good would that do any of us, Senior Group Leader? We all have jobs to perform. We all do what we must. Now, I would be grateful for your help in encoding this final data exchange protocol between Turncoat and its *selnarmic* targets."

Ossian stood in the middle of the Miharu's stateroom with a trunk open at his feet. He stared around at the Spartan, if tasteful, furnishings and wondered where to begin. He had not been in the rooms since they had both been here, having breakfast and then, unexpectedly, making desperate love on the floor mere minutes before they went to their respective posts. He to the conn of her flagship, she to the superdreadnought *Broadside* and, ultimately, her doom.

As he stood motionless, it seemed like their ghosts—his and Miharu's—came to life around him, reliving scenes of their past dinners, flirtations, laughter, arguments, and lovemaking.

The stateroom's privacy bell chimed.

The ghosts disappeared, faded into the fog of dimming memories.

"Come in," he meant to say; it came out as a strangled croak.

The door slid open; Ankaht slid in. She looked around, her eyes carefully lidded. The voice that came out of her vocoder was gentle. "I thought you might be here. Finally."

"You've been checking up on me?" He made sure it sounded jocular. Or at least he tried.

"Of course I have, Ossian. You are my friend."

He smiled at her, wished she had been human. "I know. And I am very, very glad to have you here. How did you know?"

"That you would be here? I saw the orderly leaving the briefing room, heard him sending a door release order to the security chief on the bridge." She looked around more carefully. "The admiral lived a very austere life."

"She was a pretty austere person."

"Was she? Always?"

Wethermere simultaneously longed for and dreaded the conversation he felt Ankaht was steering towards, and so was simultaneously infuriated and relieved when his comm pager toned. "Wethermere," he answered, keeping his voice carefully neutral.

"Commodore, this is Knight, aboard *No-Dachi*. I received word you wished to speak with me on a private channel?"

Oh, yeah: that. "That is correct, Captain. It looks like I'm going to be staying aboard *Krishmahnta*."

Knight uncharacteristically offered his own, unasked for, opinion: "Good to hear that, sir. It's where you're needed—and where you belong."

For some reason, coming from a veteran field commander like Knight, that meant far more to Wethermere than the assurances of Kiiraathra or Narrok. "It may be where you belong, too, Captain Knight."

"I beg your pardon, sir?"

"The engagement at Bug 27 not only cost us our commanding admiral, but our fleet tactical officer. You want the job?"

Knight was silent for so long that Wethermere began to wonder if the commlink had broken. "Sir, it seems to me you've got a lot of bright folks there on *Krishmahnta* who have genuine war experience. I suspect one of them will do just fine."

"So will you, Captain Knight."

Another silence, albeit shorter. Then: "Sir, permission to speak frankly?"

"I wouldn't have any other kind of speech from you, Captain."

"Okay. Then hear this: don't get sentimental. You know where you need me: out here. Going head to head with the threat force, close enough to feel the heat of their drive coils. That's what I do, what I've always done. I'm more likely to save lives and destroy enemies from the bridge of a fighting ship than from a well-cushioned chair in a command center."

Wethermere knew truth when he heard it. "Very well, Captain. I understand your decision. And I support it. Therefore, you will accept a reciprocal decision of mine. You are hereby brevetted to acting commodore."

"But sir—"

"I'm not done. The extraordinary circumstances allow me to confer that provisional rank upon you and so put you in charge of our new elite formation of stealth-equipped superdreadnoughts, heavy superdreadnoughts, and battleships: Assault Group Lancelot. Since you don't want to sit in the command center, you get to ride the tip of the spear, Captain. First in the breach, as it were. Sorry, but you asked for it."

"I did indeed." Knight sounded bemused, not entirely displeased. "Who'll take over the recon group, then? Zhou?"

"I figured you'd want him as your exec and tactical officer."

"I do. Thanks for leaving him with me."

"Take whom you want from the bridge crews among the recon flotilla. They'll make a crackerjack first team and know the nuances of stealth as well as anyone in the fleet. Probably better. Then send the rest of the *Wooly Impostor*'s bridge team to me."

"Will do, sir. So then who's taking over recon?"

"I'm thinking Ross. She's got good command instincts, asks the right questions. And she won't be as useful to you in Gunnery. She isn't familiar with overseeing capital ship batteries. On the other hand, being a good tactical-scale gunner, I suspect she's going to make a great tactical-scale commander."

"Yes, sir. She'd be my choice, too. Anything else, Commodore?"

"No, Commodore. You've got plenty to do, now, so get to it."

"Yes, sir. Knight out."

Wethermere closed the channel. He glanced around the compartment. "I hadn't realized that I was putting this off."

Ankaht's vocoder voice was slow, careful. "Putting what off?"

"Clearing out Miharu's quarters." He wandered over to the single old-style bookshelf, removed almost a third of the volumes. "I wasn't aware how many of my own things I had left—or moved—here. Or maybe I just forgot. Or wanted to forget."

Ankaht's question was all the more devastating because of how gentle it was: "Did you love her, Ossian?"

He kept staring at the books he had removed from the shelf. Put them back. Removed the ones that had been hers. "I had been working that out. Right up to the end."

"I am surprised to hear that."

He turned to face Ankaht. "Why?"

"Because I had the impression that you would not become physically intimate without a previously established emotional foundation—without the surety of love."

Ossian smiled to himself. "Actually, I would have said the same thing about myself a few months ago."

"What changed?" Ankaht's vocoded voice was slightly closer, just over his shoulder now. "What was different this time?"

"She was."

"I do not understand."

Wethermere picked up a press-form box and moved deeper into the stateroom's combination meeting area and office. He felt vaguely traitorous as he removed the appurtenances of Miharu's life from her desk, from shelves: mementos and a photocube cycling posed stills of her throughout her career; a paperweight; a small brass globe of her homeworld. "Miharu was . . . hard to reach. She wasn't in a rush—wasn't even particularly eager—to share her heart with anyone else."

"Do you mean to say that she was only interested in . . . in mating?"

"No, she was pretty selective when it came to sharing her body. But even so, she was much more selective in sharing her heart." Wethermere put down the box of Miharu's personal effects, realized he wasn't yet ready to venture into their—her—bedroom. "For her, I think physical intimacy was the first step toward emotional intimacy, rather than the other way around. And until she became comfortable sharing that most intimate part of herself with me . . . well, it was difficult to know how I would ultimately feel about her. So when you ask me if I loved her—" He shrugged helplessly.

"But you felt that your relationship with her was promising enough to reverse the order in which you yourself approach growing intimacy."

"Yes." He was surprised, when he looked down in the

box, at just how lightly Miharu Yoshikuni had travelled through life. *But then again, perhaps I shouldn't be surprised at all.* "I just wish—wish I'd known how she felt about me."

Ankaht's answer emerged from the vocoder with hints of a small, melancholy smile. "I suspect that you already had your answer, Ossian Wethermere." She looked around the stateroom, which seemed only partly diminished.

"What do you mean?" Following Ankaht's traveling gaze, Wethermere was surprised to realize that his own possessions had adorned half of the compartment. When had he brought all these things here? Why had he left them?

"I mean that she gave you the clearest possible sign of how she felt—the clearest that a person so private and careful as she could give. She ensured that you remained here on *Krishmahnta*. Yes, your role as a PSU representative was important, but for her, it was also providential: it allowed her to give utterly reasonable, uncontestable orders that you were to stay with the main body of the fleet. And she made those orders more explicit, more detailed and repeated, than was her wont with any others." Ankaht turned to face Ossian. "She did not want you in harm's way. And that kind of preference was not—customary—for her. Even less customary was her willingness to use her command prerogatives to act upon such a preference. Would you disagree, Ossian?"

Wethermere could only shake his head. And dread entering the bedroom.

Ankaht moved toward the door to the corridor. "She

told you in that act what she might never have been able to say in words: how very much she—cared for—you."

When Wethermere did not reply, Ankaht left the stateroom quietly, apparently obeying the peculiarly keen instincts she had for the nuances of human behavior and emotions.

Some minutes later—Wethermere was unsure how many had elapsed as he stood in the center of the compartment—he wandered to the cushioned bench-seat against the inner bulkhead, slumped down onto it. He raised his head and through the uncovered viewport, saw the stars, shimmering slightly as his eyes adjusted to the minute positional adjustments made as *Krishmahnta* traveled under the Desai drive, his brain adding in the visual gaps as in any other persistence-of-motion phenomenon.

Persistence of motion was what Erica Krishmahnta herself, his former commander and quasi-mentor, had invoked when explaining her Neo-Hindu view of how experience and lives were arrayed against the totality of the universe and time. *"We—each second of our lives, separately and as a whole—are brief intervals of activity. In themselves, those intervals are filled with disparate movements, motivations, loves, hates, longings. But together, they make up the cycle of existence that is both the journey of our individual souls and the longer coalescence of all creation back into the moment of perfect unity, of Nirvana, from which all things shall be engendered once again."* It had been a strange conversation to be having with an admiral over tea, in between desperate battles. At least, that's how it had felt at the time, almost eight years gone by. Now, that conversation seemed not merely reasonable, but almost a preparation for this moment. *Odd that I should come to these recognitions here, on the ship that bears her name.* "But still," he murmured at the far bulkhead and the stars beyond it, "I suppose even *you* never expected to see me here."

He imagined Krishmahnta's simple, smiling rejoinder, her eyes telling him that she had identified and understood parts of himself that he had yet to see, and that her faith had a label for it: *"Old Soul."* Just as she had called him, shortly before she had died.

"Or maybe," he reflected, "this is *exactly* where you expected to see me. Here, on this ship, on the precipice of pivotal events." It seemed impossible that any human should have such prescience, but when it came to Erica—

And again, he heard her voice—whether from the depths of memory or the depths of space, he could not be sure: *"All things happen for a reason; all souls fulfill the destinies that have been set for them."*

Wethermere simply stared at the stars and thought:

Let's just hope our destiny is something other than oblivion.

PART THREE
The End of Days

CHAPTER SIXTEEN

From the moment Elaine De Mornay was piped aboard *Zeven Provinciën*, Ian Trevayne could tell that something was not right.

It was nothing he could put his finger on. It wasn't a matter of merely being reserved and formal—there was nothing new in that, for she almost always carried herself as befitted a scion of an aristocratic house of the planet Lancelot. No, there was an uncharacteristic tenseness there, as though there was something she very much didn't want to say, in fact dreaded saying, but was drearily certain that it couldn't be put off forever. And, for no reason he could define, Trevayne was certain that whatever it was had nothing to do with the dire military situation in which they found themselves.

He decided not to press her on it, which would doubtless be counterproductive. Sooner or later, she would come out with it in her own good time. So he pretended not to notice, as he returned her salute, shook hands, and led her to his quarters. There he poured Scotch, which De Mornay, a very light drinker, accepted with what seemed more than usual appreciation.

"Here's tae us," he said, doing his best Scots dialect, as they raised their glasses. "Dam' few like us, an' they're a' deid." She cracked a smile, but only briefly.

"Elaine," he began, "we'll shortly have a full staff meeting. But first I wanted to meet with you privately, for two reasons. For one thing, I wish to express my personal appreciation for the magnificent job you did here at Alpha Centauri getting the Mothball Fleet ready, and are doing now at Sol."

"Thank you, Admiral. That means a great deal to me." Her eyes slid away from his as she said it, and her voice was small, as though embarrassed to be receiving a compliment from him. *No,* he thought. *Not so much embarrassed as wishing she had something better to give in return.*

"The mention of Sol," Trevayne went on promptly, to cover his puzzlement, "brings me to the second reason. I need a brief, informal evaluation of your progress there."

"Of course, sir." With something indistinguishable from relief, she turned businesslike. *Almost* too *businesslike,* he found himself thinking. "As per your instructions, the mothballed ships that were brought here to Alpha Centauri to be recommissioned and upgraded came from the various Heart Worlds with warp connections to this system, rather than from Sol. We've made good progress upgrading the ones there—a large number."

"Good," nodded Trevayne. "And the remounting of the weapons systems being ripped out of them?"

"Again, this is progressing satisfactorily. And the resulting weapon buoys and armed asteroids are being towed to the vicinity of Sol's warp point as you ordered."

"Good," Trevayne repeated. He looked somber. "The fundamental fact that we have to live with is that Sol has only the one warp point. There'll be no 'bolt-holes' for Sol's Mothball Fleet to hide in and await opportunities. So we can't plan on a war of maneuver." He didn't add the obvious: that there could be no retreat from Sol. There, they would be well and truly at bay. "So our tactics are going to have to change: we'll take our stand at the warp point and contest every inch of space from there to Old Terra. I want the space around that warp point to be a kill zone without parallel in history. Speaking of which, are the orbital fortresses being given strategic repositioning capability and moved there on schedule?"

"There we're somewhat behind. The ones you sent from here are, of course, already in position. But as for Sol's fortresses . . . The problem is that there are only a finite number of tugs in the Solar system, no matter how highly developed the asteroid belt there is. And many of them have been kept busy towing the armed asteroidal rocks. We're now in a position to take more and more of them off that job and slave them to fortresses. Andreas is doing that now. But—"

"I understand." Trevayne took a morose sip of Scotch. "What's the bottom line, Elaine? And no optimism. Be realistic."

This time she met his eyes unflinchingly. "I need another standard week, Admiral."

"I see." Trevayne finished his Scotch and set the glass

down firmly. "Actually, that's not as bad as I'd expected to hear from you. But, although we don't know exactly when the Kaituni attack is going to come, it appears very likely that Combined Fleet is going to have to fight one more battle here in the Alpha Centauri system. And after the punishing losses we've taken, I'm not sure we'd even be able to put up much of a delaying action against the armada that is going to come through the Bug 15 warp point.

"Therefore, I'm going to have to summon certain elements of the Sol Reserve. I've wanted to preserve it intact for the defense of Sol." (Trevayne stopped himself short of using the term *a fleet in being*. He was fast losing his admittedly somewhat perverse liking for the Earl of Torrington.) "And," He added quickly as De Mornay started to open her mouth, "I still have no intention of touching most of it. At the staff meeting we'll decide exactly what we need to draw on. That'll be in about two hours. For now, Elaine, why don't you freshen up. Your quarters are prepared."

"Thank you, sir." De Mornay stood up, and her strange, haunted look was back. She turned to go. Then, abruptly, she swung back to face Trevayne and spoke in an uncharacteristic rush. "Admiral, there's something else I have to tell you. *Your daughter is on Old Terra.*"

It was as though Trevayne had been struck in the chest.

"No," he heard himself say, as though from a great distance. All at once, anger flared. "No! What the devil are you talking about? What do you mean by saying something like that? She's on Novaya Rodina, with her mother's godparents."

"No, Admiral," said De Mornay unflinchingly. "They

brought her to Sol, passing through Alpha Centauri while Combined Fleet was still in Harnah. I only recently became aware of it. They told me it had been planned to take her there anyway, to start her in school."

"Well, yes, that was the plan. But—"

"And," De Mornay finished, "they thought she'd be safer there."

"Safer?" Trevayne echoed in an incredulous whisper.

To many people Han Trevayne was a symbol. Her very name made her one.

During the Fringe Revolution, Ian Trevayne and Li Han—the heroes of the loyalist and rebel sides respectively—had each been the other's nemesis, to such an extent that their names in tandem had practically become a byword for enmity. But then Trevayne had been cast into his eight decades of semi-death, awakening to find the Terran Republic an established fact, the elderly Li Han its First Space Lord . . . and the two of them allies against the Arduans of the First Dispersate.

He had also found that his old enemy had a daughter, Li Magda . . . whom, to the general stupefaction of the human race, he had married, and subsequently become a naturalized citizen of the Terran Republic whose birth he had once fought to abort.

Li Han had died in battle against the Arduans. Afterwards, naming their daughter after her heroic grandmother had seemed to Ian Trevayne and Li-Trevayne Magda the most natural thing in the world.

And now Trevayne, who had lost one family in the Fringe Revolution, stared the loss of a second in the face.

★★★

"Why in God's name didn't you inform me by courier drone?" he demanded, still furious.

"I would have, if you hadn't summoned me here. Yes, I could have done it before that, and I realized you had a right to know, but I hesitated because it seemed almost cowardly. And Admiral . . . would it have done any good?"

The last flames of Trevayne's anger guttered out, leaving ashes of desolation. "No, I don't suppose it would have. Knowing, and not being able to do a damned thing about it, might even have impaired my effectiveness." He drew himself up. "But now that I do know it, I can't let that happen—even though I still can't do a damned thing about it."

De Mornay's face held more compassion than she could permit herself to voice. "Admiral, one more thing. Your daughter's guardians are unaware as yet of your wife's . . . that is, of what happened to her. When I return to Sol shortly, what do you want me to tell them?"

Trevayne thought of Magda's godparents: Jason Windrider and Magda Petrovna Windrider, both living legends of the Fringe Revolution. Yes, that aged couple needed to know. But . . . He shook his head. "You spoke of cowardice earlier, Elaine. I won't be guilty of it either. Tell them nothing. I'll tell them myself when I arrive in the Solar system. Them . . . and Han." He turned brisk. "In the meantime, let's get ready for that staff conference. It seems I have one more battle at Alpha Centauri to fight."

And, he did not add, *I now have an additional reason why I must keep the Kaituni away from Sol for as long as possible.*

★★★

The more his fleets poured into Bug 15, the more expansive Zum'ref's mood grew. Now, with the combined armadas of seven Dispersates spread out before him on the display, he was largely over his frustration at his earlier repulse. He was even prepared to admit—though only to himself—that it *had* been a repulse, resulting from his own decision to advance prematurely. Not even the fact that it wasn't really quite seven full Dispersates, given the losses he had taken, could dampen his feeling of satisfaction. His strength was still so overwhelming that it made little practical difference.

Still, there was no reason to depend purely on numbers and neglect elementary tactical judgment. He had said as much to his Intendent and his staffers. "Once again, we will proceed without the specialized warp-point assault elements. They can follow along behind us, so as to be available for the final assault on Sol. The *griarfeksh* admiral will not attempt to make a stand at Alpha Centauri Bug 15 warp point, pinning his forces where they would not be able to escape."

(Demure, submissive agreement.) "Indeed, *Destoshaz'at*." All the staffers had echoed Inzrep'fel's *selnarmic* emanations, with an undercurrent of relief that they had no longer had to tiptoe quite so carefully around the leader's smoldering temper.

"Especially," one of them had ventured to add, "inasmuch as the Sol warp point is on the far side of the Alpha Centauri system. It will be a long fighting retreat for them."

"Furthermore," Zum'ref had continued, "there is no

need for the RAW monitors to accompany our lead elements. There are no targets for them, as I surmised and as we confirmed on our earlier incursion." He had paused slightly, as though challenging anyone to take exception to that characterization. None had. "Indeed, given the small numbers of their mobile fortresses, they too can follow along behind until the final phases of the reduction of the Solar system, when the devastators and superdevastators will have nowhere else to go. And our logistical train can, of course, remain here in Bug 15."

(Supine acquiescence) had answered him.

And now all was in readiness. He turned to Inzrep'fel with a *selnarm*-enhanced air of conscious drama and gave the command to commence warp transit.

In fact, Trevayne hadn't left the warp point totally undefended. He'd had all of the weapon-bearing asteroids that remained towed there, to within point-blank range. And he had stationed his destroyers and light and heavy cruisers—of which he had summoned a large number from the Sol Reserve to supplement those of the Mothball Fleet—around it, heavily cloaked. As the Kaituni monitors began to emerge, in necessarily small numbers at first, they came under slashing attacks from ships which, while not even remotely a match for them individually, came in swarms.

Inevitably, the Kaituni numbers began to mount up, and so did the defenders' losses. No longer able to contest the warp point, the light ships were able to use their superior speed to flee in-system ahead of their ponderous pursuers. Naturally, the Kaituni launched massed fighter strikes to hunt them down. But out in these regions beyond the Desai Limit, the fighters had no particular speed advantage over their quarry. Most of them got through the asteroid belt, and took toll of their pursuers with up-to-date anti-fighter weaponry.

Once past the belt, the snarling battle entered the Desai Limit and the Kaituni fighters had their traditional advantages. But it was precisely here that Trevayne had stationed his carriers, under Mario Leong's command. Now their fighter squadrons entered the fray, savaging their more numerous opponents with rapid-firing energy torpedoes. They fell back steadily, but the need to respond to their attack slowed the pace of the Kaituni advance.

With the twin life-bearing planets showing as a double blue dot across six light-minutes, the leading Kaituni elements came under massed long-range missile fire from Trevayne's monitors and supermonitors. Here, as had been calculated to a nicety, was the furthest forward the supermonitors—somewhat slower than anything in the Kaituni array—could be positioned and still be assured of making it to the Sol warp point ahead of any pursuit. The Kaituni were further delayed, rearranging their formations to present a maximized defense to this combined-arms attack. But they continued on their inexorable course, and Combined Fleet fell back sullenly before them, continuing its fighting retreat as the days wore on.

They passed Nova Terra and Eden so closely that the two planets showed visible discs. As those discs waxed, so did the increasingly shrill calls from the local governmental authorities there—a low-grade bunch, for the higher echelons had long since muscled their way onto the transports bound for Sol—demanding that Combined Fleet "stand and fight to the last ship." Trevayne stonily ignored them. He didn't want to look at those two fair blue words—the first extrasolar planets colonized by man, in far-off hopeful days—with their remaining billions. But he forced himself to stare, expressionless but heartsick, into the viewscreen as they dropped astern. No one disturbed him.

They passed close by Alpha Centauri A's rockball Planet III. Then, when the running battle had reached a point between the Tau Ceti and Epsilon Indi warp points, Trevayne played his last card. Courier drones flashed through those warp points and the last two "bolt-hole" task groups of the Mothball Fleet emerged and swept toward the flanks of the mammoth Kaituni armada, which slowed and realigned itself to meet these unexpected attacks.

It sickened Trevayne to have to sacrifice those aging people, who had already given as much as anyone had a right to ask. But that sacrifice enabled what was left of Combined Fleet to transit the Sol warp point in safety. A few elements of Task Group Tau Ceti managed to make it through as well. Not a ship of Task Group Epsilon Indi escaped.

By Trevayne's express command, *Zeven Provinciën* was the last ship to make transit. By then, some Kaituni monitors had almost come into extreme missile range, and their fighters were streaking in. But Trevayne spent the final minutes imperturbably receiving reports.

Combined Fleet, and the Sol Reserve elements and the tatters of the Mothball Fleet and the Alpha Centauri Defense Command, had taken heartbreaking losses. But they had inflicted considerably more damage on the Kaituni. And more important than that was what he saw in the calendar.

Gordon Singhal saw it too. "We delayed them long enough, sir."

"Yes," Trevayne nodded. "Elaine De Mornay keeps her promises."

A communicator buzzed. It was Janos Thorfinnssen. "Ready for transit, Admiral."

"Very good, Captain. Execute."

Just before the surge of warp transit took them, Trevayne spoke two sentences. Singhal didn't recognize it as a paraphrase of one of the admiral's historical heroes. "The Battle of Alpha Centauri is over. The Battle of Sol is about to begin."

CHAPTER SEVENTEEN

In the system that the humans labeled Bug 15, Cluster Leader Jadash'riz stilled the annoyed ripple in her lesser tendrils. The subordinate ship in her patrol group, the escort *Itmahar*, had not yet returned from its passage through the warp point that led to the sunless vacuum of Bug 24.

Of course, it had been the sheerest folly that fleet command had dispatched the escort there at all. When the automated courier drone stationed in the empty waste beyond the warp point arrived, reporting that the buoy they had deposited to record and scan any traffic there had failed a systems check, Jadash'riz had reported it as a matter of course. It was, to put it lightly, a minor detail, but she obediently followed the security protocols which were said to have come from Zum'ref himself—and which she had not once had to consult once since arriving in Bug 15 and being consigned to guard one of its three warp points.

231

She had expected that command would tell her to ignore the failure, and probably instruct her to send another courier drone back through the warp point with the old one so that the two could perform most of the crucial overwatch duties of the malfunctioning buoy. Ultimately, a minelayer/tender would be dispatched from the inner system to repair or replace the failing unit and Jadash'riz's patrol group of two ships would return to its normal, and utterly uneventful, routine.

But instead, command had instructed her to send the *Itmahar* through the warp point to assess the problem with the buoy and access its computer in an attempt to discern why it had failed. Although it was not explicit in command's surprisingly swift *selnarmic* response, it seemed clear that those in charge of seeing to the security of Zum'ref's rear area logistics squadrons were concerned about something other than a mere malfunction.

So Jadash'riz had sent *Itmahar* on its way, admonishing the Junior Cluster Leader who was its CO to make haste and return as swiftly as was feasible. Special out-system monitoring protocols be damned, their real mission was to stand guard on this side of the warp point. Of the two ships, Jadash'riz's much larger destroyer was tasked to intercept intruders. In the event any were detected, the diminutive *Itmahar* was tasked to flee while sending *selnarmic* reports back to the modest collection of cruisers and destroyers that had been left behind in Bug 15 to ensure the safety of seven dispersates' worth of tankers, tenders, repair ships, support craft, minelayers, and more.

But if *Itmahar* was lost, there would be but one ship to perform both tasks—and the little escort had been gone for almost twice as long as a quick inspection of the buoy should have taken. Jadash'riz glanced over at her communications second, wondered if she should send an update to fleet command. But no, she really did not have anything new to report yet, and if she was ever going to get a real combat command, she could not be pestering her superiors simply because a small craft was *almost* overdue on an utterly dull mission . . .

"Space-time anomaly detected; warp point is activating," sent sensor first with a slight pulse of both (relief) and (wariness).

One of the courier drones carried by *Itmahar* appeared, sending a *selnarmic* message as it hung in space before the warp point. Jadash'riz felt the communiqué unroll into her consciousness: the buoy had been discovered in a compromised state, intermittently activating its sensors and RF directional broadcast emitters at high power levels. It was, essentially, working like a bright, noisy beacon, sending signals out across the Bug 24 system. So the commander of *Itmahar*, unwilling to leave that kind of malfunctioning device active as it shrieked out the Kaituni presence to any craft that might wander in from the Bug 25 warp point, was taking it in tow and bringing it back through to Bug 15, thereby ending its ability to give away the proximity of Zum'ref's seven-dispersate armada.

Jadash'riz tightened her tendrils. It was the right decision, of course, and was consistent with operational security. But it was an unwelcome development nonetheless. Removing the buoy meant leaving Bug 24 unobserved and without a tripwire that could warn the fleet in Bug 15 of an approaching foe, however unlikely it was that any foe should find them at all. She gave orders for one of her own ship's courier drones to be readied for that automated sentry duty—

Just as her sensor first sent (urgently): "Warp point activating again."

A moment later, *Itmahar* emerged from the emptiness of space itself, its transponder's double ping indicating that it had returned with the buoy in tow. However, it did not emit an immediate *selnarmic* report, but rather, sent a message over lascom.

Jadash'riz frowned. "Why lascom, Communications?"

The Kaituni in question allowed (slight concern) to bleed through (puzzlement): "*Itmahar* is only sending a short, repeating message using the ancient binary distress code, Cluster Leader. It reads: 'Buoy malfunction may have been caused by embedded virus. Buoy reactivated independently once in our towing cradle. Data links monitoring buoy's status were conduits for virus attack on *Itmahar's* systems. Numerous ship's operations affected. *Selnarm* gain boosters not functioning. Environmental controls compromised. Am powering down to terminate possibility of passing virus though telemetry matching and docking datalinks. Sending hard-dock coordinates.'"

"Acknowledge their message." A flash of extra caution inspired Jadash'riz to add: "Send 'sign of the day is: *murn*,' and await countersign."

Well, this was certainly turning out to be a somewhat less routine event, Jadash'riz conceded as she grazed her mind along the edge of that belonging to her helm first: "Match docking coordinates with *Itmahar*."

Communications' *selnarmic* (concern) was diminished, his (puzzlement) giving way to (relief). "*Itmahar* has sent countersign of the day, '*vrel.*' Coordinates confirmed."

"Approach with caution. We will send an EVA team over to confirm status of the *Itmahar* before we make hard dock."

"Should I send an update to the fleet?" the communications first asked.

Jadash'riz paused. She hadn't sent a prior notice, so this would turn into a longer message: first that the Bug 24 courier came through, made report, *Itmahar* went to Bug 24, got the buoy, emerged compromised, was now going through precautionary rendezvous protocols. But despite all those details, there still wasn't any certainty that this was anything other than routine repair ops with a slight twist. No: better to leave this for the day-end traffic to be sent as a squeak just after midnight. "We do not need to trouble the fleet, Communications. Not yet. Ready EVA team."

"EVA team will be ready within the minute. They ask—"

The sensor first's *selnarm* was a fast, hard pulse: "Cluster leader, the buoy has activated and is sending a repeating, full-bandwidth emission pattern. High energy levels. *Itmahar*'s drives have reactivated, surging in offset sine-wave patterns that match the buoy's. And—"

"And—?"

"Perhaps it is affecting the warp point: the energy spikes seem to be triggering a warp point activation. Or perhaps they are obscuring one that is occurring independently."

Jadash'riz waited a moment for her sensor first to deliver a final report, grew impatient. "Well? Was it an actual warp point activation or not?"

"I cannot tell, Cluster Leader. It appeared to be, but nothing has entered the system."

Not that we can see, Jadash'riz thought cautiously. "Communication second, send *selnarmic* message only to the fleet: 'We are engaged in recovery of *Itmahar* and compromised buoy retrieved from Bug 24. Possible unexplained warp point activation. Continuing to observe.' Send it now."

"Sent, Cluster Leader. EVA team reports ready."

The helm first added, "We are in position for them to initiate free space jump to *Itmahar*. Range: one point three kilometers."

Jadash'riz's command second leaned toward her slightly. "Is the warp point anomaly not sufficient to suspend these operations and—?"

She replied with (decisive negation): "If we would fight alongside our siblings in Alpha Centauri and Earth, we must not act as though we require help at the sign of a single anomaly. However, ready the recorder buoy for launch. Keep feeding our comms and status into it. Just in case anything goes wrong, set it for automatic launch if I declare an action alert."

This did not seem to fully satisfy her command second, but he sent (acknowledgement) and set about carrying out Jadash'riz's orders. She turned her eyes upon communications'. "Send EVA team."

"EVA team underway," her communications second replied.

Three space-suited figures made a brief journey between the two floating vessels. It was wholly uneventful, but just as the EVA team was signaling that they were entering the airlock of *Itmahar*, three *murn*-tinted failure indicators illuminated on the command circuitry board. "Cluster Leader," her engineer first sent through (shock)—

"Break away, maximum speed, any direction," Jadash'riz ordered into all the *selnarmic* links on her ship, hoping that anyone who might still be able to carry out her commands would hear and act before further unexplained failures affected their systems, too.

But the worst of her fears unfolded with greater swiftness than her crew could react. The security program monitoring the link to her EVA team indicated the probable source of the software failures now ravaging her own ship: the communications units in the teams' helmets had come into the range of a virus that could be relayed *selnarmically*—but *how*?

That was when the security program itself crashed, followed almost immediately by the power plant fluctuating too wildly to be serviceable and the computer-controlled sensors going haywire, running an endless loop of pointless self-diagnostics. Other systems were showing a similar, cascading profusion of *murn*-colored failure indicators.

"Action alert!" Jadash'zir ordered at the end of her first send. "Deploy recorder buoy!"

Too late. A series of irregular shudders indicated that something had hit her ship's stern—a split second before all the interior lights and most of the bridge control panels went dark. She knew the reason before communications reported it: "Engine deck does not respond, First Cluster Leader."

Of course it doesn't, Jadash'zir affirmed to herself, as, looking up at the monitor filled by the image of *Itmahar*, she saw the escort's running lights snap on. The small ship started moving once again. Swiftly. With purpose.

Straight toward Jadash'zir's lobotomized destroyer.

Jennifer Pietchkov slipped into Bloodhound One's designated dress-out compartment on board the *No-Dachi*. She hadn't been able to get into the area three hours ago when 'Sandro and his special ops platoon were suiting up, or before he left to assault the virus-paralyzed Kaituni escort that had blundered into Bug 24, never suspecting the stealthed ships waiting for it there. The pinnace carrying 'Sandro's platoon had quickly rendezvoused and docked with the enemy craft and the Bloodhounds seized it after a short, sharp boarding action. Then, once the hull was secure, Tank had been joined by an all-Arduan prize crew commanded by *Destoshaz* Temret, accompanied by one of Ankaht's subordinate *shaxzhu* who served as a communications/intelligence specialist.

Jen had watched on the bridge monitors as the commandeered enemy ship—apparently named the *Itmahar*—had re-entered Bug 15. Precisely six minutes later, according to the ticking mission clock, a single, stealthed ship from Commodore Knight's Assault Group Lancelot—the heavy cruiser *Toshor-Prime*—slipped through the warp point herself.

The mission clock continued to tick until, at forty-two minutes and eighteen seconds, a pinnace from *Toshor-Prime* emerged from the warp point, sending a tight-beam confirmation of success. But no word on casualties. By that time, Jen was already down near the *No-Dachi*'s landing bay. Since no one on this ship knew her, and 'Sandro was not a regular part of its crew, her anonymity gave her access to any part of the hull where her clearance credentials—"secret: civilian specialist"—allowed her to venture.

So when the dress-out compartment's door to the landing bay access corridor opened, Jennifer was still unsure whether or not her 'Sandro, her Tank, was even alive. The odds were good, of course: had Bloodhound One's leader gone down in the boarding action in Bug 24 or the one presumed to have taken place in Bug 15, it was certain that she would have heard that over the comm chatter she had been privy to.

But when the door opened, she was not prepared for what she saw.

Tank came striding toward her in assault armor, the servos whining as he approached, his helmet back, his red hair spiked out from static electricity. But the mottled camo pattern on the suit was not familiar, was comprised of a strange color palette—

—until she realized: *it's blood*.

The maroon-shaded, thicker gore of the Kaituni predominated, covering him in splotches and smears from his boots on up. But horribly highlighted streaks and spatterings of bright crimson—human blood—jumped out from that background and clashed sharply with the white of the armor itself, which was scored and scraped and pocked on almost every surface.

She recoiled, felt her hand come up to her mouth.

Tank, still giving orders to his men—mostly to his platoon medics, who were in turn shouting casualty statuses to the medtechs from the *No-Dachi* as they streamed past Jen into the bay—turned to see what was blocking his way, saw her as she started to shake.

He came forward quickly, his body seeming to expand, his arms wide to conceal the scene evolving behind him: half a dozen of the Bloodhounds were being lowered to the floor of the corridor, the medtechs swarming around them, pulling off scarlet-soaked field dressings and pressing new compresses into wounds. Moans arose before anesthetic autoinjectors finished dumping their double loads into the battered and bloodied bodies.

"Jen!" 'Sandro said, his voice a strangely loud, strangled whisper. "What are you doing here? You've got to—"

But she was already half-running backward, unable to take her eyes off the man, the love of her life, who was dripping the lifeblood of both his friends and his foes on the floor behind him, the man who held Zander to him as if the little boy was a fragile lamb, the same man who must have waded hip-deep through bodies to return to her, to return looking like this.

She ran, trying to shut her ears to the sound of his voice calling after her: "Jen, Jen!"

<hr />

"How many casualties did A Platoon of the Bloodhounds take, Major?" asked Ossian Wethermere.

Alessandro's face pinched tightly for a moment.

"Seventeen, sir. Eleven KIA." He looked at the faces around the conference table in RFNS *Krishmahnta*'s flag briefing room. His own was penitent. And pained.

Kiiraathra'ostakjo's second in command, Rrurr'rao, frowned when he noticed the human's reaction to his own report. "And you captured both ships without damage to any primary systems?"

"Yes, sir."

"And took almost half of the destroyer's crew as prisoners?"

"Yes, sir."

"And secured it so that Group Leader Temret and the *shaxzhu* specialist were able to swiftly gain access to its computer?"

"Yes, sir."

"Then your mission was not merely a success, Major, it is worthy of song. I do not understand the unhappiness you display." Rrurr'rao had to fumble to find the last words of his statement.

"Commodore, it's been seven years since I lost that many men in a single engagement—when we had to storm the heart of the Arduan fortress during their occupation of Punt City on Bellerophon." The glance he bounced from Narrok to Ankaht to Mretlak was not apologetic, merely regretful. They were allies now, but they had been invaders then.

But Rrurr'rao was more confused, if anything. "Yet another battle of such valor and daring that it has reached even my ears," the Orion exclaimed, his hands suddenly outstretched. "I do not understand. Do you not consider these victories?"

"I do, sir. But these were my men. I was responsible for their lives. Many—very many—did not come back."

"Are you saying they did not die good deaths?"

"No, sir: they fought and died as bravely as any Marines it has ever been my privilege to lead. And given the soldiers I've led, I've been a very, very privileged commander, sir."

Rrurr'rao leaned sharply away from the table, glanced around the room as if he sought sanity to match his own, saw that no others shared his perplexity, not even his superior, Least Fang Kiiraathra'ostakjo.

Who smoothed his ruff and observed. "Commodore Rrurr'rao has not had enough contact with humans to understand the differences in our value systems." Glancing at his subordinate, Kiiraathra explained, "In most human societies, the honor of dying well is not felt so strongly as the misfortune of dying too soon."

"It is strange, then, that they fight so well," Rrurr'rao observed frankly. Wethermere could not be sure whether that was more insult or admiration: certainly, it contained a measure of both.

"Commodore," Tank interposed, "when we fight for what we believe and those we love,"—his eyes flicked toward Jennifer Pietchkov—"personal honor seems like a pretty weak motive by comparison. At least for us humans."

Rrurr'rao nodded slowly. He was very intelligent but did not readily understand other cultures. "I acknowledge the differences in our motivations, but struggle to find something analogous in my own culture. Even when we of the *Zheeerlikou'valkhannaieee* fight for our family and survival, we are still, also, fighting for our honor. For us, it is as inescapable as our own skins. But for you—"

"Not so much," Tank confirmed with a nod of his own as he glanced over at his wife.

Who was staring at him with wide, unblinking eyes, Wethermere noted. And then he noticed something else: that the ends of her fingernails were unusually dark. He looked closer.

There was blood under them. Ossian also saw signs of hastily cleaned stains—blood also?—on her clothes, and a thin maroon smear on the edge of one palm. When the invasion had started, back when he'd had some time to himself or for friends, Wethermere would have resolved to make subtle inquiries of the couple, find out what had left those stains on Jen's hands, had put that hundred-meter stare on her face. But that was before he'd become an admiral in all ways but title. So . . . time to move on.

"Major, your boarding action has made it possible for us to enter Bug 15 with minimal risk, and possibly, to cut off their support assets from the assault elements in Alpha Centauri, all before we begin attacking. Your actions, and the sacrifices of your personnel, were vital to their realization."

Narrok attempted to nod like a human; it still appeared as though he was having a small fit or was afflicted by a strange tic. "There is no exaggeration in the commodore's statement. The intelligence we have retrieved from these two Kaituni ships has been invaluable and has shaped our next action. The Arachnids are no longer present, and the great majority of all seven Dispersates are now engaged with Admiral Trevayne in Alpha Centauri. But most importantly, the ships in Bug 15 are overwhelmingly support craft."

Commodore Knight smiled at Rrurr'rao's sudden predatory posture. "How well are they defended?"

Knight's smiled broadened. "Hardly at all. Feel like coming hunting with me, Commodore?"

Rrurr'rao looked ready to run out of the compartment to commence the attack at once. "My only regret is that there are so few of their true warships to destroy."

Riordan shared a smile that he suspected matched Knight's. "That comes next, Commodore Rrurr'rao. But with their auxiliary craft gone, you're going to find that big game somewhat easier to hunt. The enemy's capital ships are going to be at least slightly weakened prey by the time we reach them: they'll be in danger of running out of missiles, fuel, food, repair. The Kaituni have left behind almost every hull that keeps their immense armada running and in fighting trim. And they've detailed only a few dozen cruisers, destroyers and a handful of battleships to guard it."

"A surprisingly modest force," Kiiraathra commented.

Narrok raised a didactic tendril. "It would not seem so to Zum'ref. He has scorched every system behind him down to figurative—and in some cases, literal—bedrock. His armada owns the length of the main warp line from Pesthouse to Earth and he knows he has defeated all the units in this region of space, since his advance intelligence gave him rosters of the various units arrayed here. He would not expect the warp point to Bug 24 to disgorge foes; logically, he would be looking for the Fourteenth Dispersate to come from there, or some ruined enemy units fleeing ahead of it."

"Still, his presumptions are reckless," Knight observed.

"The *Destoshaz*-as-*sulhaji* movement always had such tendencies," Narrok conceded. "The Kaituni have even greater arrogance. They also have every reason to believe they have eliminated all the opposition which can reach them for the foreseeable future. They could hardly anticipate that the entirety of the useful Rim Federation fleet might have come through a new warp point and would creep up on them from behind. The course of events which have brought us here, undetected, are unforeseeable. For which we should be thankful."

Mretlak laced his larger tentacles together. "Is there any indication, or likelihood, that the obscuring signals we rigged the buoy to emit to cover the transit of the *Toshor-Prime* would come under greater scrutiny by the main fleet elements deeper in the Bug 15 system?"

Narrok turned slightly in the direction of the Arduan intelligence chief. "No. Fortunately, the warp point to Alpha Centauri is forty light-minutes distant. It is very unlikely that they noticed any of the anomalous readings at that range. Furthermore, our Arduan prize crews are in the system now, ensuring that the two commandeered ships continue to send the correct countersigns and perform the expected functions. They should be able to deflect any suspicion for some time."

"The warp point that leads to the Harnah system, and ultimately all the way back to Pesthouse, is closer though, is it not?" asked Ankaht.

Wethermere nodded. "It is: eighteen light-minutes. But planet two lies directly between us, and closer to them. Our models indicate that the planet probably masked much of the activity around the warp point we came out of. Furthermore, the local pickets' duty rosters indicate that security back to Harnah is no greater than it is here."

"Is there a detachment in the Harnah system itself?" Kiiraathra asked, eyes narrowed.

"Probably light elements; four ship transponder codes are listed as valid traffic inbound from Harnah. We haven't matched their tail numbers to the ship roster yet, but the coding suggests that they are either escorts or destroyers." He swept a hand toward the warp point into Harnah. "A few of our refurbished Kaituni monitors will close that warp point as surely as bricking up a doorway."

Knight was smiling. "Then what are we waiting for?"

Narrok exchanged glances with Wethermere and Kiiraathra before answering. "We are waiting for all our stealthed ships to come forward. Many will be assigned to your unit, Commodore Knight. Very many."

"How many?"

"Hundreds."

Knight's eyes widened. "Oh," was all he said.

"It's an involved process," Wethermere explained. "We're trying to team up ships that don't have stealth systems with those that do. We'll be powering down the ones that have no system of their own and lashing them to the stealthed craft. That way, they can pass through the warp point concealed by the same stealth field and set course for their first way-point."

Knight nodded. "So we're trying to sneak as many of our ships into the system as we can before we start the party."

Narrok nodded. "Yes. So that by the time we bring in

the largest ships without stealth fields—such as many of our monitors—the enemy fleet will have lost crucial maneuver alternatives; our stealthed ships will be in their way."

"And how," Rrurr'rao wondered with a closed lip smile, "do you propose to accomplish that?"

Wethermere leaned forward, tried to repress a grin. "Funny you should ask . . . "

CHAPTER EIGHTEEN

Wethermere looked at the *selnarm*-updated tactical plot the moment RFNS *Krishmahnta* completed its transit into Bug 15. It revealed that battle still had not been joined. He breathed a sigh of relief.

Four hours ago, the last ships of the massively reinforced Assault Group Lancelot had entered the system under stealth and commenced making for the Alpha Centauri warp point at flank speed, several dozen stealth-refitted Arduan SDHs along with them. Included in that formation were Commodore Rrurr'rao's flotilla of smaller Orion carriers and battleships: agile craft that boasted some of the highest sprint speeds in the fleet. It was estimated that it would take them just over eight hours to reach the warp point, which was located at the twelve o'clock spot on the tac plot.

After that, an almost endless parade of stealthed superdreadnoughts and smaller warships had made transit to Bug 15—all that the Relief fleet had—and also moved briskly from their three o'clock entry spot toward the purple hoop that signified the warp point to Alpha Centauri. Hundreds of blue pinpricks were now moving steadily for it in the shape of a high, broad wave.

Just before the monitors of the fleet entered and thereby ensured that enemy sensors would soon tweak to their presence, a number of Kaituni prize hulls—half a dozen monitors and several smaller hulls—had moved through, staying cloaked as best they could. They maneuvered toward the center of the tacplot and the lavender loop that marked the warp point back to Harnah. The prize crews on board the escort and destroyer which had guarded the conduit to Bug 15 watched for any sign that the support and logistical tail of Zum'ref's armada had detected these larger craft, stood ready to send *selnarmic* messages to the Kaituni which would identify these as ships of the Fourteenth Dispersate, just arrived with report of what had transpired during their campaign in the Star Union. That story would not hold up for long— certainly not more than a few hours—but a few hours was all that was needed. After the captured Kaituni craft entered Bug 15, the entirety of the remaining Relief Fleet would soon follow them into the system. By which time it would not matter if the actual Kaituni saw through the ruse.

Forty minutes after Wethermere entered Bug 15, Knight sent a single, coded *selnarmic* squeak that indicated that Assault Group Lancelot (Augmented) had reached its jump-off point: a position just three light-minutes clockwise of the warp point into Alpha Centauri. The plot showed that enemy traffic through the purple hoop was sparse and steadily diminishing, with more of it leaving Bug 15 than entering. Almost certainly, the offensive tempo had shifted in Zum'ref's favor in Alpha Centauri. The question was: would he pause to regroup *all* his assets there, or would he swiftly carry his attack through to Earth while his logistical tail moved to take up new positions in Alpha Centauri?

Wethermere had been fairly confident that the Kaituni would follow the latter path. The records from the commandeered destroyer indicated that while Zum'ref was arrogant and somewhat hasty as a commander, he was also gifted and clearly understood that if he was to have any hope of ruining the order and planning of his adversaries, he would have to maintain unrelenting pressure. That meant giving them little time to regroup in the Sol system: logically, he would follow them through as quickly as possible.

All that remained for the Relief Fleet now was to approach as closely as it could and to watch for signs or sensor activity that indicated that the time had come to drop stealth. Before long, the advance rank of small remote-operated vehicles that were working as the Relief Fleet's *selnarmically*-linked spy eyes would show up on the enemy sensors and the fight would be on.

The conflagration commenced just where the flag staff had universally anticipated it would: near the Harnah warp point, as the monitors taken from the Fourteenth Dispersate became evident to the three pickets the enemy had stationed there. There was a brief exchange of confused communications: the prize hulls were able to convincingly refer to information gleaned from the two picket ships taken from the Bug 24 warp point, claiming that they had been admitted to bring news to commanders both further up and down the warp point. However, their attempt to explain away the fact that they were traveling cloaked ultimately broke down, and they unleashed their massive destructive energies upon the pickets. One, a destroyer, improbably survived the initial barrage—probably because of the range at which it had been necessarily unleashed—and dove for the lavender loop that was the doorway into Harnah and survival. At which point a stealthed Arduan dreadnought, warned by the Kaituni monitors, dropped its concealment and fired a barrage that literally vaporized the enemy destroyer. Collectively, the ships arrayed themselves around the warp point, weapons aimed at its ingress point: no enemy craft would be entering Bug 15 from that direction.

However, the sparse defenders of the auxiliaries and support craft that Zum'ref had left behind in the supposed safety of the system gathered together and made for these unexpected combatants. Meanwhile, the Kaituni command staff clearly desired Zum'ref to be informed of the evolving scenario: a covey of *selnarmic* courier drones began speeding toward the warp point into Alpha Centauri, the immense mass of noncombatant craft following close behind them. Since Bug 15 was no longer a safe haven, it was a predictable contingency that they should rejoin—and inform—the bulk of their seven-Dispersate armada.

But that was why Assault Group Lancelot had positioned itself alongside the warp point into Alpha Centauri before any other action had been undertaken by the Relief Fleet. Commodore Knight's ships, warned by *selnarmic* microsensors of the approaching Kaituni craft and courier drones, emerged from stealth, energy torpedoes gushing out of them as an incandescent torrent.

The primary initial targets—the couriers—were gone in three seconds; the first wave of the smaller, swifter ships that were at the head of the fleeing formation were reduced to debris or subatomic particles during the balance of that first minute of firing. While this initial slaughter stunned the Kaituni into near-immobility, the balance of Assault Group Lancelot moved to a blocking position directly at the ingress/egress cone for the warp point into Alpha Centauri. The second doorway in or out of Bug 15 had been closed.

The next three minutes confirmed the already likely outcome of the battle. Having never created a contingency for what to do in the event that *both* warp points were held against them from within the system, the Kaituni's actions resembled what Wethermere could only characterize as highly-energetic dithering. The small contingent of actual warcraft in the system paused in their headlong rush toward the Harnah warp point and then resumed their charge against it—only to run right up against the approaching blue wave that was the stealthed bulk of the Relief Fleet. As that immense formation came out of stealth, everything from monitors to cruisers figuratively jostled with each other to be able to lock on to an enemy target before the first shimmering wall of energy torpedoes wiped them all out.

Back at the Alpha Centauri warp point, the first response to the appearance of, and slaughter inflicted by,

Assault Group Lancelot was to recoil. Apparently, the senior officers on the Kaituni's actual warships had ordered them to make for Harnah in their wake, while launching all available courier drones at the warp point in an attempt to warn Zum'ref. Out of those hundreds of drones, at least one was likely to make it through and, at the very least, it would keep the suddenly-materialized human ships too busy to give the much slower and almost unarmed Kaituni auxiliaries enough time to get a head start in their withdrawal.

But the several hundred courier drones were met by more than a thousand fighters, mostly launched from Rrurr'rao's unstealthing Orion light and assault carriers. The fighters were just as fast as the couriers and more maneuverable; they made brutally short work of these unresisting targets that could do little more than head for their objective in a straight line. To no one's surprise, not one made it. Where any fighter somehow missed the courier to which it had locked on, there was another fighter behind it, to say nothing of the defense batteries of the four dozen Arduan super dreadnoughts that were holding the warp point. They had been chosen for this duty for their ability to sow at least several moments of convincing disinformation among any inbound craft and crews. Now, they proved their expert gunnery skills as well, beam weapons plucking any errant enemy drones out of space with unusual facility and speed.

Predictably, since the Kaituni did not believe in death but merely temporary discarnation, many of their auxiliaries attempted the same tactic. The numbers which elected to run the gauntlet to the Alpha Centauri warp point increased when it became clear that the exit to Harnah was decisively held against them, and, more pertinently, that the bulk of the approaching Relief Fleet was interposed between them and it (and the glowing bits of wreckage which had been the Kaitunis' scant defense squadron).

But few auxiliary or support ships are built for speed, and none carry anything beyond modest defensive weaponry. So they came on in their hundreds . . . and died more quickly and surely than the couriers and smaller craft that had preceded them to that doom. If they were counting on exhausting the Relief Fleet's supply of missiles, they had sorely underestimated the degree to which humanity in general, and the Rim Federation in particular, had converted to the energy-torpedo. Limitless as long as there was adequate power, the withering storm of fire battered each Kaituni hull into tatters until the survivors reversed and endeavored to escape to the rear and sides of the oncoming leviathan that was the main van of the Relief Fleet.

But that formation, led by Narrok (with Wethermere serving as vice-commander and strategic sounding board), had modified its shape in the hour since it had emerged from stealth. No longer a straight wave, its flanks had curved forward like horns, creating a funnel-like trap with which to catch "leakers": enemy ships that tried to slip around its sides. Less than a hundred did, mostly smaller, swifter craft that made beeline progress toward the outer system, possibly the companion star which was over one hundred fifty light-minutes distant and had no warp points of its own.

Wethermere watched the red motes scatter out of the closing trap in which thousands of Kaituni hulls were being reduced to junk and quarks as the hammer of Assault Group Lancelot crushed them against the anvil of the Relief Fleet's van. These survivors were probably pursuing the only tactic that remained viable; they were hoping to pull pursuers after them, tie up as many of the Relief Fleet's assets as possible, for as long as they could.

Narrok must have been thinking the same thing: Comms indicated that he was on secure one. Ossian waved the signal through, turned to face the small holograph of the Arduan admiral as it appeared next to his con. "Yes, sir?"

"You have no doubt noticed the smaller ships that have escaped our pocket."

"Yes, sir."

"I shall leave the matter of dispatching pursuit units to your oversight, Commodore."

"Thank you, sir. Since you're putting me in charge of that operation, I'd like to voice an opinion about it."

"Of course, Commodore."

"Admiral, with respect, I feel we should ignore the enemy ships."

"Ignore them?" Narrok sounded slightly surprised, slightly wary. Where their opponent Zum'ref had a tendency to be rash and careless with his marginal assets and security loopholes, Narrok displayed the opposite tendency: he was decidedly detail-oriented. It did not make him less bold, but sometimes, he expended time and energy to ensure optimal battlefield conditions, when victory would have been equally well-served by "good enough."

"Yes, sir. If we ignore them, what can they do? Amassed together, the Kaituni survivors can't take on even one of the monitors we've left guarding the Harnah warp point. They can head into the outer system, even go to the secondary star and its planets—but what can they do once they get there?"

"There is all sorts of mischief that several dozen ships could cause, particularly ships with crews that think nothing of giving their lives if it enables them to strike a blow against us."

"Agreed, Admiral, but as you said, in the larger strategic picture, that's nothing more than mischief. But from our perspective, we need to keep every fighting hull we have on the line. Every one we send to chase these small survivors is not only a reduction of our firepower, but a reduction of our operational scope: it reduces our footprint, the number of platforms we have for other missions, for flanking actions, for feints, for picket duty. And this battle was just the warm-up act, sir. We shot up a bunch of slow, unarmed boats in a bathtub. Next time, we'll be coming up against their real battlewagons. I don't think this is the time to diminish our numbers, sir. Not even in our lightest ship classes."

"You make a valid point, Commodore," Narrok allowed after several seconds of consideration. "But we are still leaving several large ships behind, then, to guard the warp point in and out of Harnah, to ensure that they do not exploit it."

"Sir, we'd have to guard that warp point anyway, since we don't know what might come through *from* Harnah. But since there's no way for the Kaituni on this side of the warp point to coordinate with any units in Harnah, there isn't any realistic threat that our pickets could be swarmed from both sides. And even so, those monitors are more than sufficient to do the job. However, before we push on Alpha Centauri, I want to swap out the hulls we have at the Harnah warp point and replace them with equivalent monitors that haven't yet completed their repairs from the battle in Bug 27. Mobility isn't going to matter very much to pickets, whereas maximum speed and maneuverability will be key for every ship we bring through to Alpha Centauri."

Narrok was still for almost half a minute. "We shall do as you suggest, Commodore. We shall also meet once this action is completed. In person. And with all haste. Narrok out."

Wethermere replied, "Yes Admiral," to empty air. *Is Narrok angry? He didn't sound like it, but—well, did I press too hard? Damn it, we're at battle stations: there's no time for bows and "by your leaves" and . . . Ah, the hell with it: I'll worry about that when I have the time to spare.* "Comms, raise Mretlak on secure *selnarm* two."

A three-second delay, then: "Senior Group Leader Mretlak is standing by on secure two, sir."

Wethermere nodded his acknowledgement, greeted the Arduan Intelligence chief. "Mretlak, have you identified the targets you wish to use as the field-subjects for Project Turncoat?"

"Yes, Commodore. In fact, I have already identified— and lost—several enemy clusters which would have served that purpose. Unfortunately, they were destroyed almost as quickly as I could identify them. However, several of the fleeing craft hold excellent promise. One in particular: it is a minelayer with remote drones for retrieval and servicing of mines. Those drones are currently deployed, running interference for the main hull as it attempts to escape."

"Can you catch it in time?"

"Without doubt, sir: we have a ten percent speed advantage over it and they have nowhere to hide."

"Then send me the coordinates and target codes assigned to those ships and I will send it down the comm chain that they are off limits for anyone else to pursue or engage. You have your test subject, Senior Group Leader."

"Thank you, sir. I have not had the luxury of time to assess the strategic-scale holoplot, Commodore: how is the engagement progressing?"

"Very soon, you would need to ask that question in the past tense, Mretlak. I'm going to see to the finishing touches now. Wethermere out."

Ossian Wethermere was somewhat surprised when Narrok sent word that he wished to meet aboard RFNS *Krishmahnta* rather than his own flagship. That seemed odd; usually, when a ranking officer wanted to dress you down, he or she did it aboard their own hull. Their house, their rules—including the form of spanking you'd get.

Stranger still, Narrok gave word that he had summoned Kiiraathra'ostakjo to the same meeting. And no one else. Not even support staff. Just the three of them.

Why? Wethermere wondered, *So they can execute me for not-really-insubordinate exchanges and not have any witnesses as to which one of them actually pulled the trigger? Okay, so that's an exaggeration—but by how much?*

When Narrok arrived on ship he waited for Kiiraathra down in the landing bay. Again, damned strange. After Wethermere's Orion friend was aboard and had conferred with Narrok briefly—and alone—they peremptorily instructed Wethermere to meet them in the flag briefing room in five minutes. Without so much as a single courteous word of request. Sure, they were admirals, but this was still Ossian's ship.

But maybe that will have changed before the hour is out. Wethermere sighed, got his adjutant to download the latest after-action updates to his datapad, and then left to meet with the two admirals. Or, as might be the case, to face the music.

When he entered the briefing room, Narrok was sitting on the starboard side of the conference table, Kiiraathra on the port. The only logical place to sit was the head of the table, located in the direction of the bow. Wethermere, uncertain, stopped and saluted. They rose solemnly, returned his salute, reseated themselves.

Ossian took his seat. "I have the after-action updates, Admirals."

"Very good: report," ordered Narrok.

"Yes, sir. Operational security was fully maintained; no enemy ships transited either the warp point into Harnah or Alpha Centauri. Our presence here, and all special tactics and technologies at our disposal, remain unknown to our enemies. Naturally, it also means that Zum'ref's forces will still not anticipate that we have Arduans and their *selnarmic* capabilities with us. So all those advantages have been retained in full."

"We will surely lose them in the next engagement," Narrok commented.

"Yes, sir, without doubt. And if we do not move relatively quickly, we will lose them before that. Which could be disastrous."

"Explain," demanded Kiiraathra, whose eyes glittered. Or twinkled? Wethermere could not be sure.

And he didn't have time to discern which it might be. "Admirals, we delayed our attack until we observed a decrease in the traffic between this system and Alpha Centauri. But whether or not the battle for Alpha Centauri is fully resolved, it seems certain that Zum'ref will at least be sending his more severely damaged ships back here for repair and refit. It is also likely that he will begin calling auxiliaries through to refurbish his armada once his tempo of operations in Alpha Centauri decreases. In short, we're going to have visitors soon. We can probably disappear a few of them, but from the time the first one comes through the warp point, the clock is running. And we don't know how much time we have on that clock, because we don't know at what point Zum'ref's suspicions will be aroused that something isn't quite right back here in Bug 15."

"Understood," Kiiraathra said brusquely. "Go on with your report."

"Yes, sir. In order to preserve our tactical advantages, we must therefore put a presence in Alpha Centauri to observe what is going on. As we discussed, this will mean another set of operations akin to those which allowed us to commandeer the picket ships that were guarding the warp point into this system."

"So we will need to use the Bloodhounds again."

"Yes, sir. I have already sent word to Major Magee. He has trained several platoons for these operations over the past several months. We will have all of them ready, since it stands to reason that the warp point into this system is likely to be guarded much more heavily.

"It also means that we have to pull maximum data from the Kaituni wrecks as quickly as we can. We need up-to-date passwords, signs and countersigns, force rosters: everything that will allow our q-ships of all marks to imitate our enemy as convincingly as possible for as long as possible."

Narrok raised a single, narrow tendril. "I do not yet have a complete list of the enemy hulls engaged in this system, but it is urgent that we determine if we have even the smallest bits of wreckage of a ship that mounted a relativistic assault weapon."

Wethermere nodded. "Sir, the bad news was that, going into this combat, we'd seen no evidence of any being present in their local formations. However, it turns out one of them was in system for an engine overhaul. Drive coil wear, apparently. This means we were able to take her mostly intact. Mretlak's team is crawling all over that RAW hull as we speak—right in the wake of Magee's Bloodhounds. They had to go aboard to gain control and prevent scuttling of the hull."

Narrok nodded approval. "And what of Mretlak's field test of Turncoat? Did it work as anticipated?"

"I just got the update on that before leaving the bridge,

Admiral. The short answer is yes, although there are still some bugs to be worked out of it. But since we now have access to the hardware of various Dispersates, we can see where their relevant technologies converged and diverged. That allows us to calibrate far more accurately regarding the range of software and programming environments that Turncoat is likely to encounter. Also, the earliest speculation from the technical intelligence teams currently on the RAW is that the sophistication required to build that weapon and its targeting suite apparently ended with the Eighth or Ninth Dispersate. After that, high-end science and engineering on Ardu slumped.

"So we have a better idea of which enemy command and control systems we're going to be dealing with when we activate Turncoat: those characteristic of the earlier Dispersates, which are close kin or duplicates of those employed by the attackers we encountered in the first Kaituni attacks and on which we have a reasonable amount of data."

Narrok laid his tendrils flat on the table; nothing emerged from his vocoder for several seconds. "This operation has gone quite well. Indeed, it has been an extraordinary success. Our enemy's ability to prosecute a prolonged campaign here, or elsewhere, has been gutted and Zum'ref is still not aware of it. The foresight and planning was impeccable."

"Yes, sir: the staff, at every level, has a lot to be proud of. I only wish we had the time to convene a general gathering of the—"

"Unfortunately," Narrok interrupted with uncharacteristic brusqueness, "we do not have time for such a gathering. We must collect as much information as we may on the conditions in Alpha Centauri and the disposition of our enemy. Indeed, the mere act of doing so may also, to borrow your expression, start a clock running. And so we must be ready to insinuate our stealthed warships through the warp point in hours, possibly moving directly into combat once again. So what I must now do, I must do without delay."

Here it comes, Wethermere thought.

"Commodore Wethermere, you are correct that it would be appropriate to gather the entirety of the fleet command staff—and many others besides—to offer thanks for their contributions to the success of this operation. But since we do not have time for that, Admiral Kiiraathra'ostakjo and I may only acknowledge the primary architect of the plans that we followed." His eyes rotated toward Wethermere. "Thank you, Commodore. This has been the culmination of the tactics you have championed from well before the battle in Bug 27. We are now poised to strike, undiminished and with many advantages, at the armada that threatens your homeworld and the very heart and soul of the Pan-Sentient Union."

Wethermere realized his mouth was open; he shut it with a snap that even he heard as horribly undignified. "Sirs," he said. "I—thank you. This—"

"Do not thank us yet, Wethermere," Kiiraathra literally growled. "We are not done."

Huh? was all that went through Ossian's mind.

"The admiral is correct," Narrok affirmed. "The recent operations had one key flaw, one weakness we must remedy before we proceed."

"It is a step we are loath to take," the Orion amended, "but we see no alternative." He drew a small box from a slip-pocket in his lower sleeve; because it was the one in which Orions had formerly concealed dueling daggers, Wethermere had to consciously refrain from flinching. Kiiraathra put the box on the table, pushed it toward the human. "Here. You must take responsibility for this, Wethermere."

Who looked at the box, wondering.

"Open it, human," the Orion muttered. "You have courage to fly toward enemy guns but balk at opening a box?"

Narrok's vocoder emitted a long sigh. "In all fairness, the guns are less daunting than this, Admiral."

Ossian flipped back the top of the box—and discovered an admiral's cluster of the Rim Federation Navy staring up at him. "What?" he said, then: "You can't." The rest of the world fell far away; it was only Wethermere and the symbol of rank.

"Technically, you are correct," Narrok said from a great distance. "The Least Claw's current rank is a brevet, so he may not promote someone to one grade beneath his own. I am but a provisional member of the Rim Federation Navy, and you serve the PSU, so there is another obstacle. But these are nice formalities which must be balanced against brutal realities. We are soon to enter what may be furious combat with an enemy many times our size. We will not have the luxury, or even the possibility, of commanding from the safe center of a van of monitors, because no place will be safe. If one of us"—he glanced at Kiiraathra—"were to fall, that would leave the Relief Fleet with but one admiral.

"There are too many ships, too many formations, and too many potential mishaps, for us to now go forward with only two admirals. There will not be the time—nor, possibly, even the communication links—to brevet another admiral in the midst of such a combat. Furthermore, it is folly that the person who conceived and shaped our operational plan here, and beyond, should not be involved in overseeing its execution at the highest level. Your insight and initiative is needed not as a counselor, Ossian Wethermere, but as a peer. A junior peer, perhaps, but at least as a brevet Rear Admiral. And I must point out, that since this war began, the flag ranks of the Rim Federation Navy have been all but laid waste."

"Sirs," Ossian struggled to say through a suddenly parched throat. "Even if I were to agree with your kind assessment of my abilities, I am not a member of the Rim Federation Navy. I can't possibly—"

"You can and you must," Kiiraathra'ostakjo pronounced with an air of remove that made him, for the first time that Ossian could recall, seem positively regal. "No one else may serve in this role. You have cross-trained with the Rim Federation; it was on that basis that you were brevetted to Commodore. Which rank is now made permanent, that we may brevet you to admiral—"

—and thus is insanity layered atop insanity, Wethermere thought, suppressing a physical reaction that might have manifested as a gasp, a chortle, or both—

"—but we have taken a further decisive step to confirm our action. We have spoken to the officers who've served beneath you. Those from the recon flotilla; those like Commodore Knight who command detachments under your authority; and the late Admiral Yoshikuni's fleet staff. The admiral herself evidently addressed a special communiqué to Admiral Narrok, which was relayed to him only when she was registered as deceased in the personnel database. Each of those sources told us what we already knew: that they would gladly, fiercely, serve beneath you: the only human who may reasonably share in our command of what is an overwhelmingly human fleet. Now: utter no more of your species' tiresome protestations of humility and trepidation. Wear this sign of rank and do your duty as you must."

Ossian Wethermere reached out toward the gleaming cluster and slowly affixed it to his uniform, as if in a dream. "Thank you. I think," he murmured.

"You know better than to thank us, Rear Admiral Wethermere," Narrok said. "You know all too well the impossible weight of that pin you just consented to wear. But welcome: we are stronger with you in this position."

Wethermere nodded dumbly, glanced over at Kiiraathra, who was glaring at him. "Yes?" he asked.

"I do not like to be kept waiting by irresolute humans," his Orion friend grumbled. "Now, are you going to offer us refreshments or not? We haven't much time to savor them; the great hunt is yet before us."

CHAPTER NINETEEN

Writing at the very dawn of the space age, the twentieth-century visionary Arthur C. Clarke had surprised readers accustomed to his usual optimism about the future of space travel by declaring flatly that it would never, ever be possible to have a conversation with someone on another planet.

What he had meant, of course, was a *normal* conversation. Even the two and two-thirds seconds it took a radio signal to travel from Old Terra to Luna and back imposed an irritating pause between sentence and reply—a series of speed bumps on the road of conversational give-and-take. And as for different planets, several light-minutes apart at the very least . . . !

Ian Trevayne reflected that his own present circumstances should have provided an extreme confirmation of Clarke's dictum. The orbits of Mars and Earth currently placed them on diametrically opposite sides of Sol. So they were separated by slightly over twenty-one light-minutes, with a G2v star squarely between them.

But Clarke could never have foreseen *selnarmic* relay—although, given his keen (albeit scientifically disciplined) interest in the phenomena his era grouped under the mystical heading of "paranormal," he would have been fascinated by it. Not even his imagination had seen through to the Arduans, and the still imperfectly understood quantum-mechanics-like manifestation that enabled their empathic sense to transmit—if that was the word—with an instantaneity concerning which human physicists were still in deep denial.

Thus it was that Trevayne, in the city-like space station orbiting Mars, sat before a comm screen and gazed into the huge, dark, slightly almond-shaped eyes of his daughter and waited an eternal heartbeat for her reaction to what he had just told her, dreading to see the six-year-old face dissolve into tears.

It turned out to be worse than that. She continued to meet his eyes gravely, and in a voice that held only the slightest tremor, she asked, "Does that mean that Mommy is dead?"

Trevayne forced himself to speak levelly and comfortingly. "No, Han, that's not what it means." *Actually, it probably does,* said a voice he didn't want to hear. He dismissed it firmly. "Remember what I said before: it means that no one knows where she is."

"Then can we go and look for her?"

"I'm sorry, Han. But right now we can't go back to Bug 17, the system where she was last seen. As soon as we can, we'll go there and find her." Trevayne ordered himself to add, "I promise," forcing the words out past a barrier of self-disgust.

The enormous eyes took on a pleading look. "Daddy, please come here to Old Terra. I haven't seen you in so long. I miss you."

It was almost more than Trevayne could bear. He made of his face an iron mask so that the child could not see the torment behind it. "I miss you too, dear. But I can't come and see you just now. I have . . . a lot of work to do, in order to protect you. It's work Mommy would want me to be doing. You see, she is . . . missing because she was also working to protect you. Do you understand?"

"Yes, Daddy," she said dutifully.

"Good. I'll come and see you before very much longer." *My, what an adept liar you're becoming,* said the insidious voice, which he once again thrust down into the darkness from whence it had come. "And now let me speak to your grandparents again. I have something else I need to say to them." Of course they weren't really her grandparents. But they were the closest to grandparents she had ever known, and Magda had agreed that *grand-godparents* was absurd.

"Yes, Daddy. I love you so much."

"I love you too." Trevayne managed to wait until the beautiful little girl was out of the pickup before burying his face in his hands. When he finally looked up, the faces of Jason Bluefield Windrider and Magda Petrovna Windrider were on the screen.

At a hundred and twenty-nine and a hundred and forty-nine standard years respectively, they were elderly even by the standard of Fringe World colonials, who as a matter of longstanding policy to encourage settlement were given gratis the antigerone treatments which, on the crowded inner worlds, were the prerogative of the rich and those who had placed the government in their debt. (Trevayne had often wondered if that had been one never-acknowledged source of the mutual resentments that had driven the Fringe and the inner worlds apart.) Indeed Jason's face, molded by Amerindian genes from the planet Topaz, was more seamed with age than his wife's Slavic one, even though she was the older of the two. And they, he knew, were looking into his thirtyish face and feeling the same sense of unreality he was, for they had all been in roughly the same age group when they had faced each other as enemies at the Battle of Zapata, where they had served under Li Han and he had been cast into his long cryogenic sleep.

But now their eyes met his in a communion of shared sorrow, for he had already told them about their goddaughter . . . up to a point.

"Where are you, exactly?" he asked.

"Sochi, Russia," said Magda. "A friend on Novaya Rodina has a vacation *dacha* that he let us use. It's located—"

"Yes, I know." Trevayne had been there once, in his earlier life, with his first wife Natalya. He recalled that the town was on the coast of the Black Sea, nestled at the foot of the titanic Caucasus range. It had once been a playground for the tsarist aristocracy, whose *moujiks* had performed a miracle of fertilization by getting palm trees—the very last thing anyone ever expected to see in

Russia—established there. The palaces had crumbled away during the Soviet period, but the town had later experienced a revival as a resort, aided by its breathtaking natural setting.

But it was still fairly out-of-the-way, which from Trevayne's viewpoint was a very good thing indeed.

Jason Windrider seemed to read Trevayne's thoughts, and partially understand them. He leaned forward and spoke in the still deep and resonant voice of a former Terran Republic Senator. "Ian, I'm sorry. When we brought her here, we didn't know—"

"Of course you didn't. You couldn't. And it doesn't really matter. Nowhere, including Novaya Rodina, is safe anymore—not in the long run. At least, with her here, I can tell myself that I'm personally protecting her."

"And if anyone can, Ian, you can," Magda assured him. "If you were here on Old Terra, you'd know that your very presence is one of the things that give the people hope for . . ." She trailed off, puzzled by the look that momentarily twisted Trevayne's face. If the idea hadn't seemed self-evidently absurd, she would have sworn it was look of guilt.

Jason saw it too. "Ian, what is it?"

Trevayne spoke like a man who was doing so on impulse, and was beyond feeling anything but relief at unburdening himself. "Earlier, I didn't tell you the whole truth about Mags." He had never been able to bring himself to call her that, but he knew they did. "I told you she was . . . lost commanding the rear guard covering our retreat from Bug 17. That was true as far as it went. What I didn't tell you was that she wasn't supposed to be commanding it. I was. She assumed command of it with the collusion of its task group commanders. It was mutiny."

They simply stared.

"She did it for one reason: to prevent me from putting my own life at risk. She told me essentially what you just did, Magda. Something about legend and mythic aura." Trevayne's voice held a hollow ring of self-mockery.

"Ian, don't sell yourself short," Jason said. "You owe it to her memory, after her sacrifice—"

"Her *probable* sacrifice. You see, I wasn't altogether lying to Han. I do not consider the question of her survival closed."

Magda looked at him with something like pity. "Ian," she said in gentle voice, "you told us that you received a Code Omega from her flagship, TRNS *Ark Royal*—"

"So we did. And I am aware that she is legally presumed dead. But remember: she had access to one of the new flag escape capsules."

They said nothing. The new capsules, with their capability to plunge the occupant automatically into cryogenic stasis, were far too bulky for general use. But it is one of the eternal constants of military life that rank hath its privileges. They were provided for flag officers.

But, they also knew, those capsules' bulk also precluded convenient placement, readily accessible from flag bridges. There was the small matter of getting to them in a ship being smashed to ruin in battle.

And, of course, the Kaituni advance had now left Bug 17 five warp transits behind . . .

"You mean," Jason finally said, "you think she may still

be in orbit somewhere in the Bug 17 system, in cryogenic suspension?"

"I'm not prepared to foreclose on the possibility. And if it becomes humanly possible, I *will* return to that system. And if she is alive, I *will* find her. But in the meantime . . . well, you were right, Magda. The very least I can do is try to live up to her exaggerated opinions regarding me."

Early ideas for terraforming Mars had never come to anything; by the time the project had become feasible, no one had been interested because the discovery of warp points had opened up a galaxy full of more promising planets.

So the planetscape in the conference room's viewport was essentially the same dry, ochre one that the first space probes, five and a half centuries earlier, had revealed from orbit. What was new were the space docks, construction facilities and swarming tugs that shared low orbital space with this station, which was the hub of the vast shipbuilding complex that had been located here for its proximity to the asteroid belt and its mineral riches. It was also the hub of Sol's defense network, and Trevayne had preempted it as his headquarters.

At present, his attention was not on the viewport but on the display screen filling the opposite bulkhead. It showed the inner Solar system in conventional fashion, with Sol at the center and the planets at their current positions. Earth was at an eleven o'clock bearing, Mars at five o'clock, at roughly eight and thirteen light-minutes respectively. A necklace of tiny icons around Sol at a twenty-three light-minute radius marked the asteroid belt. Mercury and Venus happened to be at opposition to each other, with both at two o'clock, where they would be irrelevant to what was about to happen. Likewise irrelevant were Jupiter and the other outer planets, which lay outside the area of the display. For at the bottom, at a bearing of about 5:30 and a distance of twenty-nine light-minutes, was the icon of Sol's lone warp point—the "Gateway" warp point, as it was called—through which the Kaituni would come, sooner rather than later. And, crawling about the display, were the green icons of Trevayne's various fleet elements.

He looked around the conference table, a long oval. Unlike *Zeven Provinciën*, this command center had the capability for virtual attendance. So, while his staffers—including Elaine De Mornay and Andreas Hagen, who had reverted to their billets as chief of staff and Intelligence officer—sat around the table in the flesh, his subordinate commanders appeared as holo images. The latter included two of his old national-component commanders from Combined Fleet, Adrian M'Zangwe and Rafaela Shang . . . but not Mario Leong, who had died at Alpha Centauri. Zheng Sha had also died in the system he had been charged with defending, and those elements of the Alpha Centauri Defense Command and the Mothball Fleet that had made good their escape were now integrated into Combined Fleet. So was the Sol Reserve, although in terms of sheer numbers this was almost a case of the tail wagging the dog.

Hagen was delivering an Intelligence briefing—a depressing one, as it dealt mainly with the Kaituni numbers revealed by probe drones. "At the same time," he added, "there has been a curious lack of Kaituni probes into this system. It seems improbable that they're trying to lull us into a false sense of security—under present circumstances, they can hardly think we're likely to fall into that."

"Maybe they just don't want to give us any warning of their attack," Gordon Singhal speculated .

"I think I know the reason," said Trevayne. "Quite simply, they don't think it's necessary. They're taking for granted that this time, for a change, they'll face a warp point defense at point-blank range. And they don't care much about that defense's precise composition. They intend to push through with their heavy assault monitors and module ships and all the rest, following a saturation bombardment with AFHAWKs and stick-hives, trusting to sheer numbers to blast away any conceivable defense."

"Maybe we ought to disappoint them," said the ebon image of M'Zangwe. "Instead of putting anything at the warp point for them to blast, withhold our forces and turn it into a war of movement."

"No," said Trevayne firmly. "I remind everyone: this is *Sol*. The time for running battles and fighting retreats is over. We have nowhere to retreat to. We have no choice but to contest every inch." He paused a moment, letting that dark truth hang heavy in the air, before resuming briskly. "However, I have no intention of putting up a static warp point defense. I plan to exploit the impression I took some pains to implant in their minds at Alpha Centauri, where we kept only a few of the Defense

Commands fortresses. I want them to expect only a few fortresses here as well."

"Whereas in reality," De Mornay put in, "between the fortresses you ordered us to tug from Alpha Centauri to Sol and the tremendous number of them already here, we have a *lot* of fortresses."

"And," said Singhal, beginning to grasp Trevayne's intention, "all of them have tugs slaved to them. And they've all been turned into practically pure long-range missile platforms, with almost everything else ripped out to make room for added magazine capacity."

"Precisely," Trevayne nodded. "Because they won't be expecting many fortresses, and because they think we'll hold our devastators and superdevastators back as we have with complete consistency so far, I believe they will bring in their RAW monitors last. They don't think they'll need them to deal with the fortresses until later because they won't know the fortresses have some limited strategic mobility thanks to the tugs, so they'll expect them to be in static orbits around Old Terra. And they know as well as we do that Sol is a dead-end system, and that Old Terra must be defended. Therefore, they'll expect out DTs and SDTs to fall back and join the fortresses in a last-ditch defense, having nowhere else to go. After which, all they'll have to do is bring in the RAW monitors, get them into range, and administer the *coup de grace*.

"Instead, we're going to deploy the fortresses just inside heavy bombardment missile range of the warp point. The DTs and SDTs will be stationed in gravitic disruptor range." Everyone looked stunned at Trevayne's words except Hugo Allende, whose virtual face lit up with ferocious and long-repressed joy. "They will lay down gee-beam fire for a short time, then fall back to join the fortresses. The two in concert will blanket the warp point with long-range missile fire, while the Kaituni are trying to wade through the close-in automated defenses: the armed asteroids and buoys, and the minefields, both of which we have emplaced in unparalleled density."

Hagen, the most junior officer present but a personal friend of Trevayne, was the first to speak up. "Admiral, aren't you taking a terrifying chance? If you're wrong about the RAW monitors being the last through the warp point—"

"There is an undeniable element of risk. But risk avoidance is a luxury we can no longer afford." Trevayne's dark eyes burned with an intense fire. "I intend to turn the volume of space around that warp point into a kill-zone whose like has never been seen or even imagined.

"Then, as the Kaituni numbers gradually build up, the fortresses and the DTs and SDTs will gradually withdraw, but staying in missile range and keeping up the bombardment, supported by the supermonitors. Obviously, the fortresses will have to set the pace. At the same time, out more mobile forces will close in from the flanks."

"And this time," De Mornay observed with satisfaction, "thanks to the Sol Reserve and Sol's Mothball Fleet, we've got a respectable quantity of those mobile forces, and a lot of fighters."

"So we do," Trevayne acknowledged. "But I want only our lighter carriers deployed outside Sol's Desai Limit. The heavier assault carriers, with most of the fighters, will be withheld, here in the vicinity of Mars, which lies in the path of any Kaituni advance."

"Because the Kaituni won't have the Desai Drive advantage over fighters there," M'Zangwe surmised.

"That is one reason. The other is this. When the RAW monitors *do* come through, I expect them to be under heavy fighter cover—and that means thousands of fighters. I want us to be able to clear a path through that cover."

There was no comment. Everyone knew that their backs were well and truly to the wall. They had come to a pass where defeat was not an option. They also knew it was hard to see any way to avoid it if the RAW monitors could be brought within range of their intended targets.

Trevayne sensed what was in their minds. He smiled slightly. "Ladies and gentlemen, while I was . . . out of commission, people convinced themselves that during the Fringe Revolution, at the Second Battle of Zephrain, I sent a certain signal to the fleet—a quote from history. In fact, when I awoke, I was appalled to see that it was chiseled into the pedestal of the stature of me they'd put up in front of Government House." *Which is now a pile of ruins marking the grave of Miriam Ortega*, he thought, remembering his old lover with a twinge of sorrow. "In reality, I never said it. But it was too late to point that out." Low chuckles ran around the table, for many of these people already knew the story. But then Trevayne turned somber, and his sheer presence seemed to expand to fill the room. "I never said it then. But this time, I *am* going to say it. *Terra expects that every man will do his duty.*"

CHAPTER TWENTY

Ossian Wethermere leaned back with a relieved sigh as the commandeered Kaituni courier drone reappeared on schedule, back through the warp point that led to Alpha Centauri. "So Zum'ref's people believed it was legitimate."

"Apparently so," Ankaht's vocoded voice replied. "But I am not so surprised as you are, Ossian Wethermere." Her voice may have been—coy? Prompting Ossian to wonder: did Arduans really do "coy"?

"Why should I have been so sure of the courier's success? Because it was you who oversaw the creation of its fake messages?"

"Have I not been sufficiently foresightful since this campaign began?"

"Oh, I guess you've been adequate," Ossian tried to deadpan, but then grinned.

Ankaht's main eye half-closed and she uttered what, to a human, would have sounded like an indignant grunt: in an Arduan, this was a chuckle. "You are most generous in your assessment of my abilities," her vocoder teased.

Okay, so Arduans *did* do "coy." "What can I say? I'm kind to a fault." Rising, Wethermere let the bantering tone slip away. "Now, let's find out what the courier's sensors discovered."

"And what it learned by eavesdropping on the secure channels to which we had access, thanks to the codes we found on Kaituni ships," she added. Gesturing that she might go ahead of him, a chivalric gesture that was as utterly alien to Arduans as most of their gestures were to humanity, they left the bridge of *Krishmahnta* to brief the rest of the command staff via secure holo-conference.

"And so," Ankaht explained as she wrapped up her part of the report, "because of the superlative work performed by Senior Group Leader Mretlak and his technical intelligence teams aboard the Kaituni wrecks, the courier drone was not only able to interact convincingly with the pickets guarding the other side of the Alpha Centauri warp point, but was tasked to carry back general updates on the situation in the system."

"Which confirms and details what the courier's own sensors were able to detect, albeit imperfectly," Wethermere added. "If you will note the tactical display we are relaying to your ships,"—he paused to allow the light-speed communication to reach the flagships of Narrok, Kiiraathra'ostakjo, Knight, and Rrurr'rao—"you'll see that Zum'ref has amassed almost ninety percent of his assets at the warp point into the Sol system."

Narrok emitted a hoarse wheeze: an Arduan reaction

signifying amazement and surprise. "He is reckless. That assault formation permits little flexibility of action."

Ankaht's vocoded voice was strong, confident. "Exactly, and there are implicit references in the orders and updates sent to the courier indicating that it is completely intentional. In short, Zum'ref seems to be willing to sustain considerable casualties to impress upon the defenders of Earth that his numbers are so overwhelming, and the outcome of the battle so assured, that he will carry the day by brute force alone."

Knight's holographic image smiled sardonically. "Sounds like someone's ego is in charge of his strategy."

"Indeed it does, Commodore," Ankaht agreed. "This is consistent with what I and the other *shaxzhu* projected: that the more pronounced the *Destoshaz*-as-*sulhaji* cultural dominance became, the more cult of personality and ego would outplace reflection and collective analysis.

"However, Zum'ref is still capable of prudence. He has retained almost the entirety of his RAW assets in a second wave, being held well back from the Sol warp point. They are clustered at the core of a defensive formation, just off the third planet."

"Which is located within twenty-four light-minutes of five of the other warp points in the system," Kiiraathra'ostakjo observed. "Clearly, a trap."

Narrok's image raised one emphatic tendril from either cluster. "If you mean that you suspect that Zum'ref has secreted response forces in several of the systems accessed by those warp points, I concur. So it is fortunate that we have so many stealthed ships at our disposal. We shall at least be able to reach the monitors carrying the relativistic assault weapons before those hidden out-system forces can respond. But after that, we may have a hard fight before us."

"We might," Wethermere agreed. "But if we can bring our various special tactics and advantages to bear upon the RAWs all at once, we may be able to defeat them so swiftly that we can then redeploy to defeat the hidden forces in detail. That would require sending stealthed detachments to some of the closer warp points, to hold them against the anticipated Kaituni ingress." He indicated two of the warp points. "These—the ones to Epsilon Indi and Epsilon Eridani, respectively—are the closest. If we can delay any forces attempting to counterattack through them by at least thirty minutes, I feel confident we will be able to prevent them and any others from mobbing us. Instead, we will knock their groups down one at a time."

"But they may be in only one or two of these systems, Admiral," Rrurr'rao pointed out. "And if it is in neither of the ones you have chosen, they will be able to bring in their full force without having to fight through a defended warp point."

"True, but in that scenario, their counterattack will not be able to reach us until we have reformed from our attack on the main body and the RAWs. And we would then be able to pull in some or all of the detachments we have watching the closer warp points as flanking forces. Lastly, they will not have seen the tactics we used to cripple the RAWs and the ships defending them. Which means we should be able to pull the same trick on the newcomers."

Narrok lowered his tendrils. "We must generate many

contingencies to account for the plenitude of variables which this scenario entails, but I agree with Admiral Wethermere. This battle will entail a set of strategic evolutions as we address one objective after another. If carried out with dispatch and precision, we should enjoy decisive numerical superiority in each of the engagements, to say nothing of the advantages conferred by our special tactics and modest technological edge. But all this presupposes that we can enter Alpha Centauri unseen and position ourselves accordingly before commencing our attack."

Rrurr'rao growled in grim agreement. "How many pickets did the courier detect, Councilor Ankaht?"

"Five, Commodore, although the detachment obligingly updated the probe with the coming changes in that roster. While there are currently three battleships and two cruisers watching the warp point to Bug 15, this will be reduced within the hour. The battleships and one of the cruisers will be pulled away; the remaining cruiser will be joined by a destroyer."

"Still, I don't think 'Sandro is going to be able to commandeer a cruiser," Knight murmured regretfully.

"I agree," Wethermere replied. "But he won't need to. Part of the data that the Kaituni sent back with the courier was a request for three support ships from the auxiliary fleet they left here in Bug 15. Specifically, they require missile tenders to top off their magazines. I propose that we send them through as requested, since we have the necessary models on hand. We captured one in this system and took several nearly identical models from the Kaituni in Bug 27.

"Once the missile tenders make transit, we'll make sure that the tender closest to the destroyer is the one we took here in Bug 15. Said tender will develop engine problems and request assistance. When the destroyer docks to put its technicians aboard, they'll discover that instead of missiles, the tender is carrying 'Sandro and all the Bloodhounds, as well as a full company of Arduans under Temret. The Arduans will be in captured Kaituni gear and should be able to stroll right up to the destroyer's anchor watch before they commence the boarding action. With the same virus disabling the engine and communications that we used on exactly the same class of destroyer in Bug 15, the odds will be even more profoundly on our side, this time."

Rrurr'rao had not moved or blinked during the explanation. "And if the cruiser grows suspicious during the boarding action or afterward?"

"Well, as Commodore Knight said, we'll never be able to seize something as large as a cruiser, anyhow. So one of our tenders will be sent without crew, flying under remote control. It will move to replenish the cruiser's missile magazines, but, at the last second, shall engage its main engines and ram the enemy ship." No one commented: a collision at five percent the speed of light was certain to vaporize both hulls. "The third tender will be carrying fighters—again, Arduan models configured to resemble Kaituni marks—ready to emerge from its replenishment bays to handle any other problems that might arise.

"As soon as the warp point is secured, Commodore Knight's Assault Group Lancelot will enter Alpha Centauri under stealth, the Arduan superdreadnoughts in the lead. With the removal of the pickets, the Kaituni will no longer have any ships close enough to detect transit changes in the warp point. The only craft nearby will be the commandeered destroyer, which, to ensure our freedom of operations, will have reported an apparent explosion in the cruiser's magazine during replenishment. The Kaituni have the same protocols that we do in these situations: to keep uninvolved ships clear until rescue and assessment operations by on-site craft have been completed. We'll obviously have the destroyer conduct a very thorough, very long, assessment.

"In the meantime, Assault Group Lancelot will maintain stealth and make for the warp point to Sol. It will stand off at five light-minutes from that destination until Zum'ref's main assault wave has finished transiting, and then take up a close flanking position, preparatory to sealing the warp point against egress and ingress."

Kiiraathra passed a hand sideways along his face, smoothing back a stray whisker. "So, a close copy of the strategy we used in Bug 15."

"Nearly an exact copy, so far as controlling the key warp points are concerned. But the similarities end there. Alpha Centauri has seven warp points, not counting the ones to Earth and Bug 15. The reports the Kaituni kindly uploaded to the courier indicate that Admiral Trevayne used those as bolt-holes for combat elements that he then sprung on Zum'ref during the battle, prolonging the engagement and giving the Kaituni both a few extra bloody noses and some real maneuver headaches. We have to be prepared for the enemy to pull the same trick on us.

"In order to trump those unexpected moves with unexpected moves of our own, we need to keep the majority of our fleet assets stealthed. In short, if they try to surprise us, we're going to have a surprise for them. But we have to accept that Alpha Centauri is going to be crawling with their sensor platforms, some probably set for passive scanning only and too small for us to detect unless and until they go active. That means that whereas in earlier battles we could remain both unexpected and unobserved until we commenced overt action, that will not be the case in Alpha Centauri. The moment we bring in a ship that is neither stealthed nor cloaked, we have to assume that the Kaituni will detect it and start to respond."

Narrok's image turned toward Ankaht. "Councilor, do the updates sent to the courier indicate when Zum'ref plans to commence his attack?"

"Not precisely, Admiral, but some of the coded communiqués we intercepted do mention a time by which all assets must be in place and ready: about five hours from now. Of course, this may not mark the beginning of the attack, but merely a deadline for preparedness."

"True, but it is unlikely that the actual jump-off time will be more than an hour after that: it is exhausting to any crew to remain poised to attack for too long. Admiral Wethermere, I understand that your staff has been calculating the probable time it will take the whole of Zum'ref's assault force to move through the warp point. Do you have a concrete number of hours?"

"We have an estimate, Admiral—and for all we know, Zum'ref may have his forces timed to arrive in the Sol system in waves. However, we estimate that, using maximum safe transit rates, it will take about nine to ten hours for his entire force to enter the Sol system."

"I do not believe there will be multiple, timed waves," Ankaht added. "The nuances in all the communications relevant to the attack convey the same subtextual impression of maximum, unrelenting assault, of generating an appearance of a virtually endless stream of craft so as to dishearten the defenders. Zum'ref has forsaken guile for directness, and I believe he perceives RAWs and the ships with them as a decisive reserve."

Kiiraathra sat more erect. "They are that and a final line breaker. Trevayne has only so many strategic and tactical options and Zum'ref knows this. He will therefore press whatever defensive line he finds, which will inevitably have its foundation in the forts and devastators in the system. The combat will inexorably force the outnumbered, smaller defenders back upon those less maneuverable hard points. And when that has occurred, Zum'ref will bring in the RAWs with a significant escort of fresh capital ships and carriers to finish the job. The RAWs will destroy those large targets and so Trevayne's line will crack and the battle will be lost."

"Unless those RAWs don't show up at the appointed time," finished Wethermere.

"Indeed," emphasized Rrurr'rao. "And there are those who believe that the elimination of the RAWs is so crucial that this waiting risks missing them: that they might move out before we can arrive."

Wethermere smiled. "Zum'ref won't move them until he's well into his attack. Given where the RAWs are being held, it will take them time to get to the Sol warp point. By that time, we'll have secured the other side of the Bug 15 warp point and Assault Group Lancelot will be half way to plugging their objective—the gateway to Sol—and sealing the RAWs in at Alpha Centauri.

"On the other hand, if we just raced through the warp point with guns blazing, we'd miss the RAWs for sure. Look at the plot of Alpha Centauri: our warp point is at the one o'clock position; the warp point to Sol is at the eight o'clock position. There's no way we can make an assault entry and catch them in time. They have only half the distance to travel that we do, and we aren't twice as fast as they are. The math is inescapable; lots of them will get through the warp point before we can stop them. And that's the *best* case scenario for a direct attack."

Rrurr'rao nodded solemnly, even respectfully. "I know this, Admiral. You do not need to convince *me*."

Ah. "So you're talking about the Relief Fleet's human crews?"

"You have heard, then?"

"I've heard them from the start, from before Bug 27. 'Why aren't we pushing forward as fast as we can to reach Earth and defend it?' And at several steps, Admiral Miharu and I shared the basic strategy with them: that when you're outgunned and outnumbered, you can't go toe-to-toe with your opponent. You'll get your head handed to you. And then where would our fine rescue attempt be? Squandered back in Bug 27, or here, or maybe now in Alpha Centauri.

"But we don't have the time for further explanations and I am not inclined to give them if we did. They're soldiers and combat crewpersons, and they'll take their orders. And once they're fighting, they'll care less about the whys and wherefores. And if some still do care, then they are entitled to their opinion—but not to an argument. This is not a democracy."

Rrurr'rao's nod was even slower this time. "But what if some do insist on arguing . . . or disobeying?"

Wethermere's response was out of his mouth with the speed of a muscular reflex: he had thought through this very question in the preceding weeks. "Then they'll be tried for mutiny and shot. If there's time for a trial, that is. This is not a peace-time navy, with all the measured responses that implies. We are at war and eternally at, or on the brink of, general quarters. We cannot—and I will not—tolerate any discord in the face of the enemy." He looked at Knight. "I presume you are of a like mind on this matter, Commodore?"

"Admiral," mumbled Knight, "even if we had a *selnarm* link between us, we couldn't be more of the same mind."

Wethermere nodded, glanced back at Rrurr'rao. "Does this answer your concerns, Commodore?"

The Orion raised his chin, nodded once. "It is the answer I was hoping for—and it was spoken as a warrior would speak it." He turned to glance at Narrok. "And among your Arduans, Admiral: is there no regret at killing so many of their siblings? No danger from hesitation or reluctance?"

Narrok aligned his tendrils and tentacles so that they all laid in neat, parallel lines. "Some regret remains among my crews, of course, but it is much diminished since we started taking more of the Kaituni prisoner."

Knight frowned. "I'd expect the opposite: that given close proximity, fellow feeling would increase sympathy."

"That is because you project human behavior onto us, Commodore," Ankaht said gently. "Bear in mind that our *selnarm* allows us to see far more deeply into each other. And what we have seen in the Kaituni is our own worst self-image: of our brutal, primitive origins. For all their technology, the Kaituni have devolved, regressed into savagery that doubts the value of *narmata*, questions the need to learn from past lives, places little value on learning itself. If they are not stopped, they would contaminate our true Arduan culture beyond cleansing. They would surely deafen us to the voice of Illudor, which arises through our *selnarm* and speaks to us from beyond the boundaries of time because *shaxzhutok* allows us to witness how His wisdom guided us throughout our history."

Two of Ankaht's tendrils swayed despairingly. "We do not discarnate the Kaituni prisoners who resist appeals to return to our community, to behold the face of Illudor as he is preserved in our memories and present experience. But nor do we have any choice but to isolate them. Contact with them is inherently unsafe—for anyone, of any race.

"That said," Ankaht concluded, "we will nonetheless grieve mightily to be the instruments whereby so many of our genetic kin shall be discarnated. Indeed, I know that some of us are already deeply troubled by our upcoming role in this final battle . . ."

CHAPTER TWENTY-ONE

Mretlak approached the secure lab knowing that he could not disguise his heaviness of spirit, the regret that suffused every iota of his *selnarmic* self. As he entered, he could feel Lentsul defensively shut his own *selnarm* down to a narrow aperture, evidently recoiling from the misery he felt emanating from his superior. The small *Ixturshaz* cautiously sent, "So, what you feared has come to pass?"

Mretlak (confirmed) Lentsul's conjecture, made his way to the primary *selnarmic* relays in the laboratory's master control pod. "It has. We cannot take the risk of merely trying to incapacitate the Kaituni fleet; we must destroy it."

"Did you try to convince them otherwise?"

Mretlak slumped into the pod, activated the communication router. With an undercurrent of (resignation), he sent, "There was no point to it, Lentsul. The admirals had already made their decision by the time that Councilor Ankaht informed me. Prepare to transmit the activation code." Mretlak began the many-tiered process that proved to the security software that he was indeed clearing the entirety of the Turncoat viral suite for access—in this case, to send it to all the Arduan and commandeered Kaituni vessels in the Relief Fleet. Within minutes, every one of them would become the most decisive electronic—well, *selnarmic*—warfare platforms in the collective history of all the known races.

Lentsul stood far to one side so that, according to protocol, he could not see the code characters that Mretlak was entering in response to the various security prompts: a *selnarmic* check routine would have further enhanced security but, understandably, none of the other races were comfortable with the creation of a clearance protocol system that their own personnel could not pass independently. The *Ixturshaz* wondered with overtones of (disappointment), "And did you not try to change Ankaht's opinion, even at this final hour?"

"When I say it was pointless to attempt to sway her, I mean that I myself can see no alternative to what the admirals have decided upon. The Kaituni are too numerous, and may have too many possible gambits, for our control of the situation to be assured. We will have to fight a battle of several stages, and failure at any one of them could be disastrous to those which follow. So we must be sure of decisive victory at every stage. And to be assured of that, we cannot afford the time nor the risk of asking for surrenders which the enemy might accept merely as subterfuges to enable later treachery. And we do not have the numbers to adequately police thousands of prisoners and their ships. Our attack would fall apart under the weight of such a challenge. No, our only reasonable path is to leave nothing unresolved in our wake, to move from victory to victory with no encumbrance upon our further actions." He finished entering the security protocols, accessed the final version of the Turncoat suite, entered the subroutine that would allow him to remove the codes which kept it from being activated.

"This outcome gives you great pain, doesn't it, Senior Group Leader?" asked Lentsul.

"It most surely does," Mretlak replied, noting the whisper of a pneumatic discharge as he did so—after which he discovered he could no longer move and could no longer feel anything beneath his neck.

Lentsul moved into his field of view; he held a pioneer tranqdart gun, the kind for controlling wildlife, in his left cluster. Peripherally, Mretlak saw a dart protruding from his own right arm. "Then I shall relieve you of the need to feel that pain. Or any other," Lentsul sent, approaching and shoving Mretlak out of the control pod. He looked at the computer panel, emitted a rush of (annoyance) when he realized that its software had locked up.

Mretlak wondered if the tranquilizer was affecting his coronary sacs or if he was instead feeling an emotional stab in response to Lentsul's treachery. "You are too late. The system is set to automatically discontinue after a short period of disuse," he sent helplessly.

"Yes, I know," Lentsul replied. He gestured to one of the data screens in the room. "That is why I rigged a camera behind that screen: to make a recording of the code you just entered. But now I will have to go through the trouble of entering it all over again."

"So that you may do what?"

"Is it not obvious? To access the Turncoat virus and insert several fatal flaws that will not be discovered until our units attempt to activate it. With that lynchpin of the Relief Fleet's current strategy removed, it will not be able to succeed—not as completely as it needs to."

"But—why?"

Lentsul paused at the midpoint of entering the code, just long enough to glance at Mretlak. "To do what you apparently could not bring yourself to do: to save our people." Feeling the wave of (bafflement) flooding out of his superior, he explicated, "Do you not remember our conversation of only a few days ago, upon learning that this outcome was likely? I said then, 'We all have jobs to perform. We all do what we must.' And so I am. Right now. I am saving our people from eventual extinction."

"No. You are *killing* your people, Lentsul. The Kaituni are no longer Arduans. They will destroy us along with the other races. And the voice of Illudor will then be forever silent, for they have forsaken His face and His words. If they triumph, they will sweep away the last vestige of what we truly are."

Lentsul resumed entering the codes. "I see a different outcome. If the Kaituni triumph and thereby eliminate the threats that have faced our race since we arrived in this region of space, then it is likely they will have no cause to remain so fearful and warlike. Perhaps the pervasive use of *selnarm* will undergo a resurgence among them, and following that, a return to *narmata* and the voice of Illudor. In that world—into which we will both be reborn,

Mretlak—our people will no longer be compelled to exist at the pleasure of semi-sapient races. And so, the true Arduan race will be rehabilitated over time. And for us, brother, time—and therefore death—is but a little thing," he finished, reciting the ancient axiom. "So when I am done here, and must discarnate you, do not think too harshly of me. And be assured that, when we have both returned to life, you will thank me for doing what you could not, even though you are *Destoshaz* and I am but *Ixturshaz*." Lentsul's tone was sincere, and yet nursed a fierce, intimate satisfaction in the caste role-reversal that he perceived himself enacting.

The door to the secure laboratory opened. Lentsul started. Mretlak felt his sudden pulse of fear and discerned the reason through his briefly unguarded *selnarm*: just after Mretlak had entered, the *Ixturshaz* had surreptitiously command-locked the door against just such intrusions.

Although Mretlak could not turn to see who had entered, he felt a strong, unmistakable *selnarmic* presence. Ankaht's send to Lentsul was gentle but firm. "Exit the command pod, Lentsul."

"Councilor, I—"

"You are not the only one who plans for unusual contingencies, Lentsul. I have had this room under remote observation for some weeks now. I had wondered why you emplaced the camera, feared it might be for some purpose akin to this."

Lentsul rose carefully from the pod.

Ankaht's order was no longer so gentle. "You will keep your clusters raised and tentacles spread." She advanced into the room where Mretlak could see her: she held one of the Kaituni handguns that fired explosive shells.

Lentsul stared at her. "Eight years ago, Councilor, it was I who held a gun which might or might not have started our race down the path to oblivion. I dropped it because your words swayed me. Will you drop yours now, if I sway you with my words?"

"I know your words already, Lentsul. You may have closed your mind to me—to all your brothers and sisters—but Mretlak remains one with us. After sharing the admirals' judgment, I followed him with my *selnarm*, through the small tendril that joins just the two of us in the vastness of our race's *narmata*. It is a slender link, but it was enough for me to have perceived what you told him in these last few minutes."

"So I was wrong to show mercy to the humans on Bellerophon. And wrong to show mercy to you."

"You may think so, but you are mistaken. Mretlak is right; what you have planned to do will kill us as a race. Our genes will persevere, but carried only by a race even more primitive than the aliens which you have always despised and which, in your inner heart, you cannot bear to tolerate."

"It is not possible that we would slip and fall to such depths as they inevitably inhabit."

"Again, you are wrong. Think, Lentsul; if the alien races are so primitive as you think, why have they not annihilated each other, once and for all, by now?"

"No doubt you shall enlighten me."

"I shall, in the hope that you will hear reason and step away from those controls. These beings you consider 'savages' persist because they have evolved the means—personal and social—to rise above their worst impulses often and long enough to build the societies you have lived among for the past eight years. They have long experience with how to mitigate their destructive instincts without the benefit of *selnarm*, or of oneness in *narmata*.

"But the Kaituni have no such experience. They have largely turned their back on the true, social purposes of *selnarm*, but have evolved nothing that replaces it as a means of keeping our race together as a peaceful community. The humans and others have climbed up out of savagery step by bloody step—and if they stumble, they may catch themselves at a lower place and retrace their path, may eventually regain what they periodically lose. But the Kaituni have no handholds, no ledges, of prior experience on which they may catch themselves as they fall. They are hurtling down a smooth chute that will end in primordial internecine strife—once they have completed their current obsession with xenophobic genocide."

Lentsul's response was undergirded by an ironic mix of (dismissal, anxiety). "And yet you would use the *selnarm* you tout so highly—the very connection that makes us what we are—to undo ninety-seven percent of our race, to make *them* the victims of genocide."

Ankaht's response was calm. "If anyone opened the furnace door of genocide, it is the Kaituni themselves, Lentsul."

"That does not matter: they are our people. Or at least,"—he stiffened—"they are mine."

"Yes," reflected Ankaht sadly, "I suppose they are. And

you will be free to exist among them. Just as soon as you step away from that control pod."

Lentsul's limbs gyrated slightly—an Arduan shrug—and he stepped away from the control pod.

But as he did, Mretlak could feel him emit a *selnarm* pulse, aimed at a control circuit which he had not known was in the chamber, and which he could read, in Lentsul's panic, as the activation switch for a suppressive gas canister—

Ankaht lowered the pistol so that it was pointed a few centimeters below Lentul's center of mass and shot the squat *Ixturshaz* three times. The first hit's explosion caused an eruption of blood, flesh, and organs: had probably killed Lentsul outright. *But,* Ankaht reasoned sadly at the edge of Mretlak's *selnarmic* sensitivity, *so dark a deed, if done at all, were best done surely.*

Mretlak reached out to her, *selnarmically* pulsing that she must shut down Turncoat's access system, that Lentsul might have co-conspirators, that the virus must not be activated until they could secure it, and to not waste time trying to find an antidote for the possibly lethal tranquilizer in him. After all, death was but a little thing—

Ankaht's response was wry, if anything. "Firstly, good Mretlak, we are quite secure, here. Ten of my personal guard followed me to your facility, and have sealed off this laboratory. And you are in no danger of death: the neurotoxin is a variety that only immobilizes. I could *shotan* that Lentsul was not only concerned about how to kill you once I had entered the room, but he was also perturbed by having to discarnate you at all. Despite the

depth of blame he placed upon you, he was as fond of you
as of any being that he ever met."

"But why did you come in alone? If you had ten
guards—"

"Ten guards are ten witnesses, ten stories that should
not be told—some of which might have been released into
our *narmata* in an unguarded moment. No, what I feared
might transpire in this room had to be kept quiet.
Lentsul's hatred, and his plan, had to be suppressed, had
to disappear without a trace." She propped Mretlak up.
"You understand?"

"Of course. If the humans ever learned of this, they
would know how perilously close they came to having just
one of our number manipulating *selnarm* to secure their
downfall, rather than their safety."

"Yes, that too. But there is also the matter of our own
people. How many harbor reservations such as Lentsul's,
simply not so strong, or simply without the ability to act
upon them? We cannot know—and so we cannot risk
having them inspired to follow him in this misguided
attempt to save us.

"If that were to happen, then our hope to rehabilitate
our race, to return it to *narmata* and the face of Illudor,
would not end with this battle. It would require that we
turn upon our own people. And would destroy us, our
trust in each other and our shared *narmata*, just as surely
as what Lentsul hoped to achieve here."

Mretlak tried to move his head, discovered that he
couldn't. "When you call your guards, get one of them to
take a sample of whatever toxin is in the darts of his gun
and discern precisely which antidote is required."

"Such haste," Ankaht observed. "Why?"

"Because as hateful a weapon as Turncoat is, I must be able to resume my work—to finish sending it to the rest of the fleet."

Ankaht sent (affirmation). "Yes. The time is short. Here: let me help you up . . ."

PART FOUR
The Seals Are Broken

CHAPTER TWENTY-TWO

Zum'ref commanded himself not to be overcome by intoxication at the spectacle of the combined fleets of seven dispersates—minus the losses one of them had incurred at Alpha Centauri, of course—arrayed for the attack.

It was *his*. His was the might of the countless millions of tons of hull. His was the inconceivable energies that lay chained in all those powerplants. His was the awful devastation slumbering in innumerable weapons—including the RAW, the ultimate weapon of the ages. All was simply the extension of himself, of his own unstoppable will. It was beyond any of the magical powers that his primitive ancestors had imagined their gods had possessed.

Is even Illudor truly my peer? he dared ask himself in the innermost privacy of his thoughts. It was not yet time to publicly unveil the . . . religious reforms he intended, giving himself the place he deserved in the Kaituni's worship.

The work of organizing this colossal fleet for an offensive through the bottleneck of a warp point had been almost overwhelming. It had so absorbed him that he had, for now, largely ignored the twin inhabited planets. Not altogether, of course; he had detached a swarm of lighter ships to destroy every spacecraft the local humans possessed. They had then crisscrossed the skies of the two planets, systematically smashing every spacefield, every military installation, every manufacturing center, every governmental headquarters, every major power generation facility and every transportation hub, leaving the humans of those planets as impotent spectators, desperately trying to stay alive amid the collapse of their highly advanced and therefore vulnerable civilized infrastructure. They could be dealt with later, at his leisure. And of course the various outposts and mining stations in the system were irrelevant, as was the terraforming operation in the system of Alpha Centauri's secondary component star.

A brief cloud passed across his mind. Amunsit wouldn't have approved. She would have made it her first priority to singlemindedly hunt down and exterminate every last *griarfeksh* in the system, and any Arduan traitors of the First Dispersate who might be present. It was, he reflected, just as well that she was far away at Zephrain, guarding against the possibility of an offensive by the enemy forces gathering at Bellerophon. Her zealotry had its uses, but she tended to let it dictate her strategy. She lacked, he thought complacently, his own rare and perfect gift for distinguishing between means and ends.

Inzrep'fel approached diffidently, her *selnarm* carefully

masked. "All elements have reported themselves ready, *Destoshaz'at*."

"Does that include the elements stationed in the systems with warp connections to this one?" Zum'ref had dispatched covering forces through those of Alpha Centauri's warp points Trevayne had used as bolt-holes. It was an elementary precaution, and a fairly minor deduction from the multitudes of ships he commanded.

"Yes, *Destoshaz'at*. They are all in position."

"Good." Zum'ref continued to gaze at the tactical display showing the disposition of his forces. For a "tactical" display, it was of exceptional scale, to encompass those ranks and ranks of ships, stacked element behind element back from the warp point with the RAW monitors in the rear together with the carriers bearing their prodigious fighter escort, and finally the logistics train. Once the assault began, they would be committed to the original plan, whatever happened. The sheer momentum of such a multitude of ships, which would surely crush through any possible defense, would also preclude any *ad hoc* changes in the order of advance.

"Ah . . . pardon me, *Destoshaz'at*," Inzrep'fel broke in on his thoughts. "Certain of the subordinate commanders have asked me to express to you—with utmost respect, of course—their concern over our lack of probing of the Solar system."

Zum'ref's *selnarm* flared in a spurt of (anger). How dare this ignominious underling spoil his, Zum'ref's, transcendent moment! He started to demand the names of the cowards and whiners who had spoken thus to the Intendent, but he checked himself. Any disciplinary action against high-ranking personnel was out of the question at this time, with action imminent. Later, of course . . . But for now, he merely addressed Inzrep'fel, choosing as he generally did to speak aloud, with *selnarm* as a mere adjunct. It lent increased emphasis, with the strength of its primitive harshness, and proclaimed the Kaituni rejection of *shaxzhu* domination and its attendant softness and decadence.

"As I have previously indicated," he began, in a soft, almost purring tone which chilled Inzrep'fel's blood, "it is not necessary. We know approximately what the *griarfeksh* will do—they have run out of options. That is why we have set our SBMHAWKs with a narrow range of prioritized targets, notably whatever fortresses may have been emplaced. But," he continued, and his voice gradually rose and his *selnarm* gradually intensified, "there is more. I don't *want* any tactical finesse! I want to make very clear that we don't need it—that we disdain it. Cleverness can always be countered by greater cleverness, so one defeated by a clever enemy still has room for hope. But the *griarfeksh* will know in the pits of their stomachs that our sheer power will overcome any obstacle they can devise, and they will know total hopelessness and despair." (Tightly controlled rage.) "Do you understand? DO YOU UNDERSTAND?"

(Empathic groveling.) "Yes, *Destoshaz'at*! I bow before your genius!"

"Good." (Mollified indulgence.) "And besides . . . the *griarfeksh* don't even know of the final surprise we have in store for them do they?"

(Grim satisfaction.) "No, *Destoshaz'at*, they do not."

"Very well then." Zum'ref drew a deep breath. "Transmit the order to initiate transit."

The order was passed. For the first time in all history, a hostile force entered the Solar system.

First came the *Urret-fah'ah*—clusters of clearing charges designed to sweep the volume of space immediately surrounding a warp point clear of mines and laser buoys. This was pure extravagance, as the Kaituni knew that the humans knew of them and therefore would emplace their area-denial ordinance further back from the warp point—and so it proved.

Next came a myriad of SBMHAWKs, vomiting missiles programmed to target fortresses. They were *not* programmed to target devastators and superdevastators, which the humans had so consistently held far back in all the systems through which they had retreated to date. And the sheer, unanticipated number of fortresses confused the tiny targeting brains, diluting the intended concentration of fire and allowing the fortresses' antimissile systems to cope with the sleet of missiles.

Then came the initial wave of ships, in transits almost suicidally closely spaced. It was a mixed force, mostly the heavy warp-point-assault monitors, their mass disproportionately devoted to armor and shields, but also including the great framework hulls that were nothing but self-propelled grids of disposable one-shot missile bays designed to belch a single tremendous volley of heavy missiles on *selnarmic* command and die. There were also the modular clusters of defensive-fire dreadnoughts, designed purely to counter the defenders' missile fire. In short, it was a force composition intended to deal with whatever defensive mix might be encountered.

It didn't.

Commodore Hugo Allende's face wore an expression of fierce eagerness.

Even since Admiral Trevayne had put him in command of Combined Fleet's DTs and SDTs, his duty had boiled down to avoiding battle. Time after time, with gritted teeth and clenched guts, he had obeyed orders to keep his massive charges far back, beyond any possibility of being brought within the range of the RAW monitors, hovering close enough to exit warp points to be assured of an escape despite their slowness. But now, at long last, there could be no further retreating and he was being allowed to use those magnificent ships as they were meant to be used.

In a voice almost crooning with unholy exultation, he gave the order to commence gravitic disrupter fire.

The power of the "gee beam" decreased with distance, out to an extreme range of twenty-five light-seconds. But that power was linked to the engine power of the ship that mounted it. The titanic power plants of the DTs and SDTs sent out space-distorting beams of force that wrenched and twisted and eviscerated Kaituni ships. From further back came a tsunami of heavy bombardment missiles, lavishly expended from the enlarged magazines of the tugged fortresses.

The first Kaituni wave was simply volatilized. Subsequent ones fared little better, but eventually a trickle of their ships survived and the total of those survivors gradually built up.

After the invaders' hull density around the warp reached a certain point, Allende reluctantly withdrew his command and joined the fortresses, to whose missile-storm they added that of their own batteries. And now the Kaituni entered the dense fields of mines—sleeper missiles, really—and came within range of the multitudes of buoys and space-rocks that bore the weapons the Mothball Fleet had given up. It was the kill-zone that Ian Trevayne had sought to create, and the advance wilted in it.

The Kaituni launched fighters as rapidly as they could. But the ranks of fortresses were interlarded with escorting cruisers armed with energy torpedoes—the plasma weapon that was fired as a ballistic projectile at lightspeed and with the range of the old standard missiles it had rendered obsolete. Now these weapons were employed in anti-fighter mode, and so far not enough Kaituni ships were lasting sufficiently long in that inferno to launch the numbers of fighters necessary to overload the defense.

Waves of conventional Kaituni ships were now coming through a warp point that was like the door to a superheated oven, and were being incinerated.

Ian Trevayne had never forgotten the American writer F. Scott Fitzgerald's chilling description of the offensive Trevayne's own British ancestors had launched at the Somme, a little over six centuries earlier in World War I: "A whole empire walking very slowly, dying in front and pushing forward behind."

Now he was reminded of it anew. There was something soul-shaking about watching anyone, even an implacable enemy, behave as the Kaituni were behaving. As though insensible to the ghastly losses they were sustaining, they continued their stolid advance in the horribly inexorable way that had appalled an earlier generation of humans when the Bugs had come on like an unfeeling, nonsentient force of nature. But this was far worse, for the Bugs *were* an unfeeling, nonsentient force of nature (at least as regards their individual units). Arduans, even the Kaituni, were self-aware individuals.

But, he reminded himself, they were self-aware individuals who believed—no, who *knew*, with a certitude beyond that of any religious believer in human history—that death was merely a temporary inconvenience.

He also reminded himself that they had the numbers to waste.

Andreas Hagen approached. "Admiral, hostile hull density in the vicinity of the warp point is now at the second stage."

Trevayne nodded somberly. The stages of accumulated Kaituni tonnage had been calculated in advance with great care. The first stage had been that at which the DTs and SDTs had ceased their gee-beam engagement and pulled back to join the fortresses, because the invading ships had begun to transit slightly faster than they could be obliterated. And now, despite all the carnage, a second tipping point had been reached. Hagen didn't need to remind him of what that meant.

"Very well." Trevayne turned to Elaine De Mornay, who had been watching the readouts and sharing his own horrified fascination. "It's time to initiate the next phase of the contingency plan."

Orders flashed across space, and the fortresses and

Allende's command began to sullenly pull back at the slow pace dictated by the former's slaved tugs. As they did, they continued to pour out heavy bombardment missiles which, looping about in their nightmarish way, sought out their targets with grim persistence. Monitor-sized Kaituni ships continued to advance through a stroboscopic region of antimatter annihilation where nothing less heavily armored and shielded than themselves could have lived. And a great many of *them* didn't live. But now they were emerging from the warp point at a significantly faster rate than they could be destroyed.

Zum'ref's staffers shrank back from the tendrils of searing *selnarm* that seeped past his iron control as he bent his lambent central eye upon the reports.

He had never anticipated that the human (privately, he permitted himself the word) admiral would position his DTs and SDTs so close to the warp point. He now knew he should have anticipated it, although of course he would kill any underling who dared to point that out. After all, Trevayne had come to the end of his retreat, and had nothing to lose. Besides which, it was in character for him to do the unexpected rather than doggedly following the ruts of established practice.

And, as Zum'ref had known from the first, it was out of the question to try to re-order his mammoth fleet in mid-advance to get the RAW monitors into Solar space any sooner than the plan called for. One might as well try to reorganize an avalanche.

He had also failed to anticipate the sheer number of fortresses, and their limited but real tactical mobility. (The lack of preparatory probing, he thought grimly, was something else none of the staffers had better mention.) Clearly, they must represent most of Alpha Centauri's fortress complement as well as all of Sol's, and the limited number they had encountered at Alpha Centauri had created a false impression—doubtless something else Trevayne had intended.

Zum'ref forced composure on himself. It was, he told himself, just as well that the RAW monitors hadn't been part of the first waves, which had died faster than many DTs and SDTs could have been targeted. And those mammoth ships were, in the long run, trapped in the dead-end system of Sol, and would be hunted down. It was obviously going to take longer, and cost more, than expected. But that changed nothing in the long run.

And, of course, Trevayne doesn't know what I know. At the pleasurable thought, his *selnarmic* emanations mellowed so markedly as to draw a quizzical glance from Inzrep'fel.

"Trevayne fancies himself the master of the unexpected," Zum'ref said, as much to himself as to the Intendent. "He has *no* idea!"

"Attention on deck!"

Ian Trevayne barely noticed. He wore a gravely distracted expression as he entered *Zeven Provinciën*'s flag bridge, followed by his staffers. He didn't even experience his usual instant of wry amusement at the irony of his flag (strictly speaking, his lights) flying from a ship whose namesake was the flagship of Michel Adriaanszoon de Ruyter, one of his own hero Horatio

Nelson's very few serious rivals for the title of Old Terra's greatest wet-navy fighting admiral. There was no room in his mind for anything but the climactic battle he was fighting, and the point it had now reached.

He had come back aboard his flagship because he was about to lead the assault carriers away from Mars, out to a point just inside Sol's Desai limit, where the fighters could operate to best advantage. It was no longer possible to realistically hope that the Kaituni could be stopped short of that.

They had, by a supreme effort, brought the invaders to another temporary halt, when the supermonitors had merged with the gradually withdrawing fortresses and the DTs and SDTs and added their firepower to the missile-storm at the same time that Combined Fleet's more mobile units had closed in and commenced their slashing attacks at energy torpedo range. They had lacerated the Kaituni flanks, aided by the fact that they'd had to deal with less fighter opposition than either Andreas Hagen or Gordon Singhal had expected. Trevayne was fairly certain he knew why that was: the enemy admiral was keeping the bulk of his carrier assets back, to provide a prodigious fighter cover for the RAW monitors when they finally appeared. But for now, it had enabled the fighters of the light carrier formations escorting the heavy missile line of battle, however depleted and weary they were by now, to deal with even their *selnarm*-controlled opponents.

He had been particularly proud of the Orions among those pilots. He knew of the undercurrents of resentment among some of their race. And, at any rate, this was not their home system. But they were still bound by the honor code of *Theernowlus*, and they had much to avenge.

But the pressure of the seemingly limitless columns of ships continuing to pour from the warp point had built up again, and the slow, stubborn withdrawal had resumed. By now it was halfway to the asteroid belt, and Trevayne saw no hope of stopping it short of that. Nor of halting it there, however densely he had strewn the belt with robotically controlled weapons.

And, sooner rather than later, the RAW monitors would materialize. And the giant missile platforms that had enabled them to hold out so far would be doomed.

As he settled into his chair, he ran his eyes over a series of displays showing views from various elements of Sol's defenses. Reluctantly, but unable to resist, he gazed at the one showing a view from Earth's primary orbital station, in geostationary orbit 22,000 mile above the surface, so the whole of mankind's cradle was visible.

He could make out some of the storied continental outlines. But what he really saw in that heartbreakingly lovely blue-and-white sphere was the face of a little girl with enormous, innocent almond eyes.

CHAPTER TWENTY-THREE

When the lead elements of the Relief Fleet entered Alpha Centauri, they passed the remains of not one, but two Kaituni cruisers. True to the military adage that no plan survives first contact with the enemy, there had either been an error in the Kaituni notification of the changed patrol composition or that the higher command echelons had changed their mind and left both cruisers behind.

Fortunately, a contingency had been created for that eventuality as well. After signaling that his missile tender was experiencing engine troubles, Temret—assuming the role of the Kaituni ship's commanding officer—indicated that he would be summoning a fourth missile tender. The rationale—that the stricken one's drive coils might be compromised, in which case it would be imprudent to bring so important a ship as a cruiser alongside—was consistent with operational protocol. And so it was not merely acceptable but completely expected when he sent a courier drone back into Bug 15 to summon a replacement craft, just before the smaller (which was to say expendable) patrol hull, the destroyer, docked to assist Temret's own "disabled" missile tender.

What occurred next had not been rehearsed, but had the virtue of being a simple plan that was as easy to execute as it was in concept. As soon as Temret's courier drone had winked out of existence through the warp point, the remote controlled missile tender accelerated to subrelativistic velocities when it was only one hundred fifteen kilometers away from the cruiser. It collided with the much larger enemy vessel before the Kaituni sensors even had time to relay their detection of the missile tender's main engines coming on-line, thereby violating the navigation protocol which stipulated that such craft use only close-maneuver thrusters to effect a hard-dock. The two ships' mutual destruction was instantaneous.

However, this event did not have the convincing appearance of a mishap, which had been the intent of the original ploy to approach to within a few kilometers, and thereby create a confusing sensor picture of the event. Predictably the first cruiser came about, charging weapons, while asking hard and pointed questions of the remaining two missile tenders—and was further dismayed to realize that the destroyer docked with one of them was no longer responding to hails.

It was in the midst of this rush of responses to the evolving situation that the cruiser's sensor officer sent her commander a *selnarmic* warning: there had been a warp transit signature the very moment of the collision. All these events taking place within the space of three seconds would have perturbed the most seasoned commander in Zum'ref's armada, but the young zealot in charge of the cruiser was relatively inexperienced and spent two crucial seconds trying to make sense of how all these occurrences might be related—and paid for that moment of indecision with his life, his ship, and his crew. A stealthed Arduan heavy superdreadnought, which had always been standing by in Bug 15 to cope with such unanticipated complications, had made its transit at the same instant as the collision. It now emerged from stealth and vaporized the cruiser with a spread of high-yield missiles. It then sent a courier back through the warp point bearing the awaited word: the gate to Alpha Centauri was open.

However, open was not quite synonymous with "clear." As expected, the destruction of two cruisers attracted the pointed attention of the system's security forces, which demanded an account of the occurrence. The sole surviving component of the warp point's security contingent—the destroyer now held by Temret and Alessandro Magee—reported that there had been some unknown mishap during the missile replenishment of one cruiser. The other had moved to assist but had been mysteriously destroyed as well. The prevailing hypothesis was that the missile tender, which also carried other physical munitions, had lost control of several mines and that the second cruiser, while drawing near, had triggered one of these.

The Kaituni found this explanation highly unlikely. Temret's *shaxzhu* specialists, one playing the part of the destroyer's commander, readily agreed with their assessment. He enthusiastically welcomed the news that

the three battleships that had left the contingent were
now being tasked to return to their prior station, both to
protect the warp point and conduct a thorough
investigation. Given the speed—even relief—with which
the destroyer's "commander" agreed, further enemy
suspicion was largely diverted: the matter became more
of a nuisance. That it was much more than a nuisance
would ultimately become evident to the three battleships
when, within several hours, they would be intercepted by
the main body of the Relief Fleet. But before then,
Assault Group Lancelot completed its entrance into Alpha
Centauri and moved with dispatch to complete the special
mission which fell to it, due both to the speed and stealth
of its smaller capital ships.

Indeed, by the time half the Relief Fleet had followed
it into Alpha Centauri, Assault Group Lancelot was
nearing its first crucial waypoint. Designated as Green
Flag, it was the point at which Commodore Knight's ships
were assured of arriving at the warp point to Sol
uncontested, even if the RAWs and their attendant
defense craft had started under way at flank speed at that
very moment.

Assault Group Lancelot was following a curved, near-
ecliptic course that turned roughly twenty degrees to its
relative port side at two way points: Green Flag and Red
Flag. While this plot compelled it to travel a total of sixty-
four light-minutes, compared to the straight-line
alternative of fifty-five light-minutes had it cut straight
across the system, Assault Group Lancelot's course also
skirted just outside the edges of Alpha Centauri's Desai
limit. Since ships beyond the Desai limit were able to

travel at twice the speed of those within it, this meant that the crooked course followed by Commodore Knight reduced the total travel time to three hours and twelve minutes, whereas cutting straight across the system—and almost bisecting the entirety of the Desai zone—would have required at least four hours and thirty-five minutes.

As Assault Group Lancelot reached waypoint Green Flag, eyes on various bridges throughout the Relief Fleet were divided between the mission clock and the status of the RAWs and their defensive flotilla, which were well within the Desai limit. If they started moving now, before Knight reached Green Flag—

But they did not. Knight, followed by Rrurr'rao's carriers, passed Green Flag, made a twenty degree turn to port and watched as the RAWs continued to wait for a summons from Sol or upon a mission clock of their own. But whichever it was, the Kaituni hulls which were equipped with RAWs—monitors—were significantly slower than those of their undetected opponents, as well as far less maneuverable. Additionally, given that over half the distance they had to travel to the warp point was within the Desai limit, the most cautious estimates still indicated that the Kaituni formation would require approximately two and a half hours to reach the Sol warp point. Once Assault Group Lancelot had been under way for one hour—which was to say, had reached Green Flag—the laws of physics dictated that they would be barring the way to Earth before the Kaituni could arrive.

Unless, of course, the enemy became suspicious and called forth forces secreted in any of the five other warp points that lay closer to the one which led to the Sol system. Bypassing these warp points constituted the second leg of Knight and Rrurr'rao's covert maneuvers, the conclusion of which was marked by waypoint Red Flag. That universal sign of danger was a wholly appropriate codename: if some mishap led to detection prior to reaching that point, the odds were all too high that the Kaituni in Alpha Centauri would call in whatever craft they had lurking out-system. In such a scenario, it would be impossible to ensure that enough of Assault Group Lancelot would make it to the Sol warp point in time to hold it against the late-arriving Kaituni.

And there were other causes for concern. Since it was likely that Zum'ref's armada had encountered stealth technology in their many engagements with Admiral Trevayne and those which had come before, detection of any one of Assault Group Lancelot hulls might lead them to swiftly and correctly conjecture that they were being bypassed by *many* unseen ships. As Wethermere and Narrok had often been at pains to point out even to senior officers and flag staffers, it was not stealth fields alone which had given Relief Fleet its unprecedented capacity to avoid timely enemy detection. Their surprise attacks had been made possible by a unique combination of factors: the near-ubiquity of the stealth generators; smaller capital hull displacements and engine output; uninterdictable *selnarmic* navigation and targeting communication; and the fleet's completely unlooked-for emergence from a rear area that the Kaituni deemed "cleared and safe." That and the fact that Wethermere in particular had taken great care to ensure that there were never any enemy craft that survived to flee and report what they had seen.

But that advantage would be inevitably and irrevocably lost when the engagement commenced in Alpha Centauri. And it would be near-disastrous if it commenced while Assault Group Lancelot was still slipping under the unseen noses of unknown numbers of Kaituni counterattackers in other systems. The Relief Fleet had not completed its thousands of transits, yet—the monitors were being held for last since they would eventually show up on the enemy sensors, even if traveling stealthed or cloaked—and the tail end of Zum'ref's primary assault force was still rushing through the warp point to Sol.

However, keeping their energy output well under the absorption rate of their stealth fields, the several hundred ships commanded by Commodores Knight and Rrurr'rao gave the other warp points as wide a berth as possible and so reached waypoint Red Flag without incident. Assault Group Lancelot made its second twenty degree turn and began its final run to the objective, code-named Checkered Flag.

More than a few commanders on bridges throughout the Relief Fleet held their breath when the enemy RAWs and their escorts began to move shortly afterward. But relieved exhales followed within the minute: the Kaituni flotilla's movement was slow, even indolent. That prompted speculation among the flag commanders over secure *selnarm* channels: were the Kaituni moving simply because they had reached M-minute on a countdown clock or because an expected summons was overdue and they were acting to ensure proximity to the warp point, if needed in a greater hurry than originally anticipated? Their casual pace was not consistent with the crisp execution of a prearranged evolution dictated in preset orders; it smacked more of an uncertain and hesitating commander's initiative in response to a somewhat unexpected scenario.

If the latter was true, that Zum'ref had not called for them when expected, then what might that mean? Had Trevayne handed the enemy armada's initial attack some unforeseen setbacks? That was to be hoped. But the reverse was also possible: that Zum'ref's initial attack had so overwhelmed Earth's overstretched defenses that the RAWs had been unnecessary. Relief Fleet's commanders watched mission clocks, studied the formation of their own van, the leading edge of which was only fifteen light-seconds behind the rearmost elements in the RAWs' formation and steadily closing the gap at flank speed.

But at last the time had come when it was impossible to hide any longer: the monitors of Relief Fleet began to enter Alpha Centauri space. It was impossible to tell if it was the three battleships making their leisurely return to the Bug 15 warp point that first detected these larger, incompletely concealed craft, or any one of dozens, hundreds, possibly thousands of small passive sensors that watched for the faintest anomalous energy emissions. Several of those sensors did go active, confirming the presence of intruders with brief radar and ladar pings before being destroyed. The Relief Fleet had been detected.

Although it took a full minute for the Kaituni to react in any unified fashion to the appearance of the unidentified craft on their sensors, once they did, all hints of their earlier lethargy disappeared. The RAW-equipped monitors accelerated to flank speed, making for the warp point to Sol. They were accompanied by approximately one-third of their defense flotilla; even after that reduction, it was still nearly equal to Assault Group Lancelot in size. The other two-thirds of the security element turned about, clearly intending to meet the newly detected enemy in the system's Desai zone. Not only would that slow down the resolution of whatever battle would be fought between the two forces, but would force the intruders to come to the dressed defensive screens of the (apparently) numerically superior defenders.

However, what those defenders did not count on—and had no way of knowing—was that they were numerically *inferior*. They just could not see the immense array of stealthed capital ships, to which they were now drawing so close that the two fleets' lines would soon be interpenetrated.

However, the Kaituni had their first reason to entertain suspicions that all was not as it seemed when the handful of small ships they had stationed to monitor the traffic in and out of the warp point to Sol disappeared like a string of exploding firecrackers. The five ships of Assault Group Lancelot that emerged from stealth to conduct the attack dealt similarly with the flurry of courier drones that had been launched to alert Zum'ref as to the rapidly evolving situation in Alpha Centauri.

The RAWs and their escorts slowed slightly in their approach, as if first taking in this unexpected appearance of a handful of enemy ships and then gradually realizing that no part of surrounding space was safe.

That was also the moment when the three battleships

returning to their picket duty at the Bug 15 warp point were gutted by concentrated fire from over thirty hulls larger than themselves, and the Kaituni rearguard within the Desai limit found itself suddenly inundated by attackers emerging from stealth in their midst, as well as quite a few that had already passed through their ranks and were thus able to attack from behind. This decided whatever enemy commander had charge over the ships in the Alpha Centauri system: the RAWs and their escorts commenced a full speed rush toward the warp point to Earth, while their rearguard, eager to enjoy the advantage of their massive numbers of fighters inside the Desai limit, scrambled hundred of triads, the remote controlled interceptors leading their robotic wingmen toward their foes. Although there were fewer fighters with the RAWs—mere hundreds instead of thousands—these too were launched, as much to serve as advance pickets as combat platforms. After all, where five stealthed ships had materialized, it was reasonable to suspect there might be others.

It was a dire enough strategic position for the Kaituni to begin with. Having split themselves into two forces, and outmaneuvered by their attackers, they knew they had a hard fight ahead of them. But they could not have foreseen what happened next.

At the prearranged activation command, the many Arduan and captured Kaituni vessels in the Relief Fleet activated the Turncoat virus in all of its separate but complimentary manifestations. Using the command and security codes embedded in the remote-operated fighters they had captured, Ankaht and her *shaxzhu* finally put months of unrelenting training into practice. Using both the *selnarmic* circuitry on their own hulls, and many more *selnarmic* transmitters and boosters which had been salvaged from Kaituni fighters of all marks, the virus reached out to locate the protocols and links that the enemy hulls were using to communicate and coordinate with each other. Those probes bounced off paradigmatically familiar countermeasures and defensive reconfigurations dozens of time before one viral package found and exploited a statistically inevitable weak point and was successfully inserted. And then another found a similar flaw. And another.

In addition to the conventionally transmitted virus that had already begun to compromise the control links that coordinated the actions of each remote fighter and its robot wingmen, a new, *selnarmically*-inserted virus raced throughout the fire control and data links that welded the Kaituni fleet into a synchronized fighting force. And being *selnarmic* in nature, it did so even faster than the speed of light: the damage—and the effects—were instantaneous.

The Kaituni craft, in order to control and coordinate actions over the immense distances of open space, utilized *selnarmic* boosters which amplified the limited signals of actual *selnarshaz* controllers into far-reaching, powerful commands that required little energy from their operators. Now, those boosters did not amplify the command signals, but instead, scrambled them.

Coordinated fire control links went off-line. Ship-to-ship communications faltered, were rerouted into lascoms, depriving the Kaituni of their accustomed instantaneous coordination. Remote control fighters tumbled, their ship-housed pilots unable to issue commands to them. Missile guidance, so *selnarm*-dependent among the Kaituni, fell back upon comparatively primitive self-homing emergency systems.

As the Kaituni struggled to fight a war without the presumed lynchpin of all their operations—faster-than-light *selnarmic* links that could span gaps of a dozen light-hours or more—the eponymous inspiration for the virus's name, Turncoat, activated its final gambit. The timing had not been left to fate, but carefully planned, striking as the Kaituni were distracted by their desperate attempts to forge direct radio links to the robotic wingmen which were customarily directed by the now-rudderless remote-control fighters. The engagement of that mostly-ignored radio control backup triggered a viral package which had lodged itself in the appropriate subsystems of each afflicted Kaituni ship, having been piggybacked upon the earlier one which had scrambled the *selnarmic* controls.

This final viral package unfolded and sent a single, very simple change to the on-board programming of each robotic wingman: all objects in detection range of its on-board sensors were immediately and incontrovertibly recoded as "targets." Following their default protocols— to prioritize targets by proximity in the absence of more detailed instructions—the robotic fighters that had always swarmed and overloaded the defenses of the Kaituni's many foes now did the same to their own masters. And in the case of those robots that were already damaged and able to approach within five thousand kilometers of a target, that meant ramming.

What followed was a surprisingly short, savage fray. As the RAWs approached the Sol warp point, their own fighters turned on them, their escorts interposing themselves and providing defensive fire—but unable to coordinate that fire as effectively as usual, due to the missing *selnarm* links. And at these ranges of engagement, with the wingmen having been launched only minutes or seconds before, the robot fighters started getting through. Frequently. All the while, more hulls from Assault Group Lancelot unstealthed; every time the Kaituni tried to maneuver or turn a flank, they found themselves flanked in turn by enemies whose appearance was announced by a punishing barrage of energy torpedoes and missiles, unleashed from devastatingly close range.

The same circumstances were suffered by the Kaituni's intended rearguard formation, except that their greater number of robot fighters produced even more chaos and mayhem. And whenever several of their hulls managed to coordinate enough to attempt to coalesce into a productive defensive formation, another set of stealthed human hulls would appear and ruin their attempt.

At some point, a Kaituni ship managed to send a signal to the buoys and couriers that floated near the entry funnels to the warp points into Epsilon Indi and Epsilon Eridani. Minutes later, Kaituni ships began to emerge from both of them.

But it was too little too late. A sizeable segment of the Relief Fleet—most of its monitors, supported by battleships and smaller marks—made directly toward the counterattackers at best speed. Given the sixteen light-minute distance between the two warp points, and with the entrance to Epsilon Indi well inside the Desai limit and only four light-minutes away from the epicenter of the engagement with the Kaituni rearguard, Kiiraathra'Ostakjo confidently predicted that he would be able to blunt and beat both forces. His strategy: to defeat them in detail, bringing overwhelming numbers to bear on each in turn.

As it turned out, he was right. An expert in the employment of carrier flight wings, he savaged the Kaituni that began to emerge from Epsilon Indi—and directly into his swarms of vengeful Orion fighters, poised and ready within the Desai limit.

In the end, the desperate rush of the RAWs and their escorts did give them a small margin of strategic success. Accepting that if any of the relativistic assault weapons were to arrive in the Sol system they would have to run a gauntlet to get there, the Kaituni did what they arguably did best: commit to a strategy which imposed casualty levels that would surely have broken the spirit of any other species in known space. Without data links to coordinate fire, and constantly fending off their own robot-fighters, the hundreds of superdreadnoughts and battleships that had been intended to protect the RAWs instead turned into a flying wedge of shielding hulls. They were swiftly reduced to gutted hulks and smaller bits of rubbish cartwheeling through the void. But in the end, eleven RAWs and two superdreadnoughts survived to make it through the warp point to Sol, every one of them streaming atmosphere and trailing flames.

The Third Battle of Alpha Centauri was officially over, but the victors did not rejoice. They were too busy examining damage reports, effecting repairs, and asking the question that had been in their mind throughout the entirety of one of the most unconventional battles in the history of space warfare:

——But what of Earth?

CHAPTER TWENTY-FOUR

The holographic faces around RFNS *Krishmahnta*'s remote-access conference table were flushed, triumphant, and yet tense.

"Do we have a fleetwide casualty count?" Narrok asked.

"We do," reported Knight, who had likened his role in the battle to shooting ducks from a blind. "We've taken nine percent Code Omegas. Disproportionately heavy losses in the lighter hulls, as we expected. Also, disproportionately heavy losses in the action against the rearguard, which we did *not* expect."

"Reason for that deviation?" Narrok insisted.

"Two factors," Knight replied crisply. "First, casualties were very low in Assault Group Lancelot because the Kaituni were focused on getting through the warp point, not fighting to inflict losses on us. Most of their capital ships were just torpedo shields for the RAWs. Second, because many of our van's lighter ships were mixed in with the rearguard when we activated Turncoat, some of them were attacked by the robot fighters, which were only concerned with target proximity. The bigger ships which destealthed in the midst of the enemy formation had sufficient defensive fire to both hold their own against a few swarms and return the fire of the Kaituni battlewagons. But the smaller ships—not so much."

"Understood. How many of the remaining ninety-one percent of our hulls remain combat effective?"

"Admiral, not to sound impertinent, but it depends how you define 'combat effective.'"

Narrok considered his answer for a moment. Then: "I define a combat effective hull as one which retains at least ninety percent of its pre-engagement speed and endurance and seventy percent of its nominal firepower."

Knight glanced at a list somewhere off to his right, frowned. "That takes an additional fourteen percent of our hulls off-line, sir."

"So, approximately seventy-seven percent of our fleet remains combat effective."

"Not to quibble, sir," Wethermere, "but we should leave some fully functional hulls here in Alpha Centauri for security. We can't be sure that there won't be more Kaituni surprises coming through the other warp points."

"Very well. Recommendations?"

"Admiral Narrok, without any prejudice against your fine fleet and officers, I recommend that we leave behind approximately half of the remaining Arduan and commandeered Kaituni craft."

"Reasons?"

"Firstly, sir, they are in the best position to recover, and provide pilots for, the thousands of *selnarmically-*

controlled Kaituni fighters currently drifting around this system. Correct me if I'm wrong, but your people should be able to reactivate them and call them in to serve under our banners, correct?"

"Correct. And since few of them even had the opportunity to engage us, they are carrying full combat loads. Excellent. Continue."

"Yes, sir. The other reason I suggest leaving a largely Arduan security force here is because we want to be sure to avoid friendly-fire incidents when we make our final attack."

"You mean, through the warp point into Earth."

"Yes, sir. We'll still need a lot of your craft with us—and all the best *shaxzhu*—to hit Zum'ref's ships with the Turncoat virus. To whatever extent they can sabotage his fighters, that will confer an immense advantage. But we also have to bear in mind that, right now, anything Arduan will be easily mistaken for Kaituni, so—"

"I quite agree, Admiral Wethermere. It is decided, then. Admiral Kiiraathra'ostakjo, as second senior admiral in this fleet, I am leaving you in charge of the defense of Alpha Centauri. How many hulls do you feel you need?"

Wethermere could tell that Kiiraathra was nursing a sudden, bitter disappointment. Had they managed to keep any Kaituni ships from leaking into the Sol system, there might have been time to gather some intelligence, estimate whether there would be more threats to Alpha Centauri from the other warp points, and whether it was therefore a quiet enough salient to leave Rrurr'rao behind with only a token force. But with word of Third Alpha Centauri reaching Zum'ref even as they spoke, the clock was ticking again, and the uncertain security in this system required the guidance of a seasoned senior commander. "I recommend you leave five out of the seventy-seven percent of functional hulls with me, as well as most of the Orion carriers. If we must defend ourselves, we will make them come to us inside the Desai limit. At Sol, you will be fighting outside the limit, so fighters will be at a disadvantage."

"Very well," Narrok decided, "and the balance of our own carriers shall be a further part of that five percent. The remaining hulls shall be drawn from the rearmost elements of the Relief Fleet's main van, so that the remaining seventy-two percent are all as proximal as possible to the Sol warp point. That brings us to the final strategic consideration." He straightened. "I invite input from all of you, for our collective fates are at stake. We have two questions to answer: firstly, do we send in a probe to gather information before attacking through the Sol system warp point?"

"No," Kiiraathra said firmly. "Subterfuge has been our friend up to this point, but it is no longer. Speed is now all that matters. Zum'ref knows we are coming, but will have uncertain data as to our numbers and our abilities. He will no doubt be attempting to find countermeasures to eliminate his susceptibility to the Turncoat virus—and we must proceed on the presumption that he has learned of it. At the very least, if he has not found a fix, he may understand enough of what transpired to limit his use of *selnarm* and robot fighters."

Narrok glanced toward Ossian. "You are the only human admiral on this staff, Admiral Wethermere. Your input on the fate of not only your race's world of origin, but your personal home planet, is essential."

"We go now," Wethermere declared. "For all the reasons Kiiraathra mentioned, and one more besides: we need to get inside of Zum'ref's decision cycle, need to take the initiative back from the Kaituni attacking Earth. The sooner we take the pressure off Admiral Trevayne, the sooner he'll come boiling out to take the fight to the invader once again: you can rest assured of that. And your second question, sir?"

"I am mindful of what you have said about friendly fire in the Sol system. Do you therefore feel that my Arduan ships should not be the first to enter?"

Wethermere suspected that Narrok was leaning in the direction of keeping the Arduans out of the front rank, and was sorry to have to disagree with him. "No, sir. They have to be the first in. They have to start hitting Zum'ref's *selnarm* links with Turncoat as soon as possible."

"And if they are eliminated by a defensive screen with which Zum'ref is protecting his rear? Every Arduan ship destroyed means we have lost that much more of our ability to infect their systems."

"Yes, sir, but let's take a close look at the clock that's been running since the eleven RAWs got through the warp point to Sol. Firstly, they will not miraculously de-infect their computers as soon as they arrive there. Meaning the RAWs and their escorts will have to send messages via lascom, not *selnarm*. That means a transmission time of ten minutes or more before their first warning reaches Zum'ref, depending upon how far he has pushed into the system. And they'll have to be careful not to infect the rest of the armada. It's likely they're not yet sure how Turncoat got into their systems. It's even more likely that they do not understand where or what it actually is, so they'll be using unhackable communications of the most primitive form. Probably they'll be using your equivalent of Morse code.

"Given that, we haven't lost as much time as it seems. And that could mean that Zum'ref really hasn't been able to do much yet to cope with our entry—particularly in regards to strengthening any security elements he might have left around the warp point on his side. In all likelihood, he felt the door back to Alpha Centauri was so secure that he just left a few light ships to watch it. So I'm not worried that our first ships in are going to be crisped by heavy defensive fire. However, the more time we spend discussing it here, the more likely it will be we *won't* catch them with their pants down."

Narrok blinked at the colloquialism but his vocoded voice answered. "Agreed. It will take us some time to get our van into a coherent formation for optimal transit—"

"Sir," Wethermere interrupted, with a glance at the mission clock, "with all due respect, I say let our ships form up on the lead elements *after* they come through the warp point. We've become pretty proficient at this exercise, so let's get on the other side of the warp point now. Assault Group Lancelot is in position to make transit immediately and can array itself to provide the skeleton for our new formation. Which will also give that bastard Zum'ref something new to worry about."

Knight smiled—surprising Ossian—and voiced what was in the faces gathered around the table. "As you say, sir, I'm all for ruining Zum'ref's pretty plans. And there's no time like the present."

Narrok stood. "Then that is what we shall do. I will communicate the operational details that are specific to my own ships. Admiral Wethermere, I will ask you to send the word to the fleet, as you will be the first admiral through the warp point."

Wethermere stood. "Sir, I would be delighted. Wethermere out." He paged his communications officer on the bridge. "Comms, I need open channel, main tactical. Send it out on *selnarm*."

"Yes, sir. You are on main channel and *selnarm* sir."

Wethermere squared his shoulders. "To all ship commanders, Relief Fleet. This is Admiral Wethermere. Your combat status for the coming engagement, based on reported damage levels, will be relayed within the minute. Within five minutes, you will receive your new orders for the relief of Sol. Warp point assault sequence and tactical details will be forwarded as they become available. Ready your ships for general quarters. We are going in."

Feeling a mix of thrill and dread, Wethermere turned—and discovered that Jennifer Pietchkov was standing right behind him, the only other person in the remote-access briefing room.

But he had to look again to make sure it was her. Jennifer did not appear to have slept in days; her eyes stared at him out of blue-grey hollows. Her hair, if it had been recently washed, had not received much grooming afterward. Her usually pliant skin sagged on her high cheekbones and her always-pronounced nose seemed not only larger than ever, but somewhat accusatory.

"Jennifer," Ossian asked quietly, "what are you doing here? Granted, you have sufficient clearance—"

"Help me, Ossian," she asked with quiet intensity. "He's going to die if you don't do something, if you don't—"

"Who's going to die, Jennifer?"

"'Sandro. Who else? Have you *seen* him when he comes back from these boarding actions? Coated in blood, his armor a wreck." She shook her head as if to clear a vision that would not depart. "The odds say he should have been dead or disabled three times, by now. And if there's any boardings during the battle for Sol, I know he's not going to make it."

"Jen, I—"

"Don't ask any more from 'Sandro, Ossian. Don't take Zander's father from him. And don't take my husband from me. Please."

Wethermere ran his hand through his hair. "Jen, I'm not sure what you'd hope I'd do about this—"

"Then let me tell you. There are a bunch of government reps stuck out on some ball of dirt and goop that the Earth or the PSU or someone is trying to terraform, out at the secondary star. For all we know, those politicos might wind up being the sole survivors of the legitimate government after the invasion of Earth. If so, they need to be protected. Right?" Her voice had an edge of truculence; her eyes were desperate and pleading.

Wethermere ran his hand through his hair again. "How'd you find out about them?"

"Does it matter? Look: will you send 'Sandro there, to secure them?"

Wethermere sighed. "I'll see what I can do."

PART FIVE
Apocalypse Revisited

CHAPTER TWENTY-FIVE

"Admiral—"

"I see it, Andreas." Trevayne waved Hagen aside and continued to glare at the displays and readouts, as though by sheer intensity he could penetrate to the enigmas they held.

By now the Kaituni armada had passed through the asteroid belt, where the swarms of weapon-bearing rocks had added their firepower to the missile storm from the fortresses and the DTs and SDTs and slowed that grim advance. Trevayne himself, with the big but fast assault carriers and their cruiser escorts, was hanging back a couple of light-minutes sunward of that, within Sol's Desai Limit, athwart the course to Earth. The Kaituni were now approaching that limit.

While he waited, Trevayne had been puzzling over certain subtle, odd, and unanticipated changes in the tempo of the Kaituni onslaught. Somehow, something seemed to be wrong. And looming above all else had been the question of where the RAW monitors were. Of course

it was understandable that Zum'ref had held them back
at first, thinking that the DTs and SDTs would be far from
the warp point as per previous practice: that had been
Trevayne's very intention, and it had worked. But surely,
by now, with the defenders forced back from the warp
point . . .

And, in fact, the miniature reconnaissance drones that
still hovered around the warp point were suddenly
reporting the appearance of those supremely deadly ships.
By now, Combined Fleet had accumulated enough sensor
data on them to make identification certain. But what the
drones were reporting only deepened the mystification.

Abruptly, Trevayne turned and faced the Intelligence
officer. Elaine De Mornay and Gordon Singhal had joined
him.

"Admiral," the chief of staff began, "the drones
report—"

"Yes, Elaine. Andreas was about to point it out to me."
Trevayne indicated the readout. "Only eleven RAW
monitors . . . badly damaged ones, as the sensor readings
make clear. And a handful of escorting capital ships, also
damaged. And then . . . nothing. None of the swarms of
carriers we expected to accompany them and provide
fighter cover. No more ships of any kind."

"Furthermore, Admiral," said Hagen, "computer
analysis indicates a certain faltering, or pause, in the main
armada's advance, starting just after those RAW monitors
made transit."

"Yes, I sensed that," Trevayne nodded, although he
seemed barely aware of Hagen's voice. His eyes held an
inward look, clouded with intense preoccupation.

Singhal's face was a study in bewilderment. "Admiral, what does it all mean?"

Abruptly, Trevayne looked up, and his eyes were clear. They also flashed with a light none of the staffers had seen in them for some time.

"It means," he stated firmly, "that something is happening in Alpha Centauri space."

"What?" and "How?" asked Hagen and De Mornay, respectively and simultaneously.

"You left out one question: *who?* If something is happening, *someone* must be causing it. But we have no way of knowing the answers to any of these questions, so we can't concern ourselves with them at the moment. We can only take advantage of the opportunity it seems to offer." Trevayne's voice took on a clipped authoritativeness that brought all three of his listeners halfway to an unconscious position of attention. "Commodore De Mornay, you will transmit a change of orders. Our forces currently engaged will discontinue their fighting withdrawal and commence Operation Beta sub *a* at once."

The chief of staff stared. "Counterattack, sir?"

"That is correct. And our carrier task groups here will proceed at once, at maximum speed, to support them."

De Mornay's eyes bulged still further. "Outside the Desai Limit, sir?"

"No; that's less than ideal for fighters. But we are no longer waiting for them to come to us here—we will meet them just inside the Desai Limit. And finally, one amendment to Operation Beta sub *a*: order Commodore Allende to bring the DTs and SDTs into gravitic disruptor range."

There was an instant of stunned silence, in the face of the terrifying risk they all knew Trevayne was taking. But only an instant. "Aye aye, sir," De Mornay said briskly. She and her two subordinates turned to go. But Trevayne stopped them with a gesture.

"Oh, one more thing, Elaine. A general signal to Combined Fleet." Trevayne smiled, and his voice took on the tone that, to anyone who knew him well, denoted a quote. "Engage the enemy more closely."

Arduans, including the Kaituni, did not foam at the mouth, but Zum'ref's spasmodic tentacle-twitching and the rapid-fire blinking of his two flanking eyes conveyed much the same effect.

"Inzrep'fel!" The grating harshness of his vocalization made the underlying *selnarmic* (rage, frustration) almost superfluous. "Find out what has happened, and who is responsible!"

"We are trying, *Destoshaz'at*." The Intendant's (bewilderment verging on panic) reflected the scene behind her in the control center. The usual smooth, quiet functioning of an organization knitted together by *selnarm* was dissolving, as frantic underlings rushed about trying to cope with the unanticipated and horrifying. "But—"

"None of your pathetic excuses! I want to know whose incompetence or treason is to blame for this!"

(Desperation.) "We are making every effort to ascertain what has happened in Alpha Centauri, *Destoshaz'at* . . . excuse me, I must receive a new report." Inzrep'fel scurried off, leaving Zum'ref seething. She returned promptly, her expression even more harried and her *selnarm* under tight control. *"Destoshaz'at*, tactical analysis indicates that the *griarfeksh* are abandoning the essentially defensive posture they have assumed so far and are going on the attack—an attack which the heavy carrier forces they have been holding in reserve are moving to join."

"What?" Zum'ref glared at a set of tactical displays and saw that it was true. "Trevayne must have gone mad. Our numbers are overwhelming."

Inzrep'fel's eyes strayed to the display covering the region of the warp point, through which eleven half-crippled RAW monitors had just emerged with a handful of equally battered escorts, followed by nothing else. "Ah . . . *Destoshaz'at,* could there be a connection between this seemingly inexplicable change of tactics and—?"

"Silence! We will simply continue our advance and cope with this forlorn hope of a counterattack. In the meantime, continue trying to get a coherent report on what has happened in Alpha Centauri."

The Intendant hurried off, and Zum'ref forced composure on himself. It was, after all, true that the change in human tactics could not alter the inevitable. His numbers really *were* still overwhelming, despite all the hideous losses he had sustained. And, he told himself, all he really needed to do was keep the attention of this system's defenders focused on his armada, to the exclusion of everything else. That was the important thing. He must, he thought, keep reminding himself of that.

He was still reassuring himself when Inzrep'fel came back, with unseemly haste, and with *selnarmic* emanations Zum'ref did not like seeping out from beneath a blanket of attempted suppression.

"*Destoshaz'at*," she stammered, "we are finally piecing together a clear picture of what has occurred in Alpha Centauri . . ."

Hugo Allende's mammoth ships surged forward, as though propelled as much by a kind of wild exultation among their crews as by their drives, and their gee-beams ripped the guts out of whole swathes of Kaituni ships. In the meantime, the missile blizzard from the fortresses continued unabated, for Operation Beta sub *a* presupposed that the time for conservation of expendable munitions was past. And the superdreadnoughts and battlecruisers on the flanks drove in grimly, spitting murder in the form of energy torpedoes. Presently they were joined by waves of fighters as the approaching assault carriers drew into launch range. Using to the hilt the speed and maneuverability advantage they possessed inside the Desai limit, those fighters wove and corkscrewed through the Kaituni formations, riddling ship after ship with rapid-fire energy torpedoes.

But the Kaituni continued to come on, and on, in their unprecedented numbers, as though unaware of—or indifferent to—any such concept as loss ratios.

Aboard *Zeven Provinciën*, lagging behind the big carriers whose top speed a superdreadnought could not match, Ian Trevayne watched the displays and readouts that told the tale of a battle of almost inconceivable scale and intensity, whose soul-shaking violence seemingly threatened to overload the very metrical framework of space itself with its titanic, wrenching energies.

It was also, he was coldly certain, a battle that he was not going to win. The odds were simply too great.

Unless . . .

Andreas Hagen came running up. "Admiral! Look at the warp point display!"

Courier drones had carried first reports back through the warp point to Alpha Centauri, but nothing prepared Ossian Wethermere for his first glimpse of the live tacplot of the Sol system.

The number of Code Omegas made his stomach plummet. A whole fleet's worth of them—Trevayne's forces—lay dead along the approaches to Earth. The number of enemy hulls was many times greater, but still not as large as he expected. Surprised, Wethermere was leaning forward to double-check the results with his Sensor Officer when the indirect answer to the missing enemy hulls came in the form of a warning from that same station: "Alert to helm and con: navigation hazard!" In the tacplot, a pink, roughly conical cloud hastily superimposed itself on the battlespace, seemed to emanate from the warp point itself, extending well beyond the entry funnel.

Wethermere's tactical officer stood, voice low. "That's hard radiation, sir. Have they seeded the warp point with dust or—?"

"Negative," Wethermere answered, understanding. "That's all that's left of two, maybe three Dispersates worth of Kaituni warships: high-level rem-emitting microparticles. The aftermath of a sustained saturation bombardment by antimatter warheads."

"But, sir," Tactics murmured, "the matter required to create that large and dense a field of particulate debris would take hundreds of ships, maybe—"

"Thousands," confirmed Wethermere. "Shields, we need hard radiation protocols right now. Heavy particle repulsion boosted to maximum. Helm, find the paths of least density through that soup. Those will probably be the wakes left by Assault Group Lancelot as they maneuvered through it."

"Yes, sir. We're following the trail they blazed, Admiral."

"Excellent. Keep at it." If there had been any defensive ships guarding the warp point on this side, they had evidently been vaporized as well—and hadn't inflicted enough losses on Knight's formation for him to bother reporting the encounter. "Looks like we have mostly clear sailing until we reach the rear of Zum'ref's van."

"That's correct, sir. With the exception of the RAWs and battleships that got past us and through the warp point. But twenty ships of Assault Group Lancelot have almost reached intercept range for those stragglers, sir."

"And our main formation here?"

"We are in good shape, sir. Given that Admiral Narrok has done a pretty fair job of organizing the rest of the Relief Fleet for fast entry on the far side, I think we could get underway, if we were willing to put some space between our two groups."

Wethermere thought: *a fleet traveling in two vans. Considering the old axiom divide and conquer, we'd be doing half of Zum'ref's work for him. Unless . . .*

"Comms, give me fleetwide secure one, on *selnarm*."

"You are live, sir."

"This is Admiral Wethermere. All fleet elements currently in system will move forward at flank speed, following the unengaged elements of Assault Group

Lancelot. They will be our stealthed vanguard. We will not, I repeat *not*, be engaging the enemy fleet at this time; we are maneuvering to draw their attention. Prepare to execute on my mark . . . and mark."

"Sir," Tactics whispered, "what's the play?"

"To get Zum'ref to worry about his rear and to send a message that Trevayne can see in his sensors—and in his opponent's changed offensive posture. We're also going to support those twenty ships Commodore Knight sent chasing after the last RAWs. I want Zum'ref to realize we'll be close enough to give him a heavy fight if he tries to send some units to pick them off. But once we've made him blink, we'll back off, wait for Narrok's formation to catch up with us, and regroup into a single formation."

"So, this is a feint, sir?"

"A credible one, with some objectives built into it, but yes—a feint. Now, have Comms spin through the channels and try to raise Admiral Trevayne in person. I know there's a ton of jamming out there, and that Trevayne doesn't have many Arduan *selnarmic* assets— maybe none—but I want to speak with him if at all possible. While you're waiting for those results, get me a tacplot update on friendly and threat force positions in the battlespace that lies along the approaches to Earth. I need to know what's happening there, ASAP."

The irruption of friendly ships from Alpha Centauri didn't come as a total surprise to Trevayne—indeed, he had based his counterattack on the supposition that someone would follow those damaged RAW monitors through the warp point.

What *did* floor him was the face that looked out at him from the comm screen when *selnarmic* relay was established.

"Yes, of course I remember you . . . ah, would that be *Admiral* Wethermere?" Trevayne had to speak up to make himself heard over the hoopla in *Zeven Provinciën's* flag bridge.

"Er, I suppose so, sir—in a somewhat irregular sort of way. You see . . . well, it's a long story."

"From my recollection of you, I will hardly be surprised at the 'irregular' part," said Trevayne drily. "And as for the long story . . . we will, with luck, have time for that later. At the moment, all I have time for is to tell you that we are most heartily glad to see you—and that I have ordered the DTs and SDTs to close the range to the point where they can use their gee-beams effectively."

"I quite understand, sir."

"Understand this, as well: our losses have been such that Combined Fleet may not be able to sustain its counterattack much longer. In other words, we may have to revert to a defensive posture—with the big ships far forward and possibly unable to withdraw out of RAW range in time, given their slowness, depending on when the remaining RAW monitors come up."

"*If* they come up, sir," said Wethermere with a tight smile.

CHAPTER TWENTY-SIX

"Admiral Wethermere, we are three minutes from reaching the limit of the outer firing envelope of our energy torpedoes. Commodore Knight reports half of the RAWs have been destroyed. The others are crippled and are veering off to evade. However, the Kaituni rearguard is pressing him and approaching us. Your orders, sir?"

So the Kaituni had maybe half a dozen RAWs left, and they were sheering off to avoid pursuit. They probably wouldn't make it back to the battle in time to intervene, and if they did, they probably wouldn't be able to inflict decisive losses, but still . . . "Get me Commodore Knight, right now. Secure one, *selnarm*."

The two second wait seemed like two hours. Then: "*No-Dachi* Actual. Go."

"Commodore, I want you to pull your ships back slowly. Fighting withdrawal. Slow down that Kaituni rearguard and keep them on you. Meanwhile, have you kept your carriers stealthed?"

"As per the OpOrd, sir."

"Excellent. It looks to me like the RAWs are sprinting—well, limping—toward the Desai limit, Commodore."

Knight's pause was pregnant. "It does indeed, sir. So am I to take it that I can tell my carrier captains, 'Good hunting?'"

"Yes, but they are to make their approach at stealth-manageable energy levels. However, on the back end of the engagement, if they have to haul ass to get out of there, they are cleared to leave their fighters behind."

"Sir—?"

"Commodore, this is Sol. Either we own the system at the end of this fight and every planet is a home port for those fighters, or we lose and they have no place left to go anyhow."

"I see your point, sir. Anything else?"

"Don't unstealth any ships you don't have to, and don't spring Turncoat on them. Not yet. From what we can tell, those RAWs have not purged it from their computers and so can't share data with anyone else without transmitting the infection. So, at most, they're just reporting on Turncoat's effects."

"A report which may or may not have gotten through, sir. Conventional commo is a mess, sir, lascom included."

"I know. So just keep your head down and withdraw to rejoin the formation—slowly. They still have no idea how many smaller capital ships we have—but in about thirty minutes, we're going to show them."

And Zum'ref, when we do, I hope you'll be wearing diapers . . .

★★★

Anger, like fear, can sometimes become so intense it defeats itself. Zum'ref had by now passed beyond fury and frustration into a state that was a kind of substitute for calmness, allowing him, at least for the present, to function coldly and analytically as was his wont.

He still had no complete or coherent picture of how these newly arrived human and Orion forces had brought about the disaster in Alpha Centauri space, only fragmentary and disjointed and frequently almost hysterical reports. But he suspected it had something to do with the command-and-control of the ROV fighters. He must find out more. There was only one way to do that—and that way would involve the sacrifice of a certain number of fighters. So be it.

In the meantime, he must continue to press forward. Trevayne had broken off his counterattack after inflicting hideous losses (but suffering losses himself that he could not afford) and shifted back to defensive tactics, drawing slowly further back from the Desai Limit. Before the enigmatic newcomers could close in from astern, his own fleet must smash through that defense—through, and out of the trap before it could close. For that, he must bring the miserable half-dozen RAW monitors remaining to him into play, despite their lameness.

He summoned Inzrep'fel and began to give the necessary orders.

RFNS *Krishmahnta* quaked once. Wethermere looked at the board down near his Shields officer; all the lights remained green as his own batteries hammered out a ceaseless stream of energy torpedoes.

"Sensors, how close are we to the Desai limit?"

"Crossing the line now, sir."

Wethermere looked at the tacplot, waited for a sudden efflorescence of magenta pinpricks: the Kaituni fighters, which would come into their own once his ships' flank speed was halved by the changed nature of space.

After ten seconds, a sprinkling of fighters emerged from a handful of Kaituni hulls, started heading toward the blue wave that was the Relief Fleet.

"Sir, do I—?"

"No: they're testing us."

"Sir, Admiral Narrok on secure one. He wants to know if—"

"Tell him I believe Zum'ref has incomplete information about what transpired in Alpha Centauri and that he is only trying to provoke a reaction, at this stage." *Because what it really means is that he hasn't found a solution to Turncoat. Because if he had, he'd play his fighter-superiority trump card now and swamp us. Instead, he's trying to find out how many he can risk and test the water at the same time. Canny. But we humans were the ones who invented poker . . .* "Tactics, when the Kaituni have deployed forty percent of their estimated fighter total, let me know."

"Yes, sir. But by then, sir, many of them will be in range. If we activate Turncoat at that point, some will choose us as their ramming targets."

Wethermere looked at the young officer. "Tactics, this is war. We take losses, too. Now keep your eyes on your readouts."

In the reaches of space between the Kaituni armada's

rearguard and the vanguard of the now-reformed Relief Fleet, ships flared like stars and were gone. On Earth, it would appear in the evening or night skies as if previously undetected stars were novaeing, twinkling, maybe even appearing in the dusk and prompting a recitation of a rhyme that was far older than spaceflight: *"First star, first light, first star I see tonight. I wish I may, I wish I might . . ."*

Wethermere hoped they were all wishing to be alive tomorrow, because at this point, nothing else really mattered anymore. There were still a staggering number of Kaituni warships grinding away at Ian Trevayne's thinning defensive screen.

Too many.

Elaine De Mornay swallowed hard and drew herself up before speaking.

"Admiral, I realize there are only six damaged RAW monitors left. But they are still coming up, and so far the, uh, Relief Fleet does not appear to be in a position to stop them. I respectfully—but in the strongest possible terms—submit that we *must* withdraw Commodore Allende's command."

Trevayne studied her. She had grown, during all the months of fire and death and desperation through which they had passed together. Once the instinctive voice of her cultural background's ingrained *élan*, she was now capable of appreciating the counsels of caution. And it took moral courage to speak as she had.

But she was wrong.

"No, Elaine," he said, gently but not inviting argument.

"In the first place, we need the firepower of the DTs and SDTs at gee-beam range if we want to have any hope of holding the line until the Relief Fleet comes up." He placed a subtle emphasis on *Relief Fleet*, as though he did not expect to hear the term preceded by "uh" again. "In the second place, on the basis of conversations I've had with Admiral Wethermere, I believe that, while you're doubtless correct about the Relief Fleet in conventional terms, he has something up his sleeve that is decidedly *un*conventional. And in the third place . . ." Trevayne suddenly flashed a grim smile. "In the third place, it's probably no bloody use anyway, considering how slow they are."

Wethermere watched two more of his ships—monitors—go from amber motes to Code Omegas. "Horseshoes of death," as the more seasoned veterans sardonically labeled them. And the rate of exchange, while strongly favoring the Relief Fleet, was still not favorable enough for Ossian to feel assured of the battle's outcome.

"Admiral," cried Comms, "signal from *No-Dachi*. Commodore Knight has restored *selnarmic* comm. He's asking for you—"

"Put him on. Commodore, this is the Flag. What is your status?"

"We're in fighting shape. Couple of close kamikazes. When do you think Zum'ref will decide to pull the trigger on the last two-thirds of his birds?"

"Wish I knew, Commodore. Any word on the carriers and the RAWs?"

"Yes, just now. Quite a fight out there. Old-style fighter

brawl. Two more RAWs destroyed, another one so battered she won't make it anywhere important."

"Our losses?"

"Two carriers, three flight wings. They're ready to go back at a word from you, Admiral."

Wethermere considered the part of the tacplot which refreshed the region where the RAWs and fighters had tangled. "No reason to send them in on another run, but I see that the fight pulled the RAWs further off course. Have your fighters harry them, nip at their heels."

"Don't know how much good that will do, sir: the RAWs are boring in straight toward Admiral Trevayne's line, come hell or high water."

"Well, have your pilots do what they can. We can't win every . . ."

"Sir!" Sensors cried. "Massive Kaituni fighter launch, all points! I estimate—"

But Wethermere wasn't listening anymore; he could see everything he needed to in the tacplot. Zum'ref, having inflicted significant damage with his fighters, had taken the bait, had decided it must in fact be safe to use them all.

Wethermere smiled. *Gotcha, you bastard.* Turning to his Comms officer he said, "Inform Admiral Narrok to send this to all Arduan operators and ships: activate Turncoat. Prepare for flank speed attack into the center of the Kaituni van." Wethermere turned back to look at the tacplot. "Because in about five minutes, there are going to be a lot more dead red icons on the grid, and we'll be ready to finish off the rest."

★★★

"You knew about it all along, didn't you?" Elaine De Mornay's tone was distinctly accusatory. "Admit it!"

"Well, not altogether." Trevayne was unable to keep a certain complacency out of his voice. "Admiral Wethermere and I didn't have the leisure for extended conversations, but he did give me some general idea of what to expect." In fact, he hadn't had any real conception of what was it was going to be like when Turncoat was activated. But he couldn't let his staffers see that he was nearly as stunned and awestruck as they were at what was happening to the Kaituni armada.

He turned brisk. "We will go back on the offensive— but at a deliberate pace, with Combined Fleet holding its organizational integrity together, so as to serve as an 'anvil.' Commodore Allende's task group, combined with the fortresses and the supermonitors, will form the main body of that anvil; the more mobile units on the flanks will remain there, in case it is necessary to 'herd' the Kaituni into the space between us and the Relief Fleet. And there is no longer any point in continuing to withhold the asteroid-based fighters. Order them to launch at once. The same goes for the ones based in Mars orbit, although they may not get here in time to affect the battle." He paused, drew a breath, and spoke so softly that the staffers could barely hear him. "Let's finish this."

The scope of the chaos inflicted by the activation of Turncoat had seemed large at the Third Battle of Alpha Centauri. But in retrospect, it now seemed like a small dress rehearsal for the devastation that suddenly afflicted Zum'ref's forces, both where they were on the verge of shattering Trevayne's lines and going toe-to-toe with the Relief Fleet. The remote-controlled fighters suddenly became straight-line projectiles, holding their last course and speed until they passed out of the battlespace and continued on, possibly beyond the heliopause if their fuel held out that long.

Their robotic wingmen, deprived of control and now targeting the closest hulls, wreaked greater havoc among the Kaituni, most of whom found, at the same moment, that their *selnarmic* datalinks had crashed. Ships that had been coordinating their defensive fire among different batteries were suddenly thrown on their own, choosing and engaging targets independently, unable to instantly consult with each other. And those robotic fighters that were closest to the ships from which they had launched doubled back, diving to annihilate the nest from which they had just flown.

With the human ships' fire coordination and communications unaffected, they also sent their own fighters into this fray—and Trevayne, seeing his opportunity, further scrambled every planet or planetoid-based bird in the system to further peck and tear at the Kaituni, exploiting the gaps that now loomed large in the uncovered areas between the larger warships, and, most particularly, their suddenly unpatrolled sterns.

From either end of the Kaituni armada, two blue grids pushed in towards each other, destroying and grinding down their stricken adversaries as they came. Trevayne's forces held, just strong enough to be a functional anvil for the Relief Fleet's hammer.

The resulting sparks and flying splinters of shattered

steel marked the slow but steady passing of the greatest collection of warships in recorded history.

Zum'ref was alone in the command center, amid the corpses and the wreckage and the acrid smoke from electrical fires. He wrapped the tentacle cluster of his one good arm around a stanchion to steady himself as the flagship shook from yet another hit and shuddered from a series of secondary explosions.

Inzrep'fel was discarnate. No matter. She had proven herself unworthy of him. So had all of the Kaituni in the Dispersates under his command. But there were still the better part of five Dispersates left, most under the command of she who would probably succeed him: Amunsit, who had the command of the Dispersates holding the bottleneck systems that made it impossible for the human Rim Federation to liberate their capitol at Xanadu. And she—though of course not to be compared to him—might yet triumph where he had not, simply because without Earth, the humans would be that much longer recuperating from the crippling losses that had been inflicted upon their fleets and their worlds. They, and their equally repugnant allies with them, would ultimately perish; otherwise Amunsit would have proven herself unworthy like all the others whose incompetence had betrayed him. And he would reincarnate to see it: he would be reborn into a universe purged of traitorous Arduans and inferior life-forms.

But those inferior life-forms were still present here, and could and would be made to suffer. He, Zum'ref, would make them suffer even after departing this incarnation. They were about to feel the lash of his genius, in its final manifestation.

He knew for certain that they were because, before the sensors had died and the display screens had exploded outward, he had seen the inconspicuous icon on the outskirts of this system, moving as theory predicted it would. He had seen it only because he had been looking for it, and had known where to look. The humans, lacking that knowledge and with all their sensors committed to the battle at hand, would have no reason to be watching that remote segment of nothingness. They would not realize, until it was too late to even attempt to do anything about it, the impending fate of their precious home planet.

Yes! he thought, his exultation banishing for a moment the agony of his wounds. *My will transcends time as well as space. I am greater than Illudor! I am supreme!*

Another spasm of secondary explosions caused even the tonnage of the monitor to tremble, and the noise began to rise to a crescendo. Zum'ref composed himself. After all, he was merely about to merge into the mind of Illudor, to await reincarnation.

But, came an unwelcome thought, *if Illudor is not truly supreme, then how . . . ?*

The poisonous doubt that had seeped into his mind seemed to expand, and its sheer existential horror was filling his consciousness to the exclusion of all else at the moment the monitor's tortured powerplant gave up its last energies in an all-consuming fireball.

Trevayne stood on the flag bridge, and a great calm began to suffuse his soul.

The battle was not over, but there could no longer be any reasonable doubt of its outcome. Tactical analysis indicated that the enemy flagship must have been destroyed or at least prevented from performing its command-and-control function; what was left of the Kaituni armada had dissolved into a formless mass of ships—or, at most, small task groups—fighting as individual units in the absence of the rigidly top-down command structure inherent in their ideology. And now Combined Fleet and the Relief Fleet were crushing that mass between them.

Trevayne sighed deeply. For the first time in a while, he dared to permit himself to glance at the screen that showed the pickup from Earth orbit, and visualize Han's face superimposed on that beautiful blue-marbled sphere.

Behind him, he heard someone approach at a dead run. Turning, he saw it was Andreas Hagen—but Andreas Hagen as he had never seen him before, wild-eyed with shock.

"What is it, Andreas?" he asked, concerned.

It was a moment before Hagen could control his voice sufficiently to speak. "Admiral, by sheer chance, we've obtained sensor reading from a scientific outpost on Charon . . . that's the moon of—"

"—Pluto. Yes, I know, Andreas; I'm a native of this system," said Trevayne, trying to calm him.

"Well, I think the data is just coming up on the strategic system display now."

Trevayne looked at that display. At first he noticed nothing unexpected.

"Look at the seven o'clock bearing, Admiral," Hagen

said hoarsely. "At about seven light-hours from Sol."

It was a scarlet icon—the kind of icon that denoted a cluster of small objects. And the glowing subscript of the screen indicated its velocity: approximately $0.6\,c$.

"Here's its projected course," said Hagen in the same haunted voice.

A dotted line grew outward from the icon, extending until it intersected Terra's orbit at the point Terra would then have reached in that orbit.

And for the first time in his life, Ian Trevayne knew what despair was.

CHAPTER TWENTY-SEVEN

"We've no time for extended discussion," said Trevayne with the kind of studied understatement for which his British ancestors had once been renowned. There was, he thought, also no time to bemoan the miserably bad luck that the little scientific station on Charon was not equipped for *selnarmic* relay, which would have notified them instantly when the intruder had been detected over seventeen and a half light-hours from Sol. As it was, almost six hours had ticked by while the tidings had winged across four billion miles by light-speed lascom. And now that intruder, whose present location showed in baleful red on the display screen, its motion perceptible even on that scale, would reach its target in 8.4 hours.

And, he reminded himself, he had no right to complain. It was providentially *good* luck that Pluto happened to currently be where it was in its two-hundred and forty-eight-year orbit. Not to mention the fact that the onrushing cluster of near-relativistic rubble was very nearly in the plane of the ecliptic.

He was addressing a hastily assembled conference consisting of Elaine De Mornay, Gordon Singhal, Andreas Hagen, and various others in comm screens, including Ossian Wethermere. De Mornay was wringing her hands, something he had seen her do very seldom, and not at all for a very long time.

"But Admiral," she wailed, clearly in the throes of denial, "the last of the showers of near-relativistic fragments of broken-up Kaituni generation ships passed through PSU space long ago, at the start of this war!"

"So we thought," said Trevayne grimly. "But there was one yet to come. And now we understand the full depth of Zum'ref's strategy—its brutal logic. We'd wondered about the deliberate, almost leisurely-seeming pace of his advance along the warp chains, and attributed it to his desire to follow the Bugs and herd them along from a safe distance, without actually catching up and falling afoul of them. But that was only part of it. It was a rendezvous of sorts. He wanted to arrive at Sol at this particular time, so that our attention—and our sensor assets—would be fixated on his fleet. We wouldn't notice until too late that a cluster of fragments was precisely targeting Earth—a cluster whose combined mass, as the data from Charon makes clear, makes it quite capable of wiping out all life on the planet, and probably disrupting its crust altogether."

"I'm surprised he didn't target Sol," said Wethermere, mostly to himself. "But no, of course not: he expected to be in Solar space himself, leading his triumphant fleet."

No one else spoke. Trevayne looked at their faces—the faces of people in the depths of a nightmare from which there could be no awakening. And they stared back at him, for they all knew where his daughter was.

Singhal gazed fixedly out into nothing. "So, after all we've done, all we've endured, Old Terra is doomed . . ."

"No!" Trevayne's voice was a whip-crack that brought them, blinking, out of their trance. He swung around toward the display and aimed a remote at it like a weapon. He reduced the scale, so only the inner system, out to thirty light-minutes from Sol, was shown. The dotted red line of the fragment-cluster's projected course showed to the left, coming in from the seven o'clock bearing, coming within five light-minutes of Sol as it continued on to intersect with Earth. At a bearing of about five thirty and a distance of about eighteen light-minutes from Sol was the confusion of green and scarlet icons that represented their present battle.

Now Trevayne manipulated other controls, and a green icon separated itself from the conflict and drew away on a nearly sunward course. As it did so, the baleful red cluster-icon appeared at seven o'clock and raced along its course. The green icon, much slower, was nevertheless so positioned by then that it was very nearly—but not quite—able to intercept the cluster as it neared its closest approach to Sol, converging on it at an angle of about twenty degrees before it passed on at $0.66\ c$.

"The green icon," he explained, "is moving at the maximum speed of our fastest ships inside the Desai Limit. Admiral M'Zangwe—"

"Yes, sir?" Adrian M'Zangwe's ebon features seemed to come to attention in the comm screen.

"—You will, without unnecessary delay, assume

command of Combined Fleet's entire complement of attack carriers—never mind their escorts—and of *Falchion* class battlecruisers." The *Falchions* were an experimental PSU class, mounting launchers for the heavy bombardment missiles that were normally reserved for ships no smaller than monitors, or perhaps superdreadnoughts. "You will depart immediately, without recovering those fighters that are currently deployed—they'll have to proceed to Mars for an emergency recovery—and follow the course I have just delineated. It's being downloaded to your flagship's nav computer now. As you see, it has been calculated that if you depart within the next hour that course will bring you to the position shown." Trevayne gave a wry look. "I'd take command of this force myself, but *Zeven Provinciën* couldn't keep up. And this is no time to be transferring my flag—there's going to be enough hasty reorganization to do as it is." His eyes met those of his chief of staff and then his operation officer. "Can you get the necessary orders out in an hour?"

"Yes, sir," De Mornay and Singhal chorused.

"But Admiral," M'Zangwe protested, "according to the display, we won't be able to intercept the objects."

"You'll come close enough to launch your fighters at maximum range. They should be able to complete the intercept course. They'll have time to engage these objects *en passant*, using their energy torpedoes to break them up into smaller chunks that will either burn up in Earth's atmosphere or miss the planet altogether." He looked for confirmation at Hagen, who nodded. "At the same time the *Falchions* can lay a barrage of HBMs across the objects' path, hopefully achieving the same result."

"What about the Relief Fleet's carriers, Admiral?" asked Wethermere.

Trevayne shook his head. "Impossible. You're too far away. No, your role is to complete the destruction of the Kaituni armada. Lacking its fighters, Combined Fleet will go back into defensive mode. Once again, we'll be the 'anvil' and you the 'hammer.'"

Even at this moment in time, Wethermere managed to smile. "Quite a hard anvil, sir, with your DTs and SDTs in it."

"Sufficiently hard, I should think." Trevayne swept the entire gathering with his eyes. "Any questions?"

"Just one, sir," rumbled M'Zangwe. "When you say *all* our carriers, does that include the Orions?"

"It does," said Trevayne unhesitatingly. "Their own home planet may not be at stake, but their honor is. Knowing them, I believe that will be enough. And now," he said with finality, "the hour I mentioned is down to fifty-five minutes. Let's *move*—for Old Terra!"

Comm screens blinked out and staffers scattered to their duties. But Elaine De Mornay paused and, when the others were out of earshot, leaned close to Trevayne and spoke softly. "We'll do it, sir. For Old Terra . . . and for Han." And she committed the astonishing impropriety of giving his hand a quick squeeze before hurrying off, leaving him gaping.

Like winged messengers of doom from the lowest depths of Hell, the kinetic projectiles—segments of what had once been asteroids, processed to make an interstellar generation ship, and then recently disassembled—

streaked across the Solar system at a velocity which, while not sufficient to greatly increase their effective mass, rendered any sort of warhead superfluous.

And ahead and to starboard of them, at the much lower velocity dictated by their reactionless drives inside the Desai Limit, Adrian M'Zangwe's flotilla of carriers and battlecruisers swept along on its converging course.

M'Zangwe marveled at the precision of the targeting calculations that would bring that jumble of starship debris to the precise point where Earth would be at the precise time it reached that point. But he didn't feel disposed to admire it.

His carriers had only about half of their normal (minus combat losses, of course) complement of fighters; squadrons had been rotating between combat and rearming in accordance with standard carrier doctrine, and the pilots of the rearming fighters had been snatching a little much-needed rest. But what he had told them of their mission had seemed to banish their exhaustion.

"We won't get all these things," he had concluded, for this was not a time for anything but honesty. *"But every one we do get will be that much less death on Old Terra, and that much less devastation of its heritage."*

At least that was what he had told the human fighter jocks. He had left it to Claw of the Khan Zhinkhaneee'houloww, his most senior Orion officer, to address his own personnel. He didn't know what Zhinkhaneee had said, but he hoped it would suffice to motivate them to protect Terra from a fate like that which had overtaken their own homeworld, only worse—a fate for which, he knew, some of them held humans to be not entirely blameless.

Despite the death-laden fragments' soul-shaking velocity, he had time to obtain more detailed sensor readings. This was an exceptionally compact cluster of debris—Zum'ref must have put special care into targeting it. And a mass of ballistic data on specific projectiles was being dumped into the fighters' computers. None of those projectiles was extremely large—and of course the largest ones would get top priority, partly because of their greater destructive potential and partly because of the greater likelihood of actually hitting them.

He spared a glance at a display of Terra's immediate astronomical neighborhood. Luna happened to be very close to the incoming projectiles' course—at least as viewed in two dimensions. Unfortunately, that course wasn't quite in the plane on the ecliptic, so there would be no real shielding effect.

Now, with Sol glowing to starboard at only five light-minutes' distance, the green and scarlet icons were drawing closer together in the tactical display, the later at an incomparably faster rate. At a certain calculated moment, M'Zangwe barked an order and the *Falchions* launched a barrage of HBMs into the path of the oncoming menace. Moments later, a second command sent waves of fighters streaking ahead of their carriers along the same intercept course.

The big missiles reached the intruders' course just ahead of them, in a tightly grouped pattern. The warheads all detonated simultaneously, and the kinetic fragments plunged through a veritable sheet of flame. M'Zangwe would have preferred to strew their path with megatons of gravel, for at 0.66 *c* any collision would result in instant mutual obliteration. But there was no way that was possible; and as it was, the ravening energies of antimatter annihilation consumed some fragments and blasted others off-course.

Then, as M'Zangwe watched anxiously, the scarlet and emerald icons slid together and touched.

If the defenders had been stationary relative to Sol—or, God forbid, on a head-on intercept course—the clustered debris would have simply flashed past too rapidly to fully register on any senses, organic or electronic, and far too rapidly for any effective action to be taken. But as it was, while the two courses weren't parallel, they were converging at a sufficiently shallow angle that that the relative velocity was reduced to a barely manageable level. And energy torpedoes struck at just under the speed of light.

It still would have been out of the question without the newer rapid-fire energy torpedoes. Those spat crackling streams of blinding plasma bolts that slashed fragments apart or, by the impact of energy exchange, sent them careening harmlessly into the interplanetary void.

Then, just before the cluster flashed onward, the fighters swept through it, energy torpedoes still blazing. In rapid succession, ghastly flowers of blinding flame opened as small projectiles collided with fighters, blasting them into showers of fine debris which, in turn collided with other projectiles, producing more mini-novae of destruction.

Watching the readouts with jaws and fists tightly

clenched, M'Zangwe saw that none of the fighters were making any attempt at evasive action. He also saw that, in percentage terms, as many Orion fighters had been immolated as human ones.

Then, almost before it had begun, it was over. The surviving fighters had flashed past into the clear, and the kinetic projectiles were already receding at their unthinkable velocity, beyond any hope of being overtaken, leaving behind a glowing cloud of rapidly cooling dust and gas and debris.

With tightly controlled intensity, M'Zangwe studied the data. As he had told the pilots, there had never been any hope of neutralizing all the projectiles that were calculated to actually hit their target; some were still hurtling toward Terra, six light-minutes away, as he'd known they would. But only a handful. More of them had been destroyed or broken up into smaller fragments or knocked off course than he had dared hope.

In just slightly over nine minutes, Terra would find out if that had been enough.

CHAPTER TWENTY-EIGHT

Luna, like Mars, was one of the Solar system objects that had figured largely in twentieth century science fiction and early twenty-first century development studies, and then been largely forgotten with the advent of relatively easy interstellar travel. Almost all the roles that the early spaceflight pioneers had envisaged for it could be more efficiently filled by orbital habitats, without the nuisance of a small but nonetheless real escape velocity. With the exception of a few scientific outposts and highly specialized mining stations, it had largely reverted to being a pretty light in the night sky of Terra.

Thus it was that only a few people died when a largish, insufficiently diverted generation-ship fragment impacted Luna at 0.66 c, with no atmosphere to burn away part of its mass by friction.

On a body without plate tectonics, there could be no earthquakes. But it was as though a solid ball of glass had been struck a sharp blow with a small steel hammer. The entire moon shuddered as a shock wave rippled through it, and a pattern of cracks spread visibly over the surface with seemingly impossible and somehow obscene rapidity. At appreciably the same instant as the big impact, a few smaller bits of accompanying debris followed. They were superfluous, save to blast even more debris into space.

Almost exactly two seconds later, the near-relativistic shower reached Terra.

Coming in from slightly above the ecliptic, the kinetic projectiles missed almost all the numerous satellites girdling the planet—only a couple of smaller ones raved into boiling clouds of superheated gas. All of the big stations equipped for *selnarmic* relay survived.

Thus it was that Ian Trevayne, and everyone else watching in horror-frozen silence on *Zeven Provinciën*'s flag bridge, were able to view the fate of Old Terra practically in real-time.

That fate could have been a great deal worse. There was, among the cluster of objects that had escaped being either destroyed or thrown off course, nothing nearly as large as the big Lunar impactor. And it was a rather tightly grouped cluster, which didn't come in perpendicularly to the surface. Instead, Terra was struck a glancing blow on its day side, with the fragments entering the atmosphere at shallow angles.

Most of those fragments were so small that, at their insane velocity, they burned up from friction effectively instantaneously, dumping a huge amount of excess heat into the atmosphere. The sky over a good part of Earth suddenly blazed with a multitude of preternaturally dazzling shooting stars, clearly visible even in broad daylight.

But no one on the ground enjoyed the spectacle. For, mere microseconds later, the objects that did *not* burn up began to smash through the planet's crust.

They were very small—the hard innermost metallic cores of the ones that had such cores inside the outer layers that burned away. But at their velocity, their impact produced the equivalent of nuclear bursts of up to fifty megatons.

The first of them struck just southeast of Rome. The eruption of Vesuvius that it triggered was a relatively trivial side effect.

As Ian Trevayne watched that titanic fireball from his indirect orbital vantage, he recalled that the PSU's governmental complex had been located in Rome, because of the city's historic associations with grandiose imperial achievement—doubtless unconsciously influenced by Virgil, however little acquaintance most modern humans (let alone nonhumans) might have with him. That, of course, was why the celebration of the "Unity" warp point had been held there—he recalled the cocktail party. Now, what he saw in his mind's eye was St. Peter's Basilica . . . Michelangelo's *Pieta* . . . the Pantheon . . . and all of what he had shown Magda and Han, what seemed like an eon ago . . . all reduced to their component molecules. And he knew, guiltily but honestly, that they meant more to him than all the politicos who had just been reduced to *their* component molecules.

By now the annihilation of the Kaituni armada had wound down to a mopping-up action, largely handled by the Relief Fleet. Trevayne had no distractions to prevent him from staring, unblinking save to occasionally clear his eyes of tears, as the hail of strikes marched east by southeast in an oval footprint, all the way to the Hindu Kush.

The Rome strike was only the first. One struck the Ionian Sea, producing a tidal wave that rushed northwest into the Adriatic Sea, which funneled and concentrated it. The exquisite, vulnerable beauty that was Venice, painstakingly preserved for centuries, vanished forever as a towering wall of water swept into and over it. That mountainous wave swept on until it lapped the foot of the Alps, meanwhile roaring along the valley of the Po through the Veneto and into Lombardy, inundating Mantua and Padua, Verona and Bologna, and not petering out until it had flooded Milan and even Turin.

On and on went the horrible rash of fireballs on Terra's surface, their tops flattening against the ceiling of the atmosphere, soon obscured by the evil growths of mushroom clouds. One struck the Peloponnese, close enough to Athens to shake the Parthenon down into gravel. Others pockmarked the Middle East, smashing down to bedrock a civilized infrastructure that had been reborn and carefully nurtured since the Great Eastern War of the early twenty-first century. A larger-than-average one landed in the eastern Mediterranean, not far from the shore of a land holy to three of humanity's great religions. Now that land was scoured by tsunami, leaving it barren of the sacred places as though they had never been. And a watery monster of destruction rushed up the valley of the Nile, washing it clean of humanity and almost submerging the pyramids.

But that wasn't the only sea strike in the Mediterranean. With tightly controlled desperation, Trevayne watched the Black Sea, whose waters lapped the city of Sochi. He did not release his breath until he saw that no strikes had hit those waters. To be sure, the crisscrossing tsunamis of the eastern Mediterranean, after completing the ruin of Greece, surged up the Aegean toward the Dardanelles. But that strait was so narrow that it somewhat contained the flow, which nonetheless poured into the Sea of Marmara and washed away Istanbul. After that brake, the Bosporus sufficed to limit the influx, so that only moderately catastrophic flooding afflicted the Black Sea coastlines.

So, he thought, weak with relief, *I dare let myself hope that Han is all right.*

By now the fireballs had guttered out, and the devastation could no longer be seen from orbit, for the lands that had once given birth to Western civilization were covered by a dense cloud of dust and water vapor, gigatons of which had been blasted into the atmosphere, and the survivors were staggering about in darkness. At the moment, it was a hot darkness, because of atmospheric superheating from mass-energy conversion. But already the winds were beginning to disperse that cloud, and would carry it round and round the globe, to obscure the sunlight and cast Terra into a years-long "nuclear winter," when snow and cold would continue through what should be summer and crops would not grow. The northern hemisphere would suffer the worst effects, but nowhere would be spared. No matter how many had died, those who lived would face the specter of hunger.

Nor was that the end of this cataclysm's secondary effects. It was a blessing that there had been no ocean strikes—but the Mediterranean was one of the world's most seismically active zones, and that zone extended outward to the west, beyond the Straits of Gibraltar. Already, reports coming in from the space stations confirmed that a veritable chain reaction of earthquakes had been activated in the planet's brutalized crust, and some of those earthquakes were under the Atlantic floor. The Atlantic coasts of Europe, Africa and the Americas would feel the lash of tsunami.

And then there was the matter of public health. With countless tens or hundreds of millions of unburied dead lying about and decomposing, especially after the floodwaters receded . . .

Yes, thought Trevayne bleakly, *the nightmare is only beginning.*

But whatever has been lost, the essentials remain. They are intangible and therefore cannot be destroyed because they are not tied to a particular place. Verona is gone, but Romeo and Juliet is eternal. Athens is gone, but the ideal of democracy will live, however infrequently the reality of entrenched party hacks may live up to that ideal. Rome is gone, but not the rule of law. Jerusalem is gone, but humans will continue to believe—even if they need to frame their belief in secular terms—in a single God of justice.

Elaine De Mornay approached and broke the silence. "Sir, we have a report from, er, Admiral Wethermere."

A wraith of a smile awoke on Trevayne's lips at that *er.* The chief of staff had changed and grown in many ways, but even at this of all moments in time she was still a scion of the planet Lancelot's aristocracy, and would be one until the day she died. "Very well, Elaine. I'll receive it."

As he turned away toward the comm station, he spared a last glance for the orbital view of Terra. The Black Sea, like so much else, was now invisible beneath the dust-pall. Just as well.

The reports were all in. The destruction of the last Kaituni ship was confirmed. Even in the unimaginable event that any of them had offered to surrender, Trevayne was coldly certain that the offer would not have been accepted.

Now Trevayne faced the same conference he had called not so very long before, in the flesh and on comm screens. Andreas Hagen was wrapping up a series of assessments.

"And finally, Admiral, we have the computer models of the effect of the Lunar impact. First of all, there was considerable ejecta thrown out, and some of it reached Luna's escape velocity. Terra's gravity field will naturally capture most of it and draw it in, and—"

"Yes, of course." Trevayne turned to the screen that held Adrian M'Zangwe's face. "Adrian, your fighter pilots have already done so much—considering what *could* have happened to Terra—that I have no right to ask more of them. But I'm asking it. You must set up an ongoing patrol of cislunar space to intercept those fragments—and it may be weeks or months before we're certain of them all. Admiral Wethermere, your carriers can help; this time we have a little more leisure."

"Aye aye, sir," they said in unison.

"Good. And now . . . but Andreas, you look like you have something else to say." *And don't want to say it*, Trevayne did not add.

"Yes, sir. We have an additional assessment from one of our astrophysics specialists. She cautions that this is, as yet, highly speculative. But . . . well, there is a possibility that the big impact may have introduced instability into Luna's orbit. Observations over an extended period will, of course, be required to verify this."

"I see." Trevayne lowered his eyes, and there was a moment of brooding silence. Then he looked up and spoke briskly. "We can't concern ourselves with that just now. We have more immediate concerns. We're already en route to Terra, and once we're in orbit our first priority must be to lend all the help we can to whatever governmental authorities are still functioning, in matters such as search-and-rescue, maintenance of order, and provision of medical assistance."

"We're still trying to determine just who those authorities are, if any," Hagen remarked glumly. "We know that the seat of the PSU government was obliterated by the Rome strike, and the Federation complex at Granyork was washed away by tsunami."

"Keep trying. And there is another matter. Admiral Wethermere . . . Ossian, we must commandeer all available civilian shipping and organize a skylift of food from Alpha Centauri."

Wethermere looked doubtful. "I must tell you, Admiral, that there may be limits to the help Alpha Centauri can provide. The Kaituni never got around to any kind of systematic genocide on Nova Terra and Eden, but they neutralized those planets by smashing their transportation infrastructure. Food distribution even on the planetary level is still a desperate problem."

"Then we'll turn to the heart-world systems beyond the Alpha Centauri warp points if we have to. We may have to fight through some Bug flotillas to do that, but they need exterminating anyway. We'll set up task forces to secure the warp links, and form relief convoys. Make no mistake: billions may have died, but billions still remain. And once the currently available supply of stored food on Old Terra is gone, they face famine. I'll not have the survivors down there eating each other."

Trevayne fell silent. They all waited for him to discuss, as the saying goes, the elephant in the room. Finally, De Mornay cleared her throat and made a timid attempt to prompt him. "Ah, Admiral, about that 'search-and-rescue' assistance you alluded to earlier. I presume you'll want us to devote special attention to—"

"We can go into the details later," said Trevayne in a subject-closing tone. He started to stand up, then paused and addressed Wethermere. "Ossian, when we're all in orbit around Terra, I shall want you to report to me aboard *Zeven Provinciën*. I'm very much looking forward to speaking to you in person. And when we meet, I shall have an important announcement to make."

On that deliberately enigmatic and tantalizing note, he departed.

CHAPTER TWENTY-NINE

"Permission to come aboard, captain?" asked Ossian Wethermere with scrupulous correctness as he came down the shuttle's ramp onto *Zeven Provinciën*'s small-craft hangar bay.

"Certainly, Admiral," said Janos Thorfinnssen, returning his salute. The massive, ruddy-faced Beauforter then turned and escorted the new arrival to meet the small group that awaited him.

Ian Trevayne stepped forward and, before Wethermere could salute, extended his hand.

Wethermere knew he had no business being struck by Trevayne's physical youthfulness, so utterly incongruous in a man who was a hero of history in addition to being a fleet admiral. After all, he knew as well as everyone else the story of Trevayne's high-tech resurrection. But he had been so struck when, several years before, he had met Trevayne toward the end of the war with the First Dispersate. And now, looking upward into that famous face—its features went with his clipped Briticisms but the faint ghost of a long-ago Jamaican ancestor lurked in its coloring—he felt the same sense of unreality come rushing back.

But now there was a difference. In an indefinable way that went beyond unwrinkled flesh and thick hair, Trevayne seemed very old indeed.

"Welcome aboard, Admiral Wethermere. I've been eager to greet you, as have we all." Trevayne introduced his staffers, who looked with a kind of awe at the man who had brought unlooked-for succor in Combined Fleet's apocalyptic hour.

"And now," Trevayne resumed, "while I know a full and detailed report of your . . . doings has already been downloaded, I would like to hear, from you personally, a summary of the story of the Relief Fleet. You warned me that it's a long story, so let's adjourn to the flag conference room."

As they departed the hangar bay, Wethermere wondered where Trevayne's wife and second-in-command was, but decided against asking.

They all sat around the long, gleaming-topped table in the flag conference room, which incorporated the extravagance of an actual viewport. That may have been somewhat unfortunate, because the curve of humankind's once-lovely, now ravaged home planet lay below. But none of them had eyes for it as they listened to Wethermere recount the saga of the Relief Fleet.

". . . And thus," he concluded, "we finally arrived at Sol."

"Right in the traditional and deservedly popular nick of time," quoted Andreas Hagen, one of whose quirks was a perverse liking for twentieth century science fiction. A murmur of agreement ran around the table.

"Indeed," nodded Trevayne. "I'm only sorry my subordinate commanders couldn't all be present to hear this tale, Ossian. But some of them will be arriving shortly—Adrian M'Zangwe, for instance, and Rafaela Shang—"

"And maybe, Admiral," said Wethermere, "I'll get to renew acquaintances with your lovely and remarkable wife. I've only met her once before, but . . ." His voice trailed to a halt as he realized that the very air of the room had seemed to congeal, and all the staffers were looking downward as though wishing they were somewhere else. Trevayne winced as though from a jag of physical pain, but he quickly smoothed out his features and spoke mildly.

"Of course you had no way to know. But Admiral Li-Trevayne was lost in action in the Bug 17 system."

Open mouth, insert foot, thought Wethermere in the depths of his sudden, gnawing regret. "Admiral, I . . . I'm sorry. And you have my deepest condolences—"

"Thank you, Ossian, but that's premature. Note that I said *lost.* She is missing, but I do not necessarily presume her to be dead. It is true that we received a Code Omega from her flagship. But we have no way of being certain that she did *not* get out in one of the flag escape pods. In which case she could still be alive, albeit in cryo suspension, in Bug 17 space."

The staffers still looked agonizingly embarrassed. But

now it seemed to Wethermere that there was a subtly different quality to their embarrassment. It was the embarrassment of people who felt, but of course could not say, that their leader was indulging in a self-deception that was unworthy of him.

"Well, Admiral," Wethermere ventured cautiously, "now it ought to be possible to go back to Bug 17 and run a careful search."

"Indeed." Trevayne suddenly turned brisk—very brisk, even for him. "And while we're on the subject, this is as good a time as any to make the announcement I mentioned earlier. As soon as we can locate a surviving governmental authority to which a resignation can be submitted, I intend to submit mine. And I forthwith turn command of Combined Fleet over to Admiral Wethermere, as senior PSU officer present. I am confident that you will all give him the same full and unstinting support that you have always given me."

For a time that seemed longer than it was, there was absolutely no reaction. It was as though what had just been released into the air of the room was so self-evident an impossibility that everyone's minds simply refused to accept the evidence of their ears.

Finally, one by one, jaws began to sag, and mouths began to work as they sought unsuccessfully to form words, for the realization had sunk home that they really had heard what they thought they had heard.

Elaine De Mornay was the first to manage semi-articulate speech. "But . . . but . . . but Admiral, you *can't!*"

It broke the spell, and a hubbub of entreaties and expostulations arose from everyone except Wethermere, who was trying very hard not to appear flabbergasted. Trevayne silenced the noise with a raised hand. But what really silenced it was a sudden change that seemed to come over him. His dark eyes became hard black ice, and his whole aspect somehow froze over. Or rather, a bitter chill that was already there but had been carefully concealed was at long last being revealed to the world.

"I assure you I am in complete earnest. I have done my duty, in the face of the political fatuity and naiveté that allowed this unimaginable calamity to occur, and brought what seemed a golden age to this horrific end. And, for the *second* time, the blind, arrogant stupidity of our rulers has cost me a family." Trevayne's bitterness was now unmistakable, for he would never have poured it forth like this before. He was, truly, burning his bridges. And they all knew the story of what had happened to his first family, in his earlier life, during the Fringe Revolution, when his wife and daughter had died in the nuclear holocaust of a rebel attack and he himself had given the orders that had caused the death of his son, who had joined the revolution. "Or, rather," he continued, "it *may* have cost me yet another family. But as long as there is any hope that they have survived, my only thought must be for them."

Andreas Hagen looked indescribably stricken. "But Admiral, we *need* you. What's left of the human race needs you."

"No, Andreas. There may have been a time when that was true. But now, to repeat, my duty is done. Or rather, I have another duty, too long neglected: the duty of a father and husband. In deep space, or amid the ruins of

Terra, or in Hell itself, *I will find them* if they're alive to be found." All at once, Trevayne smiled. "And at any rate, I have someone to whom I can turn over command with a clear conscience."

Wethermere would not have trusted himself to reply even if he had, at that moment, possessed the power of speech.

"Speaking of which," Trevayne continued, courteously but firmly, "I'll now ask you all to excuse Ossian and myself. We have things to discuss in private."

After the last of the staffers had departed, moving as though in a daze, Trevayne walked to the conference room's side table and produced a cut-glass decanter of scotch. He filled two glasses and extended one to Wethermere, who rose—very slowly— and took it. Trevayne raised his own glass, and they drank silently. Wethermere found he was badly in need of it.

"Something else you had no way of knowing," Trevayne began, gesturing at the viewport. "My daughter was down there."

"Oh my God." Wethermere breathed. He took another sip—a gulp, really—of scotch. "I gather from what you were saying earlier that you don't know yet if she's—"

"That's correct. She wasn't in any of the areas directly impacted, which is why I dare let myself hope she may still be alive. But with the general collapse of communications, I have no way of knowing without going down to the surface personally."

"And leaving me in command while you do it." Wethermere found that, ironically with the aid of the scotch, his ability to think seemed to be reasserting itself. "I'm not so sure about that 'most senior PSU officer present' part, Admiral. More senior ones will probably surface soon enough. And I'm not even sure I outrank some of your subordinates elsewhere in this system, especially given what I've told you about the slightly unorthodox way I came by my promotion."

"Well," said Trevayne with a smile, "that's open to argument. You're already in command of a fleet, which is a full admiral's billet. As a matter of practicality, we'll just have to jump you up high enough to justify your position. And under the present circumstance, I imagine personnel matters in general are going to be somewhat . . . fluid."

"A masterly understatement, sir. 'Chaotic' might be nearer the mark."

Trevayne abruptly turned to the viewport and spoke as much to himself as to Wethermere. "A dash of chaos may not be an entirely bad thing. I spoke earlier of what has seemed to be a golden age. Since its formation, the PSU has never endured the shock of a real war—a war with real consequences, a war that threatened its existence, unlike the war with the First Dispersate. So it's had the luxury of brain-dead, self-serving political leadership. Maybe it needed such a shock, to revitalize the Heart Worlds. They were great once, you know. Perhaps this will call forth greatness in them again." Trevayne turned and faced Wethermere with a wry smile. "Needless to say, I share such indiscretions with you in the strictest confidence."

"I quite understand, Admiral."

"And now I must go." Trevayne moved away from the

viewport. "If I may offer one piece of parting advice, it is this: stay well clear of the politicians in the wake of this disaster."

"Hadn't planned on getting close to any, Admiral."

"That's wise—because they are a fickle and capricious breed when their world is turned upside down. Though until now"—his tone became melancholy as he looked back out the glassteel expanse toward the savaged surface of Earth—"that has just been a figure of speech."

"I'll bear your advice in mind, sir. Although from what I hear, the PSU government complex was completely wiped out, along with almost all of its representatives. The Federation capital complex isn't in much better shape. I suspect we'll have left orbit, and maybe the system, before there are enough politicians around to reconstitute the government, let alone travel out here to make trouble."

Trevayne shook his head sadly. "Would that it were so. But like cockroaches, even the most exterminatory event never accounts for all of them. Why, just look at today's inbound roster from Alpha Centauri. A senior PSU representative—Legislative Assemblyman Morosini—was out there on some junket, so he's survived." Trevayne stared meaningfully at Wethermere. "You know Morosini's record, of course?"

"I most certainly do. You and he had some famous verbal battles at a few cocktail parties, if I remember the lore correctly."

Trevayne nodded. "We disagreed on just about everything. Except scotch; we had similar convictions, there."

Wethermere smiled. "That's good to know, sir."

If Trevayne had heard the ironic quip, he gave no sign of it. "It's good to know anything right now, since there's so much we don't know. All the most direct paths between here and both the Rim Federation and the Orion Khanate are snarled with the remaining Dispersates. Bug formations have spread out along the warp links from Alpha Centauri, throughout the gutted Star Union, and are resurgent in the old Home Hives. Of course, we must expect that the Tangri shall not fail to take advantage of this chaos, particularly considering the crippling blow that has been struck to the industrial core of the PSU."

Wethermere nodded. "Yes, sir, we're completely balkanized now. And at the same time, we've entered a new, more fluid epoch of naval combat."

"You mean, with the passing of the devastator classes—at least as the ultimate capital ships?"

"Yes, sir. But also, the emergence of the RAW means that the days of warp point forts are numbered. We're moving back toward more mobile, stealth-oriented combat, sir, and *selnarm*-links are going to accelerate those changes. Set piece slugging matches are gone for the foreseeable future, I think. No more battleaxes at high noon; we're going to be going after each other with rapiers on a moonless night."

Trevayne nodded. "I doubt the experience will do justice to the poetic terms with which you've described it." He finished off his scotch. "And now . . . 'Suffer thy servant to depart in peace.'"

CHAPTER THIRTY

As Trevayne exited, he halted briefly to return a salute to someone waiting outside the conference room, then strode off.

A figure slightly taller and far more heavy in build entered the space the departing admiral had vacated: Alessandro Magee, who stopped just inside the compartment and saluted again.

Wethermere grinned and returned the salute. "Major, I think you'd better avoid flag country after today, or you're going to wear out that arm."

'Sandro returned a boyish smile. "Sound advice—on several levels, sir." His gaze faltered, he actually glanced down at his feet for a moment. "I've a duty to discharge, sir, but before I do, I—I wanted to thank you."

"You mean, for sending you off to baby-sit the politicos out in the secondary system at Alpha Centauri?"

"Well, yes, indirectly. Frankly, I feel like I should have been present to do my duty, to lead the Bloodhounds in case—"

"'Sandro, Harry Li was glad for the chance to be on call for those missions in your place: frankly, you've been too reluctant to let him command the boardings. And as it was, we didn't need to commandeer any more ships."

"Well, yes, sir—but it's the principle of the thing. However, what I was thanking you for was helping Jennifer. She was getting sick—literally sick—with worry."

"Yes. I know. But you've no reason to thank me: I couldn't afford to have our prime *selnarm*-sensitive human at less than one hundred percent readiness, could I? So I wasn't doing anyone any favors: my motivation was to maintain maximum unit efficiency, pure and simple."

"Permission to speak freely, sir?"

"Granted."

"You're a terrible liar. Sir."

They shared a smile before Wethermere adopted that edge of formality that was the necessity he most hated about being an admiral. "You said something about having a duty to discharge, Major?"

"Yes, sir. The PSU dignitaries who I was guarding back at Alpha Centauri, they're with me. Just outside. Wanted to meet you, sir."

"Wanted to meet *me*?"

"Yes, sir. When I told them about our whole campaign, about how you had the idea to create the artificial warp point that allowed us to bring in the Rim Republic fleet from Bellerophon to aid Earth—well, they became very, very interested in you." He leaned closer. "I wouldn't be surprised if they want to give you some kind of medal— or a huge promotion. They've got a lot of empty saddles in the PSU fleet, sir, right on up through the flag ranks."

He glanced at the admiral's cluster adorning Ossian's collar. "You might need to get accustomed to wearing that particular piece of jewelry, sir."

Hmmm. . . . we'll see. "Well, I suppose we should invite them in, then."

'Sandro nodded, retraced his steps to the doorway, ushered in the two PSU reps, one a very tall patrician man whose movements were slow and grave, the other a younger woman with platinum blonde hair and lively hazel eyes. "Commodore—or would that be Captain— Wethermere?" the man asked.

Ossian smiled and shook his head. "Well, depending upon which dossier you have, I suppose it could be either of those ranks, or even—"

The tall man interrupted peremptorily. "I have the only dossier that matters, Captain: your official service record with the PSU Navy. Which lists you as a captain, promoted to that rank on recommendation of the late Admiral Yoshikuni of the RFN for your performance during your cross-posting to her fleet in the Bellerophon system."

Which seemed like a century ago, although it had only been eighteen months. "That is correct, sir." Wethermere frowned, noticed that 'Sandro was doing the same. "And I presently have the honor of addressing . . . ?"

"PSU Legislative Assemblyman Amir Morosini, and my legal affairs attaché, Ms. Dalia Latt-Patha. And we are here on official business."

"I see," Ossian responded, straightening slightly. *So: Morosini; speak of the devil, Ian. It's almost as though you summoned him to prove your point.* And the politco's tone was not promising. "What kind of official business, Mr. Assemblyman?"

"Military matters of concern to the civil government of the PSU."

"Well, I wish I had known that when you first arrived. You just missed Admiral Ian Trevayne, who has been the ranking officer throughout the recent—"

"Captain,"—Morosini was now emphasizing that lesser rank, derogatorily—"it was out of consideration for your past achievements, and the regard in which some of your staff holds you, that we did not wish our visit to coincide with Admiral Trevayne's. We see no reason to advertise our investigation into your alleged dereliction of duty before it has reached a decisive stage."

It took Ossian a moment to parse out the shocking content of that sentence, and then to reorient himself. It took that same moment for Tank to realize that his liberal praise of Wethermere had generated effects that were the opposite of the ones he had intended. He stepped forward aggressively. "Why you son of a—what dereliction of duty? The admiral—*admiral*—has been an outstanding commander, took us through some times that—"

Morosini drew up to his full, impressive height. "Major, you will mind your tongue and your tone. By your own unsolicited admission, Captain Wethermere counseled Admiral Yoshikuni and other members of the Relief Fleet's flag staff to delay attacking on several occasions during your campaign to reach Earth. In most of those cases, it is highly doubtful that any significant naval advantage was gained by those delays."

"He was gathering technical intelligence! I know; I led

the boarding actions. If we hadn't stopped to get that information, we'd never have developed the Turncoat virus, and we'd never have gotten as far as—"

"Major, those are minor details compared to the damage that Wethermere's delays caused here, today. This system has been irreparably ravaged. Billions have died. Every day, every minute, counted in the race to save us, and Captain Wethermere's counsel kept the Relief Fleet from arriving here on time."

'Sandro's face was redder than his hair, now. "You idiot! The Kaituni didn't devastate Earth with their armada; they did it with high-speed chunks that no one knew were coming! And if it wasn't for Admiral Wethermere's counsel, we'd have never have gotten here at all, much less—"

"Major, it is understandable that you feel loyalty to your commander, but do not let your overzealous defense of his misdeeds endanger your own career."

'Sandro stood very straight, stepped back, and spat once—profoundly and noisily—on the stretch of open deck between himself and Morosini. "I'm a Marine of the Rim Federation. I'm out of your chain of command—presuming you're even in the PSU chain of command, that is."

Morosini looked at the gob of saliva lying just ten centimeters from the toe of his left shoe. "Oh, I assure you, Major, that I have the authority I require—both to initiate this investigation, and to send a most uncharitable report to your superiors in the Rim Federation."

"Good luck with delivering that report."

"Why?"

"Because all the people who might have cared about it

are dead, vaporized on Xanadu a year ago. Or don't you keep up with current events?" He turned his back on the politico, saluted Wethermere with a bitter, crestfallen expression on his face. "Admiral, I think I've done enough damage to you for one day. With your leave, sir, I'll be goi—"

"Major, you are blameless in this."

"You are kind to say so, sir. But my wife is right: I've always been too optimistic a judge of character when it comes to people. And dogs." The unspoken question—whether Morosini was a member of the first breed or the second—hung like a precipice-poised boulder until Wethermere returned Tank's salute, who then marched out of the room.

"You've been unexpectedly silent in all this, Captain," Ms. Latt-Patha observed conversationally.

Wethermere knew a baited trap when he heard it. "With all due respect, if I'm actually being investigated on these—dubious charges, I think it's quite clear that you are not really interested in anything I have to say. Besides, I didn't want to start a conversation that might have kept the major from leaving, and thereby, possibly hearing things that would only put him further into your political cross-hairs."

Morosini and Latt-Patha exchanged looks. "I'm not sure I know what you mean, Captain," the former said softly.

Wethermere smiled. "Yes, well, I'm sure it's pure coincidence that you were one of the most vocal adherents of the program for building as many artificial warp points as possible. I also recall that you suggested funding that initiative by drawing down defense spending. But not the big ticket items, no: that would have cut too much of what flows into the coffers of the Industrial Worlds and earned the unwelcome attention of their political powerbrokers in the Federation, and so, in the human assembly within the PSU. So instead, you became one of the leading proponents for reducing force sizes. Reduce personnel by twenty-percent; reduce smaller capital ships by forty percent; delay the introduction of the energy-torpedo conversion program." Ossian folded his arms. "I wonder, Mr. Morosini, how that will play in the court of global opinion—and beyond—when it comes time to share out blame for Earth's near-subjugation by an alien armada?"

Morosini listened without any outward sign of reaction—other than the color bleeding steadily out of his cheeks. "Exactly what I would expect to hear from an overweening careerist who is trying to deflect attention from his own malfeasance." He drew up to his full height once again. "I have done the courtesy of informing you of our investigation in person, and in private. As of two o'clock—er, fourteen hundred hours tomorrow, we will expect you to present yourself in this place, and in the presence of at least one PSU officer of sufficient rank, to be remanded into our custody pending an initial presentation of the specifications and charges pertaining to your dereliction of duty. All of which shall determine if a general court martial should be convened." Without another word, Morosini left the room.

Latt-Patha turned, cocked a small smile at Ossian over her shoulder. "I'll see you in court. Captain."

Wethermere watched her leave and reflected: *strange how much can change in just one day.*

PART SIX
From Ashes and Dust

PART SIX
From Ashes and Dust

CHAPTER THIRTY-ONE

Low in the sooty sky, a sun the color of clotted blood dimly illuminated the ruins of Old Terra.

Gazing out the passenger-side window of his skimmer, Ian Trevayne looked down on the corrugated gray surface of the Black Sea, and drew his thermal jacket more tightly around him.

The flash of heat that had enveloped the planet as sand-to-pebble-sized debris had instantaneously burned up in the atmosphere from its own insane velocity had not lasted. Instead, there had been a wild up-and-down temperature fluctuation. For one thing, it was autumn in the northern hemisphere. For another, the insolation being received by the surface had been reduced by at least ten percent. For the moment, the abrupt shift to chill temperatures was a relief. It would soon cease to seem so, for winter was coming on . . . and would seem to last and last, most likely two or three years, although the real Siberian harshness should last only (!) through March or perhaps April. But even the "warm" season would be cooler and damper than any on record, with frequent killing frosts as far south as the edge of the subtropics.

At least, Trevayne thought, the onset of cold had helped stave off plague. If the wracks of drowned bodies left behind by the flood waters had been left to lie around in hot weather . . .

How did one of those twentieth-century science fiction writers Andreas likes put it? he thought with a defiant flash of wry humor. *"If you have a few problems you have trouble, but if you have a whole lot of problems, they start solving each other."*

The thought reminded him of his departure from *Zeven Provinciën*—he had grown fond of that ship, for all that she bore the name of the flagship of an admiral who had repeatedly swabbed the decks with the English. His staffers, with whom he had gone through so much, had lined up in the hangar bay to bid him farewell, together with Ossian Wethermere. Hagen had seemed desolate, and Trevayne himself hadn't been immune to the feeling, for they had been together almost since his reawakening in a new body. Elaine De Mornay had visibly fought to maintain her trademark aristocratic bearing—and then, at the last, lost the fight, for as he had passed by her she had whispered, "Sir, the Age of Heroes has just ended," and then turned aside before he could see her tears. Not knowing how to respond, he had moved on.

But his hardest farewell had been to Wethermere, for by then he had learned something of the latter's difficulties with Morosini and his fellow slime molds. It had almost made him feel guilty about his departure—

altogether too much like leaving the new admiral to the wolves—but he could delay no longer.

"Don't worry, Ossian," he had said gruffly. "What you accomplished with the Relief Fleet speaks for itself. And in case it doesn't, I've recorded a full endorsement of all your actions, and also your promotions."

If Wethermere had noticed that Ian had used the plural when referring to his "promotions," the younger man gave no indication of it. "Thank you, sir. But right at the moment, I'm trying to put that out of my mind and concentrate on my job as commander of Combined Fleet. You're not an especially easy act to follow," he had added with a hint of a twinkle.

"Look on the bright side, Ossian," Trevayne had told him with a twinkle of his own. "At least Combined Fleet is accustomed to having a ridiculously young *looking* commander." And on that note he had boarded his shuttle, which had gone down to Ankara, the nearest partially functional spaceport to Sochi. His skimmer had been waiting.

"Up ahead, Admiral," said his pilot, interrupting his memories. He leaned forward and looked through the windshield. Even in the mirk, the masses of the Caucasus range were growing visible, a jagged black line against the indistinct horizon. Soon they began to rear higher and higher against the polluted sky, and what was left of Sochi grew visible at their foot.

Sochi had no real natural harbor. Ever since the twentieth century it had had a succession of artificial moles starting at the mouth of the Sochi River. The current one had survived only in segments, and at any rate it had provided essentially no protection for the "Russian Riviera," whose resort hotels had been washed way or else still stood only as stumps rising above the slowly receding waters. The entire ruined city was a noisome morass, particularly the western districts along the small river, which had jumped its banks.

But the skimmer's destination was in the eastern part of greater Sochi, along the street once known as Gorkogo, where a relief station had been set up on relatively high ground. It set down in the midst of a tent city filled with misery. Trevayne alighted, to be met by a medical officer who had somehow been sent down to this particular place to coordinate search-and-rescue efforts, despite Trevayne's instructions to Elaine De Mornay that no special preference was to be given to this unimportant town.

"Admiral Trevayne?" The youngish, harried-looking woman's awe was palpable as she saluted. "Lieutenant Commander Zheng, sir. This is Doctor Igor Danilenko," she added, gesturing toward a short, stocky man in medical scrubs overlaid with a sheepskin jacket against the chill. "I've been working with him to try and deal with . . ." She gave a helpless, frustrated gesture that encompassed the refugee camp. "Well, anyway, sir, we heard that you were coming, and . . . I'm sorry to have to tell you that we have no definite news as to your daughter's whereabouts. However, we have a possible lead. In connection with which . . ." She swallowed hard. "We have a couple of bodies that we would appreciate if you would identify."

"Yes, it's them," said Trevayne tonelessly, staring somberly down at the two lifeless bodies on the tray.

Zheng gave a peremptory gesture in the direction of the orderly, who slid the tray out of sight. "We found them on the northeast fringes of Sochi proper, where they had naturally been trying to get away from the flooding of the river, toward the foothills."

"Naturally," Trevayne echoed. *But they were old . . . old. No matter what antigerone treatments could do.*

"When we found them, they were . . . holding hands."

"They would be." *Jason Bluefield Windrider and Magda Petrovna Windrider . . . living links to the Fringe Revolution, my old enemies, later the godparents of my wife, the daughter of my supreme enemy Li Han, who was sometimes accused of being a bit of a bore on the subject of her own alleged unworthiness.*

Now I know those accusations were on the mark. For it is I who am truly unworthy.

Elaine De Mornay was wrong. The Age of Heroes ended when these two aged people died, hand in hand, struggling up a mountain path to try and bring my daughter out of a calamity that I was unable to prevent.

But then there swam into Trevayne's mind's eye a face with the pure features of Old Terra's East Asia—the face of an enemy, younger than he, who had by extraordinary convolutions of fate become his mother-in-law. And the black eyes—literally black, not the dark brown that novelists usually call "black"—twinkled, and she smiled. *"Why, Ian! And people thought I was always too insistent about blaming myself for things no one else blamed me for! If it weren't for you, no one would be alive on Old Terra. As it is . . . my granddaughter may still live."*

"Ah . . . Admiral Trevayne?" Zheng's hesitant voice broke in on his reverie.

"I gather," he said aloud, drawing himself up, "that the body of a six-year-old girl was not found with them."

"That's correct, sir," said Zheng, a little too emphatically. "But there's one other thing. Senator Windrider was still alive—barely—when we found them. There was nothing we could do; he died very shortly, and practically none of what he tried to say was audible. But he managed to make one word just barely understandable: *Izmaylovka.*"

"What does that mean?"

Doctor Danilenko spoke up. "It's a tiny town a short distance to the northeast of here, up in the foothills. A popular center for winter sports, before . . . Well, it's been swamped with refugees from the coast."

"Is it possible," Trevayne asked Zheng, "that he was trying to say that was their destination?"

"That was our first thought, Admiral."

"Then it's also possible that, once they realized they could go no further, they told Han to go on ahead, alone, and try to reach it." *Which,* Trevayne thought, *would explain why Jason Windrider used his last dying breath to gasp out that town's name, hoping someone would understand, and know where to search.*

He tried to imagine the scene, though his mind flinched from it: the terrified, bewildered little girl, ordered by her beloved "grandparents" to leave them and continue on alone. It must have seemed to her a hurtful rejection. She must have resisted, and begged to stay with them. But somehow they had persuaded her to abandon them before she could see them die, and follow the straggling crowds of the dispossessed, up into the higher, colder altitudes.

Was it actually possible that a six-year-old girl, alone, could have struggled up there, amid the chaos of a breakdown in law and order? Trevayne knew what depravities of human nature could surface in such a breakdown, freed from the restraints of civilized society, for all the fatuous braying of Rousseau and similar jackasses.

But he also knew of the equally human attributes of pity and generosity that the sight of a helpless child was apt to trigger. Perhaps there would have been those who would have helped her. Just possibly . . .

"Doctor Danilenko," he called out over his shoulder as he turned and strode toward his skimmer, "I will be obliged if you will accompany me. You doubtless know some of the medical people at Izmaylovka."

The distance was short, but Trevayne ordered the skimmer to stop at every clearing along the way where people were in evidence, to search and inquire, always unavailingly. Night was falling when they reached Izmaylovka.

The town—little more than a village, really—lay just southwest of the first escarpment, with the permanently snow-capped masses of the western end of the Caucasus range looming beyond. The flood waters hadn't quite reached this altitude, and Izmaylovka wasn't the sodden wreck that Sochi was. But Danilenko hadn't exaggerated the degree to which it was overwhelmed by refugees.

Harsh electric lights, powered by portable generators, revealed a scene of despair and stunned horror.

Danilenko spoke to the local relief coordinators and hurried back to Trevayne. "They can't be certain—there are so many children. But of course you're welcome to search."

The last trace of dust-filtered light departed from the sky, and the chill deepened. His breath frosting in the air, Trevayne went from one huddled, shivering child to another, sweeping a flashlight over each in search of a particular Eurasian face. A dead sense of defeat began to rise in him.

Danilenko touched his shoulder. "There's a small warehouse they're using to shelter children who need special care, because they're physically injured or else in a state of shock. Naturally I'd hoped we'd find her short of that. But if it's the only hope left . . ."

The interior of the warehouse was warmed by small portable heating units—and by body heat, for the overcrowding was hideous. Heart-rending wails and whimpers filled the stuffy air as a few desperately overworked adults tried to dispense what comfort they could. But some of the children made no sound at all; they merely stared with unblinking eyes into the worlds to which they had withdrawn to escape a real world that had become intolerable.

Stepping gingerly among the small bodies that carpeted the floor and calling upon a lifetime's self-discipline, Trevayne made himself look into the pain-wracked faces of even the most horribly injured children. The faces that were merely blank were, in their way, as bad. But he recognized none of them. The hollowness that had been growing within him threatened to swallow his soul.

He turned to go . . . and noticed a small form huddled in a corner, legs drawn up tightly, inconspicuous because so still and so quiet.

All at once the whole scene of mass tragedy seemed to vanish, for his vision—his entire world—had narrowed to that single form.

Moving as though in a dream, he approached her. Yes, it was her face, underneath all the grime and all the expressionlessness. There was no mistaking her, even through the mist that blurred his vision. He went to his knees and leaned close, looking into the huge dark unseeing eyes. "Han?"

She flinched back, clasping her knees even more tightly. Her eyes remained empty of recognition.

"Han," he repeated through a constricted throat, "it's *me*. Remember I promised that I'd come back, and that we'd go looking for Mommy?"

For an agonizing instant, he thought she hadn't even heard him. But then she blinked several times, and her eyes cleared.

"Daddy? *Daddy!*" And her arms were around his neck and she was clinging to him, wetting his shoulder with her tears.

"Daddy, you were gone so long!"

"I know, dear, and I'm sorry. But now it will be as I promised. We're going to go and look for Mommy—and we'll go together."

CHAPTER THIRTY-TWO

Waiting for Assemblyman Morosini and his legal aide Latt-Patha, Ossian Wethermere finished the physical paperwork, which actually required his signature. His witness—a lieutenant commander from a PSU light cruiser that had stumbled across Relief Fleet in the weeks immediately following the invasion, looked on as Ossian first signed off on the accuracy of after-action reports, and then the transfer of Fleet Command to Commodore Knight until such time as an RFN flag officer could take over. Which, unfortunately, meant that Relief Fleet would have to head home immediately, and by the same circuitous route it had followed to Earth. All other paths were still blocked by the remaining Kaituni fleets, to say nothing of possible Bug incursions.

As Wethermere's wrist-comp alarm announced that it was now 1400 hours, Morosini and Latt-Patha swung around the doorjamb, four grey-suited subordinates trailing them like the retinue of nobility. Wethermere smiled. "Very punctual, I see. Did you serve in the military at some point, Mr. Morosini, Ms. Latt-Patha?"

"Certainly not," Morosini said crisply. Latt-Patha simply rolled her eyes.

"Well," Wethermere said, signing the last hard-copy, "no real surprise there. Since you seem unwilling to reconsider your decision despite Admiral Trevayne's deposition and confirmation of my brevet rank as permanent, I am ready to come along if you have no further—" Ossian stopped, looking for the requisite security guards that invariably escorted persons off a hull over which they had lost command. "I am grateful that you elected to forego the security detachment," he commented.

"If that is a joke, it is in very poor taste," Morosini replied haughtily.

"A joke? I don't understand."

Latt-Patha frowned. "Your Marines would not allow our security detachment to board the *Krishmahnta*. 'Admiral's orders,' they told us."

Wethermere blinked. "I did not issue any such orders."

"Then if you didn't—?"

"I did," said Narrok's vocoded voice as he came around the same corner the PSU politicos had just turned, gesturing that a combined Marine/Arduan guard force remain outside the chamber. Following him in and taking up positions to either side of Ossian were Ankaht, Kiiraathra'ostakjo, and the much-scarred Rrurr'rao. Narrok drew himself up, his golden skin unusually iridescent. "I am Narrok, the admiral who gave the Marines the order to bar your security detachment from boarding."

"On what grounds? How dare you!" Morosini almost lost his composure—but not quite.

Kiiraathra'ostakjo bowed deeply. "We dare on these grounds: that you lack adequate authority to initiate the investigation which you propose, and that the charges and specifications reflect more ignorance than knowledge of the relevant events."

Morosini fixed Ossian with an icy glare.

Who hoped his response would annoy the politico even more. He shrugged. "Sorry, Mr. Assemblyman, they didn't hear about your kangaroo court from me."

"We were informed of these proceedings by Admiral Trevayne, shortly after they were brought to our attention by Major Alessandro Magee," Ankaht explained. "And we thought it best not to prejudice your reaction by involving Admiral Wethermere in our plans to be here for your arrival. Indeed, we have not consulted him on any of the matters that we have taken under consideration in light of Major Magee's report to us."

Morosini grew somewhat taller, if that was possible. "I am delighted to have this chance to meet with the most senior representatives of our indispensable allies, but this is a most unfortunate time and circumstance in which to begin a collegial conversation. I must cordially ask that you cease obstructing our lawful removal of Captain Wethermere from his command."

"And I must repeat that we refuse to do so," Kiiraathra said with inclined head.

"Sir, you are trying my patience. We have the authority in this matter."

Kiiraathra looked up, eyes bright. "Do you, Mr.

Morosini? I am the ranking Pan Sentient Union naval officer in this fleet, and my authority over naval matters is absolute. By comparison, your line of accession to—authority—is unclear. At best. Indeed, until you have conducted a thorough cataloging of the survivors on Earth and elsewhere in this system, you cannot be sure that your represent the senior voice of the PSU, much less have either the position or precedent to speak for it autonomously. It seems to us that your authority here is—how shall I put it?—ambitiously presumptive."

Wethermere couldn't keep from raising an eyebrow and thinking; *Damn, Kiiraathra could be a politician yet.*

The Orion admiral continued. "On the other hand, and in the absence of any news to the contrary, I am the ranking naval *and* political *Zheeerlikou'valkhannaieee*—or, as you style my species, 'Orion'— who survives in this system." His tone grew grim, morosely introspective. "It is possible this is my status even in regions far beyond, as well. Possibly in the entirety of the Khanate." He looked up again. "But what is certain beyond dispute is that my word is law in this matter, and I, who have had daily personal contact with Ossian Wethermere throughout this campaign, attest that your accusations are, at best, wildly inaccurate misconstruances. He has been a credit to your navy and species throughout these times, and a leader and strategist of the first order.

"However,"—Kiiraathra'ostakjo cast a desultory hand to indicate his surroundings— "although we are on a Rim Federation ship, we are in *your* home system. Which is the capitol of the PSU, no less. It would be imprudent of me to press this matter to the point of armed dispute.

However, you might wish to bear this in mind: as we rebuild the Pan-Sentient Union, you will want the good opinion and cooperation of the *Zheeerlikou'valkhannaieee* and the Khan, whomever the new one turns out to be. And you may be assured that I will have his ear, given my role in what is, I remind you, an ongoing conflict. If you choose, here and now, to ignore the rule of law which our two races forged together when we initiated the PSU, you cannot hope that I will tender a positive report of you or your species unto my leader and my people."

"And how much could such a report really mean, since you make it on behalf of a long-standing comrade in arms?" Morosini did not quite sneer. "Your history with Wethermere dates back to the first war, against the Arduans. Your voice will be uniformly known to be prejudiced in his favor. And if your leaders are unaware of your preference for him, then we shall acquaint them with that fact."

Kiiraathra smiled . . . and a hint of one tooth showed. Rrurr'rao's stance changed to one that was subtly more ready for action. *Holy shit*, thought Wethermere, *is Kiiraathra going to filet this jerk right here in my conference room?*

But the Orion merely smoothed his whiskers, and in so doing, covered the errant tooth which indicated to any who truly knew his culture that the smile had not been a smile at all. "Assemblyman Morosini, I think you have made two incorrect assumptions. In the first place, you do not understand my people if you believe that my prior knowledge of and association with Ossian Wethermere will diminish their confidence in my account of him and his character. In my species, those we call friends share bonds not merely of affection but debt and duty. His dishonor is my dishonor, and mine his. And so it is with honor, as well. Consequently, the collateral I offer my people to validate the witness I bear to his abilities is my own honor, my own stature. And so, my prior association with Wethermere does not weaken my testimony on his behalf, but greatly magnifies it in the ears of both the Khan and his counselors.

"But the more erroneous assumption you have made is that my opinion of Ossian Wethermere shall sound as a solitary voice in a great hall." Kiiraathra smiled a closed-mouth—and therefore, safe—smile. "Shall I summon my crews, so that you may ask their opinion of this human? I shall absent myself, if you wish, and I shall give them no advance warning of what you wish to ask them.

"But if you decide to use this method to discover their opinion of Wethermere, I give you two pieces of advice. Firstly, that you bring ear-plugs, for my people are not mild and meek in their passions—and for them, Ossian Wethermere is the only surviving human admiral who was present in the Khanate after the Kaituni despoiled it, was the only one who took the fight to the invader, and who did not attempt to deflect nor avoid the ire of the *Zheeerlikou'valkhannaieee* when they learned that Earth had closed the artificial warp point whereby her own fleets might have come to our aid."

He held up a hand to forestall the Assemblyman's protest. "I do not claim Earth did ill in eliminating that warp point. If anything, it corrected a prior problem: the strategic inadvisability of creating such a portal to begin with—whose most vocal opponent was none other than the hero of this hour, Admiral Ian Trevayne." Kiiraathra's smile became a more sardonic curl. "As you know all too well, Mr. Morosini, according to both news and rumor.

"However, my people generally lack that strategic context. They only know that in their hour of need, Earth was there in the shape of one person: Ossian Wethermere, who was instrumental in leading them here where they could avenge their families, their Khanate, and the PSU." Kiiraathra leaned back, arms crossed. "So I believe you will find my crews and my people uncommonly vocal— and loud—in their support of the admiral."

Morosini looked mildly disgusted. "Well, that explains the ear plugs. You said you had a second piece of advice?"

"Yes. You must also bring guards—or the weapons with which you mean to answer the challenges my people would make to defend Wethermere's honor should you so impugn it. Since you are not *Zheeerlikou'valkhannaieee*, you are not bound to accept challenges. But they may perceive motives other than military justice behind your accusations, and they will make their outrage known."

"Are you threatening us, Admiral?" Assemblyman Morosini asked.

Kiiraathra had to work at keeping his lips over his teeth as he smiled. "I do not threaten, Mr. Morosini. I make vows. And I keep them. But I am doing neither here. I am simply pointing out what is likely to happen if you attempt to illegally contravene my authority in this matter. And you should be aware of—and prepared for—the political consequences. Both for your world and for yourself."

Ankaht stepped forward. "Of course, there is an advantage to be gained by all parties, if you accede to Admiral Kiiraathra'ostakjo's wishes," she said, the vocoder making her voice sound almost musical.

"Indeed?" Latt-Patha said and was then conspicuously quiet, one eyebrow raised.

"We all understand, of course," Ankaht soothed, "that what Earth needs at this moment of terrible loss and confusion is calm, not more strife. And what could come of pursuing this issue but the most disruptive strife possible? There would be accusations and counteraccusations at the very highest level of the few surviving PSU authorities, the very persons whom this planet and the Union itself must look to for steady-handed guidance. However, since you evidently feel that—for whatever reason—Ossian Wethermere's presence would complicate the already turbulent situation here, then perhaps his departure would be a better alternative than a rancorous investigation."

"What exactly are you proposing?" Morosini asked.

"I simply observe that he is much needed elsewhere, by persons who have no reservations regarding his abilities or character, and who would be grateful to the PSU for making his services available to them. Because I assure you, there are many planets which have urgent need of the skills possessed by Admiral Wethermere."

"*Captain* Wethermere," Morosini corrected. "It may have been Admiral Trevayne's intent to see that the captain's brevet rank was both legitimated and then vested in full, but Trevayne announced his resignation prior to issuing those directives. I have it on legal authority"—he glanced somewhat anxiously toward Latt-Patha—"that in the current state of crisis, we are within our rights to construe anything he supposedly 'ordered' after his statement of resignation to be subject to confirmation by the appropriate authorities. This is made more especially pertinent since, although Admiral Trevayne's command of the Defense Fleet was not contested, it was somewhat irregular in that he had not been a flag officer of the PSU for some time. He was and remains a member of the Terran Republic Navy—which has no power over our command structures. So I'm afraid Captain Wethermere remains simply that: a captain."

"Now on that point, we must disagree, Mr. Assemblyman," Ankaht insisted gently yet firmly. "And you would understandably be unable to anticipate why, since the definitive rationale and reason that legitimates my assertion preceded our entry to Alpha Centauri.

"You see, Ossian Wethermere's brevet rank of admiral could not be conferred by Admiral Kiiraathra'ostakjo, who was only one rank above him, and who was himself brevetted to that. The only flag officer with sufficient actual rank was Admiral Narrok, who, in order to promote Commodore Wethermere to admiral, had to do so under the aegis of the Rim Federation Navy. This required a more formal arrangement of dual service with the navies of *both* polities, even though the commodore was already on detached duty with the RFN when the invasion began. Fortunately, as a PSU flag officer, Admiral Kiiraathra'ostakjo *did* have the authority to agree to that dual-service agreement.

"So you see, Mr. Assemblyman, those actions which

you feel make Mr. Wethermere's courage and abilities suspect were not carried out, nor were they ordered, by him as an admiral of the PSU, but as an admiral of the Rim Federation. For which I am the senior political authority present. And I may assure you, we feel no ambivalence about the admiral's role in this battle or any part of the campaign which led up to it."

Narrok stepped forward, his posture rigid. "As you no doubt know, I am the senior military authority present for the Rim Federation. To the best of my knowledge, I am the senior admiral left in the entirety of its formations."

Latt-Patha smiled faintly. "I believe Arduan membership in the Rim Federation remains provisional."

All three of Narrok's eyes narrowed as they bored into the human. "I suspect that status may have already changed, given our role in supporting this war effort with our *selnarmic* skills as well as our ships. Or would you dispute that projection?"

Latt-Patha was silent, shook her head once when she realized that Narrok was not going to continue until he had received some response.

"Therefore, in my role as the senior acting military officer in the Rim Federation, I hereby formally request that Admiral Ossian Wethermere's assignment to our polity be made of open-ended duration, and that his rank and privileges be considered equal in both services. And before you hasten to object, Mr. Morosini, you might consider that this reprises the course of Admiral Trevayne's own career—a precedent you would be at pains to dispute at any time, but particularly given his current popularity. And which the admiral reprised in

Ossian's second promotion: as having equal standing in the navy of the Terran Republic as well—thereby putting him in direct, legal command of the Combined Fleet currently protecting this system."

And with that, the entire group of them turned and saluted Ossian. Who, too stunned to do anything else, did the best thing he could have: he returned their salutes.

The assemblyman chewed his lower lip for a long moment, then shrugged. "Very well. We shall set aside our resolve to mount an investigation. But with one proviso: that 'Admiral' Wethermere shall immediately relinquish his command of what was the former Defense Fleet to local command and shall remain . . . er, at his assignment in the Rim Federation for at least three years from this date. Any return to PSU space before that would be . . . politically provocative."

—And would upset your careful recontextualizing of events to deflect any inquiries into your pre-war advocacy for building artificial warp points at the expense of adequate defenses, Wethermere reflected with a bitter grin—

Ankaht's posture suggested that she was ready to agree—on Wethermere's behalf—to his three-year exile when, wholly unforeseen, Rrurr'rao stepped forward aggressively. "No. I say 'no' to this banishment of Wethermere from all the worlds of the PSU."

Surprised eyes—including Kiiraathra's—waited for an explanation.

"Is my reason not obvious?" Rrurr'rao growled loudly. "Wethermere is a great strategist, and yet these kin-of-*chofaki* would keep him from our worlds, though the

Khanate lies ruined beneath the heel of its invaders? I mean no slight to Least Fang Kiiraathra'ostakjo, whose name and rank and line will grow prodigiously in the days to come, I predict. But in all the hero-lays of my people, the greatest warriors are invariably twinned, either as literal or figurative brothers. They face perils together, craft cunning plans together. And so we see that, as great as they are individually, their unified prowess is so much greater than the sum of its parts." He stared frankly at Wethermere. "This human is my Least Fang's hero-brother. Together they are greater than either one alone. And in going forth together to rid the Khanate of the Kaituni scourge that still sits upon it, the songs sung of them will help rebuild our opinion of Earth, and of your race."

Rrurr'rao paused, then his brow lowered. "It is no secret to any gathered here that my opinion of humans was not—charitable—when my broken ship first happened upon the small flotilla that had gathered around the Least Fang and Wethermere. But in time, and despite occasional examples to the contrary,"—he shot a meaningful glance at Morosini—"I learned the error of my judgment about your species. Yet now you wish to banish Wethermere from the world of his birth? My reaction is this: if your cowardly scheming requires that he must either be made a scapegoat or be forgotten, that is your sorry affair. But do not forbid him to come fight for the other worlds of the PSU, and the Khanate in particular. We have need of him." He looked directly at Wethermere. "Indeed, if I were to serve under a leader other than the Least Fang, it would be him."

Morosini had bristled at the words "cowardly" and "scheming," but, consummate politician that he was, he also understood that he was struggling against a current, and against adversaries, which he could not overcome. So, ever a creature of his class, he swayed the other direction. "Given the unanimous support that Commo—er, Admiral Wethermere seems to enjoy among you, I feel it would be prudent to not merely shelve, but terminate and permanently indemnify Admiral Wethermere against the PSU's investigative initiative. After all, the chaos of the current situation may have led my researchers to see various of his actions without sufficient context, and so, they may have misperceived his culpability. And, having thus withdrawn our legal proceedings, we would not want to detain Admiral Wethermere here at Earth when he is so urgently needed elsewhere by our cherished allies."

Morosini turned to Kiiraathra'ostakjo. "Since you are the ranking PSU flag officer in this system—indeed, within the range of sure summons—I will leave it in your capable hands to process the official side of the admiral's unusual dual assignment."

"It shall be my pleasure," replied Kiiraathra with the slightest possible hint of a bow. Even so, the Orion managed to make it look like a gesture of dismissal.

Annoyed but without any recourse to a commensurately retaliatory gesture, Morosini left the conference room, his assistants fluttering behind him.

Kiiraathra's smile widened to show a tooth as he leaned sideways toward his collar communicator. "Major Magee, did you hear all of that?"

"Sir, yes, sir." Although Tank's voice was small through

the micro-speaker, he still sounded as though he was ready to chew rivets like they were popcorn.

"Then please 'escort' Mr. Morosini and his party back to the ship which brought him up here. Ensure that his ride is as comfortable and swift as a person of his station deserves."

"Sir, that would be my everlasting pleasure. And Admiral Wethermere?"

"Yes?"

"Oo-rah, sir. Magee out."

"I think," Ankaht mused, her breathing slits spasming in the Arduan equivalent of suppressed laughter, "that Assemblyman Morosini is going to have a very memorable return trip."

"And you, Wethermere, are going to have a very interesting return to Khanate space," Kiiraathra'ostakjo observed gruffly. "Although why I endangered my reputation by vouching for you, I shall never understand. You don't even speak the Tongue of Tongues that well— and after years of trying, too."

Wethermere smiled. "Well, I knew you weren't keeping me around for my linguistic gifts."

Kiiraathra almost snarled. "So true. The problem is that I can't seem to recall *any* gifts so profound that they make you worth keeping around."

"Oh, I don't know. You've always found my strategic insights stimulating."

"Stimulating? Does that human word also encompass the meanings of your words 'terrifying' and 'deranging'?"

"Oh come on, my plans aren't all that bizarre. In fact, just yesterday, I was thinking about a way we could dislodge the Second Dispersate from Zarzuela, if we can just—"

But Kiiraathra heard no more: hands over his ears, a rictus of anticipated pain on his face, the Orion strode swiftly from the room.

Ossian Wethermere turned to look at the others, who were still gathered around—and staring at—him.

"What?" he asked innocently. "Was it something I said?"

EPILOGUE

The warp chain from Sol to Bug 17 was clear of Kaituni and Bugs alike, and Ian Trevayne had protested that Ossian Wethermere needed all the combatant ships he had to form relief convoys through possibly Bug-infested space. Nevertheless, Wethermere had insisted on providing him with a substantial escort—"gunslingers" in the parlance of survey work.

However, the ship Trevayne and his daughter rode was a mere scout cruiser. Firepower wasn't required just now; sophisticated sensor equipment and scientific instrumentation were. And certain enhancements had been made to PSUNS *Kiowa*'s sick bay.

Now, having crossed the inner system from the Bug 16 warp point, passing close to the yellow sun and the two lifeless innermost planets, she and several other ships of her class were deploying in a search pattern outside Bug 17's asteroid belt, toward the region of the warp points leading to Bug 05 and Bug 21.

For Trevayne, these were haunted spaces. Magda had been fighting a desperate (and highly irregular) rear-guard action against the Bugs at the Bug 05 warp point to allow the main body of Combined Fleet to escape when a second, previously unsuspected Bug horde had emerged from the Bug 21 warp point, trapping her. It was here that he had received her flagship's Code Omega.

He stood on *Kiowa's* small bridge, gazing at the forward viewscreen. Han was at his side. A young aide Wethermere had assigned to him stood deferentially to the rear. Han stared at the star-blazing infinity in the screen.

"How will we find Mommy?" she wanted to know.

"Well," Trevayne explained in terms he hoped she could understand, "her ship was destroyed near here—or what passes for 'near' in space. We're hoping that she was able to get out first." He laid a slight but definite emphasis on the word *hoping*. "You see, there is a special model of what is called a life pod for flag officers—uh, that means very high-ranking officers—which, once it's launched, automatically puts whoever is inside into cryostasis."

"Like your first body." Han was familiar with the story.

Trevayne smiled. *It is getting to be a family tradition, isn't it.* "Well, if Mommy was able to get to the capsule, it's a sure bet she wasn't nearly as banged up as I was. And another thing about this kind of life pod: it has what's called a transponder, which sends out a signal that shows where it is. But the signal is short-range—that means you have to be pretty close to be able to pick it up. So we and the other ships are searching the volume of space where a life pod ought to still be. But by now that's a *big* volume of space."

Han nodded gravely, with an apparent understanding that Trevayne hoped wasn't deceptive. "Why did Mommy's ship get blown up?"

"Well . . . she was trying to save me—in spite of myself."

"Yes, she was," came a small voice from behind them.

Surprised, Trevayne turned to face the aide—a lieutenant named Victor Menocal, whom Trevayne hadn't had time to get to know. He flushed and came to attention. "Sorry, sir."

"No, that's all right. But what made you say that?"

"Well, sir, at the time, I was her aide."

Han brightened. "You knew my Mommy?"

Menocal smiled down at her. "Yes, I did."

"But," asked Trevayne, perplexed, "how is it that you're . . . ?" He left *still alive* unsaid.

"I was with her aboard *Zeven Provinciën* when she planned her . . . unofficial action." (*Which,* Trevayne thought, *sounds rather better than "mutiny."*) "In fact, she sent me to gather her task group commanders together so she could persuade them to join her. I didn't know what was going on," Menocal added hastily.

"Of course not," Trevayne deadpanned.

"But afterwards, when she returned to her flagship, she ordered me to remain behind on *Zeven Provinciën*. I didn't understand why. Afterwards, I did." There was a long pause, during which Han looked back and forth between the two men, puzzled by what had been said and what had been left unsaid. "Anyway," Menocal finally said, "I asked to be assigned to this expedition. Admiral Wethermere granted my request."

"That sounds like him," said Trevayne with a smile.

They all fell silent and resumed waiting. Negative reports continued to come in from the sensor operators, and also from the other scout cruisers. Routine began to shade over into gloom. Han began to fidget, and looked up at her father with eyes that pleaded for reassurance. He held her tightly in his arms as the time continued to drag.

All at once, a series of lights flashed on a board, and *Kiowa*'s skipper turned to Trevayne with a face that told him everything he needed to know. "Admiral, *Sarmatian* has picked up a transponder signal. She's moving to get within tractor range. *Tangut*, the nearest ship, is moving in to assist if necessary."

"Thank you, Commander," said Trevayne in a barely audible voice, as he hugged Han more tightly.

The worst part came after *Kiowa* rendezvoused with *Sarmatian* and the life pod was transferred and taken to the revival chamber that accounted for the expansion of the sick bay. Trevayne knew better than to joggle the elbows of doctors at work, so he and Han remained in the background, giving each other comfort.

Finally, Doctor Gopal, the chief surgeon, approached them with a gentle smile. "Admiral, we've completed all bioscans. Aside from a few possible bruises, she was uninjured at the time she escaped in the pod. And the cryostasis functioned perfectly."

Trevayne, weak with relief, could not form words.

"The thawing process is about complete," Gopal continued. "If you'd like to come with me . . ."

They entered the revival chamber. The pod was open, and Li-Trevayne Magda lay serenely on her back.

"Mommy! Mommy!" squealed Han, and started to rush forward. Trevayne restrained her.

Gopal studied instrument readouts. "She's just about to regain consciousness, Admiral . . . ah, Admiral . . . ?"

Trevayne stepped forward past him and leaned over the pod. As the last of the readouts flashed green, he kissed her with enormous gentleness.

At the instant their lips touched, her eyes—the ebony eyes of her mother—fluttered open.

With a wisdom beyond her years, Han stayed back, and smiled.